The Mouth
of the Gods

Book 3 of the Vampire Queen Saga

William Stacey

E-book cover by Isabel Robalo – IsaDesign.net
Formatting by Polgarus Studio www.polgarusstudio.com
Map by Steam Power Studios www.steampowerstudios.com.au

Part 1:
The Fist of Wodor

Chapter 1

Owen

"The Fist of Wodor, ho!" screamed the lookout at *Fen Wolf*'s prow, holding tightly to the wooden figurehead of a snarling wolf's head as the ship climbed through the waves. Other crew members took up his sighting, repeating it down the length of the eighty-foot Fenyir warship, alerting the skipper that their destination lay ahead.

Farther back, his vision blocked by the large mast and its full, flapping square sail, Owen Toscovar balanced precariously upon the gunwale, one hand lightly gripping the rigging as he leaned out over the freezing water of the northern Promiscuous Sea. Although he looked much like the other men aboard the longship with his blond hair and newly grown beard, Owen was no ruddy-faced Fenyir clansman but a Kingdom of Conarck man-at-arms, sworn in service to the noble Dain family. Despite his mainlander origins, he had taken to seaborne life as if born to it, finding in himself an unexpected love for the sea. Ignoring the rushing waters below and the cold spray in his face, Owen watched the ship's prow rise above the waves, revealing the towering rock pillar rising out of the ocean— the Fist of Wodor.

The Fist sat upon a towering rock formation the others had called a stalk, a pillar of weathered cliff at least a hundred feet high. Ages ago, the stalk had clearly been the far tip of the headland that extended out from the Hishtari coastline on their right-hand side— or steering-board side—but the never-ending onslaught of the waves had battered it free of the cliffs, so that it now stood as a tower of rock surrounded by the ocean. The summit of the tower flared wider, like the head of a war mace—*No,* Owen corrected himself, *like a closed fist sitting atop an arm thrust into the air.* The rocks at the bulbous summit even had the appearance of tightly clenched fingers. Owen swung back onto the ship, dropping lightly upon its wooden deck. *No one back home in Wolfredsuntown would ever believe me if I told them of this place.*

Fen Wolf rocked slightly as the longship's prow swung to port, angling away from the Fist and the headland to maneuver around it. As the sun dropped below the cliffs of the headland and the shadows grew over the waves, he knew they'd need to find a place to beach the ship soon, or risk spending a night at sea. And, after weeks of sailing with the Fenyir, he well understood their unease with such a practice; what you couldn't see in the dark could easily tear your hull out.

Lady Danika Dain, the last of her family and Owen's new liege-lord, sat farther forward on a rowing bench near the ship's mast, a thick wool blanket wrapped around her shoulders. Gali, the young Hishtari woman who had saved their lives in Daenipor, sat beside her, idly chatting away in her stilted trade common. The two women, equally out of place aboard the ship, had found comfort in each other's company. Their discomfort wasn't because of their sex— slightly less than half of *Fen Wolf*'s eighty-some crew members were women—rather, it was their mainlander heritage, which couldn't have been more different. Lady Danika's family was nobility and had ruled the northern Duchy of Wolfrey in the Kingdom of Conarck for generations, whereas Gali was a Hishtari pickpocket who had grown up on the rough docks of Daenipor, stealing to stay alive.

Watching them together, Owen was glad for whatever comfort Lady Danika could find. The brave noblewoman had lost everything—her father, her younger brother, and all her servants but Owen. Months ago, she and her brother had mounted an armed expedition to Greywynne Island in an attempt to recover a priceless heirloom, the magical sword Sight-Bringer, buried in the catacombs beneath the ruins of an ancient fortress. Instead, they had inadvertently set free a monster—Serina Greywynne, the Blood Queen of legend who had almost destroyed the kingdom a half century earlier. In the bloodbath that followed her escape, Owen and Lady Danika—the only survivors of the ill-fated expedition—had fled for their lives, pursued by Serina's servants, the traitorous Greywynne Islanders. They had stolen a small fishing boat and headed out to sea with the shattered remains of Sight-Bringer, now only a white-stone hilt and a half foot of jagged steel. Fioni Ice-Bound, *Fen Wolf*'s beautiful but volatile redheaded skipper, had saved them. Serina had been pursuing them ever since.

He watched Fioni now, standing on the steering platform at the rear of the longship, her hand lightly resting atop the tiller, her short red hair flapping in the breeze. Fioni Ice-Bound—the dreaded "Red Wolf," scourge of the shipping lanes that ran along the Fenyir island chain between the Kingdom of Conarck and the Empire of Hishtar. At her feet, as always, lay her massive wolfhound bitch, Ekkie, her long tail slowly flopping against the deck in a measured, happy cadence. Fioni was near Owen's age, still in her early twenties. But where Owen was a simple soldier, the younger son of a horse-breeder, Fioni was like royalty among the barbarian Fenyir clans, the great-granddaughter of the legendary Fenyir chieftain Serl Raven-Eye and the daughter of the Waveborn clan's murdered yarl, Taios Oak-Heart.

Fioni laughed suddenly, her face lit up with a dazzling smile at something her first mate Kora Far-Sails had just said. A tight knot formed in Owen's gut as he watched her. Fioni was as beautiful as the sea she loved, but twice as dangerous. The same night she had saved Owen and Lady Danika, Fioni had slipped naked and uninvited—but very welcome—into Owen's bed. Since then, though, Fioni had acted as if the tryst hadn't even happened or—worse—was of no special significance. Tall, muscular, and handsome, Owen knew women found him attractive. Growing up in Wolfredsuntown, he had certainly taken advantage of that attraction, seducing more than his share of the local daughters, but never before had he felt so... *used*.

It wasn't a comfortable feeling.

Kora said something else, and the smile disappeared from Fioni's face, and she shook her head sadly. Unlike Fioni, Kora Far-Sails would never be described as a pretty woman—in truth, she was harder than tempered steel—with short blond hair, lean hard muscles, and tattoos of leaping dolphins on either side of her forehead. A formidable warrior, she had saved Owen's life twice already. Standing next to her, picking his teeth with a bone sliver, was Rolf Fork-Beard, a heavyset, bearded warrior in his fifties with a disfigured patch of skin from an old burn on his right cheek. A good man and an excellent fighter, Rolf had been the leader of Fioni's father's house-herd, his personal warriors... until the night Fioni's hated cousin Galas Gilt-Mane had murdered Fioni's father, stolen his position as yarl of the Waveborn clan, and chased Fioni and her crew to sea. Now, Galas served Serina.

All their enemies, it seemed, had joined forces.

The hull and sail ropes creaked as Fioni tacked the longship, bringing it around the Fist of Wodor and back toward the shoreline. As they circled the towering rock formation, Owen saw the rope bridge atop the Fist's summit that spanned the waters, connecting it to the headland a bow's shot away. *How old is that bridge?*

"See you ever anything so pretty?" a young woman asked him. Turning about, he smiled at Gali, who had left Lady Danika to her solitude to come join him.

"Never," he admitted. "Nor did I ever think I would." He looked past Gali, at Lady Danika. "How is she?"

Gali's smile fell. "She… her body heals, but… I fright what is unseen."

Owen's throat felt thick, making it hard to swallow. Less than a week ago, they had sailed to the Hishtari city of Daenipor, a major trading port, in a misguided attempt to bargain for an old shield that hid a map showing the location of Torin Island and Serina's magically removed heart, which they needed to find in order to kill the seemingly immortal blood fiend. But Serina's reach was long, and she had set a trap for them in Daenipor. Kalishni'coor, the ancient necromancer known as "the Blue Man," had been waiting for them. In the ambush that followed their arrival at the city's Rose Palace, Kalishni'coor had captured Lady Danika. By the time Owen had managed to rescue her, she had suffered unimaginable torment at the hands of his torturers. The responsibility for keeping her safe had been his—and he had failed.

"Where… where are gulls?" Gali suddenly asked, drawing Owen out of his melancholy.

Owen stared at her for a moment before wondering the same thing. For days now, the ever-present screams of the gulls had followed them along the shoreline. Now, an eerie silence had fallen upon them. "I don't know," he said. "Odd they'd just… disappear like that."

As they came around the far side of the Fist, a natural bay and sandy beach with a thick forest came into view. On the southern side of the bay, a rock wall hundreds of feet high connected the beach to the headland. Running diagonally up the rock face was a twisting lip of stone, a slumped cliff created when a portion of the cliff face had fallen away.

Kora moved among the crew now, ordering the sail lowered and the oars placed in the water. As they sailed alongside the cliff face and lost the wind, a hideous screech cut through the air, echoing from the Fist behind them. A chill ran down Owen's spine, and he turned and bolted to the rear of the ship, launching himself up the stairs to the steering platform, rushing past the wide-eyed Fioni. Ignoring her, he climbed up onto the sternpost, staring up at the dark summit of the Fist in their wake. Despite the gloom, he saw what he had been dreading—several impossibly large winged creatures circled the summit before disappearing from sight. He swore beneath his breath, dropping back down onto the steering platform, where Fioni stared at him.

"Well?" she demanded.

He sighed, meeting the challenge in her sea-green eyes. *Now we know why there are no gulls.* Like most northern men, Owen had grown up an experienced woodsman and mountaineer. He had lost friends to those damned creatures, ripped from the side of a mountain by a storm of wings and talons.

"What?" she said.

"Harpies," he answered. "There must be a nest up there."

Her eyes narrowed. "Wodor's balls."

Chapter 2

Owen

They anchored *Fen Wolf* close to the beach, where the crew could climb over the prow and walk ashore. Owen splashed down into the freezing water and then helped Lady Danika, lifting her around the waist and carrying her to the shore. She had always been a slight woman, but there was even less to her now after weeks at sea. They both wore Fenyir clothing: thick wool and linen tunics and breeches, high otter-skin boots, and fur cloaks. While he carried a curved Hishtari sword and dagger—taken as plunder from the Rose Palace—the only weapon she carried was Sight-Bringer in a makeshift sheath in the small of her back, covered by the cloak. She rarely let the sword out of her possession, as it was their only chance to stop Serina.

The crew made camp on the beach, setting up tents and starting a bonfire. Kora supervised, posting sentries at the forest's edge as well as a watch on the skies over the Fist of Wodor. While Owen approved of sentries, harpies were unlikely to attack an armed camp, preferring safer prey such as sheep or, on rare occasions, cows. *Unless,* Owen noted, *someone was foolish enough to threaten their nest.*

The beach was strewn with seashells. Streamers of seaweed rolled in the surf, washing up on the sand among small skittering crabs that Gali and some of the others were trying to catch for dinner. Out in the bay, whitecaps slapped the surface of the black water as the waves rolled inland before dissolving into foam on the beach. The nearby forest was dark and silent, with long cattails swaying before the pine trees. The bonfire, stoked with armloads of driftwood, popped and crackled, and the crew began to congregate around it, laughing and conversing. Owen stood watching the cliff-face with the path created by the sunken trail that led up to the headland, several hundred feet above the bay. From that height, a fall would shatter bones and crush organs. *If the harpies hear Fioni and the others coming, they'll wait until they're near the top, where any fall into the waters below would be lethal.* Once again, he heard a harpy screech echoing in the night, and for a moment, the conversation around the bonfire stopped as men and women glanced nervously in the direction of the Fist.

In the north, discovery of a harpy nest was always a cause for concern. If they were found anywhere near a settlement, every healthy man, and most of the older boys, would band together to burn it, driving the beasts into the mountains. If left alone, the harpies would become bolder and begin to kill children. They hadn't seen a Hishtari settlement along the coast for some days, so the harpies probably had free rein to hunt whatever they could find. *Would that make them careless?* Owen had participated in three nest-destroying excursions, but always in daylight, always when the adult harpies were out hunting. No one hunted harpies at night, which was, unfortunately, exactly what Fioni wanted to do.

She sat nearby, perched atop a piece of driftwood, softly conversing with Kora and Rolf. She held her great-grandfather's battered journal open on her lap, jabbing a finger at an open page. Her voice rose slightly, carrying across the sand. When Fioni noticed

Owen watching her, she stared at him in challenge. "You've the look of a man with something to say, Owen Northman."

Days ago, the crew had taken to calling him "Northman"—a *name-gift*, Kora had called it. While not terribly imaginative, it was a much more flattering nickname than the derogatory "Horse-Boy" the other northern soldiers had given him. He quickly looked away, intent on minding his own business, when Lady Danika slid up next to him and placed her hand on his forearm. "You know more about harpies than any of them, Owen. If you've something to say, tell her."

He met her eyes and nodded. *No one tells Fioni anything*, he thought sourly, but he and the noblewoman approached the three Fenyir. Rolf rose from his stump and gave it to Lady Danika to sit on. Owen met Fioni's challenging green eyes. He inhaled deeply and then began. "This plan of yours, to take the path in the dark up to the headland and the Fist tonight..."

Her gaze narrowed. "What of it?"

Rolf's eyes darted from Fioni to Owen. Rolf and a dozen of his men, the former house-herd to her father, Yarl Taios, would join Fioni this night—and *only* those men, which made no sense. Rolf's men were older, each past his prime and too old for midnight climbs along cliff faces.

"I don't understand this," Owen said. "Why go up there at all?"

"Because we have to," she replied.

"Even without the harpies, taking that path at night is needlessly dangerous. A fall from that height will be fatal, and harpies love to pull men from cliffs. If they hear you coming, they'll wait until you're most vulnerable."

"Won't they be asleep?" Kora asked.

"Not as soundly as you may think," Owen insisted. "There's a reason no one attacks harpy nests at night."

Fioni leaned forward. "Owen…"

"Please, Fioni," said Lady Danika. "We have experience with these monsters in the north. Listen to him."

Fioni sighed. "I am listening, my lady of Wolfrey, but you're not. We *have* to go up there."

"Why?" Owen asked. "This is the Hishtari coastline, not the Fenyir Island chain. Let *them* deal with these creatures."

"It's not about territory and responsibility, Owen—although the Fist of Wodor is a *Fenyir* holy site, no matter whose coastline it sits on. We're going up there because that withered ball-sack Kalishni'coor destroyed the map Serl hid on his shield—a map that would have provided a nautical course for us to follow into the Feral Sea to Torin Island."

"But you have the Raven's-Eye *and* Serl's journal," insisted Lady Danika.

Fioni hefted the journal. "Aye, I do. And Serl left detailed notes of his voyage in his journal, including where he started from—the Fist of Wodor."

Lady Danika watched her. "Then you intend to—"

"Retrace Serl's voyage," Owen said.

"Yes, Owen. I'm going to follow Serl's voyage as closely as I can. With luck—a great deal of luck—we'll find Torin Island and Serina's heart."

"Okay, I understand that, but why make the climb to the Fist? Why risk the harpies?"

"The Fist," said Kora, "is holy to us, a special place where one can ask the gods for their help." Kora and Rolf nodded solemnly. "But there's another reason."

"Us," said Rolf. "My men and I, the surviving members of Yarl Taios's house-herd, we would transfer our oath-bond to Fioni."

"I don't understand," said Owen.

Fioni sighed. "That much is obvious."

Kora frowned at Fioni before addressing Owen. "An oath-bond is a serious matter to us. We do not give it lightly. Traditionally, when a yarl dies, his house-herd will lay down their arms and live out the rest of their days on their farms, drinking beer and growing fat."

"That path," said Rolf bitterly, "is closed to us, thanks to Galas. Even if we wanted to ignore the death of our yarl—which we could never do—Galas can't let us live."

"It's true, Owen," said Kora. "Galas would kill these men. He would have killed them the same night Taios died had they not escaped with us. But if they can't go home, they need to find a new master. So they will transfer their oath to Fioni."

Rolf nodded, his gaze solemn.

"But such a thing is rarely done, and never without first asking the blessing of the gods," said Fioni. She glanced up toward the Fist. "This night we ask the gods for their support."

"And your gods will hear this?" Owen asked.

Fioni shook her head. "No, but the Fist of Wodor is a holy place. And this night, the woodland wights will be present, unseen but watching. They will hear us and tell the gods for us."

Rolf stroked his beard, his eyes shining. "*Orkinus*, the sea god; *Fenya*, the brave warrior maiden; even *Wodor* himself, the great-father. They will all bless our request. If the gods are truly pleased, mayhap they will even grant us our vengeance against Galas Gilt-Mane."

"It is our way," agreed Kora. "The strongest of oaths are made on this site."

"'Tis truth," said Rolf. "Thirty-two years ago, when we were all young men, we made this climb with Taios." He smiled at the memory. "Under the witnessing eyes of the woodland wights, we swore our oaths. In return, Taios gave us these armbands." Rolf gestured to the silver band clasped about his thick bicep. "This night, we shall all of us give these bands back to his daughter and make the oaths anew."

"And I will give them back," said Fioni, "binding these men to me for the rest of their lives."

"We'll never make these oaths again," said Rolf.

"All right," said Owen. "I understand, but why at night? In the morning—"

"We can't wait for morning," said Kora. "The ceremony must take place when the shades are present so they can tell the gods. But the wights will only come out when Fenya's shield shines upon the land."

Owen stared at her. "I... what?"

"The light of the full moon, Owen. Tonight. Besides, tomorrow morning, when the sun rises, we sail west for the Feral Sea. Even with my great-grandfather's journal and his Raven's-Eye, I will need to ask the gods for their help. Otherwise, we might sail right past Torin Island in the fog."

"What about Serina?" Lady Danika asked.

The three Fenyir warriors exchanged nervous glances. Unlike Owen and Lady Danika, they had never actually seen Serina. Perhaps they only half believed the infamous Blood Queen even existed. "She can't find us," said Fioni, perhaps a little too quickly. "And even if she is hunting us, once we enter the Feral Sea, we'll be free of her. She can't come after us."

"Don't be so certain of what she can and can't do," said Lady Danika. "Her reach is long—as we all discovered in Daenipor. Kalishni'coor, the Blue Man, was her ally, as, apparently, is your own cousin, Galas."

Fioni leaned forward, her gaze cold. "I will give Galas the death he has earned; trust me, my lady of Wolfrey. But even Galas can't come after us, not without a way of finding the sun within the fog."

"Fioni has the truth of this," said Kora. "Galas will not dare the Feral Sea."

"Does Galas know of this place?" Lady Danika asked.

Fioni, Kora, and Rolf exchanged meaningful glances. *Of course he does,* Owen realized. *It is a Fenyir holy site, after all. And Serina is Fenyir—older, more steeped in Fenyir lore than anyone now alive is.* He inhaled deeply. "Fioni, this is madness. We should sail now, this very night!"

Fioni shook her head, her expression resolute. "Not before the oath-swearing."

Out to sea, thunder rumbled and dark clouds gathered. It would be raining within the hour, he guessed. Their luck couldn't be worse. Not only would Fioni, Rolf, and the others have to make their ascent along the narrow ledge in the dark, but it would also be wet and slick. "Fioni," he said, searching for the words that would change her mind. "I understand, but…"

"We're going, Owen," she said with finality.

Lady Danika stood up abruptly. "Very well, then. So is Owen."

He turned to her in surprise. "My lady, my place is with you."

She raised her hand, cutting him off. "You are a soldier of Wolfrey, and I am now Wolfrey. *Your place* is wherever I choose it to be."

Fioni's eyes darted from Lady Danika to Owen. "My lady, thank you, but this is a… holy ritual for Fenyir."

"Make an exception," Lady Danika insisted in a tone that was more command than request. "Owen is an experienced mountaineer and woodsman. No doubt, he already has experience clearing out harpy nests."

"I have," Owen admitted.

"I will lend you Sight-Bringer, of course," said the noblewoman. "Its magic will help you find your way in the dark."

"Yes, my lady," said Owen, accepting her mind was decided.

"Good," she said, turning away. She paused and met his eye over her shoulder. "But I do need to talk to you in private, Owen, on a matter of some importance."

#

He followed the small dark-haired noblewoman back down the beach, his face heating with shame. He already knew what she wanted to discuss and had been dreading this conversation. When there was no one within earshot, she stopped and waited for him, pulling her cloak tighter around her shoulders. "Owen, I need to ask you something, something I couldn't bring up before on the ship… with all the others nearby."

Behind him, the surf crashed against the beach, the waves washing within feet of them before receding. "I… I know what you're going to say, my lady. *I'm sorry.* I failed you. I betrayed my oath and left you to those people. It's my fault they hurt you."

"What—no!" Her voice rose in startled confusion, and she stepped forward, placing her palm on his chest. "No, of course it's not your fault. Had you stayed, you would have died as well. *You saved me*, and I'm so grateful for that. I had given up all hope. That pig, Modwyn, would have done far worse than just hurt me. I owe you my life."

Relief coursed through him, causing his knees to shake. "But I—"

"Thank you, Owen. I'm sorry I took so long to say that, but thank you. I've been… I've been trying to find myself after what they… what they did to me, hurt me. But that's no excuse. I should have told you right away how grateful I was that you came back for me." She stood on her toes and kissed him on his bearded cheek. Then she hugged him, burying her face in his neck. "Thank you for my life, my dignity."

Uncertain what to do, he tentatively placed his arm around her. "You're welcome, my lady. But what, then, did you want to talk about?"

She pulled away, moving once more to a respectable distance. "The night you came for me, you told me I should 'thank Keep-Captain Awde.' What did you mean by that?"

He turned away, staring out to sea and watching the dark waves. He remembered that night so clearly: Brice Awde's ghost beckoning him on into the shadowy recesses of the Rose Palace, wordlessly leading him to the tower where Danika was held prisoner. There had been more than a few rumors in Castle Dain about Lady Danika and the Keep-Captain, but he had never truly believed them—or hadn't until that night. "I saw him," he finally said, so softly it was almost a whisper. "Or, rather, I saw his shade."

"You… you saw Brice? Truly?"

"He led me straight to you, all without saying a single word or stepping out of the shadows."

"If he was in the shadows, then how do you—"

"It was him, my lady. I know it."

"Oh, Brice," she whispered, her voice breaking as she fell to her knees in the sand, her head lowered, sobbing.

He thought again of that horrible night when Serina had sent her ghouls to attack Stron's Watch, the Dain fort on Greywynne Island. Just before sunrise, Serina had sent Brice Awde, now an unholy blood fiend like her, against the fort to steal back Sight-Bringer. But, when he had had the chance, instead of killing Danika, Awde had impaled himself on the sword, driving it through his own heart. At the time, Owen had thought his sacrifice a final act of loyalty to the family he had served all his life, but he now understood he had been dead wrong.

It had been love.

Chapter 3

Owen

When Owen and Lady Danika returned to the others near the bonfire, Fioni was waiting for him. "I have something to give you," she said simply, before brusquely turning away, clearly expecting him to follow her.

She stopped before her tent, where a large sea chest sat in the sand. Kneeling, she lifted the lid, revealing her possessions: combs, tools, clothing, and several battered books, which she quickly pushed aside. As she reached into the chest, Owen heard the distinctive rustle of ring mail. "Here," she said, using both hands to pull a heavy ring-mail coat out, dislodging many of her possessions, including a battered old doll with wooden discs for eyes. She quickly threw a wool sweater atop the doll before climbing to her feet and holding the heavy ring-mail coat out to Owen. "If you're going to come with us tonight, you'll need this. And it needs a new owner, someone large enough to wear it."

The rings of the coat were black with varnish or paint. And unlike kingdom castle-forged ring mail, where the sleeves stopped at the upper arm, the sleeves on this coat were long enough to cover the wearer's entire arms to the hands. There was even a hood hanging from the back, to protect the head and neck. The hem was longer than he was used to as well, stopping just above his knees. Thick whalebone plates called "baleen" were bolted to the shoulders, providing additional protection. Intricate Fenyir runes covered the surface of each piece of baleen, creating a breathtakingly beautiful geodesic pattern that looked to be inlaid with traces of silver. He knew whose coat this had been—Vory Eel-Gifted, Fioni's former first mate, murdered by Kalishni'coor. "How?" he asked as he trailed his fingers over one of the rings.

"We found it in the Rose Palace's armory, along with my own coat that I left atop that damned tower we climbed down."

"The Hishtari weren't using this?"

"I doubt there was a man among them who could have filled it."

He shook his head. "I can't take this. It was his."

Sorrow flashed through her eyes, replaced a moment later by cold determination. "Whale shit, you can't. He'd want you to have it. Gods know why, but Vory liked you." She smirked, the corners of her mouth curling. "Probably because you knocked him down the first time you met." She thrust the coat into his chest, held it there as she examined them both, making a noncommittal grunt. "You'll grow into it."

"The rings are smaller than ours."

"Smaller but stronger, I wager. Vory had it built to his specifications in Lyr. Cost him a fortune, or at least that's what my father told me. It's more than twenty years old but still perfect."

He took it from her, hefting its considerable weight in his arms. "Thank you."

She slapped him on the shoulder and then turned away. When she spoke, there was a tremor in her voice. "Let's go kill some harpies."

#

19

They departed before midnight with Owen, holding Sight-Bringer, leading the way. Over his shoulder, he carried one of the heavy crossbows they had taken from the Kur'teshi mercenaries, as did Fioni, Rolf, and the other twelve warriors. The powerful weapons had helped them immeasurably in the battle for the Rose Palace, shredding the massed ranks of the Hishtari soldiers. Owen wore his new armor. Fioni and her father's house-herd wore theirs as well. In addition to the crossbows, each man carried axe and spear, but none carried shields; moving up the slick cliff face would be hard enough without cumbersome shields. Besides, it was always best to kill harpies from a distance rather than letting them get close enough to grasp and pull with their talons. A full-grown harpy could easily pull a man into the air before dropping him to splatter against the rocks. Two of the men also carried sacks filled with bundles of pitch-soaked straw that they would use to set the nest ablaze. Each man carried a handful of fire-strips—a special type of tree fungus pounded flat into strips the length of a man's finger and then boiled in urine. When set ablaze and then tightly rerolled—as they had done before leaving camp—the strips would smolder without burning for hours. To bring a flame to life again, all they'd need to do was to unroll the strips and blow on the embers.

With Sight-Bringer's magic helping him see, Owen easily found the rocky end of the sunken trail at the far end of the beach. Torches would have helped immeasurably, but animals were attuned to the smell of smoke, and the last thing they needed this night was to warn the harpies they were coming. If the harpies swarmed them on the treacherous cliff face, it would be a massacre. Instead, they took their time, moving slowly but quietly. He led Fioni and the others up the twisting rocky path, picking the safest route he could find. The rain drizzled down upon them, masking the sounds of their climb but making their footing much slicker. Several times already, a man had slipped, only to catch himself at the last moment. Owen moved slowly, often stopping to point out to Fioni where to place her feet on the path. In turn, Fioni passed the word down the line to the next man. As they climbed, the waves washed against the rocks below them.

Despite appearances, Vory's armor was lighter than he had expected, but the sleeves rubbed against the heavy padded cloth of the gambeson he wore beneath the armor. Owen was a large, powerful man, but there were at least three fingers of space between the sleeves and his biceps. Vory had been a beast of a man.

In places, thick, grasping bushes grew out of the cliff face, forcing them to push their way past. Burrs clung to his breeches and boots, prickling and irritating his skin, driving him crazy.

Although they moved slowly, as quietly as they could, the Fenyir were clearly not woodsmen and occasionally made too much noise. At these times, Owen would stop the trek and hold his breath as he listened for any indication the harpies were awake. So far, though, he heard nothing but the wind and the strained breathing of the men. He moved forward once more, slowly placing the outside of each foot down and then rolling his foot forward along the outer edge.

An hour or more later, they finally reached the summit of the headland, coming out onto a wind-swept grassy promontory that looked out toward the Fist and the sea. The moment he stepped onto the summit, he smelled the harpies. The pungent scent of rot and bird shit was like being smashed in the face with a shield. Breathing through his mouth, he fought down his revulsion. It had been years since he had burned his last harpy nest, but the smell brought him right back to that day.

He slid forward, keeping low as he entered the tall, wet stalks of grass upon the headland. Far out to sea, lightning flared once more, hitting the sea and illuminating the surrounding terrain. East, the headlands sloped downward before running into the forest that surrounded the beach. He closed his eyes and listened, concentrating on the night's noises. Fioni stumbled into him and then dropped down on one knee beside him, her breathing strained. "Where?" she whispered.

He pointed to the west, where he could just make out the shape of the rope bridge that crossed over to the summit of the Fist. He saw no sign of other animals, not even a squirrel, nor did he expect to. An adult harpy weighed less than a hundred pounds but could eat twice its weight in prey every three days. Harpies ate everything they could catch, slowly widening their hunting expeditions. In time, the harpies would have to move the nest or starve. The wind gusted, blowing cold rain in his face. *At least we have the wind in our favor. It'll mask our movement and scent.* Minutes later, the last of Rolf's men climbed over the summit and joined them in the grass of the headland.

Owen slipped Sight-Bringer back into its makeshift sheath, his senses immediately returning to normal, making him feel both deaf and blind, but the sword's magic had done its part. Now, more mundane but no less lethal tools were called for. They un-slung their crossbows and began to quietly load the weapons. Placing his foot inside the stirrup at the end of the weapon, he slipped the hook attached to the sinew string onto his belt. As he straightened his legs, he spanned the weapon, locking the string into place with a soft click against the walnut release device attached to the trigger lever. He held his hand between the lever and the stock to make sure he didn't accidentally release the string. This close to the nest, the snap of a crossbow's arms would almost certainly wake the harpies. He took one of the metal-tipped wooden bolts he carried in a sack on his belt and fitted it into the weapon's groove so that it lay flat, its nock fully caught against the catch. When they were all ready, he eased himself up and placed the crossbow's stock tightly into his shoulder.

Fioni met his eye and then nodded. Together, they slipped

through the tall stalks of grass, moving silently toward the rope bridge. As they reached the peak of the headland, the cliff narrowed, pointing out to sea. The ropes creaked in the wind, softly swaying in place. In the dark, it was impossible to judge how sturdy it was, but Rolf had insisted the Fenyir came here often enough to swear oaths that it had to be serviceable. If so, the harpies must have built their nest recently, which, given their migratory nature to pursue prey, was entirely possible. The summit of the stalk on the other side of the bridge was higher than the headland, so that the bridge ran up at a slight incline; but it also hid the top of the stalk and the nest from view. *When we cross over, we could blunder right into the nest.*

Nothing for it, Owen. Get a move on.

He inhaled deeply and prepared to step out onto the bridge, when Fioni slid in front of him, holding her crossbow with one hand while she gripped one of the support ropes with the other. The boards creaked under her weight but held. She took another step, and then another, moving steadily across the swaying bridge. Owen wiped the rain and sweat from his eyes, peering into the darkness as Fioni moved farther out of sight. When the bridge stopped swaying, he realized she must have stepped off onto the other side. *Okay, my turn.* He tentatively stepped out onto the bridge, slowly placing his weight on the creaking boards. He was much heavier than Fioni, and sweat ran down his spine in rivulets as he took another step, this one creaking even louder. He froze, but the bridge held. As Fioni had done, he held onto his crossbow with one hand and the support rope with the other and moved across the bridge. Far below, he could hear the waves crashing against the rock face. Keeping his gaze fixated on the end of the bridge, he focused on placing one foot and then the other, ignoring the swaying of the bridge. When he reached the other side and stepped onto the rocky stalk where Fioni waited for him, it came as almost a surprise.

He had made it.

Dropping down on one knee beside Fioni, he placed the crossbow into his shoulder again and focused his attention on the Fist of Wodor while the others crossed the bridge, one by one. Hundreds of paces wide and dotted with stunted, windblown bushes, the summit was wider than he had realized. In its center, a ring of man-high stone obelisks ringed a single massive oak tree that stood majestically atop the summit, its thick branches reaching into the sky. Staring at the tree, he couldn't help but believe this was indeed a holy place, even if he didn't worship the Fenyir's gods. And while he couldn't see the base of the tree through the ring of dark obelisks, he knew from the stench that he'd find the nest built up around the tree.

Once the others were across, Fioni rose and, crossbow raised, began to inch her way forward. Owen followed to her left, with Rolf on her right. The others moved into line where they could release their bolts without fear of striking their own. Fioni edged around one of the obelisks and then paused. Owen, moving around another stone, also stopped in his tracks.

The base of the oak tree was empty.

There was no nest, no harpies.

This made no sense. He had seen them earlier circling the summit, heard their unmistakable cries. Even now, he could smell their stench. His eyes met Fioni's. She shook her head in confusion. Holding the crossbow in one hand, he drew Sight-Bringer again. The moment his fingers touched the white stone hilt, its magic flowed back into him, invigorating him, but also vastly increasing the stench of harpy dung. Motioning for Fioni and the others to remain in place, he entered the ring, approaching the oak's trunk. As expected, bones, massive feathers, and other detritus—all coated in harpy shit—covered the ground beneath the tree's thick branches. *What am I missing? The nest* has *to be here.*

Owen circled the trunk where he saw a build-up of bones on the tree's ocean side leading past the ring of obelisks to the far edge of the summit. His hunter's intuition screamed in warning. Placing each foot carefully to avoid the brittle bones, he stepped up to the edge of the cliff and slowly peered over it.

There was the nest.

Less than ten feet away, an enormous pile of detritus, interlaced branches, bushes, and feathers sat on a stone lip extending a dozen paces from the side of the cliff that would make it impossible to see from below. And huddled together, sharing heat, were at least a dozen harpies, each smaller than a man was, but vicious and deadly with their clawed talons and grinding beaks. They slept with their wings wrapped around them, like a ball of feathers. When extended, their wingspan would be more than ten feet across. Although clearly avian, the upper half of their bodies looked eerily human, with four pendulous breasts covered in thick down. Even their heads were vaguely simian with savage womanish faces, albeit with small beady black eyes set on either side of a savage beak that could pull flesh from bone. That similarity, however, ended with their lower torsos, which were entirely birdlike, consisting of stick-thin scaly legs tipped with inch-long talons.

Owen slid back, praying the beasts remained sleeping. His heartbeat racing, he held his breath and waited, listening for any sign they were waking. When he heard nothing, he considered what to do next. They had been lucky so far, but eventually, the animals would catch their scent and wake. Then a plan began to form in his mind. It would be stupid and dangerous but, if successful, would make short work of the nest. Fioni and the others stood back, watching him. He slowly moved back to join her and placed his lips next to her ear. "The nest is just below, but I have an idea."

"What are you thinking?" she whispered back.

"Lower me." He bent down and placed his loaded crossbow on the ground.

Her eyes widened, but he pointed to one of the warriors carrying the bundles of pitch-soaked straw, and she seemed to understand, bobbing her head. Owen approached the man and removed several of the straw bundles, stuffing them beneath his ring-mail coat and holding them in place with his sword belt. When ready, he approached the cliff's edge once again, slipping Sight-Bringer beneath his belt. Rolf and one of the larger warriors, a stout bald-headed fighter named Asger, each took one of his arms as he backed out over the edge of the cliff. They took his weight, slowly lowering him down to the lip upon which sat the nest. One of the harpies rustled in its sleep, and the men froze, holding Owen in place. At any moment, Owen expected to feel the claws of a harpy on his back, but after several moments, nothing happened. Rolf, his face strained, grimaced, and he and Asger lowered Owen the rest of the way. His boots softly touched the rock, and they let go of his wrists.

Owen turned, staring at the mass of harpies from only feet away. Their breathing this close was raspy and loud, but they were still sleeping. Moving as quietly as he could, he removed the straw bundles from beneath his armor and carefully placed them inside the outer edge of the nest. When they were all in place, Owen backed away from the nest, met Rolf's eye, and nodded. Rolf and Asger reached out again and took Owen by the wrists. As they began to raise him back up, one of the harpies suddenly screeched in warning, an earsplitting shriek of rage and fear that forced Owen's heart into his throat in panic. Rolf and Asger heaved him back up and over the cliff just as something ripped into the back of his legs. Sudden pain flared through his calf muscle, but he ignored it as he scrambled back and away from the cliff. Just then, a spark-streaming bundle of fire whipped past his head as it fell over the cliff and onto the nest.

Moments later, the pitch-soaked bundles Owen had placed caught flame, lighting up the night, setting free a cacophony of enraged shrieks and pounding wings.

Crossbow strings snapped, sending bolts flying into the air. Harpies screamed in fear and pain. Owen threw himself forward, grasping at his crossbow. He rolled over, bringing the weapon up just as a huge harpy descended on him, its wings trailing sparks, and released the firing lever. The bolt hammered into the harpy, throwing it back over the cliff in an explosion of feathers. Nearby, a man screamed, his voice trailing away.

Someone's fallen.

Flames from the burning nest roared upward at least twenty feet high, highlighting the men and harpies, the heat pushing the men back. Above the flames, burning harpies screamed, trailing fire as they dived and swooped. Owen reloaded his crossbow and shot another harpy, sending it spinning toward the ocean. All around him, Fioni and the others were shooting at the beasts. At least two of the men were now wielding spears, keeping the harpies back. Owen tried to reload his weapon, but another harpy came right for him, its talons outstretched, so Owen smashed his weapon into its face, hearing bone crack and sending it tumbling back over the edge of the cliff and into the raging fire below. When he saw one of his crossbow's arms was now broken off, Owen dropped it and drew his Hishtari sword. Another harpy lay nearby, clearly wounded and still thrashing about dangerously. He cut down at it, severing its head. He looked about for another foe but realized that the battle was over. All the harpies were either dead or dying. The fires from the nest now roared up from below, lighting up the entire Fist of Wodor, no doubt visible for dozens of leagues away.

But they had done it.

Rolf clapped Owen on the back. "Well done, Northman. You've got bigger balls than a whale."

"Whales don't have balls," said Fioni, smiling in the light of the fire. "But it was impressive nonetheless."

"I heard someone scream," Owen said.

"Figlif," said Rolf. "Saw it myself. One of the beasts pulled him from the cliff."

Fioni, her eyes grim now, reached out her hand and gripped Rolf's shoulder. "I'm so sorry. He was a brave man."

"Aye, he'll be missed."

As the warriors took stock of their injuries, Owen's fingers drifted over his belt. He stared about him, sudden panic welling within him.

Sight-Bringer was gone.

Chapter 4

Danika

Danika dreams.

A small part of her subconscious recognizes the dream for the fantasy that it is, but she can easily dismiss such an uncomfortable truth when the fantasy is this pleasant. She's with Brice, the only man she's ever loved. They lie in bed together, naked, her thigh draped over his, her body warm with the afterglow of their lovemaking. She rolls over on her stomach, lying atop his hard muscles as she playfully tugs on his thick mat of chest hair. She sighs, loving this moment, never wanting it to end. "Danika," he says, pulling her from her bliss.

And then she's no longer with him.

Now, she stands alone on a beach. The air is warm and moist, caressing her skin. She turns about, seeking her lover. The forest behind her is thick with pine trees. A huge flat-topped mountain rises in the background. The sky directly overhead is blue and clear, but in the distance, thick clouds ring the mountain.

Island, *she realizes, not knowing how she knows this but certain that it is true.*

I'm on an island.

"Danika!" Brice calls her name again, more urgently this time.

He's standing a dozen paces away before the forest's edge, watching her, a look of profound sadness on his features.

"Why are you over there, love?" she asks. She tries to go to him but can't move. Looking down, she sees she stands in the surf, ice-cold water lapping at her bare calves. Why can't she go to him?

"I can't stay anymore," he says softly, sadly, his voice breaking with emotion.

And that frightens her. Nothing has ever *stopped Brice Awde.*

Except death, she suddenly realizes. "What is this place, Brice? What's happening?"

"I don't want to cross the Golden Veil without you, but I can't stay any longer. Forces are pulling at me, incessantly demanding I move on. I'm sorry, my love, but I have to *go." He steps back a pace, and a shadow falls over his features.*

"Brice, wait! Come back."

He's into the tree line now, almost out of sight.

"Brice, I want to go with you."

But Brice was gone.

Danika bolted upright in her blankets, a thick coating of sweat over her skin. The night was black, and rain pattered on the tarp above her. She groaned, rubbing her chest, which felt as though she had just swallowed a block of ice. "Brice," she whispered. "I'm sorry. I should have gone with you when you asked."

The only answer was the wind rippling the tarp, the soft snoring of the others lying nearby. Sighing, she rolled out from beneath the tarp, recognizing she'd get no more sleep this night. The dream had felt so… real, as if she could have touched Brice. Was it only a dream? Brice's shade had already visited Owen; she was certain of that.

"I can't stay anymore." That's what he said.

A log in the bonfire cracked and split apart, sending sparks into the air. Someone sat on a lump of wood before the fire, highlighted by its glow. *Kora. It's Kora,* she realized. *Fen Wolf's* first mate must be waiting for Fioni, Owen, and the others to return. Danika dressed, pulling on her boots and wrapping her cloak around her shoulders as she made her way over to the fire. Ekkie lay on her belly near Kora, her eyes glowing red in the firelight. Kora was shifting embers about the fire with a stick as Danika joined her. "Can't sleep either, my lady of Wolfrey?"

She shook her head. "Danika, please. We're a long way from Wolfrey."

"Long way from everywhere... Danika."

"The others?"

Kora glanced up at the Fist of Wodor in the bay, and the fire still burning atop it. "We won't know for sure until they come back… or don't come back. But"—Kora paused, smiling slyly—"harpies don't start fires."

Danika lifted another log and sat down as well, basking in the heat from the fire. Ekkie rubbed her head against Danika's thigh, and she scratched behind the dog's ears. Kora handed her a small metal flask filled with sloshing fluid. The top was open, and Danika recoiled from the pungent, nose-clearing alcohol smell. She shook her head and handed the flask back to Kora. "Take a sip," said Kora. "As you said, we're a long way from your kingdom. I won't tell the other noblewomen."

Danika lifted the flask to her lips, taking just a taste. Immediately, she coughed violently, thrusting the flask back to Kora. Kora laughed as she pounded Danika upon the back before upending the flask and drinking from it herself. Danika, her eyes watering, held her hand out once more, and Kora gave her back the flask. She took another sip, this time feeling a warm glow build in her toes. "What is it?"

"Flame-rot. From Greywynne Island." She smirked at Danika. "Your family's island, is it not?"

"Not any longer," said Danika bitterly.

"Not ever," said Kora. "Don't get me wrong. We Waveborn don't much like the toads. They've lost their way. But lost or no, they're still kin to us. Still more like us than you—despite what you may believe in your kingdom."

"Your kingdom, too," said Danika.

Kora snorted. "Think so, do ye?"

Danika sighed. "Maybe not. Much of what I once knew to be truth... isn't." Her vision was a tad blurry. When Kora offered her the flask again, she shook her head.

Kora shrugged and sipped again. "From ignorance comes wisdom. Least that's what my great-grandmother always told me."

Danika glanced up at the Fist. "How long do you think... before we know?"

"Not before sunrise, even if all is fine. But don't fret. Fioni is harder than tempered Lyrian steel. And your knight...? Well, he's a tough fish, isn't he?"

"I think we both know Owen is no knight."

Kora snorted. "Knew that the moment you said he was. I like Owen. We *all* like Owen. He's no fish-up-the ass, knighted nobleman—no offense offered."

"None taken," said Danika, reaching down to scratch Ekkie's ears again before holding out her hand for the flask once more.

Chapter 5

Fioni

When Owen dashed forward, trying to throw himself at the roaring flames, Fioni tackled him around the knees, bringing him down. A moment later, Rolf was on top of him as well. "Let go!" Owen yelled, frantic.

"Idiot!" snapped Fioni. "You'll burn."

"The sword."

She tightened her grip on his thrashing legs. "It's steel, Owen—Illthori steel. The fire *can't* get hot enough to harm it." He stopped struggling, perhaps understanding she spoke the truth. She understood his fear. Sight-Bringer was the only weapon they possessed that could harm Serina's heart. In his journal, Serl had noted the various attempts he had made to destroy the heart: wooden stakes, fire, even trying to cut the heart to pieces—nothing Serl had possessed could even mar the heart's flesh. Whatever magic Serina had used to remove her heart also kept it beating, kept it indestructible. If Sight-Bringer was lost, so was their chance to kill Serina.

Owen groaned in frustration.

"Are you calm?" she asked.

He lay still, breathing heavily. "Aye," he finally said.

When they let him go, he sat on the ground, grim-faced, staring at the fires shooting up from the ledge. "She trusted me with it," he said.

She knelt beside him and squeezed his shoulder. "If it's down there, it'll still be there when the fires burn out. You'll see." She turned to Rolf. "Begin the preparations."

Rolf grunted and went about his tasks.

As Owen climbed to his feet, he winced, hobbling in place. Fioni examined the back of his leg, seeing the blood soaking through his breeches. "You're hurt. Let me look at it."

Nearby, one of the stone obelisks had fallen over, and she helped Owen hobble over to it and sit down. Kneeling in front of him, she yanked his boot off and then ran her fingers up his leg. He winced, glaring at her. "Don't be such a guppy," she said.

He muttered something beneath his breath she didn't catch. She rolled the hem of his breeches up, examining the wound. There was a cut, but it was less than an inch wide and not that deep, although it bled profusely. "Not so bad. Won't even need stitches, which is good, because I've always been a poor seamstress."

He frowned at her. "Just bind it tightly with a strip, then."

She shook her head as she traced the outside of the puncture with her finger. "Harpy talons are filthy. If we leave it, it could become foul. When we get back to the ship, ask Kora to put a salve of boiled goat urine on it."

As she pulled a small metal flask from her belt pouch, he eyed her suspiciously. "What's that for?"

She made a noncommittal shrug and then sighed. "Usually drinking." Without warning, she poured some of the contents of the flask over his wound. He cried out, bolting upright and almost kneeing her in the face.

He glared at her in indignation. "What in the name of Father Craftsman are you doing?"

"Oh, grow up. It's far better than filling with pus and becoming feverous." She grabbed his hips and forced him back down before tightly wrapping the wound.

He sighed, looking around him. "So this is the Fist of Wodor then? Strange, that a Fenyir holy site is on the Hishtari coastline."

"Wasn't always Hishtari coastline." She stood up again, hands on hips, and let her gaze sweep over the monuments with their carved Fenyir runes. "Once, all this land belonged to our gods and their servants, including men and women, us Fenyir."

He rolled his pant leg back down over the bandage before pulling his boot back on. "I thought you had to travel to Torin Island, this *Gateway to the Gods*, in order to talk to them."

She sat beside him on the stone, enjoying his discomfort as she invaded his private space, and he wriggled away from her. *These kingdom types are so strange,* she mused. *Such prigs.* "You can speak to the gods from anywhere, Owen. They just don't listen—or perhaps they simply ignore us. I think we're like pets to them, or livestock."

"Our Father Craftsman loves us," he said.

"Of course he does," she said with a forced smile as she patted his thigh, feeling the dense mass of muscle through the cloth. *Gods, he's like a horse.*

"So why here then?"

"Trees are special to us, Owen. We're master carpenters. Our ships, our homes, everything comes from wood, from the forests. Even Wodor was born from the roots of the world tree, Hrandruil, as was his brother, the Dark Shark we do not name. When Fenya's shield shines down, it allows the wights to interact with our world, to see and hear us. And wights are notorious tattletales. They will always rush off to tell the gods what we mortals are saying and doing."

"And Torin Island?"

"Ah." Her smile dropped. "That's different. Once, eons ago, the gods themselves lived on Torin Island. It was from Torin Island that they departed our world for the stars. That's why we call it the Gateway to the Gods. Our priests—men like my uncle Denyr—say that on Torin Island a trueborn Fenyir warrior can speak directly to the gods, bypassing the wights. Although..."

"Although what?"

"This is all legend, Owen. Few among us have ever been to Torin Island and returned to speak of it—Serl, Kora's grandmother, those who sailed with Serl, and perhaps a handful of others over the centuries, usually blown off course by storms into the Feral Sea. Only by luck did they find the island, and only by even greater luck—or, perhaps, the will of the gods—did they find their way home again."

"Because of the fog?"

"And the storms. Not for nothing are those waters named the *Feral Sea*. At the best of times, fog covers it, making navigation impossible. At the worst, ship-killing storms rise unnaturally fast."

By now, the others had set small fires before each of the obelisks. The effect was eerie, evoking in her supernatural awe. The flames seemed to flicker across the runes carved into the obelisks, giving them a silver sheen. Even the harpy stench had died off, their filth burned away by the fire, which was now only embers. She began to pull her boots off, first one and then the other. Owen stared at her. "Aren't you going to go look for your sword?" she asked, rubbing her toes. "Gods," she whispered, "I'd sleep with a bear for a hot bath."

He stared at her in confusion for a moment before sudden understanding filled his eyes. He jumped to his feet and ran to the edge of the cliff, where smoke rose, highlighted by the glow of embers in the nest. She joined him, the ground cold on her bare feet. "I didn't think it would take long to burn out. Rolf!" she called out. "Some help?"

A bare-chested Rolf, his thick chest covered in gray hair and scars, joined her. Owen stared at him in surprise, but before he could say anything, the two of them lowered him back down over the cliff again onto the ledge. The nest was gone, leaving only ashes and red-hot coals, but Owen kept back on the rocks, using his boots to shove the embers away. While he searched for Sight-Bringer, Rolf untied the laces at the back of Fioni's ring-mail coat and helped her pull it over her head and shoulder. Then she stripped off her sweaty gambeson and under-tunic. The night air was cool on her skin.

Owen whooped in glee from below. "It's here, thank Father Craftsman. It's still here, and it's unhurt, barely even warm."

Glancing over the edge, she saw he now held aloft the broken blade, a toothy, satisfied smile on his handsome features. *Thank the gods for that.* "Maybe you should come back up before you fall off."

When they pulled him back up, he stared wide eyed at her and Rolf, and then the others—all naked now—their armor, weapons, and clothing neatly piled on the ground. She faced him, naked, hands on hips. "Well?" she said.

He stared at her in stunned silence. "What?"

"Come now, Owen. There are no witnesses to our oath-swearings. If you're here, you're contributing. Remove your clothing. Be as the gods made you."

"I... naked?"

"Did your mother birth you fully clothed?" She walked away, perhaps exaggerating the sway of her hips a bit more than necessary. She paused, looking over her shoulder and enjoying the emotions storming across his handsome features. "*Completely* naked, Owen."

#

As *Fen Wolf*'s master, Fioni was the "head of the family" and led the ceremony. She and each of her father's former warriors, as well as

Owen, had used harpy blood to paint a Wodor's Hammer on their chests. The blood glistened wetly on her skin, running in a streak across her breasts from nipple to nipple and then down her stomach to run in rivulets between her thighs. When it dried, it would be impossible to wash clean, but traditions were traditions, and she didn't want the wights whispering that she and the others had failed to show respect to Wodor.

She stood before the others at the base of the oak tree, swaying in the firelight. Owen stood back, watching the row of warriors—each old enough to be her father. His face registered his confusion and unease. He was clearly uncomfortable, and perhaps a bit embarrassed. She hid her smile, focusing on the task before her.

Wodor was chief among their gods, but it wasn't his blessing she sought this night, nor did she call upon his oldest son, Orkinus the sea god, master of Nifalgen, the alehouse beneath the dark waves. This night was an oath night, and they sought the blessing of the goddess Fenya, daughter of Wodor and namesake of their people, the goddess of lightning, thunder, storms, war, and courage.

The warriors swayed and chanted, on occasion breaking into an impromptu dance or throwing themselves chest first at their mates. All were old, middle-aged, with too much gray hair and too many scars. It broke her heart that such brave men, men who had already fought, bled, and killed for her father so many times before, could not now live out their lives in peace. *Damn you, Galas! Damn your treachery, and damn your ambition.*

A brass bowl they had carried up the cliff in a sack lay on the ground before her. A foot wide, it was filled with fresh grain, sprinkled over the top with salt, and into which she had just poured a goatskin filled with ale. Placed on the ground around the bowl were twelve silver armbands. There had been thirteen, but Figlif no longer needed one. His duty was over, and no doubt, a brave warrior like him was already in Nifalgen, mayhap drinking with her father. She found that thought pleasing. She had always liked Figlif. When she was a little girl, she had ridden on his knee, pretending to be a ship tossed about by a storm as he bucked and thrashed, making stormy noises. Distracted by the memory, she almost missed the moment when the chanting reached its peak. *Now,* she knew. *It must be now. The wights must be watching.* Rolf smashed his chest against another of his men, sending the man staggering backward, his eyes fervent with religious joy.

She bent down and picked up a sharpened bone dagger placed before the bowl. Holding her forearm over the bowl, she placed the edge of the blade against her skin. "Fenya, war mother, hear us this night. Accept the oaths of these brave warriors who have outlived their yarl. They are honorable men, who through no fault of their own cannot yet accompany their master to Nifalgen. I, Fioni Ice-Bound, daughter of Taios Oak-Heart, would take up their oaths. I will feed them. I will house them. I will treat them with honor."

"Hear us, Fenya!" the men screamed, their eyes wild, spittle running from the corner of their mouths. "Witness our oaths."

"But, most of all"—Fioni raised her voice—"I will bring them to the revenge they need."

"Bless us, Fenya!" they screamed.

"Take my blood with theirs," said Fioni, cutting her forearm with the bone dagger. The cut, although neither wide nor deep, still filled with blood, dripping down her arm and fingers and into the grain-and ale-filled bowl.

"Take our blood! Take our blood!" the men chanted.

Rolf stepped forward, his body trembling with excitement. Rolf thrust his arm out over the bowl, and she cut it. His blood mingled with hers in the bowl. She bent down, picked up the first silver arm-ring, and used it to stir the now-bloody grain, before holding the arm-ring out to Rolf. "What say you before the wights, Rolf Fork-Beard? What say you to those who would whisper your message to the ears of the gods, to Fenya herself?"

"I say I swear to serve Fioni Ice-Bound, the daughter of Taios Oak-Heart. I will obey her orders. I will fight for her. I will kill for her. And—if necessary—I will die for her."

Fioni grabbed Rolf's arm and thrust the bloody, grain-covered silver band all the way up his arm to his large bicep, jamming it in place. "I accept your oath, Rolf Fork-Beard. I offer you ale and salt for the rest of your life."

Rolf reached out and hugged her fiercely. The others cheered, and she felt giddiness for the first time since the death of her father. *This is a good thing. Amid all the death, the oath of a good man is a blessing.* She thought of Vory, and his loss shivered through her.

The others came now, one by one, to cut their arms, mingle their blood with hers, and receive their armbands. Only Owen stood back, a look on his face of half uncertainty, half awe. *He swore his own oath to the Lady Danika. Can his people transfer oaths?*

After midnight, the ceremony complete, they cleaned themselves as well as they could and dressed again, strapping their armor back in place. She tightened her sword belt as the others kicked out the fires, once more plunging the Fist of Wodor into darkness. The rain still drizzled down, but the storm was moving farther away. Then, far out over the sea, the lightning flared once more—in its sudden illumination, revealing the shapes of the three longships now sailing past the Fist of Wodor and into the bay. She stared wide eyed at Owen.

"Serina," he said softly. "She's found us."

Chapter 6

Danika

Danika's head jerked up as what sounded like an entire pack of coyotes began howling in the woods behind the beach. Ekkie stood, staring out to sea and growling. Danika felt a prickling in her scalp, the hair lifting on the back of her neck. The night was black, and the huge fire atop the Fist of Wodor had long since burned out. Rain continued to patter about them, and far out to sea, the occasional flicker of lightning flashed in the night sky. Kora watched Ekkie. "What's up your ass, girl?" she muttered softly.

"Something's wrong," Danika insisted, leaning forward to meet Kora's eye. "The dog… the coyotes. We should send someone to check on Fioni and the others."

Kora shook her head. "It's too dangerous." She scratched Ekkie's rump, but the dog only began to growl more aggressively and bark at the sea. "There's a storm at sea. The thunder spooks animals, that's all."

"I don't think so. This… feels different." She reached out and placed her hand on Kora's forearm. "Please. Break the camp."

"You must be calm. No one knows we're here. And even if the Hishtari navy—"

41

"It's not the Hishtari that scares me," Danika insisted.

Kora bit her lip. "Even if Serina could find us, *Fen Wolf* is the fastest ship in the Promiscuous Sea."

"*Fen Wolf* is anchored, her crew is sleeping, and her skipper is away," insisted Danika, hearing the strain in her voice. "Look at Ekkie. Listen to the coyotes. Something *is* wrong. Break the camp!"

Kora stared at her in silence. *She's not going to listen to me.* Then Danika saw the momentary flicker of uncertainty in the other woman's eyes.

Chapter 7

Owen

Owen stood beside Fioni and the others, staring over the cliff and down into the darkness below. He drew Sight-Bringer, immediately feeling the rush of magic that heightened his senses. His vision suddenly as sharp as an owl's, he saw the three longships again as they sailed around the base of the stalk and entered the bay. The largest ship was more than twice the size of the others—*Iron Beard*, the Waveborn clan's prized drake-ship. Once, the massive warship had belonged to Fioni's legendary great-grandfather Serl, before passing on to her father, Taios. Now, it belonged to their enemy. "It's *Iron Beard*," Owen said. "And two other ships."

"Galas," Fioni said bitterly. "One of the other two must be *Thunder Killer*, but how did Galas get a third ship? You and Kora burned *Blood Raven*."

Behind them, Rolf lit a torch, showing the concern on the faces of the others. "They're heading for the beach," Owen said. "We need to warn them."

"Rolf, the horn," she urged.

Rolf handed his torch to her before drawing an intricately carved bone horn tied to his sword belt. Raising the horn to his lips, he blew a single, braying note, shattering the night's silence. In the woods to the east, Owen heard coyotes howling. As Rolf lowered the horn, light suddenly flared into existence around each of the three ships far below as their crews—understanding someone had seen them—lit lanterns. From here, Owen could see the light of the bonfire on the beach, but nothing else, even with Sight-Bringer. They could do no more to warn the others.

"What orders, Fioni?" asked Rolf.

"We need to get back and get underway. We can't fight three ships."

Fioni, still holding the torch, took off at a trot, with Owen and the others close behind her. They traversed the rope bridge much quicker this time, practically running over it. The bridge swayed and rocked beneath their weight, the ropes creaking in protest, but it held. In moments, Fioni scrambled back onto the sunken cliff leading back to the beach. The three ships were already ahead of them, rowing along the cliff as Fioni and the others scrambled down the path above them. One of the men ahead of Owen slipped on the wet rocks. Before Owen could even reach for him, the man disappeared, screaming as he fell. Fioni spun about, anguish in her eyes.

"Keep going!" Rolf yelled from behind Owen. "If they beat us to the beach, we're dead anyway."

Fioni turned away, continuing their mad dash down the trail.

From here, Owen could look down on his left, peering right onto the lantern-lit decks of the three longships, their oars pulling them along the cliff face. Rows of warriors standing shoulder to shoulder packed *Iron Beard*'s wide deck. *Too many fighters,* Owen realized. *Something's wrong here.* Then one of the smaller longships broke away and turned to port, heading away. *Iron Beard* and the other longship continued along the cliff face, headed for the beach.

"*Thunder Killer*," Rolf said behind Owen. "Where's she going?"

Owen, with Sight-Bringer's magic aiding him, gazed out over the bay. It was almost too far to see, but he could just make out a sleek dark shape moving quickly toward the mouth of the bay and the open sea. "*Fen Wolf!*" Owen cried, stopping Fioni and the others in their tracks. "Kora's already underway, making a run for the sea."

Thunder Killer was trying to intercept *Fen Wolf*.

"Are you certain?" Fioni demanded.

"I am, but I don't understand how they knew to get underway. Rolf only just blew the horn."

"Don't know," said Fioni. "But I've learned to never underestimate Kora Far-Sails."

"What do we do now?" Owen asked.

The others stood panting and wheezing on the trail behind them. "We head inland," said Fioni. "Kora will come back for us when she can."

Out on the bay, a drum began pounding, keeping cadence for the rowers. He could no longer see *Fen Wolf*'s shape, only the glow of the torchlight from the pursuing *Thunder Killer*. "How fast is *Thunder Killer?*" he asked.

"Fast," Fioni practically spat. Just then, she stiffened in alarm, gripping his bicep and squeezing it. "Look!" She pointed with the torch.

Iron Beard had drifted to a halt ahead of them, parallel to the cliff face. On its massive castle-like steering platform, a single person—a tall blond woman—was staring up at them. A wave of terror washed over Owen, threatening to unman him. He recognized it and its source in a moment—Serina and the Dread that surrounded her, a dark aura of fear. Twice now, he had experienced this same crippling fear. The first time had been in the Great Crypt when Modwyn had woken Serina from her decades-long slumber, feeding her with the blood of Palin; the second time had been when they had tried to kill her in Port Eaton's alehouse.

"Gods," whispered Fioni. "What's happening?"

The others were shaking in fear as well, their eyes reflecting their terror. In his grip, Sight-Bringer throbbed, sending a pulse of warmth up his arm, washing away the worst of the terror. Gripping Fioni's arm, he spun her to face him and then shook her violently. "Fioni. We can't stay here."

"I...how...what?"

He shook her again. For a moment, she stared at him in confusion, her mouth opening and closing like a beached fish's. Then purpose filled her eyes, and she gazed past him to the ship below. "Look!"

As one, the mass of warriors on *Iron Beard*'s deck surged forward, headed for the gunwale facing the cliff. Without hesitation, they clambered over the ship's hull and dropped into the frigid waters. Cold realization washed over him. "Ghouls," he whispered.

"There's no such thing," said Rolf weakly.

The first of the living corpses had reached the wave-soaked rocks of the cliff face. Gripping the wet stones with immeasurably strong fingers, the ghoul began to climb, like a human spider, toward the sunken trail and the path. In moments, dozens more followed, moving quickly up the cliff. The first ghoul reached the path between them and the beach and, without hesitation, began shambling inexorably toward their party. "We're cut off," Owen said.

Fioni, her face pale, looked up the trail. "We go back up."

The men turned and retraced their path. His stomach roiling with doubt, Owen turned and hurried after the others.

Chapter 8

Danika

Standing on the stern platform with Kora, Danika peered past *Fen Wolf*'s sternpost at the pursuing longship. "Careful," cautioned Kora, her hand upon the tiller. "If they've archers…"

Danika ducked back behind the gunwale, her heartbeat pounding as several arrows flashed overhead. While some of the crew fought to raise the sail, the others pulled at their oars, desperately trying to get past the other ship and to the open sea, where they could catch the wind. If Kora had not listened to Danika, the enemy ships would have caught them on the beach. As it was, they had just barely gotten underway in time, abandoning their tents and supplies on the beach when they heard the alarm horn from the Fist of Wodor. Just beside her, Ekkie barked furiously, vibrating with anger.

Kora glared over her shoulder at the approaching ship, coming at them from their port side. "*Thunder Killer*. Skippered by that skinny, ugly bastard, Ullyn Tangle-Beard. Almost killed him once. Wish I had."

Fen Wolf's new oar-master, a thickset, dark-haired woman named Bryndil, stalked between the ranks of rowers, urging them to greater speed. *Fen Wolf* cut through the waves. But *Thunder Killer* was almost on them, less than three boat lengths away on their left. "They're going to ram us," Danika said.

Kora snorted. "They're going to try."

Armed warriors crowded the sides of *Thunder Killer*, screaming obscenities at *Fen Wolf*, but a single warrior stood alone at the other ship's prow, separate from all the others. Something about him sent shivers down Danika's spine, but with the lantern light behind him, she could only make out his dark shadow, silent and unmoving. And then she understood: unlike the others, he wore a gleaming ring-mail coat. The Fenyir didn't wear armor at sea. To fall overboard in armor was certain death. Something about him seemed familiar…

Ekkie snarled.

"Now!" Kora screamed.

The six crew members armed with the remaining Kur'teshi crossbows rose up over the gunwale, where they had been hiding out of sight, and aimed their weapons at *Thunder Killer*'s elevated stern platform, just barely visible at this angle. The enemy warriors, recognizing the danger, tried to duck down but mostly fell atop one another in a tangled heap. The crossbow-armed warriors released their devastating volley. Impossibly fast, the lone warrior at the prow dropped out of sight as the crossbow bolts whipped across the length of the longship, splintering wood and skewering the two men at the tiller. Just for a moment, *Thunder Killer*'s high prow seemed to hang in the air, and then it began to swing away.

Fen Wolf's crew cheered as the longship darted past the other vessel, headed for the open sea.

Chapter 9

Serina

Serina watched her ghouls make their way along the sunken cliff. Some fell as they climbed, splashing back into the freezing waters without a sound, only to resurface moments later and once again begin to scale the cliff face. She watched them with a satisfied smile, knowing nothing could stop them. Out in the bay, *Thunder Killer*, with her childe Dilan aboard, pursued *Fen Wolf*. The map that had been hidden beneath the marsh-tick plates on Serl's shield had brought her to this place, but somehow her prey had gotten underway before she could take them on the beach. If she knew for certain where the niece of Stron was, she wouldn't have split her forces and pursued both the ship and those who had climbed the Fist of Wodor. Her fury was a cold frost seeping slowly over her entire body, turning it to ice. As she squeezed the gunwale, it burst into shards. *Be calm,* she told herself. *Be a queen. You've waited fifty years to destroy the Dain line—another hour or two won't make any difference.*

Behind her, she heard the approaching footsteps of several men. The first to speak was Yarl Galas Gilt-Mane, the tall, handsome

Fenyir warrior with long, flowing locks of blond hair. "My queen," he said with a nervous tremor in his voice. "What orders?"

She turned, once again in control of her emotions, and considered her servants. Two men stood just behind Galas. The first was Galvin, a heavyset, bearded man who had been the former barrel-maker in Port Eaton before demonstrating himself to be an ambitious and capable leader. The remaining Greywynne Islanders, several dozen men, had deferred to his authority, choosing him to lead them. She had given him command of *Hard Stone*, the ship that had once belonged to Yarl Vengir Flat-Nose—before she had taken his life and destroyed the Windhelm clan for their treason. The other man was her new blood thrall, Kory'ander Dey. The one-time Hishtari Moon Lord of Daenipor was young, boyish in form, and with the dark, pretty eyes she liked in her toys. He was only human, but she had altered him, giving him the gift of her blood milk, her mother's milk, making him faster and stronger in order to serve her better. Her last blood thrall had been her ill-fated great-nephew Modwyn, dead now, murdered in Daenipor while trying to bring her the niece of Stron. Modwyn's death was no great loss, but killing him had been an insult to her. *Yet one more reason to kill this... Danika Dain. Gods damn that family!*

Dey watched her out of the corner of his eye. His blue-painted lips—denoting his status as Hishtari royalty—quivered as if he wanted to say something, but instead he cast his eyes down, staring at her feet. Still new to his condition, he had yet to come to grips with the full range of his... *responsibilities*, but that would come soon enough. New blood thralls were like pets; they needed proper training. She held her hand out to Dey. "Come forward, my pretty one."

He hesitated only a moment and then rushed forward. Equal parts fear and love filled his eyes as he gripped her hand with both of his and fell to his knees before her. "Command me, my queen."

He still hobbled slightly when he walked. The night she had claimed him, he had been abed, recovering from a spear wound in his thigh. As well as enhancing his physical abilities, her milk had also sped up his body's healing. Had he been like her and Dilan, a true blood fiend, he'd have completely healed in a single day. But he was still only human, not worthy of her dark master's gift of immortality.

She ran her palm over his smooth cheek. "You will take your soldiers aboard *Hard Stone*. Master Galvin will take you to the shoreline and wait for you while you hunt our enemies. Follow the ghouls. Capture those who were on the Fist of Wodor. If the niece of Stron is with them, you will take her alive. The others you can do with as you please."

"My queen," said Galas, stepping forward, alarm in his eyes. "Fioni might be among them. She's the great-granddaughter of Serl Raven-Eye. I need her to legitimize my rule."

"No, you don't, Yarl Galas. All you need is *my* support."

Galas, his lips trembling, nodded. "Yes... yes, my queen."

"But you have served me well, so if this Fioni is among those we hunt, you are welcome to her."

"Thank you, my queen," said Galas.

Dey stumbled forward. "My queen, I don't have enough soldiers to fight the Red Wolf and her warriors. After her attack upon the Rose Palace, I have only several score, not enough to—"

She raised her hand, cutting him off. "With my ghouls, you have more than enough for a handful of warriors. Hunt them down, capture them if you can, but bring me both the niece of Stron and Sight-Bringer. I must have that blade back, where it can't threaten my kind. It can't harm me, but fifty years ago, Stron used it to butcher my childes." Her gaze swept all three of them. "Do you *all* understand?"

"Yes, my queen," they parroted.

"Hurry," Serina said, glancing to the east. "The dawn comes sooner than you might think."

She turned away from them, staring out at the open sea where her childe Dilan pursued the other ship. She felt his presence through the connection they shared as master blood fiend and childe. *Bring me the niece of Stron. Kill the others.*

She felt his thoughts in a moment, sensed his bloodlust. *Yes, Mother.*

Chapter 10

Owen

Owen and Fioni came up onto the headland last, joining Rolf and the others. In the east, the sky was beginning to lighten, but the night was still dark, and rain continued to patter around them. Owen watched the path along the sunken ledge. The closest of the ghouls was still several hundred yards away. "What are we going to do, Fioni?"

"We have the height advantage here," Fioni said, but she sounded uncertain, as if she was trying to convince herself. "They have to come at us one or two at a time. With the crossbows, we can—"

Owen shook his head. "Did you not hear me? They're ghouls. Crossbows won't even slow them down. You need to cut them to pieces or burn them."

Her eyes wild, she rounded on him. "How do you know?"

"Because I fought them once already—from behind the walls of Stron's Watch, and we barely held then. You can't hold them here. They'll just pull you off the cliff with them."

Rolf glared over the edge of the cliff at the two ships below. "Fioni, that other ship looks like—"

"*Hard Stone*," answered Fioni. "Yarl Vengir's ship."

"*He* betrayed us?" Rolf asked with incredulity. "Why would he do such a thing?"

"He said himself he'd have no choice but to bend knee if Serina came," Fioni said bitterly.

"It doesn't matter," said Owen. "We need to move down the headland, to the forest at the base of the cliffs. If we go east, we'll lose the ghouls in the hinterland."

"If we go east, we'll move away from the beach. Kora will come back for us when she can, but she'll never find us if we move away from the coast."

"If we stay here, we die," Owen insisted.

"This isn't our land, Northman," Rolf said. "Any Hishtari settlements we come across will treat us as enemies."

The closest ghoul was now less than fifty feet away on the trail below, moving steadily forward. Others followed along closely behind on the narrow trail. As the first ghoul came closer, within the light of their torch, Fioni stiffened in alarm. "Oh gods," she whispered, anguish in her voice. "He didn't betray us."

The ghoul was Yarl Vengir Flat-Nose, his dead black eyes shining in the torchlight as he stumbled closer.

Fioni spun about, hurrying down the sloping headland, speaking loudly over her shoulder as she went. "We head for the woods," she said. "You'd better be right about this, Owen."

Owen and the others hurried after her.

#

Fioni led them east down the headland, moving at a quick pace. The ground became rockier, more treacherous, but the sky began to lighten, improving their visibility and helping them stay ahead of their pursuers. The ghouls were still coming, Owen knew. He had seen them only minutes ago, spread out in a line across the headland, forestalling any attempt they might have made to get around them and return to the beach. *They're driving us inland, pushing us north,* he realized. *Why?*

Fioni led the others down a stony gully and into the thick forest. On this side of the cliffs, the woods were much drier, the branches cracking and breaking noisily underfoot, causing Owen to grimace. The Fenyir were wonderful mariners but poor woodsmen. He slipped back, dropping behind a tree and watching the gully they had just traversed. He still held Sight-Bringer, letting its magic flow through him. Far faster than he had expected, he saw the first of the ghouls coming down the gully—an old woman wearing a torn dress, revealing skin the color of burned wood. Another ghoul shoved through the trees on her left, and then two more on her right. And then he saw something he truly had not expected: men, *living* men— coming from the north where the beach lay—followed the line of ghouls. He stared at the men in disbelief. There were at least a dozen of them, all wearing the heavy red-and-blue cloth gambesons and animal masks of Hishtari soldiers.

What is happening here?

One of the soldiers bent down with a lit torch and examined the ground Owen and the others had just traversed. *A tracker,* he realized. *They have a tracker.*

Another man, wearing a thick dark cloak, stood behind the tracker, asking him something. The tracker, in turn, pointed in Owen's direction, and Owen felt a surge of panic but forced himself to relax. They couldn't possibly see him in the dark at this distance. Owen stared at the man in the dark cloak, feeling a certainty he had seen him somewhere before. And then he remembered where—the throne room of the Rose Palace. The man in the cloak was Kory'ander Dey, the Moon Lord of Daenipor.

And now he's serving Serina.

The last time Owen had seen Dey, Fioni had thrown a spear through his leg. The man hadn't even been able to stand, yet here he was, leading the hunt for them. Something had changed, he knew, something he needed to figure out—quickly.

Bent over and moving with all the stealth he could manage, Owen slipped away, hurrying to catch back up to the others. *At least now, we know why the ghouls were driving us north. They were pushing us toward the Hishtari soldiers.* The knowledge wasn't the least bit comforting.

Chapter 11

Kory'ander Dey

Kory'ander Dey slipped through the woods, a jeweled scimitar in his grip. Once, he had been weak and thin, as befitted nobility, but now he was outpacing his soldiers. What had Serina done to him?

And why did he need to please her so badly?

While one of his men, a former hunter, examined the ground, the rest, several dozen, watched the ghouls, their eyes wide with terror. Even after days at sea with the ghouls in *Iron Beard*'s hold, the men remained terrified of them, and Serina. Nor did they understand why they sailed with Fenyir pirates. But what they liked or didn't like was of no interest to Dey. They were his to do as he commanded. The hunter looked up. "They're not that far ahead, Moon Lord. Perhaps a dozen men."

"We must go faster," Dey snapped. "I want to catch them before sunrise." After that, Serina had told him, when she went to sleep, the ghouls would only act on her last command. Without her will driving them, they'd become near-mindless creations of dead flesh.

Another guardsman, a captain, pushed his way past the other soldiers, sweat coating his face. His name was Kor'islim, Dey knew.

He came from a lesser but still noble family. Kor'islim stared at the backs of the ghouls as they moved forward in a line, entering the woods. "Moon Lord, now is our chance. There is a large village only some hours' march to the south. There will be men there. We can find help."

Dey stared at him in confusion. "What do I care for some dirty village?"

"Moon Lord." Kor'islim's dark eyes darted to the other soldiers watching. "What are we doing here? Why do we serve our enemy? And these dead things are an abomination. Worse, that—that Fenyir woman they call *queen*—she is a monster. We must flee."

At the mention of the queen, Dey's pulse began to pound behind his eyes. "Captain, do you question my orders?" he said slowly, softly.

"What? No. No, of course not, Moon Lord. It's just that—"

"The queen wants those we hunt. So *I* want those we hunt."

"What queen? Not *our* queen. Just another Fenyir she-bitch. I don't understand why we're here."

Some of the soldiers began to bob their heads and mutter in agreement. Dey's gaze swept over all of them before returning to the captain. "You will not speak of her that way," he said through clenched teeth. He began to squeeze the hilt of his scimitar so tightly, the bones in his hand creaked, sending pain running up his forearm.

"Moon Lord," Kor'islim said forcefully, drawing strength from the support of the other soldiers. "We must—"

"Must?" Dey shrieked as he lunged forward. Before the other man could move, Dey thrust his scimitar through his right eye so forcefully that the weapon's point exited the back of the man's skull. Still standing, the captain turned his left eye inward, so that it seemed to stare cross-eyed at the blade through his head. Dey yanked his blade free—pulling Kor'islim's impaled eye with it—and his body fell, his legs jerking. The other soldiers stumbled back, staring at Dey, their faces white. Joy rushed through Dey. He flicked his scimitar, casting away the bloody chunk of eyeball. "Those we now hunt attacked us, raiding the Rose Palace itself—an act to shame your ancestors! Now, they flee from us, hiding in our own land, seeking to avoid justice for their crimes." He pointed his scimitar at their faces, turning in place as he addressed them. "Know this—the Fenyir are not the only warriors in this land. We Hishtari are more than a match for anyone. Your ancestors know this. They are watching you now, judging you. This coward"—he hawked and spat upon the corpse—"was an insult to his ancestors. Do you wish to be like him?"

The soldiers stared at the corpse in silence.

"Good then," said Dey, wondering just how strong and fast he was now. "Let's go kill some Fenyir."

Chapter 12

Owen

The ghouls pushed them east, always farther into the hinterland and away from the shoreline. Twice now, Fioni had tried to lead them around the line of ghouls in an attempt to sneak past them and head back to the beach. Each time, though, the ghouls had seen them within minutes and—seemingly moving as a single entity—had begun to converge upon them, once again forcing them east. Owen glanced at the horizon, now turning red. The sun would be up within an hour or two, maybe a bit less. Would the ghouls turn back then, as they had when they attacked Stron's Watch? Maybe, but for some reason, he doubted it. Some of the men wanted to try fighting their way through the line of ghouls, but Owen had talked them out of such a desperate course of action, describing what a ghoul could do to a man. *We may have no choice soon,* Owen mused, wishing he wielded an intact Sight-Bringer once again instead of the broken shard it now was.

The forest around them was eerily devoid of animal life, frightened off, no doubt, by the unholy presence of the ghouls. Wind whistled through the trees, blowing against their sweaty faces. Their progress became more difficult, the forest floor strangely thick with underbrush and fallen trees. Even the air carried the rot of decaying leaves and wood. Something was...*off*, but he couldn't put his finger on it. Then, as the shadows began to recede, he now saw that they had somehow blundered into a small valley; that was why the wind was howling, it was blowing in from the east, captured by the valley's steep sides. "Fioni," he called out.

She and the others paused, turning to look back.

"We're in the mouth of a valley. We need to go back—now!"

She looked about her and then swore bitterly when she realized he was right. She moved to slip past, intent on leading the others back out.

"Quickly," Rolf urged, "before the ghouls cut us—"

"Wait," said Owen, grabbing her forearm. "Do we still have any of the straw we used on the harpy nest?"

Her eyes narrowed, and then she glanced about her, at the high, sloping, tree-lined valley and the thick, dry underbrush caught in it. She took a sudden deep breath and turned to Rolf in excitement. "Well?"

"Four bundles," Rolf answered after conversing with the others. "We used the rest on the nest."

"Is that enough?" she asked Owen. "You're the woodsman."

Bending down, Owen broke off some of the underbrush and cracked it between thumb and forefinger. "The underbrush is dryer than I'd expect this late in the year—and thicker. The valley's walls must shelter it from the weather. With the wind blowing through the way it is, it'll only take a small fire to become a death trap. I'm amazed it hasn't gone up yet from a lightning strike."

"What do you recommend?" Fioni asked Owen. "We're running out of time."

Owen bit his upper lip and looked about him, excitement

beginning to course through him. "There," he said, pointing to a streambed near the valley's entrance. Thick brush lay collected within the bed and along its banks. "We hide there. The ghouls funnel in after us, and then we burn them."

Fioni shook her head. "They'll see us."

"Not if someone draws their attention, leads them away," Owen said. "They're ghouls, mindless corpses. If they see someone—"

"It might work, Fioni," Rolf said.

"What then?" Fioni asked.

"The same person who leads them farther into the valley can set the fire-bundles."

"What are you talking about?" asked Fioni, surprise in her eyes. "It's *your* plan; you're the only woodsman here. Only you can set the fires and get away."

A lump formed in his throat. He shook his head, answering her in a wooden, distant voice. "I… I can't, Fioni. I have to get back to Lady Danika. Somebody else needs to volunteer."

"Owen," she said, a surprised, pleading tone in her voice.

He looked away, unable to meet her gaze. He felt the heat of her stare, but he had no choice. His loyalty was to Lady Danika, and he had let her down once already, abandoning her to torture. He couldn't keep his promise to see her safely home if he died in this forest—and without knowing for certain if there was another way out of this valley, he just couldn't take that chance.

"It's all right, Northman," Rolf said softly, kindly. "I understand. It's not your place, anyway. I'll do it."

Fioni glared at Owen while shaking her head. "No. You're too old to run from ghouls, Rolf. Give me the straw-bundles. I'll do it."

Rolf snorted loudly. "You're right about one thing, Fioni Ice-Bound: I *am* too old to be running through the woods. So instead, I'm going to stay here and burn some ghouls. Don't worry. I'll catch up."

Fioni grabbed his forearm. "Rolf."

Rolf patted her hand, grinning at her and exposing a gap in his front teeth. "Go on. Let me do this little thing for you."

She stood there, indecision on her features, then rushed forward and hugged Rolf fiercely. "Light the damned fires, but then run! Catch up to us at the beach. We need you."

He threw the sack containing the pitch-soaked straw over his shoulder. "Get moving." He turned and began to run farther into the valley.

Owen led the others to the streambed, where they quickly hid themselves, lying on their bellies in the underbrush. The sounds of the ghouls crashing through the woods grew closer. Fioni made a point of not looking at Owen, and he could feel her resentment roiling from her. *She's furious, but I had no choice. I can't let Lady Danika down, not again. I have to get back to her.* The stench of dead, rotting flesh wafted over him a moment before he saw the first ghoul, a dead girl no more than fifteen or sixteen with one of her arms hanging only by a string of sinew. As she stumbled forward, the arm spun one way and then the other. More ghouls followed, and soon there were dozens bunched together, funneled into the valley's entrance. As they came alongside the streambed, Owen felt his heartbeat race. *All they need do is look this way...*

Then, farther ahead, Rolf appeared, waving his arms and screaming obscenities at the ghouls. He turned and disappeared into the trees, and the ghouls fixated on him, marching right past the streambed. Soon, a long stream of ghouls slipped past, all focused ahead of them. Then they saw the Hishtari soldiers, including the young Moon Lord, Kory'ander Dey. The soldiers loped along behind the ghouls. One of them dropped down onto the trail, only about thirty feet away from them, peering at the ground. The other soldiers, Dey included, ran ahead of him, following the ghouls. The tracker stood, turned about, and stared back in their direction, his face registering his uncertainty. He opened his mouth, as if to yell, when Fioni popped up on one knee, a crossbow in her shoulder, and released her bolt. It hit him in the forehead, shattering the back of his skull as it went clear through it. His corpse flew back through the air, smashing into a tree trunk, staining it with his blood and brains. In the trees ahead, the other Hishtari soldiers carried on, oblivious to what had just happened. Fioni lowered her crossbow and faced Asger, Rolf's second-in-command. "Let's go."

Asger turned to the others. "Quickly—and quietly," he whispered.

They rose and began to run, heading back the way they had come. Behind them, Owen smelled smoke.

#

A short time later, they came upon a softly gurgling creek, and Fioni called for a short halt while everyone drank and recovered their strength. They had been moving quickly, running when they could through the thick forest, desperate to outpace the forest fire behind them, although Owen doubted it would spread far past the sheltered valley and its thick deadfall; this late in the year, forest fires tended to burn out quickly in the damp woods.

As he cupped his hands in the cold stream and drank greedily, Owen scanned the faces of the others. They were all older men, older even than the garrison had been in Stron's Watch. But like those grizzled veterans, these men were still tough and hardy. The strain of the night, though, was beginning to show in their lined faces, in their trembling limbs. Even Owen was growing tired. Vory's armor, while lighter than he would have thought, was still becoming a burden. He had long since sheathed Sight-Bringer. Its magic had limits, which he had reached during the battle at Stron's Watch, and he didn't want to exhaust it now.

While the men drank, Fioni moved back into the woods, staring behind them, her body rigid. *She's looking for Rolf.* There had been no sign of the other man. As he stared at her back, he felt a thickness in his throat. *Was I right not to stay behind and set the fires?*

What would Dilan have done?

He approached her slowly, racking his mind for something to say that could make her understand. Smoke obscured the woods behind them and stung his eyes. Despite the smoke, the sky was still getting lighter; it would be daylight soon. He stopped in place several feet behind her, when he saw Fioni's shoulders tremble. Once again, his guilt crashed against him. He inhaled deeply, hating himself. "Fioni, can we—"

Without turning, she raised her hand, cutting him off. "There's someone coming. I think it's Rolf," she said excitedly.

Then he also saw the shape moving through the smoke, and a sense of giddy relief washed through him. *Thank you, Father Craftsman.*

"Rolf," Fioni called out, taking a step closer.

Yarl Vengir Flat-Nose stepped into view, flanked by two more ghouls. His hair was gone, burned away by the same fires that had blackened most of his skin and charred his clothing. The stench of burned flesh assaulted them, almost a physical thing, and Owen stumbled back, bile rising in his throat. Yarl Vengir's black eyes seethed with hatred as he came forward, his hands outstretched for Fioni. The other two ghouls, a young girl no more than twelve and an elderly man, their skin charred, stumbled forward as well.

Fioni stood frozen.

Having seen firsthand what a ghoul was capable of, Owen grabbed Fioni's shoulders and threw her behind him. Yarl Vengir smashed into him, knocking him onto his back, and falling atop him. He just managed to catch the former yarl's wrists, desperately trying to hold his grasping fingers away from his face. He heard Fioni's sword, Wave's Kiss, hiss from her scabbard, followed a moment later by her cry of rage, but he couldn't spare any energy for her. Yarl Vengir glared at him without a trace of his humanity as he pushed his clawlike, fire-blackened hands closer to Owen's face. As the ghoul's black fingers came closer, Owen let go of one wrist and threw an off-balance punch, connecting solidly with the ghoul's chin and snapping its head back. The blow had done nothing but give the ghoul a moment's pause, but in that moment, Owen gripped Sight-Bringer's hilt and drew it free of its sheath. Owen stabbed Sight-Bringer's broken blade into the ghoul's side, sliding it between the ribs. In an instant, Yarl Vengir ceased moving, stiffened, and fell away from Owen, smoke drifting from the wound in his side, the stench of burned flesh stronger than before. During the siege of Stron's Watch, Owen had learned that Sight-Bringer was anathema to the undead and could destroy ghouls with a single cut—*if* one could survive long enough to use it. Owen staggered to his feet.

The other men rushed past him, throwing themselves at the remaining two ghouls, one of which, the young girl, was now pulling herself along the ground, her left leg cut off at the knee by Fioni. Yarl Taios's warriors—no, Fioni's warriors—smashed into the remaining ghoul, knocking it down before standing around it, hacking it and the young girl to pieces with their fighting axes. He rushed over to Fioni, who stood holding her sword before her, its bloody blade shaking. She stared at him in confusion. "Fioni, are you all right?" he asked.

When her green eyes darted to the corpse of Yarl Vengir, sorrow replaced the horror. She stared at the corpse for long moments. "Rolf's not coming, is he?" she finally said.

He shook his head, his shame threatening to unman him. "No," he mumbled through thick lips. "Fioni… I—"

She turned away from him. "We go now."

Chapter 13

Danika

The sun hadn't yet broken the horizon, but its glow presaged its imminent arrival, chasing away the night and revealing the longship pursuing them and the coastline flying past. Danika pulled herself up on the sternpost, watching *Thunder Killer* in *Fen Wolf*'s wake. Both longships were now running with sails raised and oars in the water. A stocky, dark-haired woman named Herla High-Eye gripped the tiller while Kora stood beside her, overseeing the crew and the operation of the ship. The ropes creaked, and the huge sail crackled with wind. Danika climbed back down just as *Fen Wolf* hit a large wave, splashing her with cold seawater.

In her weeks at sea, this was by far the fastest Danika had ever seen the longship move—so fast, she half thought *Fen Wolf* would fly into the air. But, as fast as they cut through the waves, *Thunder Killer* was still following, unable to close the distance but unwilling to give up the chase. The Hishtari coastline was thick with forests of dark pine on their steering board side as they sailed north away from the bay and away from Owen, Fioni, and the others. The sky was turning red in the east, chasing away the night.

"Can we out-sail them?" she asked Kora.

Kora looked back at *Thunder Killer* and chewed on her lip, her face thoughtful. "In time, yes, but *Thunder Killer* is a fine ship. And—much as I hate to admit it—Ullyn knows his business. It'll take some hours to get away from them, maybe even a day or more."

"Owen and Fioni don't have that long," Danika insisted.

Herla snorted. "Never thought I'd hear Kora Far-Sails compliment Ullyn Tangle-Beard."

"I didn't compliment him," Kora said. "Least I don't think I did." She made a sour face. "Gods, maybe I did say something nice about him. This has been a hard voyage."

"Well, what do you want to do?" Herla asked.

"I don't know yet. Something clever. Do you have any ideas?"

Herla laughed. Danika watched them both in disbelief. They could have been discussing what to have for dinner. Ekkie, standing nearby, barked and then turned about several times before lowering herself to the deck. Kora's eyes narrowed as she watched the dog settle.

"Well," said Herla, "whatever you decide, bear in mind we have a strong port tack right now."

"So does Ullyn," said Kora as she climbed up and balanced alongside the sternpost, watching the ship to their rear. She turned, squinting to their front now. "There are seagulls diving into the water, maybe a league to the north." She hopped down onto the deck, smiling impishly, and punched Herla in the bicep. "I'm going to rub Ullyn's balls."

Herla frowned at the now-grinning Kora.

"Rub his what?" asked Lady Danika, staring at Kora in confusion. "Never mind. What's this about seagulls?"

"They dive for fish that swim in warmer currents," said Herla. "Sometimes"—she paused and looked down her nose at Kora, as if the other woman were incredibly foolish—"where there's a sandbar, the water is shallow, warmer."

"There *is* a sandbar," insisted Kora. "I feel it in my toes."

Herla snorted, tossing her head. "None of us have ever sailed this far north. Maybe you're feeling something else in your toes."

"I don't understand," Danika said.

Kora cupped her hands over her mouth. "I need sharp eyes at the prow now!" she yelled to the crew.

A young man darted forward, climbing onto the wooden wolf's head on the stempost, watching the sea to their front. *Fen Wolf* continued to rise and slam back into the waves, but the sailor remained perched atop the wolf's head. Once again, Danika was amazed at the Fenyirs' ease with seaboard life. "Take us in closer to the shoreline," Kora said to Herla.

Herla shook her head but did as Kora had asked. "Even if there is a sandbar, with such a strong tack, we'll be head-to-wind before we can come about. They'll catch us amidships."

"The day that ugly runt Ullyn catches me floundering head-to-wind is the day I give up sailing to raise babies," scoffed Kora, now leaning precariously out over the gunwale to their port side in an attempt to see.

"No, it'll be the day you die," said Herla.

"Not today," answered Kora with a flash of white teeth.

Many years ago, when she had been a teenaged girl and had accompanied her father to their family holdings on Greywynne Island, Danika had learned to sail small boats, but as she listened to the two women converse, she felt as if they were speaking in an entirely different language. "If there is a sandbar close to the shoreline," said Danika, standing on her toes in a futile attempt to see, "shouldn't we move farther out to sea, not closer to the shore?"

"Probably," answered Kora in a distracted manner, still hanging far out over the gunwale, her gaze fixed on the seas ahead of them.

"What will happen if we run into it?" Danika asked.

Kora glanced back at her in puzzlement as if she had just asked if water was wet. "We'll run aground."

At that moment, the young man hanging onto the prow turned back and yelled, "Turtles ahead, less than five ells!"

"Ha!" barked Kora. "Ramming speed!"

Bryndil, the oar master, increased the cadence, and *Fen Wolf* shot forward. Ekkie rose again and began barking furiously. "Be ready!" Kora yelled to the crew as she dropped back beside Herla on the steering platform. "We're going to rub their balls."

The crew cheered, and Danika saw the excitement on their faces in the early-morning light. Kora moved to the sternpost, where the anchor, a metal hook attached to a wooden crossbeam, hung attached to a long coil of rope. Kora took up a small hand-axe and braced herself near the anchor, her gaze intent on the ship to their rear. "Come on, Ullyn," she said softly to herself. "Come take the bait."

"I don't understand what you're doing," Danika said.

Kora's eyes darted to her, then at the deck near her feet. "You'll want to watch your feet, my lady of Wolfrey."

Danika glanced down, saw she stood with a foot atop the coiled rope, and quickly moved off, suddenly understanding. "You're crazy."

Kora barked in laughter. "Ha! *Thunder Killer* just matched our speed. That idiot Ullyn thinks he has us."

"Maybe he does," mused Herla. "If we rip out the keel…"

"We won't rip out the keel," said Kora, shaking her head, the affection clear in her voice. "*Fen Wolf's* a tough bitch. Besides, I've always wanted to try this, but Fioni never wanted to."

"Maybe for good reason," Herla said.

"Seaweed ahead!" the lookout yelled, near panic in his voice.

"Now!" Kora screamed. "Port oars up. Hard to steering board."

As one, the oars on the left hand side of the ship rose as the crew detached them from the oarlocks and lifted them upright. The rowers on the right kept pulling, if anything straining even harder as the ship suddenly began to skew, tipping over on the right as the ship turned—far faster than a ship should have been able to. Herla, both arms wrapped around the tiller, screamed as she hauled on it, turning the rudder. Danika's stomach lurched, and she fell against Ekkie, trapped against the hull as the ship rolled into the turn. The prow lifted out of the water as the entire ship swung suddenly toward the shoreline, the wooden hull screaming in protest. Danika, wedged in tightly next to Ekkie, could only pray as the ship's entire port side rose out of the water. Ekkie licked her face. When she pulled herself up by the gunwale, Danika's eyes opened wide at the sight of the other longship, now bearing down on them with its iron-tipped prow. *It's going to hit us,* Danika realized in horror. *Cave in our hull.*

Kora swung her hand-axe, cutting through the rope securing the anchor. The anchor fell, the rope whipping past so fast it burned a groove into the gunwale. Danika had only a moment to stare in astonishment before the line ran out, stretched taut, and *Fen Wolf* shuddered under the sudden jarring impact. Once again, she fell forward, sliding down the deck on her belly as *Fen Wolf* whipped about—now completely facing the opposite direction. Kora roared in triumph and cut through the anchor rope. The sail, filled with wind a moment ago, now hung limp, but the ship's prior momentum kept it moving forward. "All oars row!" Kora screamed, spittle flying from her mouth.

The port oars dropped back down, and *Fen Wolf* leaped through the waves again just as *Thunder Killer*, unable to turn in time, sped past twenty feet away at least. Without having to be told, Danika understood they had just "rubbed Ullyn's balls."

Then, impossibly, Danika saw the warrior in ring mail she had seen earlier launch himself through the air at them. No one could possibly jump that far, but the warrior somehow made it, smashing into *Fen Wolf*'s hull, where he hung from it one-handed. The closest rower jumped up, pulling his oar with him as he tried to hammer the man loose. Instead, the warrior grasped him with his other hand and pulled him over the side. Kora drew back and tossed her hand-axe. It spun through the air before striking the warrior's hand, severing several of his fingers as it drove into the wooden deck. The warrior fell back into the water, disappearing from sight.

Danika stared in horror at the gouge marks in the gunwale where the warrior had gripped it, tearing furrows in the wood, and then at the severed clawlike fingers lying on the deck. The fingers turned to ash and blew away before her eyes. Her heart was pounding, her skin drenched in sudden perspiration. Although she had only had a brief glimpse of his face, with his red eyes, she had recognized the warrior. It had been Dilan Reese, a man-at-arms in her family's service. Dilan had helped Owen bring Sight-Bringer back from Serina's fortress. Dilan had led the defense of Stron's Watch. Dilan had driven Sight-Bringer through Serina's chest. And Dilan had thrown himself onto Serina's back, slowing her down long enough for Owen and Danika to escape the disaster at the alehouse in Port Eaton.

Dilan was a hero.

Dilan was a blood fiend.

A moment later, there was a shuddering crash behind them as *Thunder Killer* struck the sand bar and came to a sudden halt, tipping over to lie at an angle. The screams of its crew reached across the waves.

Kora flashed her teeth at Herla. "Told you *Fen Wolf* was a tough bitch."

Chapter 14

Fioni

Fioni led the others west through the forest, retracing their path back to the beach where they had moored *Fen Wolf* the previous night. When Kora returned—and Fioni knew she would—she would come first to the beach, even if *Iron Beard* and *Hard Stone* were still in the bay. They had outpaced the fire and the smoke and had seen no more ghouls. With the sun now over the horizon, the forest was eerily quiet. They could still smell the smoke in the distance, though, and pushed on as fast as they could through the woods. Soon, they came upon another streambed, and Owen suggested they follow it, guessing it would flow into the bay.

Rolf was dead. She was sure of that. Twice now, Owen had made plans that others had had to carry out for him. It had been his plan to climb the walls of the Rose Palace and open the Water Gate for the others, but once inside, Owen had abandoned Fioni to go off on his own and save Lady Danika. Now, although he might have been able to set the fire and escape, Owen had refused, forcing Rolf to volunteer in his place. Once again, his service to that damned noblewoman had come before Fioni. A sudden thought made her pause midstep: *Does he love her?*

And do I care?

Asger stopped beside her, watching her. "Is everything all right?"

"We need to keep moving," she said. Not waiting for a response, she stalked forward, moving quicker along the streambed. Soon she could smell the sea, strong enough to wash away the stench of the smoke on her clothes.

#

Fioni, Asger, and Owen lay on their bellies at the forest's edge, spying on the beach and the bay beyond it. The others hid farther back in the trees, waiting out of sight. Owen had been right: the stream cut across the sand, flowing into the bay where they had camped the night before. In place of *Fen Wolf*, Yarl Vengir's longship *Hard Stone* sat in the water, its prow resting against the sand. It was a serpent-ship, like *Fen Wolf*, but smaller, easily beached but also easily put back out to sea, the work of only moments—if they could capture it from the large group of armed men left to guard it. *At least it's only men and not more ghouls,* she mused. Farther out in the bay, *Iron Beard* lay at anchor. She guessed its hull was too deep to bring it in closer to the beach. It was a wonderful warship but so impractical for raiding. Fioni chewed the inside of her cheek as she considered both the armed men on the beach, and the two longships. *Hard Stone* would be much faster than *Iron Beard*, but *Iron Beard* sat between the beach and the sea. All Galas need do was to stop *Hard Stone* from slipping past. *Iron Beard* didn't need to be fast or maneuverable to do that. She considered waiting until nightfall when she could steal *Hard Stone* and slip past *Iron Beard* in the dark but discarded that idea almost immediately. *Whatever we do, we need do it right now, before the ghouls and the Hishtari soldiers come back and trap us between two forces.* As much as she wanted to believe it, she very much doubted the fire had killed all of them.

Several hundred feet away, the men on the beach sat about campfires, while others lay sleeping in the sand, clearly in no hurry to be about their day. *They must be waiting for the ghouls and the Hishtari,* she realized. What piqued her interest the most, though, was the large group of men, several dozen, who sat about, separated from the others, under guard from six men wearing gleaming ring mail and leaning on spears.

"Prisoners," whispered Asger. "But who?"

"Those men are wearing Wolfrey ring mail," said Owen bitterly. "Those are Greywynne Islanders. They've stripped our dead."

Fioni gasped, suddenly recognizing one of the prisoners. "Erik," she said. "Erik Gull-Song, Yarl Vengir's oldest son. Those men are Windhelm clansmen."

"Aye, you're right," said Asger. "I recognize at least a couple of the others as well."

"Why prisoners?" Owen asked.

"The Greywynne Islanders are mostly fishermen, have been for generations now," explained Asger. "It's not an easy thing to sail a serpent-ship, not when all you're used to is fishing boats. They've kept the Windhelm clansmen alive to row—and maybe help them sail." Asger met Fioni's eye. "Those men are like brothers. We can't let this stand, Fioni."

"We're not going to," she said with conviction. "*Hard Stone* has fifteen oars per side; let's say thirty men then, maybe some spares."

"I can't count 'em the way they're bunched together," said Asger. "But I think they outnumber the toads. They don't look tied up."

"Because they're unarmed," said Owen. "They can't just attack men with spears and swords with nothing more than their hands."

"You think they have swords?" Fioni asked with concern.

Owen nodded, glaring at the beach. "Castle-forged steel to go with their castle-forged armor—an entire fort's worth."

Asger sighed. "That changes things, then."

"Not necessarily," said Owen. "They still have no training, and we have Kur'teshi crossbows. They'll punch right through armor, even Wolfrey armor."

"We used most of the bolts on the harpies," said Fioni sadly. "We have only a couple dozen bolts remaining. There's *Iron Beard* to consider as well. If we charge the toads…"

"Don't charge, then," said Owen. "That's the obvious tactic. Never do what the enemy expects."

"We have to attack," said Fioni. "If we don't take *Hard Stone*, we can't get off this beach. Besides, I won't leave the Windhelm prisoners."

"Will the prisoners fight?" Owen asked.

"I'm sure of it," said Fioni, "especially Erik."

Asger grunted. "The Windhelm are Fenyir. They'll jump at any chance for revenge."

"Okay," said Owen. "I have a plan."

Chapter 15

Owen

Owen, Asger, and four others had crawled forward from the trees and were hiding now in tall grass about a hundred yards from the beach and the campfires. Armed with the crossbows, they had split the remaining bolts between the six of them, four bolts each. They'd have to make each shot count. Owen's bolts lay before his face in easy reach. He met Asger's eye. "Ready?"

Asger snorted. "Since before you had fuzz on your balls, Northman."

Owen smiled and rolled over onto his back. Placing his foot in the crossbow's stirrup, he pulled the string back, locking it into place with a soft click. Then he rolled back onto his stomach, fitted one of the bolts into place, and took careful aim on one of the Greywynne Islanders guarding the prisoners. Each of them had already determined among themselves which of the six guards they'd fire upon, so as not to waste the precious bolts killing the same man twice. Owen's target leaned over his spear, the iron spearhead digging into the sand.

"When I loose," he said just loudly enough for the other men to hear him.

Asger grunted, holding his own crossbow tight against his shoulder.

Owen raised his head slightly, trying to see how far Fioni and her force of four fighters had made their way, crawling on their bellies, down the stream's bed, hidden from view of those in the camp, but from his vantage point, he couldn't see her or the others.

"She'll be ready," Asger said, noting where he was looking. "Fioni Ice-Bound does what she says she'll do—just like her father."

Owen exhaled and nodded. The moment he and the others engaged the guards, Fioni would need to charge. Their success would depend on timing, surprise, and maximum violence. As far as plans went, this one was simple: free the prisoners; kill the islanders. But then Keep-Captain Awde had always said the best plans were the simple ones.

He aimed at the guard leaning on his spear. As he inhaled and exhaled, the iron-tipped bolt rose and fell. On his third breath, Owen paused as he exhaled, and the bolt once again fell on the center of the guard's body.

He squeezed the firing lever.

The weapon jumped in his grip as its wooden and bone-reinforced arms snapped forward. His target spun about and fell backward without a word. The other guards stared at him in confusion, but then Asger and the others released their own bolts, and three of them also fell. Owen reloaded as the guards began screaming. Owen loosed another bolt at one of the two remaining guards, but he couldn't tell if he hit the man. Then a Fenyir war cry erupted from the hidden bank of the stream as Fioni and her team rose and charged toward the prisoners, who were also jumping to their feet, making it impossible to shoot at the remaining guard. Owen transferred his aim to the confused mass of islanders around the campfires, who were now screaming and yelling, kicking those still asleep awake.

"Get up, get up!" yelled Owen, rising to his feet.

The others joined him. The time for hiding was over. He wanted the islanders to see them. He loosed a bolt at the men, seeing at least two of them fall. He loaded his last bolt. More of the islanders fell under the shots of Asger and the others, and the men with Owen began screaming insults at the islanders. Fioni and her fighters had reached the prisoners, who were now picking up the guards' fallen weapons or pieces of driftwood, and began forming a rank with Fioni and her men in the center.

"Waveborn, Windhelm!" Fioni yelled, thrusting her sword in the air. The others also took up the cry.

Then the islanders did exactly what Owen had been hoping they'd do. At least half of them, almost a dozen men, broke away and charged straight at Owen and the other crossbowmen. A large dark-haired bearded islander screamed at the men, waving his sword and ordering them to come back, but Owen saw they were too angry to think clearly, their attention entirely focused on the men shooting at them from less than a hundred feet away. When the islanders hit the loose, dry sand farther up the beach, they slowed down noticeably, as if now running in water. This time, Owen took careful aim with his last bolt, sending it flying into an islander's face, shattering it. Taking his time, he placed the crossbow down and drew his Hishtari scimitar as the surviving islanders, their faces now showing their exhaustion, struggled forward through the loose sand.

Asger and the others joined him. "I think I like your plan, Northman," he said then swung his axe down upon a terrified islander, cleaving the man's head in two.

Owen and the others charged into the handful of men that had made it across the sand, shattering any hope they had of cohesion. The first man Owen came up against awkwardly thrust a castle-forged Wolfrey sword at his face, but Owen batted it aside before killing him with a reverse cut against his throat. Owen swept down from the high guard, cutting another man's sword-hand off at the wrist as he inexpertly lifted it in a half-hearted attempt at a parry. Owen's next cut split the screaming man's skull to his jaw. Once, a lifetime ago, Owen had wondered if he could ever take another man's life. Now he did so with ruthless efficiency.

The last of the islanders who had charged across the sand lay on the ground, Asger's fighting axe buried in the back of his skull. Asger, blood dripping from his beard, wrenched it free and faced Owen. "What now, Northman?"

On the beach, Fioni and the prisoners fought a desperate battle against the remaining islanders, more than a dozen of them. Owen pointed his scimitar at the mass of islanders. "Now we kill them all."

Asger barked a rough laugh. "Ha! I love this plan, Northman."

Owen and the five others moved to engage the islanders fighting Fioni and the prisoners. Unlike their enemies, they took their time crossing the sand, moving at a steady, determined walk. As they came closer, Owen saw that the better-armed islanders were savaging the Windhelm prisoners, few of whom were armed with more than a piece of driftwood. At least a half dozen Windhelm bodies lay on the blood-soaked sand. If not for Fioni and the other four Fenyir warriors, the islanders would have broken their line already. As it was, they couldn't hold much longer.

They wouldn't need to.

Owen, Asger, and the others smashed into their unprotected rear. Before the islanders even realized they were there, they had killed a man each. Some of the islanders turned to face this new threat, including the heavyset bearded islander, the leader who had been screaming orders at the others. This man charged straight for Owen, bearing a wooden round shield in one hand and a shining longsword in the other. He smashed into Owen like a wave thundering against cliffs and, unlike the other islanders, possessed enough skill with both shield and sword to force Owen onto the defensive. Owen fell back under the onslaught, deflecting each of the man's attacks, but without a shield of his own, he was at a decided disadvantage. The heavyset attacker paused, breathing heavily behind his shield, his sword raised in a hanging guard so that its point threatened Owen's face.

As his eyes ran up that blade to the lion of Wolfrey etched into its fuller just above the cross-guard, a chill of recognition flashed through Owen, burned away a moment later by hot anger—he knew that sword.

Owen took up the middle guard, and the two men began to circle one another. Around them, the battle raged, but their attention was only on each other. Months ago, Keep-Captain Awde had used that very sword in the courtyard of Castle Dain to demonstrate the principle of countertiming—the intuitive recognition of the crucial moment when an opponent was about to launch an attack. "*If you could recognize that moment,*" Awde had said, "*you could preempt it with your own strike. To the untrained eye, it appears as though you both attacked at the same moment, but his attack fails while yours luckily succeeds—but there's no such thing as luck or fate in battle. What's truly happened is that you've anticipated your opponent's attack and moved in such a way that—even without parrying—his strike misses and yours hits.*"

Effective countertiming was, Owen now understood, *the* defining mark of a master swordsman.

When the islander darted forward, thrusting with his sword point, Owen was already sliding to the right, his scimitar flashing around the other man's blade in a thrust cut. His opponent's blade swept past Owen's face, so close he heard it whistle by his ear, but before the other man could react and alter his blow, Owen was already sliding back into the hanging guard, his blade dangling over his eyes, blood dripping from it. The bearded man's eyes widened. He stumbled forward, falling to his knees and dropping his shield and sword as he grasped at his neck, blood spraying from the severed artery. He stared at his bloody fingers in disbelief, not quite understanding what had just happened. Owen finished him with a single sword thrust through the back of his neck.

He had been a competent foe.

The remaining islanders broke, running for the forest. His breathing wild, his blood pounding, Owen stared at Brice Awde's sword lying on the beach. His Hishtari scimitar fell from his fingers, and he bent down and picked up the finely crafted longsword, gifted to the Keep-Captain by old Duke Oskaley himself.

Owen took a quick assessment of their situation. The fighting had been vicious. The corpses of at least a dozen Windhelm prisoners lay about. Fioni's small team had been able to help the prisoners stand and fight, but it had been costly. Two more of her herdsmen had fallen—as well as one of the men who had fought with Owen—leaving Fioni now only six men left of the thirteen who had sworn oaths the night before. Asger still lived, although he was limping, his thigh bleeding.

The young blond man they had seen from the woods, Erik Gull-Song, Yarl Vengir's oldest son, rushed forward and hugged Fioni. "Gods bless you, Fioni. Where did you come from?" The man was tall, with a warrior's physique. He was handsome, with long hair and a plaited beard, and intricate tattoos covered his chest and shoulders.

"Fioni!" yelled Asger. "*Iron Beard.*"

They all turned and stared. The massive drake-ship's oars were in the water as it turned to face the shoreline. "Galas can't come in this close," Erik said.

"He doesn't need to," said Fioni, pulling away from him. "He has us trapped here. Leave everything but the shields and the weapons and get to *Hard Stone*. If we're going to survive this day, we need to fight our way past my cousin."

The survivors, some two dozen Windhelm and Fioni's half dozen herdsmen, rushed to the beached serpent-ship. The men threw shields and weapons over its hull and then shoved it back into the water.

"Too slow!" Asger yelled.

He was right, Owen saw with mounting desperation. Even now, the massive drake ship was ready for them. Armed men stood along its hull, screaming insults. Among them, Owen saw Galas Gilt-Mane. Arrows began to fall into the water.

"Push!" Fioni yelled.

Hard Stone slid off the beach and onto the surf. Thigh-deep in the cold water, Owen and the others helped the wounded aboard, before clambering over the hull themselves. "Oars!" Fioni screamed.

Hard Stone slipped away from the beach, its oars rising and falling, and it began to turn toward the massive drake-ship. Fioni was right: they'd need to fight their way clear if they wanted to live. He picked up one of the round shields lying on the deck and slipped his arm through the straps before joining Fioni, Erik Gull-Song, and Asger, all of whom had also picked up shields. Arrows whipped overhead, with several hitting the rowers. The man at the tiller tried to maneuver *Hard Stone* past *Iron Beard*, but it was too late. *Iron Beard* bore down on them.

"Stand by for impact!" Fioni screamed.

The crew scrambled away from the benches and rushed to pick up shield and sword, axe and spear. They formed massed ranks near the prow and down the steering board side. As *Iron Beard* came forward, Owen again noted the elaborately carved wooden figurehead of a beastlike woman, her arms reaching forward, her catlike face snarling in hatred. The resemblance between the figurehead and the white stone hilt of Sight-Bringer was remarkable, but then there was no more time for such thoughts.

Iron Beard's prow smashed into *Hard Stone*, caving in its hull and sending the warriors falling back. Only the press of the other warriors around him kept Owen on his feet. Water sprayed their faces as the wooden hull splintered and fell apart. The enemy crew cheered and rushed forward, jumping over the prow to land atop the ruined deck of the much smaller longship. Fioni screamed and rushed forward to meet them, followed by Owen and the others. In moments, the deck was a writhing mass of warriors, locked in a death struggle, pushing and straining against one another, trying to strike over the tops of their shields or shove their opponents back into the water. Aboard *Iron Beard*, men threw grappling hooks attached to ropes against *Hard Stone*'s broken hull, lashing the two ships together. More and more of the enemy jumped down onto their deck, while others shot arrows directly down on them with frightening accuracy. As the defenders fell, the attackers pushed them inexorably back. In the surf, with neither ship under oar now, both ships began to spin about, turning *Hard Stone*'s stern out to sea. *We'll never get underway again*, Owen realized with sinking resignation. *We're all going to die.*

An arrow struck the baleen plates over his collarbone, shattering the shaft but sending a shard of it flying up to cut his cheek. Fioni remained on his right, their shields locked together, with Asger on his left. One of Galas's warriors came at him, but Owen shoved his shield into him, throwing him to the deck. Another man took his place, screaming in rage as he came at Owen. In the press of bodies, Owen managed to maneuver his sword—Brice Awde's sword—over his shield and then drove its point right through the man's open mouth, severing his tongue.

But for every man Owen put down, three more took his place.

Asger went down under a spear thrust that slipped beneath his shield. The fighting pushed them back, and now they fought beside the keelson, the huge block of wood that held the ship's mast in place. More and more of the defenders fell, leaving only a handful now. Owen's lungs burned, and his shoulders were on fire. They couldn't possibly win now, yet not a man surrendered.

"Ship!" a panicked voice called out. "There's another ship coming to take us from behind."

Thunder Killer, Owen realized, unable to take his eyes off the men attacking them. *They've come back to finish us.* A huge fat man came at him, forcing him back under his powerful attacks. Then, bizarrely, he heard a dog barking. "It's *Fen Wolf!*" Fioni yelled. "I told you Kora would come back. Fight on, fight on!"

Out of nothing, hope surged in Owen, lending him the strength to keep going. "Wolfrey, Dain!" he screamed as he lashed out at the fat man, splitting his skull to his shoulders.

Fear and uncertainty flitted through the eyes of the enemy as they realized they were now fighting two ships instead of one. They faltered, falling back. Owen caught a quick glimpse of Galas Gilt-Mane, standing on the deck of *Iron Beard*, screaming at his men to press the attack. *Hard Stone* shuddered as *Fen Wolf* ran right into its stern, shattering it and sending those fighting on its decks reeling. Then volleys of crossbow bolts hammered into Galas's men, savaging them, forcing them back farther and opening up space between the two forces. Kora was screaming at Fioni and the others to climb aboard *Fen Wolf* before *Hard Stone* went under.

A hand-axe flew through the air, coming right at Owen's face—a moment later, pain lanced through his skull, and he was falling. He hit the cold seawater already pouring over *Hard Stone*'s deck. He couldn't see properly. Something—blood—was in his eyes, blinding him. He lay on his back in the seawater, waving Brice Awde's lion-marked sword and babbling incoherently. Then someone grabbed him and lifted him up, and the world spun around him before a familiar young woman with strawberry-blond hair peered down at him, asking him something. He blinked in confusion, desperate to understand how his little sister, Tanda, had somehow gotten here.

Part 2:
Black Fish

Chapter 16

Serina

Serina awoke in darkness with the press of dead flesh upon her—an entirely familiar sensation. She lay beneath her corpse pile in *Iron Beard*'s musty hold, feeling the gentle rocking of the hull and listening to the soft creaking of its strakes. The air thrummed with the sweet stench of decaying flesh. Above her, she heard voices conversing on the deck and the thump of boot steps as the crew went about their business. As always, her hunger gnawed at her, but there'd be time for blood later. Now, she wanted to see the Dain woman and make sure her servants had recovered that cursed Illthori blade, Sight-Bringer. She sat up, pushing the corpses away. In the darkness, she heard a single heartbeat pounding wildly.

She smiled, running her tongue over her fangs. *My toy awaits.*

With a flick of her fingers, she cast a minor spell, a cantrip, and a single flame flared up on the wick of a nearby candle, casting flickering light over the terrified face of Kory'ander Dey, standing near the foot of the wooden steps leading up to the deck.

When she saw the terror in his eyes, she knew that he must be expecting her displeasure, which could only mean he had failed.

Damn it, and damn him. "Tell me," she said softly. "Where is the niece of Stron?"

His heartbeat quickened. "Gone, my queen." Unable to look her in the eye, he stared at the filthy wooden deck.

"Gone?"

"Sailed away, my queen, with the Red Wolf, Fioni."

She sighed, pulling her blood-splattered bare legs out from under the corpse of a young boy, and sat up. As always, she slept in the nude, covered in the dripping gore and excrement of the dead. Water gently sloshed against the side of the hull. *We're stationary,* she realized. *Anchored still.* Thick spiderwebs hung from the corners of the hold, but there were no longer any vermin on this ship. Rats, mice, roaches, even spiders fled from her presence. Animals would sooner drown than remain near her. It was the Dread, a gift from her dark master, Ator—the greatest of the Fenyir gods—that maintained fear and loyalty among her servants. Usually, that fear kept them faithful and loyal, but when she grew angry—as she did now—the power of the Dread multiplied. The smell of fresh feces suddenly filled the hold, and Dey, trembling like a leaf, fell to his knees. *This one will not last long in my service, I fear. The pretty ones rarely do.*

"Where are we?" she asked, holding her hand out to him.

Dey, white-faced, rose again and scrambled forward. Taking her hand, he helped her climb down, his gaze averted from her blood-drenched body. "Still anchored in the bay, off the coast of the tower of rock, my queen."

"Your mission?"

"Not my fault, my queen. The Red Wolf set the woods on fire. Your ghouls, they... they didn't stop. They walked right into the fires. My men and I barely escaped. But by the time we made it back to the beach, the Fenyir scum had already captured *Hard Stone* and were battling *Iron Beard.*"

She fought down her rage; it would be undignified to take out her anger on a blood thrall. "Yet they escaped?"

"The other ship, my queen, the one that slipped away as we arrived. It came back, and the Fenyir jumped aboard it. By the time that Fenyir dog of yours, Galas, managed to cut his way free of *Hard Stone*, the Red Wolf and the others were already out of the bay."

"So, no prisoners, no sword—yet we remain here, at anchor. Why?"

"It was too dangerous, my queen. You were sleeping, and the other longship, *Thunder Killer*, never returned. Its crew must be dead, so I felt it best to be prudent. But Galas, that insolent scum, insisted we rush after them. I knew better, so I countermanded his orders, told him you'd want us to stay in place until I spoke to you. It nearly came to blood, but the cowardly Fenyir scum did as I commanded. His kind always backs down. He should be punished, though, taught his place."

She stared at Dey for long moments. *He has no idea who I truly am, my background. Surprising considering who his great-grandfather was. I do believe I actually feel sorry for Kalishni'coor.* "You should have listened to Yarl Galas," she said softly. "Now we've lost an entire day."

Dey looked crestfallen, his demeanor like that of a mistreated dog. Shaking her head, she approached one of the huge water barrels placed against the hull. The barrel reached her waist and probably weighed three hundred pounds. She ripped free its nailed-shut lid and then easily lifted the sloshing barrel over her head, holding it there as she turned in place and faced him again. "My ghouls are all gone?"

"Yes… yes, my queen."

"What of Galvin and the islanders on *Hard Stone*?"

"Most are dead, my queen, including Galvin."

"Dead? How many dead in the fighting, both on the beach and the ship?"

Dey paused. "Dozens, I imagine, my queen."

Serina slowly poured the contents of the barrel over her head, washing away the bloody filth. *There will always be setbacks,* she told herself, *but as long as there are dead, I shall have an army.* She set the empty water barrel back down.

"My queen," Dey said, "what will you do about Galas? That Fenyir dog—"

She swept forward. As fast and as strong as her milk had made Dey, he was still only mortal. In moments, she held him by the sides of his head and lifted him into the air, his feet dangling and his face red. "*I* am Fenyir, you Hishtari turd. Insult my people again, and I will crush your head like a barnacle caught between a ship's hull and a pier."

"Yes... yes, my queen," he squeaked, his eyes bulging.

She dropped him, and he collapsed near her dripping feet, gasping.

"Do you have anything at all to show for your failure?" she asked, her voice dripping with scorn.

"Yes, your majesty." Dey scampered away to a sack that sat on the deck beside the stairs. Still on his knees, his hands trembling, he undid the opening and withdrew a severed head—a middle-aged Fenyir warrior with a huge burn scar on his right cheek. "This one tried to slip past us, but I killed him for you, my queen."

"And can you interrogate a decapitated head, fool?"

Dey's blue lips opened and closed. "I... I—"

She batted the severed head from his hands, sending it rolling across the wooden deck. Bloody water dripped down her body, pooling between her thighs and then running down her long white legs. He remained kneeling, his head down, his shoulders trembling.

Serina ran her fingers through his long hair, and he shuddered. "Do you think me cruel?" she asked in a soft voice.

"No, of course not, my queen," he whined. "It's just that… I'm not like the… the others. I am the Moon Lord of Daenipor. My family is ancient. My bloodline is royal—"

Her fingers tightened in his hair, and he yelped in pain. "Your bloodline is insignificant—as are you. You are a thrall now, nothing more, a slave."

He squeaked in fear. "Majesty, wait!"

She pulled his face between her thighs, held it there, grinding his nose against her filthy pubic hair. "Lick me clean, *Moon Lord of Daenipor.*"

When he hesitated, she ripped a handful of his hair from his scalp. He howled in pain, but moments later, she felt his tongue between her legs. When he began to gag, trying to pull back, she ground his face against her sex. If he failed to please her, she'd crush his skull and throw his corpse atop the pile with the others, one more ghoul. When she felt his tongue again, she moaned in pleasure, spreading her thighs wider. "That's it. That's it."

He continued to cry and whimper, but they usually did; she was deaf to such things now. Closing her eyes, she sent her consciousness out, seeking Dilan. In moments, she made contact, overcome with relief that he was safe. Dilan was not like Dey. Dilan was a warrior, a hero. "*Where are you, my childe?*"

"*North, Mother.*" His thoughts drifted to her, sounding far away. "*But I can't come to you.*"

"*No matter. I shall come to you.*"

Chapter 17

Owen

Owen winced as Kora drove the wooden needle and the catgut sutures into his scalp. Gali stood behind her, helping her, as she had with all the other wounded. Once again, he marveled at how like his sister Gali looked. It had been Gali's face he had seen before passing out, not Tanda's. Tanda was still back home in Wolfredsuntown. *Will I ever see her again?*

Lady Danika stood next to Gali, commiserating with Owen as Kora sewed his wound shut. The noblewoman had been present and holding a bandage against his scalp when he had finally woken up, his head throbbing. While he slept, she had even removed his heavy ring-mail coat, stowing it in their sea chest for him. Purple bruises covered most of his chest, but there could be no doubt that Vory's ring-mail coat had saved his life in the worst of the fighting. Sight-Bringer, she had taken back for safekeeping and now wore on her belt.

A spasm of pain cut through his skull, and he winced, drawing back from Kora and her needle. She shoved his head back against the hull, holding him in place as she shoved the needle through his tender skin. "Be still. It's not that bad. You were lucky."

He was. As the least badly wounded, he was the last to receive treatment. Gali and Kora had been tending wounded men all day, many of whom had already died. Out of the two dozen or so Windhelm prisoners they had rescued, only Erik Gull-Song and a handful remained unhurt. Worse, of the thirteen house-herd warriors who had transferred their oath to Fioni the night before, only Asger still lived—and he was dying, an arrow still lodged in his lungs. Fioni knelt beside him now, holding his hand and waiting as *Fen Wolf* rocked in the waves, its sail lowered.

The longship drifted in the currents, some leagues yet from the eastern boundary of the fog bank, which seemed on fire now with the light of the setting sun behind it, glowing through it. They had sailed west all day, approaching the Feral Sea before lowering their sail. In the morning, when Fioni could make use of the Raven's-Eye to find the sun, they'd enter the Feral Sea. For the first time since he and Lady Danika had joined the crew, they'd spend the night at sea and not camped on the shore.

And however many more nights it took after that to find Torin Island.

The other wounded, just under a dozen men, sat huddled together or resting between the rowing benches. The battle against *Iron Beard* had been the most bloody, one-sided fight in which Owen had ever been involved. They'd have all died had Kora not come back for them. With *Iron Beard* and *Hard Stone* lashed together with the grappling hooks, Galas had been unable to maneuver to stop Kora from taking on the survivors and rowing away again.

"Done," said Kora, twisting his head one way and then the other to examine her work. "The cut isn't that bad, but you might get sick or become dizzy. Don't climb the mast for a few days, eh?"

Owen gingerly touched the sutures in his scalp. His head

continued to throb but not as badly as it had earlier that day. "Aye. Thank you, Kora."

"Good thing for you that whoever threw that hand-axe didn't know what they were doing, or it would have been buried in your skull."

"I'm lucky it wasn't you."

"You're right about that." She slapped him on the back as she moved away to check on the others. Gali trailed behind her. The young Hishtari woman had been helping Kora all day.

Lady Danika sat beside Owen. They both watched Fioni and Asger. The large bald warrior lay covered in furs now, his breathing wet. Ekkie lay beside the kneeling Fioni, her head resting on Fioni's lap, her brown eyes filled with sorrow. Owen watched Fioni's face for long moments. *When Asger dies—and it will be soon now—every single man who participated in the ceremony last night will be dead.*

Ale and salt… for the rest of their lives.

Fioni's gods are cruel.

Gali came back, an open wooden jar of salve in her hand. "Kora say me to rub in your wound."

Lady Danika took the jar from her hand. "Go get something to eat, Gali. I'll do that."

Gali slipped away, heading to the prow, where a small hearth burned and the smell of stew drifted through the sea air. Lady Danika began to smooth the ointment into Owen's scalp. "Owen, the sword you were holding."

"Keep-Captain Awde's, my lady. I took it from the leader of the Greywynne Islanders. It's yours, of course. I know how much he meant to you."

A flicker of sorrow passed through her large brown eyes. She bit her lower lip and tried to smile. "Keep it. He'd want you to have it."

"Me? Why?"

Finished with the salve, she sat back again, pulling the flaps of her cloak tighter around her shoulders, sitting beside him in silence for some moments before she finally answered. "Because he liked you, Owen, thought highly of you. I think, maybe, that's why his shade led you to me in the Rose Palace."

He shook his head. "I'm just a soldier, no different from the others."

Her smile was a sad thing without true joy. She shook her head. "If we're being honest with one another, Owen, I should tell you that at first I thought the same thing. I know how you came into my family's service, what you did to your own brother. Because of that, I assumed you were just another dumb brute. I was wrong. You're very different from the others. Brice saw it. I see that now, too."

"I don't understand."

"Brice was mentoring you, Owen. He thought you could become a lieutenant to Warin Sayer."

"Me?"

"He wanted me to run away with him. But he needed someone to take his place. Personally, I always thought Warin to be a weak choice as Keep-Captain, but I suspect Brice considered him a temporary replacement—until you could become Keep-Captain."

"That's crazy," he whispered. "I'm no leader." But even as he spoke, he thought back to all the impromptu discussions Awde had held with him. While Owen hadn't been the only man-at-arms to receive the keep-captain's special attention, he couldn't remember anyone else who Awde had singled out as often or as consistently for long discussions on the finer points of logistics, tactics, leadership, and duty. He felt a sudden breathlessness spread through him as he realized the truth. *Awde had treated Owen differently and had elevated his training over all the other soldiers.* Maybe that was why the more experienced men, including Sayer, had been so cold to him, why they called him Horse-Boy.

They had been jealous.

"Owen," said Lady Danika, hesitation in her voice. "There's something else. Something I need to tell you. I saw… someone on the other ship. I think, maybe—"

Nearby, Asger began to thrash. He coughed, spitting up a mouthful of dark blood. *His lungs are filling with blood,* Owen knew. *Any moment now…*

Asger tried to lift his head but failed, so Fioni held it for him in her lap. His eyes were wide, frightened, his lips moving feebly. Kora knelt next to Fioni, her eyes filled with sorrow. "He needs to go," she said softly.

Fioni closed her eyes and inhaled deeply. When she opened them again, they were filled with determination. She drew her father's beautiful pattern-welded longsword, Wave's Kiss, and placed it in Asger's hand, closing her fist over his. In the last light of the setting sun, the red blood gem embedded in the sword's hilt seemed to shine. "Go, warrior," Fioni said softly, leaning in and placing her cheek against his. "Join your friends in Nifalgen. Your duty is over, your oath fulfilled."

Asger's eyes remained open and staring in death.

Erik Gull-Song stood behind Kora, his chest rising and falling, his eyes solemn. "A brave warrior, Fioni. He'll swim straight to Orkinus's mead hall. I know it."

Fioni remained like that for some minutes and then pried her sword from the dead man's grip. She stood, her chest heaving, pain filling her green eyes, and faced Owen. "This is your fault."

His head snapped back as if struck. "But I…"

"It was *your* plan to burn the woods that cost me Rolf. It was *your* plan on the beach to split our forces and go after *Hard Stone.*"

"We… we had to do something." He felt them all staring at him now, judging him.

"I curse the day I took you from the sea. My father is dead. Vory is dead. My home taken. And only after I met you. Owen *Northman*? I name you Owen *Ill-Luck*."

"Fioni," said Kora, pulling on her arm. "This is not the time for such—"

Fioni wrenched her arm free and spun away, pushing past the watching crew. Erik Gull-Song followed her, glancing back at Owen with cold, hard eyes.

Kora stood before Owen, a crestfallen look on her face. "She doesn't mean it, Owen. It's just… all her father's herdsmen..."

Owen's face burned, and he stared helplessly at his hands. "No. She's right. It *is* my fault."

Chapter 18

Galas

Galas Gilt-Mane stared down at the Windhelm prisoners, several dozen young women and a handful of boys, who were bound hand and foot around *Iron Beard*'s massive keelson, the block of wood that held the towering mast in place. At first, there had been almost fifty of them, but each night that Hishtari guppy who insisted others call him "Moon Lord" led several down into the hold, and only Dey returned. Now, this group of prisoners was all that remained of the once-proud Windhelm clan. Serina had made an example of them, and once word spread to the other clans, Galas doubted any of them would refuse when Serina called upon them to join her army and make war once again on the Kingdom of Conarck. This time, he knew, the kingdom would fall.

But before that war could start, they needed to capture one ship.

Unfortunately, Fioni and *Fen Wolf* were proving tough prey, which in turn angered the queen and put Galas's own life at risk. *Damn Fioni! How can one woman be so much trouble?*

He squatted down beside one of the prisoners, a young woman with light-brown hair and a horn-shaped birthmark on her cheek.

Like the others, she sat silently, staring at nothing, her eyes vacant and glassy. Previously, they had only been under a light guard; after all, they were on a ship at sea. But yesterday one of them had simply stood up and climbed over the gunwale, disappearing beneath the waves before anyone could do anything. *What horrors did they see, I wonder, the night Serina sent her ghouls into Voria Bay?* He pulled the girl's shirt open and placed his palm on her naked breast, her soft nipple rubbing against his calloused palm. As expected, she didn't move, nor did her expression change. *What do they see down in the hold?* He placed his ear against the skin of her chest, listening to her heart slowly beat, almost as if she were sleeping. Then he sat back and slapped her so hard she fell over onto her side, a raw palm print on her cheek.

She didn't even blink.

He sighed, standing back up, his fingers gently pulling on the stone carving of a black fish hanging from a knotted cord around his neck. The black fish was the hereditary sigil of the Waveborn yarls, and Galas had ripped this carving from around the neck of his dead uncle the morning after his attack on Welmen Town. "It would be a kindness," he told the girl, "if I were to cut your throat right now."

The girl's eyes remained empty.

He felt Serina's presence then, a cold chill that swept through his bones. No matter how often he felt the Dread, he'd never grow used to it. He saw the same fear spread through the faces of the others, his Waveborn warriors, the Hishtari soldiers, and the handful of Greywynne Islanders who had survived the fighting on the beach. Galas hurried to take his place before the hold, grasping his hands before him to stop them from trembling.

The doors flew open, smashing back, and Serina stepped out into the night, highlighted by a moonbeam so that her pale skin seemed to glow with a silvery hue. Around her shoulders, she wore a fox-fur cape, its collar high against her slender neck. As always, her hair was tightly braided in the old style, interwoven with silver chains and small gems. Behind her scurried that guppy, Dey. Blood and filth stained his face, his gaze fixed upon the wooden deck.

The corner of Galas's mouth curled into a sneer, but he quickly hid his pleasure, dropping down on a knee before the queen. His men immediately followed his example, followed moments later by the others, including the Hishtari soldiers.

"My queen," Galas said.

Serina stepped closer. "Our enemy is far to the northwest now, Yarl Galas, so far. While you've remained here, they've slipped away from us—again."

"I apologize, my queen." Galas glared at Dey. "Your servant said—"

"My *slave* was mistaken, Yarl Galas, nor does he speak for me. *Never* forget that again."

"Yes, my queen."

"I need you to set sail now. Head north. Follow the coastline."

North? He glanced up at her in confusion, wondering if he had somehow misheard her. "But *Fen Wolf* sailed west, my queen."

"Yes, but my childe is north—and so is your ship. I'm assuming you wish it back, yes?"

Galas's fear spiked, his heart throbbing in his chest. "My... my queen..."

"Say your words, Yarl Galas. Loyal chieftains have nothing to fear from speaking truth to me."

Galas inhaled deeply and then averted his eyes from her tattooed, masklike face and her unnatural bloodred eyes. "My queen, I fear we have been betrayed. Ullyn Tangle-Beard… I fear that coward must have murdered your childe and then fled with my ship. *Thunder Killer* is fast. I can't catch it in *Iron Beard*. Nor do I think Ullyn would have sailed north. There's nothing north. He'll sail south and then east, likely make for Xi'ur."

Serina approached, her boots stopping before his eyes. She cupped his cheek with her hand, almost tenderly. "No, of course Ullyn has not betrayed us, Galas," she said softly, as if lecturing a small child. "You, he might betray—*if* he felt he could profit by doing so—but me? No. Even Xi'ur is not that far away."

Galas shuddered. If she noticed, she gave no indication. "I have a matter requiring your attention," she said, turning her gaze upon Dey. "Show him."

Dey scrambled forward, a bloody sack under his arm. Thrusting his hand into the sack, he pulled out a bearded man's severed head. The eyes were open and staring, the mouth locked in a rictus of pain. An old burn mark covered a portion of the dead man's right cheek. As Dey held up the head, recognition spread through the Fenyir ranks. "You know this man, then?" Serina asked him.

"Aye," Galas said. "All my life. He taught me to fight. Rolf Fork-Beard, leader of my uncle's herdsmen, as fine a warrior as any Fenyir ever born." Galas glared at Dey. The fact that Galas had planned to kill Rolf himself was unimportant. Galas *had* to kill Taios's house-herd; such things were expected, but he would have done so honorably and quickly. *For a man like Rolf to die at the hands of this Hishtari guppy…*

"Rolf Fork-Beard," Serina repeated. "An all-too-common name among our kind, I'm afraid. Do you know his father's name?"

Galas paused, rubbing his chin as he searched his memory. "Gael, I think it was." He looked to his new first mate, Aegrism—who had filled the position vacated by Galas's former first mate, Hringol, murdered by Fioni in her attack upon the Rose Palace. Aegrism was a tall, dim man with a pleated black beard and a bald head that was almost completely covered in tattoos of octopus tentacles. Aegrism stared at Galas wordlessly for several moments and then bobbed his head in agreement, mouthing the word "Gael." "Gael Gods-Man," said Galas with conviction, remembering him now. "A holy man. Been dead since I were a boy, though."

Serina took the head from Dey's hands. She held it by the hair against her thigh as though it were a sack. "You speak as though death is a barrier." He said nothing, and she continued. "Sail north. Three leagues, no more. You'll find your ship grounded atop a sand bar. I'm assuming you can pull it free?"

How does she know this? "Yes, my queen."

She turned away, heading back to the hold. She paused, looking back over her shoulder at Dey. "Bring me one of the prisoners, then leave me."

"Yes, my queen," Dey squeaked, bowing obsequiously.

Cold sweat coating his skin, Galas continued to pull on the smooth stone black fish around his neck.

#

Hours later, Galas looked down upon the moonlit waves before them. Getting the drake-ship ready for sea had taken far longer than it should have, but they were finally sailing north along the coast, as the queen had demanded. Like all Fenyir, he disliked sailing at night, but he knew he'd also dislike having Serina rip his spine from his back.

"Ship ahead!" the lookout yelled.

Galas joined the small crowd jostling near the prow platform. He shoved his way past them and leaned out over the prow. *Thunder Killer* drifted before them. From up here, he could look down upon its empty decks. Aegrism joined him, and they stared wordlessly at one another. "She said it was grounded on a sandbar," Galas said.

"Tide's risen," answered his new first mate. "Must've drifted loose. We should be careful we don't run aground ourselves."

"Aye," Galas said. "Lower the sail. Bring us alongside."

As they drifted closer, Galas saw that *Thunder Killer* wasn't deserted after all. The other blood fiend, the young kingdom man called Dilan, stood like a statue, staring up at them. A tremor of fear ran down Galas's spine. *There were thirty men on that ship. What happened to them?* Once again, he felt the cold rush of fear presaging Serina's presence. She glided across the deck toward the prow, Dey scuttling along behind her. Galas dropped onto a knee and lowered his head. There was a smear of fresh blood across her chin and over her ample cleavage. In her hand, she still held the head of Rolf Fork-Beard. Just for a moment, the head's open eyes seemed to move on their own, but that had to be a trick of the moonlight. Serina casually tossed the severed head over the hull to fall into the waters below with a splash. "Rise, Yarl Galas," she said. "We have weighty matters to attend to, it seems."

"Yes, my queen."

"Our enemies plot to kill me—me—their queen!"

The anger in her voice almost loosened his bowels. "They'll fail, my queen," he said, his tongue thick in his mouth.

"Yes, but it would seem they have another Illthori artifact, one I knew nothing about. What else remains hidden to me, I wonder?"

"Another Illthori artifact?"

"The Raven's-Eye, a sunstone. It will permit our enemies to navigate within the fog of the Feral Sea. This Fioni—the Red Wolf—she is full of surprises. But I also sense the foul machinations of Fenya here, once again playing her cosmic game against her brother, Ator—at my expense! She will fail."

At the mention of the Dark Shark's true name, Galas's eyes darted about as if he expected to see Wodor and the other gods appear and punish them. Clearly, Serina had no qualms about naming the Dark

Shark, though. *She is his servant.* "My queen, they don't have Serl's map. You do. How can they—"

"It seems she also has Serl's journal detailing his voyage. Now, their visit to the Fist of Wodor makes more sense than simply holding an oath-taking ceremony. They intend to retrace Serl's voyage fifty years ago to Torin Island."

"We'll need to stop them before they enter the fog. Once they're within it, we can't follow."

She raised her hand, cutting him off. "Yes, *we can.* I need no Raven's-Eye to know where the hated sun is—even when it's behind fog. My childe and I have an affinity for such things now. And, as you pointed out, I have the map. We'll find that ship, or we'll find the island. Either way, I will have my heart back."

"But—"

"But nothing. Have courage. You are a Fenyir warrior. Besides, our foe thinks the fog will hide them from me—but I have a special surprise for traitors."

"And Fioni, my queen?"

"I have promised her to you, and I keep my word. I only desire the niece of Stron and Sight-Bringer. No one and nothing else matters. But I think you'll soon find the blood of Serl Raven-Eye to be of little value among the Fenyir. Before I'm done, all the clans will curse his foul name. If you find you no longer want or need this Red Wolf, give her to me. I can always use brave warriors."

"Yes, my queen."

Iron Beard's hull ground against *Thunder Killer*'s. Galas leaned over the hull—and then stumbled backward, reeling in horror. A mound of corpses lay near the mast, the sail still partially covering it. Lying atop the mound had been Ullyn Tangle-Beard's gaunt face, his dead eyes shining.

"Rejoice, Yarl Galas Gilt-Mane," Serina said. "I told you your man didn't betray you."

"I… why?"

"Sacrifice is necessary in war. Out at sea, without a hold to hide from the sun, Dilan couldn't take any chances."

The blood fiend Dilan climbed atop *Thunder Killer*'s gunwale and then launched himself against *Iron Beard*'s hull, gripping it with his fingernails as he quickly scaled its side. When he climbed over the gunwale, the crew fell back, scrambling away from him. Dilan rushed forward, dropping to his knees and wrapping his arms around Serina's waist.

She pulled his head in tightly against her bosom, stroking his hair as if he were a babe. "Have the corpses placed in the hold," she told Galas. "While sacrifice is necessary, waste is not."

"Yes…yes, my queen," Galas stammered.

"And put a new crew aboard that ship."

"I no longer have the men to crew two ships."

"Nonsense. Use the Hishtari and the remaining islanders. You'll only need enough to sail the ship. My childe shall do the rest."

"Yes, my queen."

Chapter 19

Owen

Before noon the following morning, *Fen Wolf* approached the eastern edge of the fog bank marking the boundary of the Feral Sea. Owen leaned over the gunwale, watching the fog with more than a bit of trepidation. The Feral Sea was a place of dark legends, rumored to be the abode of monsters. According to the Fenyir, their gods had once dwelled within it.

Torin Island, the Gateway to the Gods.

Wisps of mist danced along the outer edge of the fog bank, like ghostly tendrils. The strong nor'easter wind that had been with them for days had now become a gentle breeze. As they approached the grayness before them, the silence amplified the soft crackling of the sail, the creaking of the ropes, and the splashing of the waves against their hull. The crew stood watching in silence as they drifted closer. Even Ekkie trembled against Fioni's leg. Owen turned to Lady Danika, standing next to a wide-eyed Gali. "Seems like a dream," he said.

"A black dream," said Gali, trembling like a newborn foal.

"It's just fog," said Fioni. "It can't hurt us," she said loudly for the crew. "Serl sailed within this sea, and so shall we."

Fen Wolf entered the fog bank, instantly plunging them into a vast, unending grayness so thick that they could only see a hundred feet in any direction. The sun was gone. The air turned suddenly chill, so that the crew could now see their own breath as they muttered nervously.

"Remember who you are," Fioni called out loudly. "Remember your parents. The wights are watching us now, have no doubt of that. They will tell the gods if we are brave, and they will tell if we are not. So be brave."

Erik Gull-Song placed a hand possessively on her shoulder. "Try it, Fioni."

"Aye," said Kora. "Before it's too late to turn about and leave again."

Fioni drew the bowl-shaped metal shield boss slightly larger than a fist from a pouch attached to her belt. The boss had been painted in the image of a raven's golden eye. A small hole, the width of a finger, had been bored through the top of the boss. Bolted to its hollow interior was an Illthori sunstone, a golden, opaque glass disk that magnified the sun's rays. Fioni held the Raven's-Eye up to her face now and peered through the back of it, slowly turning in place. Lowering the Raven's-Eye, she beamed at the others. "It works! I see the sun clearly, four and a half hands port of the sternpost."

"Ha!" barked Kora. "Thank you, Grandmother."

"We'll keep the same course for two hundred ells," Fioni said, beaming at the crew. When her gaze fell on Owen, her smile vanished. "After that, we'll tack north."

Gali stared at her with wide eyes. "You know where you are—in this blanket of sky?"

Fioni gripped Gali's shoulder and squeezed it. "Not exactly, but I know where we *were* when we entered the fog bank. I know that at this time of the year, at this latitude, the sun will be almost due south at midday. And Serl left detailed notes in his journal, so I know which course he took fifty years ago. With that, I can make a reasonable estimation of our own route."

"I don't understand," said Gali. "How can you follow writings in a book?"

"Even at sea," said Fioni, "there are signposts, clear indications if one knows what to look for: the direction and strength of currents, waves, and wind; the flight of sea birds; black fish breeding grounds; even the cloud formations and stars in the night sky. All of these signs are like landmarks to us Fenyir."

"And you can follow these signs?" Owen asked.

"Better than you could track on land, I'd wager. At any rate, you'd better hope I'm a more skilled navigator than you are a tactician."

"But in this fog," interjected Lady Danika, "how many of those signs can you find?"

Fioni bit her upper lip. "Not as many as I'd prefer, admittedly. But with the Raven's-Eye, I can at least determine direction."

"But not at night," said Owen. "You can't see the sun at night?"

"No, Owen," said Fioni, glaring at him now. "I can't see the sun at night. Can you?"

Lady Danika stepped in front of Owen. "We don't doubt you, Fioni. It's just..."

"I know. I wish I had the map Serl left behind, but Kalishni'coor destroyed it. I can't change that. I've studied Serl's journal, and I think we have a chance, maybe even a good one, of retracing his voyage. All we need do is find the Godswall."

"What is Godswall?" asked Gali.

"Yes, what?" asked Lady Danika.

Fioni approached her sea chest, rummaged through it for a moment, and then came back with the battered journal of her great-grandfather. "According to our legends—and confirmed by Serl's journal—Torin Island is surrounded by a vast ring of cliffs called the Godswall." She thumbed through the journal, finding a specific page with a drawing of an island upon it. A ring of cliffs circled the island.

Owen leaned over Lady Danika's shoulder, peering at the map. "There's a gap along the southern part of the ring," he noted. "It looks like… teeth."

"The Mouth of the Gods," said Fioni, "the only way through the Godswall."

"Fioni," said Kora, before anyone could say anything else. "The wind…"

Owen stared at her for a moment and then realized the sea was now utterly still and silent. The sail hung limp. Even the ocean's surface was calm and unmoving.

"Fenya's tits," said Fioni. "We're becalmed."

Chapter 20

Owen

Owen lay on a rowing bench, his head propped up against the hull as he watched Fioni use the Raven's-Eye for what seemed like the hundredth time. Nearby, Kora leaned back against the gunwale, watching Fioni as well. They had been drifting all day now on the still waters of the Feral Sea, shrouded in fog. He guessed it must be late afternoon. Fioni lowered the Raven's-Eye, a worried frown on her face.

"Well?" he asked.

Without looking at him, she pointed to the steering board side. "The sun is over there, west. We have five, maybe six hours of daylight remaining."

Owen snorted. "You call this mist daylight?"

Kora, a sour expression on her face, said, "We're drifting."

"Aye," admitted Fioni, joining her, leaning out over the hull and staring into the still waters.

So that's it then, Owen thought bitterly. *With the sea becalmed, we're drifting off course, away from Serl's path.*

Some of the crew stood around the small cooking hearth near the prow, warming their hands and softly conversing. Others sat or lay about, wrapped in leather sleep sacks. Some played at dice or a board game, while others groomed themselves. Lady Danika slept nearby, wedged between two rowing benches, with only her dark hair visible beneath the blanket she had pulled over herself.

"Why don't we row?" Owen asked.

Fioni snorted, shaking her head.

"Rowing is hard work, Owen," said Kora. "Even for a man with shoulders like you. We row when we have to, but we can only keep it up for a few hours. Best to wait. The wind will return. It always does."

"If it doesn't," said Fioni, "you'll soon get your chance to pull an oar."

"How will we know if we're near this... Godswall?" he asked. "We can only see... what, a hundred, two hundred feet in any direction. We could sail right past it and never know."

Fioni shook her head. "According to Serl's journal, we'll see the lightning first—from leagues away."

Owen stared at her. "Like a storm?"

Fioni flicked a lock of hair away from her eyes. "No, Owen. Like magic. There's *always* lightning over the Godswall. Every day, every night, never-ending."

"That's not possible," he said. "Even in the north, in the mountains during the winter storms, the weather is ugly, but..."

Fioni shrugged and began cleaning her fingernails with a small knife. Kora frowned at her and then began to explain. "You're not Fenyir, Owen, so there's no way you could know our legends. Torin Island isn't just an island. Nor is the Godswall simply a ring of cliffs. Ages ago, when the world was new, the gods themselves lived on Torin Island. Wodor stood atop the mountain on the island and, pointing out to sea, turned in place. The Godswall rose up out of the ocean, answering Wodor's call, creating a shield to guard the home of the gods. And on Torin Island, the gods created men and women to serve them—us, the Fenyir. Then, because the Fenyir were hungry, the gods created fish and birds, and all other animals. For a time, all was bliss and happiness… but only for a time."

"The Dark Shark," said Fioni. "Serina's master."

"Aye," agreed Kora. "The Dark Shark, the younger brother to Wodor, the Father of Lies. He was jealous and filled with hatred for his brother. In secret, he began to turn the hearts of the Fenyir away from Wodor, Fenya, and the other gods. There was a war… and the gods—enraged that their creations turned against them—abandoned us. Almost all of the gods left Torin Island, departing for the stars. So, you see, Torin Island was the Gateway to the Gods. Because of this, because of the island's connection to our creators, the island is special to us. Torin Island is the only place in the entire world where the Fenyir can speak to the gods without going through the wights. And—if one is pious enough—perhaps the gods might even answer."

"You said *almost* all of the gods."

Kora nodded. "Orkinus, the god of the sea, he who loves us best. Orkinus defied his father, Wodor, to remain behind and watch over the Fenyir. He resides beneath the sea in Nifalgen, his mead hall. There, he collects the souls of fallen Fenyir warriors and judges those worthy of special reward, another chance at life, albeit a different life."

"Orkinus was not the only god who remained," said Fioni softly. "There was one other, one that does not love us."

"We do not speak the Dark Shark's name," whispered Kora. "But it is said Serina serves him."

"Owen's heard his name already, Kora. My father spoke it in his study—the night before he died."

Owen remembered now—*Ator. Did Taios bring about his own*

death by naming their dark god? Owen shivered. "In Conarck, we do not share your beliefs. We worship only one god, Father Craftsman, but we know of one other, Old Grim. He sounds much like your Dark Shark."

"Worship whichever god you want, Owen," said Fioni. "I don't think they care one way or another. The point that Kora is trying to make is that Torin Island, the Gateway to the Gods, is a mystical place. It resides between our world and that of the gods. Nature and the elements behave... *differently* over that island. If lightning forever strikes the peaks of the Godswall, it is because the gods will it so. When we get closer—"

A huge wave of water fell over Fioni and Kora, soaking both women and causing them to jump away from the gunwale in surprise. Behind them, on their port side, a giant black fish—more than half the length of *Fen Wolf*—leapt from the water once again to fall back with another splash that drenched the ship, eliciting cries of surprise from the crew. Then three massive heads—each larger than a wagon, with small shining black eyes—bobbed in the water, watching the longship, their huge tooth-lined mouths open wide, as if they were laughing at the consternation they had caused in *Fen Wolf*'s crew.

"Black Fish!" Kora cried out in wonder.

Owen's breath caught in his throat, and he rushed to the gunwale, leaning out and staring at the creatures. One of the monstrous fish swam lazily past the hull, so close that Owen could almost reach out and touch its pebbly dark flesh. Although almost completely black, each fish had a patch of white flesh above and behind their shining black eyes, as well as a larger white patch on their bellies next to their fins. Along their backs rose a single huge dorsal fin, similar to a shark's but larger, some taller than a man. The crew rushed excitedly to the gunwale as more of the massive heads surfaced, bobbing on either side of the still waters, staring at *Fen Wolf* and its crew. Now, Owen saw much smaller fish with yellow tints to their white patches—*calves*, he guessed. But even the young were at least eight feet long. None of the black fish seemed hostile, despite the rows of sharp teeth, nor did the crew seem at all concerned. In fact, they were all smiling and pointing excitedly.

One black fish lifted its tail and splashed, sending a wave to rock the ship. Lady Danika, awake now, gripped Owen's arm, a glowing smile on her freckled face. The same black fish that had just splashed them opened its massive mouth, filled with rows of razor-sharp teeth, and sprayed water at the crew, drenching them. The creatures cried out, screeching to one another in excitement.

"They're talking," said Lady Danika in wonder as seawater dripped from her face.

"They're a good omen for us," said Fioni.

"Do you hunt such creatures?" Lady Danika asked.

"Never," said Fioni quickly. "They are *special* to us."

At that moment, one particularly large brute leaped out of the water at least fifteen feet into the air. It spun about in a midair somersault before diving back into the water again. "Very special," she said with a smile.

Another black fish shot out of the waters. But, at the very height of its jump, the waters beneath it erupted as a giant serpentine form thrust up, catching the black fish in midair in its huge jaws. Then, in a frenzy of bloody bubbles and foam, both serpent and black fish disappeared beneath the waves.

"Vole serpent!" Kora screamed.

Another of the monstrous serpentine heads broke the surface of the water, this one holding a still-thrashing black fish calf in its mouth. Eellike in appearance, the vole serpent was at least a hundred feet long, its bloated body covered with glistening blue-and-green scales. Massive bulbous yellow eyes sat on opposite sides of an eel head crowned by thick spikes.

"Ancestors, save us!" cried Gali, staggering back in horror.

In one savage bite, the monster bit the black fish calf in half, letting its severed tail end fall free. As it ate, the vole serpent's head thrashed violently, sending waves of frothy gore to rock *Fen Wolf*. The other black fish were gone, scattered beneath the waves in a desperate attempt to escape the monsters.

A snapping noise resonated nearby, and a shaft flew through the air, hitting one of the vole serpent's bulbous yellow eyes. A crew member raised his crossbow into the air and cheered.

"No, you idiot!" screamed Fioni, running toward him.

She made it only two steps before the wounded vole serpent exploded out of the water, drenching them all and violently rocking the longship, throwing Fioni and the others to the deck. As Lady Danika fell back against the gunwale, Owen desperately grabbed at her arm, stopping her from going over the side. The vole serpent lifted its tail and smashed it down upon the waters, sending a wave that lifted the ship up, sending it skidding sideways. The crew screamed and grabbed at anything they could as the ship spun about. Owen, holding onto Lady Danika's wrist with one hand, gripped the rigging with the other and held on with all his strength. They had just stopped their mad spin when he saw the vole serpent, half-submerged, swimming straight for their hull, its wounded eye streaming blood.

It's going to ram us.

"Brace yourselves!" Fioni yelled.

The serpentine head slipped beneath the waves as the monster dove beneath the hull. *It's not going to hit us!* His relief was short lived, because the entire ship shuddered, rising out of the water as the vole serpent slammed up against its hull from below. The longship fell back upon the waves. Cold water sprayed through broken wooden thwarts in the deck, but the creature made no further attacks. As the seconds passed and the ship's violent rocking settled, Owen began to hope the monster had swum away.

He heard screams coming from the water. "Hang on to the rigging!" he yelled to Lady Danika as he sprinted to the ship's stern. There, bobbing in the waters behind them, was a white face—one of the crew, a young woman named Lenta. "She's fallen overboard!" he cried out, pointing to her.

Erik Gull-Song joined him. "Where?"

Owen pointed to where he had seen Lenta, but she was no longer visible. Someone was screaming that the ship was taking on water. Looking about the dark waters frantically, Owen saw no sign of the vole serpent. Without another word, Erik climbed atop the gunwale and dove headfirst into the water, sliding through it like a fish.

"Kora!" Fioni yelled. "A rope. Everyone else bail."

Kora dashed to Owen's side, a coil of walrus-hide rope in her hands. He couldn't see Erik anymore. "They were just there," he said, pointing. He gripped the gunwale, preparing to dive in himself.

Kora stopped him. "Wait. Erik's the best swimmer I know."

Then both Erik's and Lenta's heads broke the water. Kora swung the rope, tied with a loop at the end, around her head and then threw it far out over the water. It hit only feet from Erik, and he easily grabbed it, pulling it over Lenta's head and arm.

"Pull!" Kora ordered, and she and Owen began to draw the woman in.

Erik swam easily beside her. Others ran over and began hauling on the rope as well, pulling Lenta in toward the hull. She was dead weight in the water, with blood streaming down the side of her head. As they began to haul her up the side, Fioni leaned over the hull, holding an oar for Erik, who gripped it and pulled himself up, falling onto the deck with a splash. When they had pulled Lenta most of the way up the hull, Owen reached over and gripped the woman by the armpits. Her head lolled to the side, but her closed eyelids fluttered. *She's still alive!* Bracing himself, he had her partway over the gunwale when the vole serpent exploded from the depths beneath them, filling Owen's vision with rows of giant bladed teeth. He yanked Lenta over the side as the ship shuddered under the impact, once again sending everyone reeling and falling to the deck, including Owen, who held Lenta against his chest, as the ship slid through the turbulent waters.

"It's gone again!" someone yelled almost hysterically.

Thank the Craftsman, Owen thought. As the ship's rocking eased, Owen became aware of a strange warmness soaking through his lower torso. Lenta's eyes were open now, and she was staring at him. She opened her mouth and said, "Oh." Then her eyes rolled up into her skull, and her head fell against his chest.

Her entire lower body was gone from the waist down.

Chapter 21

Dilan

Dilan stands once again on that damned bridge high above the gorge, the river roaring far below. A battle rages at one end of the narrow bridge as an army of rebels try to force their way past the scores of men desperately trying to hold them back. Men scream, men fall, men die—both attacker and defender. But soon the fighting moves onto the bridge itself as the outnumbered defenders give way. Dilan stands shoulder to shoulder with his comrades, elite soldiers of the Rams—blooded killers all. Next to Dilan, fighting like a demon, is his older brother, Artur, the best man Dilan has ever known.

Soon, it is only Dilan and Artur still on their feet, still fighting. The attackers pause, preparing themselves for the final assault. Dilan's helmet is gone now, ripped loose in the fighting. Blood seeps down his arm, and his lungs burn with exertion. It's almost over, he knows. He can't do any more; no man could. But there are worse ways to die than standing alongside a man like Artur.

Pain lances through his skull, and he's falling, going over the side of the bridge. He jars to a sudden stop, his arm wrenching with agony as Artur grips his wrist, holding him as he swings over the gorge and the river. The enemy rush behind Artur, hatred in their eyes.

"Let me go! Save yourself!" he pleads.

"Never!" screams Artur—a moment before the iron-tipped spearhead comes through the front of his throat.

Dilan falls.

And falls.

…falls.

"Wake, my childe," a woman's voice calls to him. The bridge fades away from his memory. His brother's face fades away…

Dilan bolted upright from the corpse-pile, sending bodies tumbling down its side. All was darkness around him. Nearby, a single candle flared into life, illuminating the curved walls of the hold. Dilan pushed away the naked corpse of a young Windhelm girl with straw-colored hair and a horn-shaped birthmark on her cheek. The two deep puncture marks in her throat drew his gaze. *I did that. I killed her.* It had felt… *good.* He remembered her moaning in pain and ecstasy as he drank her blood. He had been so hungry, ravenous even.

As he was now.

He stared at his left hand, now whole and complete again. The fingers he had lost had regrown, like a sunfish when cut in half. He dropped down onto the blood-soaked deck, his toes sticking to the congealing blood. Then he reeled, almost falling, as weakness rushed through him, causing his legs to tremble. He grasped at the corpse-pile, holding himself upright by gripping the cold, dead shoulder of the young woman he had killed. A moment later, Serina caught him and held him against her naked chest. She was so beautiful, painfully beautiful. "Mother," he mumbled, swaying. "Something is wrong."

"It's the sun," she said as she held his cheek against her breast. "It's daytime still."

"How… why?"

"We've entered the Feral Sea. The sun cannot reach you through the fog. But while it cannot kill you, it will make you weaker—slow you down. The worst of the dizziness will soon pass, but you must be careful. In your weakened state... well, you shall remain strong enough for the task at hand."

Dilan stared at her in confusion. His thoughts were lethargic, as if he was still sleeping, or drunk. "I don't understand, Mother."

"Gird yourself for war, my battle captain. Those we hunt, I now know where they are."

"What must I do?"

"Do what you do best—kill."

Chapter 22

Owen

Owen watched as Kora, naked and dripping seawater, climbed back over *Fen Wolf*'s hull onto the longship. Fioni wrapped a blanket around her shoulders as Kora, shivering, rubbed her arms. Her body was all lean muscles and old scars, her breasts small but firm. When Kora saw him watching her, she grinned and tossed her shoulders back, thrusting her breasts out. He looked away quickly, his face red, and Kora and several of the crew snorted with laughter. Erik Gull-Song looked from Kora to Owen with confusion. He and his fellow Windhelm clansmen weren't yet in on the joke: the Fenyir, remarkably indifferent about nudity, often stripped naked in full view of the others without a second thought. In the weeks he had been aboard *Fen Wolf*, Owen had seen more naked women than at any other time in his life. But, as soon as the female crew members had realized how uncomfortable that made him, they delighted in using every opportunity to strip before him, often asking him to help them with their grooming. Even the men found it endlessly amusing.

"Well?" Fioni asked Kora.

Kora shook her head. "At least two of the center strakes are split—it may even be worse."

"Fenya's tits," swore Fioni.

"What can we do?" Lady Danika asked.

Kora dressed quickly, her skin pebbling with the cold as she stepped into her breeches. "For now we can ram caulking into the gaps below the deck-boards, but what we really need to do is to find land, haul *Fen Wolf* out, and re-caulk the boards."

"No," said Fioni. "What we really need to do is put her up on blocks for a few weeks and replace the strakes entirely—maybe some of the older ones as well."

"But we're still becalmed," said Owen.

Fioni looked down her nose at him, as if he were a stupid little boy. "Yes, Owen. We're still becalmed. I had no idea you kingdom types were such natural mariners."

Erik snorted, and Owen glared at him. Lady Danika pushed past Owen to stand before Fioni. "What then? How far are we from Torin Island?"

Fioni sat back on a bench, resting her back against the hull. "In truth, my lady, I don't know."

"But your great-grandfather's journal—"

"Isn't a map. I know heading and sea and wind conditions when Serl sailed, but he was never becalmed. And despite how still the water looks, we've been drifting all morning."

"What about the Raven's-Eye?" Lady Danika asked. "Surely it can help."

Fioni bit her upper lip and shook her head. "Even knowing the sun's location, I can only guess as to where we are. At this time of the year, the current should be pushing us southeast. But..." Her voice trailed off.

"We row then," Owen insisted.

Kora was fully dressed now and was once again strapping her Lyrian short swords to her back. "What do you think, Fioni?"

"Do you even know how to row, Northman?" Erik asked.

Owen's back stiffened, but he ignored the barb.

"He can row, Erik," said Kora as she adjusted the handles of her swords. "*And fight.* Be thankful for that, or you'd still be a slave."

Erik's smile vanished. "I meant no offense."

"None taken," Owen lied.

Fioni watched Owen and Erik, a sparkle in her green eyes, an amused tilt to her lips. "As much as it pains me to say this, I think that this one time, Owen is right. We've waited all day for the wind to return. With the state of the strakes, we can't wait any longer. We row."

"But which direction?" Kora asked.

"Southeast. Serl wrote of a black fish breeding area, a landmark, and—more importantly—land to the southeast of it."

"How can a spot of water be a landmark?" Owen asked.

"Such 'spots of water' are remarkable to the children of Wodor, Owen, in the same way that you mainlanders note a particularly tall hill or odd tree. Such things are passed from generation to generation—if for no other reason than to avoid where the vole serpents hunt the black fish."

"So what does that mean, then?" Lady Danika asked.

"It means, my lady of Wolfrey," said Fioni, "that despite losing the wind and drifting all day, we may not be as far off track as we think. Serl passed the black fish breeding grounds—"

"What if Serl referred to another black fish area?" Owen asked.

"There wouldn't be two such sites, not so close," said Kora.

"Which means Serl came this way," said Fioni. "And in his journal he made mention of an atoll to the southeast of the black fish site. So we row southeast and hope for the best."

"An atoll? An island?" asked Lady Danika.

"Yes—but perhaps not as you'd describe such a thing," said Kora. "An atoll is often little more than a rock rising above the sea."

Fioni stood. "But it might be large enough for us to beach *Fen Wolf* while we fix the broken strakes."

"In this fog, we might row right past it," said Kora.

"And if we don't make land soon—even a rock rising above the water—we're going to sink. We have to try," said Fioni.

"Agreed," said Kora.

"Well, Northman," said Erik, clapping Owen on the shoulder. "Looks like you're going to get to row, after all."

#

They rowed in shifts, slowly hauling the ship through the still waters. As the ship took on more water, it grew heavier, more cumbersome. Fioni stood at the stern, her hand upon the tiller. Every half hour or so, she'd use the Raven's-Eye to find the sun and then make minor course adjustments. Owen, pulling an oar beside Kora, had slipped into the same long, slow strokes as the others that were necessary to maintain a steady tempo. Those who were not rowing, including Lady Danika and Gali, were frantically bailing, using buckets, helmets, whatever worked, to drain the water. Yet the water continued to pool around their ankles, slowly rising. The crew had removed some of the deck boards, and now several worked on hands and knees in the cold water, trying to stuff a mixture of hair, moss, and a tar-like tree resin into the broken strakes. No one said anything, but Owen felt the tension, saw it in the crew's eyes. *We're running out of time.* In every direction, all he saw was fog. It was early afternoon yet, but when the sun went down, they'd never find the atoll. *Can we even stay afloat until daybreak?*

"Bird to port!" a lookout yelled.

Owen looked to Kora's face, saw the excitement in her eyes. "Does that mean—"

"Land to port!" the lookout yelled again.

This time the entire crew cheered. Most dropped their oars to rush to the port side, Owen among them. He saw the dark shadow appear through the mist—land, a small island. Birds circled overhead, a type he had never seen before with long black feathers and a sharp beak.

"Shrikes," Kora said. "Unless you all wish to swim the last bit, get your asses back on the rowing benches!" she yelled.

Then, absent all day, the wind came back, brushing against his sweaty face. Owen sighed and flexed his sore shoulders. *Great. Now that we don't need it anymore…*

The breeze pushed the fog back, vastly improving visibility in only moments, exposing more of the atoll. Even from here, he could see that it was so small it would probably take less than a half hour to cross it on foot. A single large hill dominated its interior with a stony black beach surrounding it. Kora had been right: it was little more than a rock rising above the water.

But it was the most beautiful rock he had ever seen.

Chapter 23

Owen

The entire crew, including Gali and Lady Danika, beached *Fen Wolf*. It took more than an hour because the entire ship needed to be unloaded by hand, the provisions and supplies carried through the surf and onto the rocky beach. Then, when the ship was as light as it was going to get, they all dragged, pulled, shoved, and rocked the waterlogged longship far enough onto the shore to get at the broken strakes. The seawater began to drain. It would be much easier to push the lighter vessel back into the water now, and would only take minutes at best. Owen watched silently behind Fioni and Kora as they examined the broken strakes.

He was amazed they had made it without sinking. The damage had been far worse than Kora had described. Four of the central strakes were broken, not two—with one shattered. There were no real trees on this atoll, certainly nothing that could replace a strake, but *Fen Wolf* had carried more supplies stored away under the deck boards than Owen would have thought possible: hammers, axes, saws, bundles of iron nails, and wooden jars filled with moss and tar—and, *thank Father Craftsman*, long wooden beams stacked together atop the keel. If they had to, according to Kora, they could also use some of the deck boards. While not ideal, they would keep most of the seawater out. As she was first mate, the task of repairing the ship fell on Kora, who was explaining to Fioni what she intended to do first. Fioni, however, kept interrupting her, pointing out how she would do it.

It was no business of his, so Owen wandered away.

The crew were happily chatting and laughing as they set up tents, built a small fire, and started cooking dinner. Owen moved away, considering the large hill at the center of the atoll. While he saw no trees, there were green bushes growing at its base, as well as thick vegetation on the summit of the hill. *Is there a stream up there, fresh water?* Kora and Fioni's voices rose in volume as the two women clearly began trying to talk over one another, with Kora jabbing a finger into Fioni's chest as she spoke. The crew wisely drifted away, pretending not to see them, and Owen continued to examine the hill's summit. The shrikes they had seen earlier seemed to be roosting up there, further reinforcing the possibility of fresh water. The summit appeared... *odd*, as if a portion of it had been broken off.

Lady Danika joined him. "I've never seen those two argue before."

He pointed to the summit. "My lady, what do you see up there?"

She squinted and then drew Sight-Bringer. Her breath caught in her throat. "There are stone blocks, broken pillars among the bushes." Her eyes were wide as she turned to face him. "Ruins, Owen. There are ruins up there."

"How is that possible?"

"The Feral Sea is a place of legends, Owen. The Fenyir may be the best mariners in the world, but even they don't come here. If not for the Illthori Raven's-Eye, we wouldn't be here either. Who can say who once lived here or what they left behind?"

Owen felt his excitement grow. "We should go take a look. If nothing else, maybe we can find fresh water."

Danika hesitated and then nodded. "Let's talk to Fioni."

#

"You want to do what?" Fioni asked them.

Fioni and Kora had seemingly been near blows when Owen and Lady Danika had interrupted them. Now, both women stared at them, their faces red.

"A quick look," said Owen. "Even if there isn't a creek, we may find a pool of rainwater."

"It'd be stagnant," said Fioni.

"We can boil it," said Kora. "This might be a good idea."

"Ruins, you say?" Fioni repeated, staring up at the hilltop in the distance. She turned about, sniffing the air. "The weather's turning bad. I think a storm is building."

To Owen's eye, the sky was the same grey mist it had been since entering the fog bank. "Are you sure? It looks—"

Fioni's face darkened, but Kora put a hand on her forearm. "If Fioni Ice-Bound says a storm is coming, then a storm is coming. But we do need more water—even if it is brackish. Wouldn't you agree, Fioni?"

"I suppose so. Go ahead, but take someone else with you—and maybe one of the crossbows."

"*You* should go, Fioni," said Kora.

"No. You need me to—"

"No. I don't. I really don't," said Kora with finality. "You are *Fen Wolf*'s master. You choose the course and the prey we go after, but *I* run the ship—and that includes fixing her. Go with your guests, and leave *Fen Wolf* to me. Trust me; I'll get her seaworthy again."

Fioni's eyes flashed in indecision. "I should—"

"Fioni, I love you like a sister," said Kora. "But if you don't get out of my hair, I'm going to kill you myself."

Fioni looked away. "Fine. As long as we're not gone long."

"I'll go as well," said Erik Gull-Song, now joining them. The young man smiled, flashing his too-white teeth at Fioni. "I could use a chance to stretch my legs."

"Probably a waste of your time," said Owen.

"Nonsense," said Fioni, glancing from Owen to Erik. "If there is water up there, we can use a strong back to help us carry it."

#

They ate first, wolfing down stew with dried fish chunks, while Kora oversaw the repairs on *Fen Wolf,* glaring at Fioni whenever she came too close to the work. Within the hour, though, Owen, Lady Danika, Fioni, and Erik had loaded themselves up with empty water skins and were trekking toward the hill. The hike was quick and easy, and they soon found themselves at the base of the hill, where, just as he had expected, they found a muddy, brackish creek. Owen paced the creek's bank for several minutes, looking for dead birds or other signs that the water was bad, but found nothing. They filled all the water skins, stacking them along the bank. Fioni wiped her wet palms on her breeches and peered up the hill. "You're sure you saw ruins?"

"You can't see them from this angle," said Lady Danika, "but they're up there."

Erik bit his lip, looking ill at ease. "This close to Torin Island, what if—"

Fioni snorted. "The gods wouldn't live on a bird-shit-stained little rock like this. I don't know who lived here, but it wasn't our gods."

"Only one way to find out," said Lady Danika as she brushed past the other woman and began to climb the hillside.

Worried but happy to see her more active, Owen held his

scabbard in place with one hand while hurrying after her. Whatever they found up there, it might help her forget the horror she had experienced in the Rose Palace.

The hill's slope was mostly barren and covered in rock, but as they neared the summit, they saw more and more thick green bushes and small windblown trees. Erik took up the rear, carrying one of the heavy Kur'teshi crossbows in case they saw anything worth killing and bringing back for dinner, although Owen doubted such a rock could support anything larger than a turtle or bird.

Fioni paused, sniffing the air once again. "Definitely a storm brewing. Thank the gods we found this atoll when we did."

As Owen reached the summit behind Lady Danika, he saw the ruins clearly for the first time. The shattered remains of walls lay about the level surface of the hill. Once, a huge multi-storied structure with walls and towers had sat upon the hilltop, but now all that remained was its broken shell, half-overgrown by weeds and bushes. The wind whistled through the broken masonry.

"Gods," said Erik, awe in his voice. "Who builds homes from stone and not wood?"

Owen scrambled up atop one of the broken walls, using the elevation to look down upon the ruins. "Not homes," he said. "See the remains of a tower there and there?" he pointed to several piles of stone, barely recognizable now. "This was a fort."

"Like Stron's Watch?" Lady Danika asked.

"Exactly like Stron's Watch," he answered. "Although the masonry is... different." He stared at the remains of what must have once been a window but built as an inverted triangle, the point facing down. *Who builds windows like that?* He met Fioni's gaze. "Did the Hishtari ever settle in the Feral Sea?"

She shook her head. "The Hishtari are not an... exploratory people."

"In their past maybe, a long time ago?"

"Not ever, Owen. The only people that would have sailed here are my people—and we've *never* worked in stone. We're woodworkers."

"Whoever it was," said Lady Danika, "they abandoned this place hundreds of years ago. These ruins are ancient."

She was right, he saw. The elements had almost completely reclaimed the summit. A thick carpet of moss, weeds, and bushes strangled the bricks and walls, looking like a new skin. "I'm not so sure they abandoned it, my lady," he said.

"What do you mean?" she asked.

"Look, the walls, the towers—they've all fallen in. This place was broken."

"A cataclysm of some type?" suggested Fioni.

"Or the wrath of the gods," said Erik softly.

The wind howled louder now.

Owen carefully edged his way up another pile of broken stones, precariously balancing upon the rubble. He froze when one of the blocks began to suddenly shift and teeter, sending pebbles scattering. He leaped higher up onto another.

"Careful, Owen," said Lady Danika.

"If not for the fog," he said, spinning in place and staring out at the sea around them, "you could see for a dozen leagues from up here."

"What do you see?" Erik asked him.

"The fog is clearing somewhat, but the waves are growing rougher," he said.

"Yes, that tends to happen during storms," Fioni snapped.

Owen was about to climb back down when something strange caught his eye. It hadn't been easy to see before, but from this height, he saw that a portion of the rubble near one of the collapsed towers seemed… open, as if the stone had fallen around something. "There's something over there."

"Over where?" Fioni asked.

Moving carefully, Owen jumped from stone to stone, sending several more skittering and sliding down, and made his way to a hollow space created by fallen blocks of stone. "Here," he said, gazing down at a pattern in the ground, a white triangle several feet wide surrounded by black stone, with weeds growing over them.

He carefully climbed down into the hollow, an open space of perhaps fifteen feet. The others joined him. "There are runes carved into the stone," said Fioni, dropping down on one knee and yanking the brush clear, exposing strangely familiar runic markings.

Lady Danika rested her hand on his forearm. "Owen! They're the same as on—"

"Sight-Bringer," he answered breathlessly.

She knelt down and placed the broken Illthori sword alongside the markings on the stone, comparing them to those on the blade. Clearly, the same people who had made Sight-Bringer had also etched the symbols around the edges of the white triangle.

"What does this mean?" Fioni asked.

"It means," said Lady Danika, wonder in her voice, "that these are Illthori ruins."

Fioni's mouth dropped open. "Is that even possible—"

"The sword! Look," insisted Erik.

In comparing the markings, Lady Danika had touched the blade against the stone. Now, the runes carved into the metal blade and white triangle began to glow with a soft blue-white light. Lady Danika snatched back the broken sword, and the markings on both blade and stone began to fade. "My lady," said Owen, a note of trepidation in his voice, "perhaps…"

Ignoring him, she bent down again, bringing the broken tip of the sword near the markings once more. As she did, the eldritch glow returned, and Lady Danika inhaled deeply in wonder and then began to run the tip of the sword over all three sides of the triangle, lighting all the runes up.

"This is an evil place," said Erik. "We need to go back."

When the last of the runes on the stone was glowing, the ground began to hum and vibrate, sending all four of them scrambling back in fear. The white stone triangle sank into the earth, and a cloud of dust exploded out, making them all choke and cough. When the cloud drifted away, they saw the triangle begin to turn beneath the ground, pivoting away to reveal a dark opening and a flight of dark, glasslike stone steps. A soft green glow shone upon the stairs.

Chapter 24

Owen

Owen stared down at the dark, glasslike stone steps and the green light coming from below. The steps extended as far as he could see, dozens of feet beneath the earth. From here, he could just make out another tunnel at the base of the steps. Impossibly smooth black walls ran on either side of the stairs.

"What... what have you done?" Erik asked Lady Danika.

Now that the portal was fully open, the glowing runes around the portal's edge and the sword blade faded away once again. "I didn't know *that* would happen," Lady Danika said softly, wonder in her voice. "These must be Illthori ruins."

"The air smells... *wrong*," said Fioni.

"It was the same in Greywynne Fortress," said Owen. "After we unsealed the catacombs, the air stank of rot and mildew. Modwyn warned of *foul vapors*, said they were dangerous."

"Modwyn was a liar and a traitor," said Lady Danika. "There's no such thing as foul vapors. He was only trying to trick you into covering your faces with his poisoned cloth."

"Perhaps," said Fioni. "But the air does stink. And this *feels* wrong. I don't think whatever is down there is meant for our eyes."

"Fioni's right. We should go back to the ship," said Erik.

"No," said Lady Danika. "Sight-Bringer's magic somehow opened this portal for a reason. We need to go down there—even if we only take a quick look. You Fenyir are always speaking of destiny. What else could this be?" She looked to Owen, her eyes pleading.

"We don't know that," insisted Erik.

"She has a point, Erik," said Fioni. "Think about it. Just when we need shelter, we find this atoll. Then we find these ruins. And Sight-Bringer not only kills the undead, but is also a magical key? Tell me you don't see the hand of the gods in all this. If this isn't fate, then I don't know what is."

Erik shook his head. "It's not the hand of the gods I'm worried about, Fioni. It's one god in particular. This may be a trap of the Dark Shark."

"I'll go down there, my lady," said Owen. "You wait here. I'll only take a quick look."

The noblewoman shook her head. "I'm going as well."

"Are you addlepated?" asked Erik. "This is an unholy place. I can feel it. We need to leave!"

"No," said Fioni. "She's right. This is fate. I'm going as well."

"Fioni," said Erik, a tremor in his voice, his eyes pleading.

She reached out and gripped the back of his neck, pulling his forehead in to rest against hers. "I *have* to, Erik. You must see that? I want you to wait here. If something happens, bring Kora and the others. Okay?"

Erik moved away, shaking his head as he sat upon a fallen block of stone. He stared at his hands and mumbled something beneath his breath.

Owen stood at the top of the stairs, staring down at the dark passage below. "Let me go first, and follow once I've reached the bottom." Owen stepped onto the stairs. Despite looking like glass, the surface of the steps was surprisingly firm, not at all slick. He took another step and then another, dropping below the triangular opening. He hesitated, his breathing wild, his face drenched in sudden sweat. He disliked the underground and always had. If the portal closed again...

"Are you all right, Owen?" Lady Danika asked.

He wiped the stinging sweat from his eyes. "I'm fine, my lady. I'm fine."

He forced himself to keep going, the fingers of one hand trailing along the wall as he descended. Conscious of the ground seemingly closing in around him, Owen reached the base of the steps and the large passageway. The tunnel was hexagonal, six-sided, and lined with a type of stonework he had never seen before. Metal pipes ran along the tunnel's ceiling, at least twelve feet high. *Why build a tunnel so high?* It extended before him, at least a hundred feet or more. The light was coming from a series of glowing runes that ran the length of the tunnel, although only every second or third rune glowed; the others remained dark. His breath caught in his throat as he stared at the light. *Magic! Lady Danika was right. These must be Illthori ruins. Only they could create such wonders.*

Little was known of the long-dead Illthori race. Their civilization had vanished long before the rise of men, and all that now remained were the rare magic relics they had left behind, such as Sight-Bringer and Serl's Raven-Eye. *Not only do we now have two Illthori relics, but also we've somehow stumbled upon an Illthori ruin—the first I've ever heard of. Lady Danika and Fioni are right. This has to be fate.*

At the sound of descending footsteps, he glanced up to see Lady Danika slowly descending the stairs. Fioni followed closely behind, holding the crossbow Erik had brought with him. When the two women reached him, they both stared in wonder.

"I know," he said softly. "I know."

"We should come back with torches," said Fioni. "Just in case the lights…"

"We'll just take a quick look," said Lady Danika. She turned, looking up the dark steps. "Even if the lights die, we'll still see daylight through the opening."

The air stank of chalky dust, mildew, and stone. Water slowly dripped from the rusty pipes overhead, creating stagnant pools along the tunnel's stone floor. Glistening spiderwebs stretched entirely across the passageway. Owen inhaled deeply. "Just a short way, then."

He began to make his way down the tunnel, his boots splashing in the puddles. He paused before the spiderwebs stretched across the tunnel, watching the spiders—some as large as his thumb—scurry away. Owen drew his longsword—Brice Awde's longsword—and used it to pull away the spiderwebs, clearing a path for the two women.

Lady Danika placed her palm against one of the walls and then drew it back again immediately. She stared at Owen with wide eyes. "The walls—there's something… *moving* behind them."

He placed his ear against the dark stone, immediately hearing and feeling a light vibration, as if the rocks themselves were trembling. A moment later, the sensation just stopped. He met the women's eyes and shook his head.

"Let's just go a bit farther," whispered Lady Danika. "To come this far…"

Owen gritted his teeth and continued to pull away the spiderwebs. Before they had gone a dozen paces, gossamer webs completely covered the steel blade all the way to the cross guard. The stale underground air reminded him of the corpse-lined catacombs beneath Greywynne Fortress.

Just ahead of them, a large portion of the ceiling and tunnel wall had fallen inward, creating a pile of rubble almost blocking the entire passageway. He turned sideways to slip past it. When he came out on the other side of the rubble pile, he saw something almost completely buried beneath the stones. At first, he thought he was looking at an old pile of rotting clothing or garbage. The light was poor at this spot. Dropping down on one knee, he sifted among the stones and began clearing them away. A chill ran down his spine when he suddenly realized what was buried beneath the rubble.

"It's a corpse," he said softly.

Lady Danika knelt beside him. "This is no person," she said softly.

She was right. Covered in mummified skin looking like dried leather, the corpse was clearly not human. It lay on its back, with the entire lower torso still covered by heavy rocks. The exposed upper torso, however, was far too long, the arm bones articulated at an odd angle and twice the length of a man's. The head was also strangely shaped, with a feline face, overextended jaw, and rows of sharp feline teeth, many now broken off and missing. The eyes were long gone, with only dark, empty pits set too closely together on either side of what had once been a muzzle of some type. Shards of dark clothing still remained but fell apart under Owen's touch. Lady Danika stared at the corpse, her eyes wide. "Owen, I think... I think maybe this is an Illthori, the first anyone has ever seen."

"How..."

She drew Sight-Bringer, held the white stone handle carved in the likeness of a beastlike woman in her palm. "It's the same face, isn't it?"

"How is that possible?" asked Fioni. "The Illthori disappeared hundreds of years ago. They should be nothing but dust now."

"I don't know," said Lady Danika. "Perhaps being underground preserved the corpse somehow."

"Look at the chest cavity," Owen said, pointing toward a massive circular hole, the width of his fist where the heart would be. "It may have been trapped when the wall fell upon it, but someone finished it off. A spear thrust, perhaps? Did the Illthori war among themselves?"

Uncertainty flitted across Lady Danika's face. "No one knows."

Owen bit his lip and nodded, once again leading the two women down the passageway. For the first time, they passed several chambers set on either side of the tunnel. Like the corridor, the doorways were six-sided and far too high for men. While cave-ins completely blocked the first two chambers, a portion of the third remained intact—although the far wall had fallen in, knocking over a massive stone structure that reminded Owen of the vaults in the Great Crypt of Greywynne Fortress. Once, the structure had been shaped like a pyramid, easily ten feet high with a flat, narrow top; now, it lay on its side, two of its thick walls shattered. As he stared at the broken pyramid, Owen's skin itched, as if spiders crawled over him. He backed away, rubbing his arms. "What is that?" asked Lady Danika.

"I don't know," Owen answered, "but I don't even like looking at it."

"Maybe we should head back now," said Fioni. "I'm starting to think maybe Erik was right. Maybe this place is haunted."

"There's one more chamber up ahead," Lady Danika said. "I don't think there's anything else."

They moved on. Lady Danika was right—the tunnel led to a single final chamber. At its hexagonal-shaped doorway, Owen looked in upon a large chamber. As with the other chambers, portions of the ceiling and wall had also fallen in, creating piles of stone rubble. Holding his arm across the doorway to block the women, he stared up at the ceiling, where he could make out large cracks in the portion that remained intact.

"Fioni," said Lady Danika. "Your sword…"

Wave's Kiss, the wave-pattern-welded longsword that had once belonged to Fioni's great-grandfather Serl, hung from Fioni's waist. Fifty years ago, Serl had had one of the blood gems taken with the chest containing Serina's still-beating heart embedded upon the hilt of his sword. That red stone now glowed softly, as if a candle flame burned within it. "That's something new," she said in a hushed whisper. Holding her crossbow against her hip with one hand, she drew the sword, holding the gem up to her eye, bathing her face in a red glow. "In his journal, Serl wrote that the blood gems in the chest... glowed."

"In Daenipor, when I was a prisoner of Kalishni'coor, he bragged about the blood gems he gave to Serina, claiming they retained magical properties from the nell spiders from which they're harvested."

"What are spiders doing with gems?" Owen asked. "I would think—" He paused when he saw another red glow coming from a far corner of the chamber behind the rubble created by the fallen ceiling. "That wasn't there a moment ago," he said softly, feeling coldness spread through his core.

"This is otherworldly," Fioni whispered.

Owen's heartbeat pounded in his skull as he slowly entered the chamber, sliding among the fallen stones. The two women followed right behind him, so closely he felt their breath on his neck. As he made his way across the chamber, he kept one worried eye on the fragile ceiling above them. He edged around the fallen stones and looked down upon yet another mummified Illthori corpse. Unlike the other, this one lay completely exposed. Its legs definitively inhuman, the knees bent wrong, covered in what looked like rotted fur, and ended in split hooves. The glow they had seen came from beneath one of the corpse's oversized, clawlike hands.

Slowly, Owen dropped down beside the corpse and lifted its dead hand, gently prying the fingers open. A single glowing red stone rolled onto the ground. Owen picked it up, holding it between thumb and forefinger. Small silver threads the length of his finger dangled from the back of the stone where they seemed to be growing from it, like hair.

Fioni bent over his shoulder. "Is that…"

"Another blood gem," Owen answered.

"May I see that?" Lady Danika asked him.

He handed her the gem and then continued to search the immediate surroundings, shifting some of the rocks away. He stopped when dust and pebbles cascaded from the ceiling. *We need to go,* he thought. *This structure is ready to come down.*

"Owen," said Lady Danika, "there's something else here, buried beneath the collapsed wall."

Owen joined her as Lady Danika dropped down on hands and knees and began to shift several of the rocks. Dust drifted down from the ceiling. Owen's concern spiked. "We need to go, my lady. Now!"

"There's… ash, a huge pile of ash beneath the stones," Lady Danika said. "And some… some… *thing* else." From where he stood, he saw what looked like a narrow strip of cloth, smaller than his hand and partially buried by the rocks. Gripping it with both hands, she pulled it free. As it did, the rubble shifted. Stones and dust began to fall around them. A moment later, a loud crack resonated along the length of the ceiling, followed by a deep rumbling.

"Run!" Owen yelled, gripping Lady Danika around the waist and hauling her to her feet. As the ceiling began to fall in on them, he thrust her through the doorway and into the passageway.

"Owen!" yelled Fioni from behind.

He paused, seeing her stumbling about in the dust. He grabbed her by the shoulders, spun her about in the right direction, and shoved her after Lady Danika. "Go!" he screamed. "Get to the surface before everything collapses!"

A moment after he stumbled through the doorway, the entire chamber fell in upon itself with a thunderous roar, sending a choking cloud of dust around them, obscuring their vision. The rest of the complex seemed to be falling in upon itself, and rocks continued to fall around them. The ground shook. Choking and coughing, barely able to see, they stumbled back down the tunnel, desperate to reach the stairs and safety. The glowing marks along the walls vanished, plunging them into complete darkness. Owen reeled off a wall and stumbled, falling face first on the floor. He climbed to his feet and once again staggered forward, praying he was still going the right way. He only made it another dozen paces before he tripped again, falling and smashing his knee on the stones. He cried out in pain, his fear almost overwhelming him, when he realized he could just make out daylight through the dust above him.

He had tripped on the stairs.

His heart pounding, he began to crawl up the glasslike steps, the walls shaking and rumbling around him. Rocks hammered into his back and shoulders, and he felt fresh blood seep into his eyes. He tried to rise and fell again.

I'm going to be buried alive.

Then hands grabbed him and pulled him to his feet. Someone was half-dragging, half-carrying him up the steps. Daylight grew stronger, and then he was out of the underground, a fresh wind on his face. He fell onto his hands and knees near the portal and then saw Lady Danika and Fioni nearby, coughing but otherwise safe. Erik knelt down next to him and stared into his face. "Will you live, Northman?"

Owen wiped the blood and dust from his eyes. "Thanks… thanks to you, Erik," he finally managed, still coughing.

Erik went to check on the women. The ground beneath them continued to shudder and roar, and dust continued to pour from the portal. Then a final ear-shattering crack reverberated around them, and all went silent. When he trusted himself to stand once more, he stumbled over to the women. Lady Danika stared at him with concern. "You're bleeding, Owen."

He touched the side of his head, wincing. "I think the stitches reopened. I'll ask Kora to tie them again. Are you all right, my lady?"

"I am. Fioni got me out."

"What was it you found beneath the stones?"

She opened her hands up. Lying across her palms was a huge black feather, but far too large for any bird he had ever seen—even a harpy didn't have feathers that long. "What does this mean?" she asked him.

He trailed a finger over the feather. As he touched it, it began to fall apart, to disintegrate, and drift away on the wind. Whatever it was, it couldn't survive above ground. He shook his head, sighing softly. "I don't know, but we're alive. Let's be grateful for that."

Erik came back and handed him a waterskin and a strip of cloth to hold against his head. After a few minutes, the bleeding slowed and then mostly stopped. Erik lifted the cloth and examined the wound. "The catgut came loose in all the excitement. That's what you get for letting Kora Far-Sails tend your wounds. She never could tie a knot worth shit," Erik said with a wink.

Owen snorted, thinking that *maybe* Erik wasn't that bad after all.

Fioni sniffed and then stared up at the sky. The fog was drifting away, revealing black clouds from horizon to horizon. "Storm's starting," she said. She climbed out of the hollow created by the rubble and stood atop the fallen masonry. "I think you were right about this being a fort, Owen. With the fog drifting away, you can see for leagues now." She turned in place, slowly scanning the horizon. "Surf's getting rough. I hope the others have tightly lashed down the tents. Otherwise, we'll have a miserable—"

Owen stared up at her. "Miserable what?"

"Fenya's tits," she said softly.

Jumping to his feet, he climbed up beside her and followed her gaze out to sea. She had been correct. With the storm pushing the fog back, he could now see for leagues in all directions. And there, on the far side of the atoll, fighting its way through the turbulent waves, was *Thunder Killer*, sailing straight toward them.

Chapter 25

Owen

They ran, slipping and sliding back down the hill, leaving the full waterskins where they had piled them next to the creek. Fioni said *Thunder Killer* had been tacking against the wind, and that they'd have some minutes before it rounded the atoll, but *Fen Wolf* was beached, its crew helpless. Owen's head was bleeding again by the time the four of them staggered back onto the beach. Someone must have seen them running, because Kora and a handful of the others were waiting for them, loaded crossbows at the ready. "What's wrong?" Kora demanded.

"*Thunder Killer...* is... here," gasped Fioni, gripping Kora's shoulder for support as she tried to catch her breath. "We get underway now!"

Without a word of protest, Kora spun away and began screaming orders at the watching crew. In moments, they rushed to the beached ship and began to shove it back into the waters. Owen, his heart pounding, ran to help them, all the while keeping an eye on the horizon for *Thunder Killer's* sail. Because all the supplies were still sitting on the beach, *Fen Wolf* easily slid back into the water, taking only moments to reverse what had taken almost an hour earlier. This time, though, the ship heaved in the surf. "She's too light!" Kora yelled to Fioni. "We need more ballast. How long do we have?"

"Not long enough," Fioni yelled back, stopping to watch the far shore of the island. "Leave everything but the weapons and the water."

"Wodor's balls!" swore Kora, but she began yelling orders to the crew, who began haphazardly throwing shields and weapons onto the longship.

Owen had just thrown Vory's ring-mail coat over the gunwale—leaving everything else in the sea chest behind—when Fioni grabbed Kora's arm, turning her to face her. Both women were waist-high in the freezing waters. "The strakes?"

Kora shook her head. "We replaced the shattered strake and recaulked three others, but..." She paused, her gaze darting toward the dark clouds and turbulent waves. "I thought we'd have until after the storm."

Owen approached the two women, the water pushing him off-balance. "What about fighting? It's just *Thunder Killer*." He glanced up at the dark clouds. "Despite the storm, it's not nightfall yet. We won't have to face Serina. We'll have a fair chance."

Fioni shook her head. "We don't know how close behind *Iron Beard* is. If we become tied down fighting *Thunder Killer* and Galas closes on us…"

"He has a point," said Kora. "Without more ballast, the waves will hammer the hull."

"*Fen Wolf* is a tough bitch," said Fioni. "You've told me that enough times. She'll hold."

"Here comes *Thunder Killer*!" yelled Owen, pointing to the far shore of the atoll where the other longship had now come into view, its oars in the water as it pulled through the surf, heading toward them. Even from here, Owen saw the ranks of armed warriors at its prow.

"Everyone aboard now!" screamed Fioni. "We're out of time."

The crew pushed through the waters and began to climb aboard the longship. Owen gripped Gali around the waist and easily lifted her up and onto the ship to Erik. He helped Lady Danika up next before looking back at the shoreline, the rocky beach littered with stacks of supplies, barrels of water, and tentage. A campfire burned, its flames gusting with the wind.

"Time to go, Northman," said Erik as he leaned over the hull, his open hand held out.

Owen jumped up and caught Erik's hand. Erik hauled him over the side of the ship. Fioni climbed aboard last, glaring at the approaching longship. She ran to the tiller, taking it from Herla. In moments, Kora had the oars in the water, and *Fen Wolf* began to pull away from the atoll. But now, *Thunder Killer* had closed much of the distance and was coming on fast. Arrows whistled overhead to splash into the rough waves or shudder into the ship. Picking up one of the round shields, Owen slipped his arm through the rungs then drew his longsword, which still trailed spiderwebs in the strong wind. Fioni turned *Fen Wolf* out to sea, but *Thunder Killer* was close behind, less than a hundred feet away. Owen used his shield to protect Fioni at the tiller, watching the hate-filled faces of the enemy warriors as *Thunder Killer* rowed closer. "Fioni!" he yelled over the wind. "They're closing fast. We're not going to—"

"I know!" she replied, her eyes tight. She raised her voice so that Kora could hear her. "Prepare to repel boarders!"

Ekkie barked furiously.

From amidships, Kora turned and, white-faced, stared back at her. Then she hurried down the line of benches, pulling every second man or woman away and sending them to the stern. The warriors scrambled to arm themselves before taking up ranks and forming an impromptu shield wall. Owen remained with Fioni, covering her with his shield while she operated the tiller. Kora and five other crew members armed with the last of the Kur'teshi crossbows stepped out before the shield wall, taking aim at the approaching longship. Some of the enemy threw lit torches through the air, but in the tossing waves, all of them fell into the water. Just behind the mast, Owen saw Lady Danika and Gali huddled together behind a shield, which was as safe as they were likely to get this day.

"Ready!" Kora screamed. The ship rose and fell in the stormy waves. *Thunder Killer* was now only a ship's length away. "Loose!" Kora yelled as she squeezed the firing lever. The arms of the Kur'teshi crossbows snapped forward, sending a half dozen bolts whipping past Owen and Fioni and into the warriors massed at *Thunder Killer*'s prow. From this close, the powerful bolts shattered both shields and the men holding them, in some cases killing the men standing behind those in front as well. This close, Owen now saw that many of those men wore the colorful bright padded-cloth-armor gambesons and animal facemasks of Hishtari soldiers. *Why use Hishtari soldiers on a Fenyir longship?*

Screams of pain and fear cut across the waves.

"Again!" Kora yelled. "Again!"

Having already tasted the devastating impact of the heavy crossbows, the enemy crew fought to move back, away from the carnage, but in the press of bodies, there was nowhere to go. A second volley of crossbow bolts smashed into them, sending them into a panic. Men fell and were trampled by their fellows. Some even fell overboard—or jumped. *They'll drown in those gambesons,* Owen knew, as he almost had.

Fen Wolf's crew cheered, but *Thunder Killer* was almost on them. With no more time to reload, Kora and the other crossbow-armed crew members stepped back behind the shield wall. An arrow hammered into Owen's shield, and he cut it loose with his sword. "Fioni, leave it!" he yelled.

Her desperate face darted from his to the ship about to ram them, and then she slipped away from the tiller. After she took a shield handed to her, she and Owen joined the shield wall, locking their shields together.

"Brace for impact!" Fioni yelled.

Thunder Killer's prow crashed into *Fen Wolf*'s stern, just forward and port of the steering platform. Several feet of the wooden gunwale caved in, tearing loose boards and sending shards of wood flying. Owen fell back against the others under the jarring impact, but the press of bodies kept him upright. Grappling hooks flew through the air, latching onto *Fen Wolf*'s hull as the enemy pulled the two ships together—a chilling reminder of the disastrous battle against *Iron Beard*.

As if waiting for this moment, the storm's full fury let loose, darkening the sky and pelting them with stinging rain. The enemy rushed forward, jumping from *Thunder Killer* onto *Fen Wolf*. Thunder boomed. As the first of the enemy came at them, Owen and the others met them in a single cohesive wall. Owen, screaming "Wolfrey!" hammered his shield into the jaguar-masked face of a Hishtari warrior, hearing bone crunch and sending the man flying back through the air. The enemy, coming at them in a disorganized rush, fell apart against the shield wall.

"Now!" screamed Fioni. "Send 'em into the sea!"

As one, the shield wall shoved forward. Owen put his shoulder behind his shield and sent another man—a Greywynne islander—skidding back to slip and fall upon the rain-slick deck. They moved forward, stepping over fallen enemy soldiers, and Owen stomped down on one before shoving another man over the broken hull to slip between the two hulls and disappear into the water. Ekkie buried her teeth in a man's groin, whipping her head back and forth as he screamed. Owen couldn't tell who broke first, the Hishtari soldiers or the Greywynne Islanders, but in moments, the enemy warriors turned and fled, desperate to return to the safety of *Thunder Killer*.

Few made it.

A cheer broke out among *Fen Wolf*'s crew. Exhilaration coursed through Owen, and he shook his sword—bloody now, although he couldn't remember using it—at the frightened faces of the enemy crew, jostling to find cover behind *Thunder Killer*'s hull.

Fioni cut a grappling hook from *Fen Wolf*'s gunwale. "Cut us free. Hurry!"

As the crew severed the other grappling hooks, *Fen Wolf*, with half its crew still rowing, began to pull away from *Thunder Killer*. After the beating they had just endured, the enemy fighters were unable or unwilling to come against *Fen Wolf*'s crew again. Owen whooped in joy, his heartbeat racing. He felt like hugging someone.

That joy vanished when the ranks of the islanders slipped away, revealing the ring-mail-clad warrior with the short dark hair and thick eyebrows. Owen froze, his hands falling to his side, his mouth open. *Dilan—it's Dilan!*

But Dilan died...

When Dilan opened his mouth to reveal two long fangs, the hair lifted on Owen's neck and arms, and a chill washed over him, freezing him. He understood then: Serina hadn't killed Dilan; she had turned him into a blood fiend.

Oh, Dilan...

His one-time friend exploded into action. Moving impossibly fast—faster even than Modwyn had been—Dilan leaped across the widening expanse between the two ships and landed with a jarring thud on *Fen Wolf*'s deck, smashing into the shield-bearing warriors and scattering them. Owen watched in stunned disbelief as Dilan began lashing out at the others, moving so fast his body blurred. With a single sweep of his hand, he ripped away most of a woman's face, before tearing out another man's throat, sending bright arterial blood spurting. Another man, he disemboweled with his clawlike hands; the man's intestines spilled out, falling onto the deck. The crew fell back in horror, leaving only Owen before Dilan.

The two men faced one another, Owen's thoughts a chaotic whirlwind of disbelief.

Dilan had saved his life more than once. He had even leaped onto Serina's back, slowing her down long enough for Owen and Lady Danika to escape the alehouse. They had been friends—best friends. Owen shook his head, his shield and sword still hanging at his sides. "Dilan, wait—"

Dilan bared his fangs, and Owen knew with absolute certainty his friend was about to kill him. But then, Dilan spun about, a crossbow bolt punching right through the ring-mail armor over his chest—but just a fraction too high to have hit the heart. Owen saw Kora furiously trying to respan her crossbow. Dilan hissed at her, turning toward her with hatred in his bloodred eyes—and Owen finally moved, slamming his shield into Dilan's back, smashing him against the gunwale. Dilan spun, beating his fists against the shield and smashing it to splinters, before gripping Owen and lifting him high above his head, as if he were a child. Owen flew, colliding with Kora and knocking her down. A bright flash of light obscured his vision—he must have hit his head again. He tried to rise but couldn't. Then, through his blurry vision, he saw Lady Danika's face before his. He realized a moment later that she was now shielding him with her own body as Dilan reached out for her…

Dilan's face contorted in pain, and he spun away, grasping at his hand.

Owen saw the glint of light coming from Sight-Bringer's broken blade in Lady Danika's hand. *She cut him.*

Dilan stumbled back against the gunwale, holding his right hand against his chest. Tendrils of black smoke drifted from his palm. Another crossbow bolt smashed into his stomach, pinning him to the gunwale. Once again, Dilan bared his fangs and hissed in rage at Fioni, who had picked up the crossbow Kora had dropped and was now respanning it. Dilan's red eyes swept the others also now advancing on him. He screamed in inhuman rage as he pulled himself free of the bolt, ripping his body away from the bloody gunwale. Another crew member rushed forward with a spear, but before the man could strike, Dilan leaped onto him, wrapping his legs over the man's shoulders and bearing him down to the deck. As they fell, Dilan squeezed the man's head with his thighs, crushing it like a pumpkin. The crew fell back in horror once more. But as Dilan rose, another crossbow whipped past him to strike the deck. Dilan lifted the nearly headless corpse and held it before him as a shield.

"Get around him!" yelled Fioni. "You have to hit the heart."

"Take it," Lady Danika said, thrusting Sight-Bringer into Owen's hands. "Finish him!"

Magical energy coursed through Owen, clearing his vision and giving him the energy to move. Owen, holding the broken sword in both hands, advanced on Dilan. "Dilan, stop!" Owen cried out.

"Get out of the way, Owen," Fioni yelled, her crossbow in her shoulder, Owen between her and Dilan.

Before Owen could move, Dilan threw the corpse at him, knocking him back into Fioni. The two of them fell entangled as Dilan jumped up onto the gunwale and then ran lithely along its length, like a cat. At the last moment, Dilan jumped once again across the waves, landing on *Thunder Killer*'s deck. A moment later, Dilan was out of sight, protected by the enemy warriors.

"Row!" Fioni yelled, jumping to her feet and grabbing the closest crew member, thrusting her onto a sea bench. "This is the only chance we're going to get."

Fen Wolf pulled away from *Thunder Killer*. The other ship began to pursue *Fen Wolf*, but it was clear its crew was having difficulties; the ship moved sluggishly through the water. *"Iron Beard* to our stern!" someone screamed, their voice breaking in panic.

In the heavy deluge of rain, the massive drake-ship was a vast dark shadow, just now coming around the far shore of the atoll. "He's too late to the fight!" Fioni screamed into the pelting rain. "Galas will never catch us now. Row!"

The waves grew much rougher, throwing the longship up before smashing it back down again with a teeth-jarring impact. "Half-sail now!" screamed Fioni, once again at the tiller. The crew shouted her orders forward, repeating them, as others struggled to lower the sail. Behind them, *Thunder Killer* was just a dark shape in the rain, and *Iron Beard* was lost from sight.

Owen fell down next to Lady Danika, his mind a whirlwind of conflicting thoughts and images as he handed Sight-Bringer back to her. Dilan was a blood fiend. Although he had been new to the garrison, Dilan was by far the best man-at-arms in service to the Dain family, a former member of the kingdom's elite Rams. Now, he was an obscenity.

This *couldn't* be.

"Owen, are you all right?" Lady Danika screamed at him, water running off her face.

Owen looked past her, at the dark roiling clouds around them. Lightning forked down on the port side less than a hundred feet away, leaving bright spots in his vision and an acrid stench in his nostrils. Moments later, thunder boomed around them. *Old Grim's laughter,* he thought miserably. When he could see again, the waves now towered above the deck on either side. *Fen Wolf*'s prow rose and fell, smashing back into the waves.

"What do we do?" Gali screamed, clutching at Lady Danika, who shook her head, her eyes darting to Owen. Owen stared at the young Hishtari woman, as if he didn't understand the question.

"Owen!" yelled Lady Danika, gripping him by the chin and turning his face toward hers. "What should we do?"

"Pray," he answered.

Fen Wolf sailed into the heart of the storm.

Part 3:
Sentinels

THE WHITE BLIGHT

FERAL
SEA

EMPIRE OF
HISHTAR

DUCHY OF
WOLFREY

DAENIPOR

KINGDOM
OF CONARCK

PROMISCUOUS
SEA

KINGS
HOLD

PORT
OLLECHTA

GREAT
DRAKE'S
HEAD

FENYIR
ISLANDS

GREYWYNNE ISLAND

TORIN ISLAND

N

W   E

S

Chapter 26

Owen

The rain continued to hammer down in freezing sheets, interspersed with the occasional lightning bolt that boiled the seas around them and lit up the dark, angry clouds overhead. Owen clung to the mast with one arm while gripping Lady Danika with the other. The noblewoman in turn held onto the terrified Gali. The crew secured themselves to whatever they could, only moving about when necessary—and even then, only from one handhold to another, lest they be washed overboard. Some of the waves were so high they towered over *Fen Wolf*'s mast, threatening to capsize the longship. Mist and foam sprayed their faces, and water constantly poured over the hull, pooling around their feet, drenching them in freezing water, stealing their warmth and strength. Lady Danika screamed something at him, but her words were lost in the tempest.

All this time, Fioni remained at the tiller, fighting to keep the ship facing the worst of the oncoming waves. Each time, the ship would claw its way up the oncoming wave until it reached the gray-bearded crest, only to hang for a moment before tipping forward and beginning the stomach-churning descent to smash into the waters below. Each time they struck, Owen was certain the impact would rip apart the damaged hull, sending them all to a watery death. But each time, *Fen Wolf's* prow would rock upward once again, and he'd breathe a heavy sigh of relief. But always, the worry nagged him. *How much longer can the hull withstand this pounding?*

Nearby, her arm wrapped around a guide rope, Kora threw her head back and howled like a wolf. He stared at her in disbelief. Kora, seawater dripping from her chin, flashed a smile at him. "The wave beats the high benches!" she screamed above the wind. "The keel cleaves the sea. Will the ugly sea break the beautiful ship?"

Above them, the sail, still only half-raised, crackled as the wind tore at it. The mast creaked ominously, waving under the stress. "I don't understand!" he yelled back.

Kora, her eyes dancing, reached out and gripped Owen's tunic, pulling his ear closer to her lips. "The spinster-crones have already spun out the threads of your life, Owen Northman—whether you believe in our gods or not. You can't escape your fate, so you might as well be adventurous."

A sweet, pungent zing filled his nostrils, and a moment later, a massive bolt of white lightning struck the sea less than a half-league away, exploding around them.

Kora howled once again.

#

Time lost all meaning.

They fought on through the storm for what felt like hours as night fell. At one point, the sea became so rough, Owen tied a length of rope around himself, Lady Danika, and Gali, and all three huddled together for warmth, shivering miserably. Yet, despite the cold, the constant soaking, the waves, and the ever-present threat of breaking apart, he recognized a sense of wild abandon coursing through him, invigorating him. He had never experienced anything like this in the north. By comparison, free-climbing snow-covered mountains seemed dull.

Then one of the wooden shroud pegs snapped, freeing a guide rope to whip about in the wind. Kora's eyes grew wide, and she let go of her handhold, dashed to the side of the hull, and leaned far out, grasping at the flying rope, missing it by at least a foot. Owen slipped free of the rope securing him to the women and rushed over to help Kora, slamming into the hull and almost falling overboard in the process. Kora yelled something, but he couldn't make it out. A moment later, she gripped him around the waist, and he understood. Letting her hold onto him, he leaned dangerously over the hull, straining to catch the rope with the wooden shroud still attached to it. Water sprayed his face, obscuring his vision, and he knew if Kora's fingers slipped, he'd be over the side and gone in a moment. He groaned, reaching out farther, his fingers straining. Then, just when he was certain he'd never catch it, the wind shifted and threw the rope back at him. He gripped it as tightly as his numb fingers would allow. Kora and another crew member hauled him back over the hull. They took the rope from him and quickly reattached it to another shroud along the gunwale. Kora slapped him on the back. He saw other crew members nervously eying the remaining mast shrouds. One of the crew members scrambled up to Kora, pointing at Fioni as she put her lips near Kora's ear. Kora squeezed the woman's arm and then looked about at the nearby crew members. When her eyes fell on Owen, she scuttled over to him, keeping her center of balance low as she yelled into his ear, "We need to run ropes around the hull! Can you help?"

Lady Danika and Gali stared at him in terror, but he nodded. He secured both women to one of the nearby rowing benches. "I'll be back when I can!" he yelled at Lady Danika.

Kora grabbed a dozen other select crew members, and together they began to slip wide rings of rope around the prow. Then they pulled and tugged the ropes, dragging them as far back along the hull as they could before pulling them tight. Tying knots in such conditions was desperately difficult work, made harder by the constant pounding the sea gave them, but somehow they managed. The hull creaked and groaned. One of those helping, a thin, bald man named Eigley —or Egg, as the crew called him—who had a long, drooping mustache, yelled something to Owen. Owen didn't catch his words, but the thumbs-up and smile Egg gave him was clear enough. A moment later, a wave washed over the hull, sending both men reeling. Owen fell against a nearby bench, cracking his shin against it and sending a bolt of pain up his leg. When he staggered back to his feet, Egg was gone. He ran forward, sliding up against the hull where Egg had been a moment before. He leaned over the hull, screaming for help, but saw nothing in the roiling waters. Kora was beside him in a moment, her eyes tense with concern. "Egg went over!" he yelled.

Peering at the waves, she gripped the wooden Wodor's hammer she wore on a thong around her neck, looked into Owen's eyes, and shook her head. He looked away, scanning the waves once more, but saw nothing. His heart thudded dully in his chest as he stared at the dark, heaving waves, an empty feeling in the pit of his stomach. Infinitely tired, he turned away, stumbling back hand over hand along the gunwale to the two women, and joined them again without a word.

#

Sometime later, the wind just died down without warning. Even the waves, although still rough, became noticeably calmer. The transition was so abrupt, a current of excitement ran through the crew as they leaned over the hull, staring at the sea around them, as if looking for something. Kora ran to the stern platform and began to converse excitedly with Fioni, who was pointing directly ahead of them. Owen staggered to the prow and then peered past the wooden wolf's head, staring out into the dark night. Lightning flared in the distance, highlighting a vast shape rising before them. Kora rushed forward, excitement on her face. "Hoist full sail and pray to Orkinus!" she yelled to the crew.

Owen grabbed her arm, stopping her. "What is it?"

"We're in the lee of an island. It's sheltering us from the wind. Fioni wants to push on now and sail for it at best speed."

"We're safe?" he asked with incredulity, having been certain they'd die this night.

Kora barked in laughter, shaking her head. "Not even a little bit, Northman. With the sail raised, we'll be far less maneuverable. If we broach to, we'll founder stern first or slew broadside and capsize." She punched him in the shoulder, her eyes flashing. "But what an adventure, no?"

Owen helped the crew, hauling on a guide rope. As the bright-green sail extended to its full height, the winds gripped it, snapping it full—and *Fen Wolf* shot forward like an arrow. Owen leaned over the hull, trying to make out the looming shape of the island through the rain. Mist sprayed his face and ran into his beard. Unable to help himself, he threw his head back and laughed.

Both Gali and Lady Danika were watching him with concern.

"Tidal streams to port side!" a lookout screamed.

Other crew members relayed the warning, yelling it back to Fioni, who pulled hard on the tiller, turning the ship's prow away from the port side. When lightning flared again, Owen saw a whirlpool in the water, bigger than the ship and not a bow's shot away. Had they kept their initial course, they'd have sailed right into it. The hull creaked in protest, but *Fen Wolf* slipped past the hazard. Minutes later, the worst of the storm seemed to just… end, eerily, abruptly. The dark clouds parted before them, revealing a night sky filled with stars, highlighting vast black cliffs, like a wall, rising before them. Kora, standing near the prow, turned and yelled to Fioni. "It's the Godswall!"

The crew cheered. Owen looked at Lady Danika and Gali, who seemed as confused as he was. The waves, so huge and threatening only minutes ago, were now only gently rolling. The tall, knifelike peaks, hundreds of feet high, stabbed into a clear, star-filled night sky—but only over the cliffs. In all other directions, the sky remained dark and angry. Behind them, thunder crackled as the storm raged on. He stared at Kora in confusion. "What does this mean?"

She jumped down onto the deck and wrapped her arms around his waist, actually lifting him off the deck several inches as she whooped in joy. "It means, Northman, we've found Torin Island."

Chapter 27

Danika

Danika stood before the hull, watching the cliffs speed past as *Fen Wolf* sailed around the Godswall. Surprisingly, the air was far warmer than it had been in weeks, almost balmy, like a warm summer night. Despite the ocean being much calmer near the island, the helmsman maintained a safe distance from the cliffs, where the waves might throw them against the rocks. Out to sea, the storm continued to rage, but all was surreal and still near the Godswall. Bright stars and a half moon shone down, bathing the ship in silver. Danika still couldn't believe it. It was beyond surreal; it was impossible.

But it was true, nonetheless.

The storm swept around Torin Island and the Godswall, avoiding it.

Earlier, when the seas had calmed, Gali had left her to help with the wounded. Five crew members had died during the fighting with *Thunder Killer*. At least one of the wounded—Herla High-Eye, the woman who had so expertly operated the tiller during Kora's maneuver to slip past *Thunder Killer*—would die before the sun rose. It had been Herla whose face Dilan had slashed, shearing away her nose, one of her eyes, and most of her cheek. She had been suffering for hours now. When she passed, it would be a blessing.

Owen sat alone on a rowing bench, his back against the hull, his knees pulled up to his chest, staring at nothing. Seeing Dilan as a blood fiend had affected him deeply, she knew. It had been the same with her and Brice. What Serina did to others was a… foul thing… far worse than just killing them. She stared at Owen now, her guilt eating at her. *I could have warned him—I should have warned him. Why didn't I? Did I want to spare him the pain I suffered, or was I just too frightened to bring it up? Who was I protecting—him, or myself?*

She heard a rustle behind her as Kora slipped next to her and stared out at the Godswall. For long moments, the two women watched in silence as the dark cliffs slipped past. "Have you ever seen anything like this before?" Danika broke the silence, looking from the clear night sky to the dark clouds that ringed the Godswall. Lightning suddenly forked down, striking the cliffs, leaving a bright afterimage in her eyes for a few moments.

Kora shook her head. "No, but my grandmother did, when she came here with Serl. I've sailed through many a storm—and some of 'em were real ship-killers. Sometimes, you'll sail into an eerie calm in the heart of the storm—but not like this." She looked out to sea, at the turbulent dark waves. "Storm's moving away, heading nor'east, but the clouds sweep *around* the Godswall, like sheep avoiding a campfire." Kora gripped her Wodor's hammer, held it tightly in her fist. "This… this is the will of the gods."

Despite the warm, balmy weather, Danika shivered.

#

The Godswall was far larger than Danika had realized. Hours later, they were still sailing around it. Eventually, the storm that surrounded them began to abate, and as it did, the fog bank returned—but like the storm, the fog avoided the island. The lightning strikes along the peaks continued, seemingly at random, but ceaseless. Danika had never seen anything like it. Most of the crew slept now, but despite wrapping herself in a fur, Danika found sleep impossible. At the base of the stern platform, where the wounded slept, a single lantern shone, illuminating Fioni, who sat beside the dying Herla. Danika rose, pulled her boots on, and then carefully stepped past the sleeping crew members, slowly making her way to the stern. As always, Ekkie lay on her stomach alongside Fioni. At Danika's arrival, the dog briefly opened her eyes to watch her, and then almost as quickly went back to sleep. Ekkie snored softly, and Fioni scratched behind the wolfhound's massive pointy ears. Fioni watched wordlessly as Danika lowered herself next to Herla, sitting across from Fioni. Danika sadly gazed upon Herla. A blood-soaked cloth had been left atop the woman's face, covering most of it, but leaving her one remaining eye exposed. That eye was closed now, hopefully in slumber. Herla's breathing was wet and slow. Danika watched the wounded woman. "Does she…"

"She sleeps, thank the gods," whispered Fioni. "But I think she'll move on soon. She has another journey to make."

"I'm sorry. I barely knew her, but I liked her. She's… fierce."

Fioni softly snorted, the trace of a smile on her tired face. "She is that."

The lightning struck the peaks again, this time illuminating what looked like a… tall structure of some type—one sitting atop the cliff's peaks.

"It's odd, no?" Fioni said. "Seeing lightning but hearing no thunder afterwards. I knew to expect it, but each time I see the flash, I expect to hear the thunder, the booming of Wodor's hammer in the sky."

"There's something up there," said Danika, certain she had seen something manmade atop the cliffs.

"Giant towers. Made entirely of steel. Serl wrote of them in his journal. When the sun comes up in the morning, we'll see them more clearly, set all along the cliffs at regular intervals, like watchtowers. Which only makes sense—the Godswall protects Torin Island."

Towers, atop cliffs? Danika shook her head, wondering at the engineering marvel that must be. *Perhaps Fioni was right; maybe Torin Island was once the home of gods.*

A spasm seemed to course through Herla, and she moaned in pain. Fioni gripped her hand with both of hers. "It's all right, sister," she whispered. "You don't need to keep fighting. You've shown us all how to be brave."

In response, Herla's eyelid fluttered weakly.

"Were you close?" Danika asked her.

Fioni sighed sadly. "All of our lives. Herla, me… Kora." Leaning forward, she traced her fingers through Herla's dark hair. The barest hint of a smile curled up the corner of Fioni's mouth. "You two have the same long dark hair. It's so rare among us Fenyir, you know. Have you noticed the men stealing glances at you? I have. It was ever the same with Herla. I was so jealous, so I used to torment her mercilessly. I told her she wasn't really one of the Fenyir but the drunken get of a kingdom sailor who had lain with her mother. The last time I made that joke, I was… eight maybe. By then, Herla had had enough of my stupidity. She punched me in the nose and knocked me on my ass. Before I could do anything, she sat atop my chest and ripped a handful of hair from my head. The pain was… glorious. I was crying. She was crying. The servants were running about, screaming for our mothers. And Herla, dragged away by her mother, waved a handful of my hair at me, yelling, 'See? Now I have red hair, too.'" Fioni laughed, an exhausted, barely recognizable thing. "But I never mocked you again, did I, Herla?" She sobbed, looking away as she wiped her eyes with the back of her hand.

Danika smiled dutifully. That may have been the first sign of vulnerability Danika had ever seen in the woman.

They sat there in silence for long moments. When Fioni finally spoke again, steel laced her voice. "I have so many reasons to kill Galas. How does he keep finding us, I wonder?"

"I don't think it's your cousin. Before she became a blood fiend, Serina Greywynne was already a sorcerer, a master necromancer. Who knows what evil spirits she can call upon."

Fioni rested her chin on her palm, her elbow on her knee. "And this is our destiny: blood fiends and necromancers?" She shook her head. "The spinster-crones are having a fine laugh at our expense, I'm afraid."

"I'm sorry for all you've lost, Fioni Ice-Bound: your father, Rolf, now your childhood friend. The price for helping us is… *too* high."

"No. You shame me, my lady of Wolfrey. I need to apologize to you… and Owen. I was angry earlier. None of this is your fault, nor his, truth be heard above the wind. Our fates are preordained—me, my father, Rolf, Herla… even you kingdom types, I suspect. All we can do is bravely play out the tapestry of our lives." Her lip trembled as she stared at her friend. "But you, Herla, you were so brave. You fought a blood fiend. Who among the clans now alive can boast of such an act?" Fioni closed her eyes again, running her palms back over her face, through her short red hair. "Gods, save us. Blood fiends, ghouls—and *Serina-fucking-Greywynne*! Who lives through such times?"

Silence once again settled over the two women. They remained like that for long moments. Lightning again struck the cliffs, highlighting another tower. When Fioni spoke again, her voice was barely a whisper. "What… what happened to Owen? I've seen him face death without the slightest hesitation, but he was… shaken today, unnerved. Who was that man—that *thing*?"

"Dilan Reese, one of my family's men-at-arms." A slight gust of wind blew Danika's hair before her eyes, and she brushed it away. "He was once Owen's friend, maybe his best friend." She felt broken inside, as she had when Brice had driven Sight-Bringer through his own heart. She choked back a sob. *Damn Serina!* "Dilan was brave and noble and kind and responsible and… and a hundred other things that no one will ever know about or remember—because he's a soulless monster now. Serina destroys everyone around her." Danika looked away, tears now running down her cheeks. *Brice, it's all too hard. Please, come back.*

Everything is too hard.

"We Fenyir believe," whispered Fioni, "that if we die bravely, perhaps Orkinus will choose to bring us to Nifalgen. There, we drink and eat and fornicate all day and all night." She winked at Danika. "But some of those heroes—the bravest, the finest—are reborn, returned to life as black fish, to once again swim the seas we love."

Danika wiped her tears and smiled. "That's a pleasant belief. Our kingdom scripture says that as long as we honor Father Craftsman and live by his laws, face our end with courage and dignity, we will find peace in the afterlife. We can even be with those who have crossed the Golden Veil before us. I'd like that."

Fioni leaned over Herla and squeezed Danika's knee. "That, too, is a pleasant belief." She sat back, once again holding Herla's hand in both of hers. "Although, no insult intended, my lady of Wolfrey, I'd rather spend eternity drinking and screwing."

"And who says there won't be time for lovemaking across the Golden Veil?" said Danika, thinking now of Brice. Lightning struck the cliffs again, this time much farther away, on the far side of the Godswall, snapping Danika from more pleasant memories. "Your uncle, if he's still alive—he's been living alone on Torin Island, guarding Serina's heart for almost fifty years."

"He'd be almost seventy by now, but you have a question?"

"Why? Why do it? Why spend a lifetime alone with that foul thing?"

"Duty," she said softly. "Duty to his family. Duty to his clan. Duty to the gods. According to my father, Denyr was a very pious young man."

"But… fifty years?"

"It was never supposed to be that long. Serl meant to come back for him after he was certain Serina was truly dead. But Serl foolishly tried to sell a handful of the blood gems taken with Serina's heart to Kalishni'coor."

Danika sighed. "And Kalishni'coor was the one who had given those gems to Serina to begin with. He had been expecting her heart, as well. But the ship never arrived."

"But Serl and a handful of the gems did. So that odious ball-sack betrayed Serl and murdered him—before he could make Serl tell him where the heart lay hidden. And Serl never had the chance to return for his grandson. I'll be honest with you. I hope my uncle is long dead. Sometimes the cost of duty is far too high."

"Duty," Danika repeated softly. "Someone once told me, 'Duty is a double-edged sword. It cuts both wielder and foe.' Duty to family drove me to accompany my brother to Greywynne Island. Duty pushed me on this voyage. Duty stopped me from… from going away with someone I loved when he begged me. If I could only have that moment back…"

Fioni watched her in near silence, the only sound the water lapping against the hull, the creaking of the rigging, the snapping of the sail, and Herla's ever weaker, ever less regular breaths. "Could you have lived with yourself, my lady of Wolfrey, if you had abandoned duty to run away with your lover? Do you think you'd have been happy knowing you had let your family down?"

"We'd have had each other."

Fioni leaned forward, her eyes shining in the lantern light. "You'd have hated yourself within a month. Within a year, you'd have hated your lover. Resentment would have poisoned your happiness. No, the painful, horrible truth is this: our hand may be on the tiller, but sometimes the current takes us where it will. This is fate."

Danika sat back, considered the other woman coldly. "If you know so much of love and happiness, tell me, why are you so angry with Owen all of a sudden? You liked him well enough to sneak into his bed the same night you met—or was that just to shock me?"

Fioni stiffened, and she looked away quickly. "*You?* Of course not. It's just… well… Owen is not who I thought he was."

"Because of Rolf and your father's herdsmen? I'm sorry they died, but that's on Serina, not Owen. This is a war. It may have started fifty years ago, but Serina has never stopped waging it. If we don't succeed tomorrow, if we don't find and destroy Serina's heart, thousands more will die."

Fioni shook her head, her eyes tight and cold. "I admit, I'm angry about Rolf and the others, but that's not it—at least not *all* of it. I've known men like Owen, and they always end up letting you down."

"I thought him nothing more than a brute at first," Danika said. "But I was wrong, wrong about everything. Someone I trust had faith in Owen."

Fioni snorted, shaking her head. "I'm no fool. I recognized Owen's potential the same day we fished the two of you from the water. I know he's no dummy. He may have the body of an overgrown bull, but his intellect is sharp and true. But that's never been Owen's real fault. His true weakness is that he lacks commitment, lacks confidence to take charge when it's most important. He knows the right course to tack but refuses to put his own hand on the tiller."

"Give him a chance."

"I have, and men died carrying out *his* plans."

"Not true. Owen's risked his life many times. He scaled the Rose Palace to save me. If not for Owen, Modwyn would have burned my eyes out and given me to Serina."

"Granted, but ask yourself this: why did Owen risk his life to save yours? What was in it for him?"

Danika's eyes narrowed in confusion. "I don't understand."

"Kora reads lips. She was watching when we fished you from the sea, when you made your little deal. I see what you don't. Owen serves you out of selfishness, because you promised to release him from his oath if he helped you get home and warn your king of Serina's return. I understand why *you're* here. Duty compels you. Your family has a blood feud with the Greywynnes. Each of you represents the last of your bloodlines. But something other than duty compels Owen."

Her heart racing, Danika thought back to that day. Certain their lives were at risk, Owen had been plotting escape from Fioni and her crew, but Danika had wanted to make a deal with Fioni, to barter for their freedom. She needed to warn the king of Serina's return. If Owen had done something foolish, he might have put that warning at risk. She had been desperate to get him to obey her, so she had promised to release him from his oath once they reached King's Hold. But she hadn't been completely honest with him, either. As the last living member of the Dain family, by law, Owen's oath passed to her, but females could not wield power in a household in the Kingdom of Conarck. Once she arrived in King's Hold and delivered her warning, the king would find her a suitable husband. Owen's oath, as well as her family's lands and wealth, would pass to that man. While she had every intent to honor her promise, she also knew that any future husband—whomever that might be—would be under no such legal obligation. But she had needed Owen's help. She still did.

I had no choice.

Fioni was watching her with guarded eyes. Something *else* was going on here, something hidden. Danika bit her lip, considering her words carefully. "I don't know, exactly, why Owen risked his life for me, nor why he continues to do so, but I refuse to believe it's just for personal gain. He's just not *that* kind of man. And I suspect you know that, as well."

Fioni stared at her hands. "Maybe… maybe he *loves* you?" she said in a soft whisper.

Danika sat back, breathless, sudden realization coursing through her. "Fioni—"

Then she paused, suddenly aware of a strange noise that had been growing as they argued. It sounded like distant thunder but constant and growing quickly in volume. The two women stared at one another in confusion, but then, Herla's body stiffened, and she cried out in pain. Fioni, her face pale, bent over the woman and kissed her forehead. "Wait for me in Nifalgen, my friend," she whispered as she slid the handle of her sword into Herla's fingers then held them closed over it with her own.

And Herla died.

#

Leagues away, in the darkened hold of *Iron Beard*, Serina sat naked and cross-legged atop her corpse-pile, her eyes closed in meditation. A ghost of a smile curled the corners of her lips. "Herla," she whispered. "Hello. I have questions."

Chapter 28

Owen

Owen's eyes opened. For several confused moments, he lay between two of the rowing benches where he had been sleeping. He had been dreaming of a tall waterfall back home, once again standing in the freezing pool beneath the cascading waters, listening to the roar of the water as it fell upon the rocks. Although awake, he still heard the waterfall. Still lying on his back, he stared up at a clear, star-filled night sky. Was he still dreaming? No, he definitely heard the roar of thrashing water. He sat up, rubbing his eyes and looking about the ship. Most of the crew still slept, huddled together even though the air was unseasonably warm. The sail crackled overhead, catching what little wind there was this night. The only light on the ship came from a lantern near the stern. A single crew member operated the tiller, but Lady Danika and Fioni were also awake, staring out over the hull. *Something's going on.* He stood, pulling on his clothing and boots and then tucking his sword belt under his arm as he made his way past the sleeping crew members, approaching the two women. The sound of crashing water came from their steering board side, but in the darkness, he saw nothing but the shadow of the cliffs. *It's not a waterfall,* he realized, *but waves churning against rocks. But how?* At his approach, the two women turned and watched him. Lady Danika gave him a slight smile. Just behind them lay the corpse of Herla, the woman whose face Dilan had mauled. He looked sadly down upon Herla's dead face. "When…"

"Not long ago," said Fioni, her voice raw with sorrow.

"I'm sorry."

"Thank you."

He stepped up to the side of the hull and stared out into the darkness. The sound of the waves crashing against rocks was growing stronger. "What is that sound?"

"The Mouth of the Gods," said Fioni, a tremor of awe in her voice.

The roaring grew in volume as they sailed closer, waking other crew members as well. More of the crew woke and made their way to the steering board side of the vessel, staring out into the darkness.

Lightning struck the nearby cliffs, arcing out into the sky and exposing the opening in the Godswall. Owen only saw it for a moment, but the sight of tall, fanglike peaks thrusting out of the water shocked him to his core. "That's not possible."

As they sailed closer, they were able to see the Mouth clearer, even with just the moon and starlight. A gap stood between the cliffs of the Godswall, at least a hundred feet across, but dozens of needlelike rock spires thrust out of the turbulent waters between the cliffs, looking like fangs. And in this narrow obstacle, the waves beat upon the spires, throwing mist into the air and churning the water around them.

"It's exactly as Serl described it," Fioni said. She turned to face the woman at the tiller. "Hold us here until sunrise. Keep at least five ells from the Mouth. I don't want to go anywhere near that gap while the tide is low."

"What is it you intend to do?" Lady Danika asked in disbelief, her hand clutching her chest.

"Courage, my lady of Wolfrey. This is the only way past the Godswall."

Owen shook his head, breathless, as he stared at the thrashing waters within the Mouth. There was a path through the spires, he saw, but it was far too narrow. "You can't be serious. The waves will smash us against those fangs of rock."

"There is no other way," insisted Fioni. "But the tide is low right now. When it rises, the gap will become much wider, the water less… wild."

He stared at her, his mouth hanging open. "But…"

"Fifty years ago, Serl passed through the Mouth—and he sailed *Iron Beard*, a much larger, far less maneuverable ship. Trust me, Owen. When the tide rises, we will slip through the Mouth easily enough—although I warrant it will be a frightening experience."

"We have no choice, Owen," Lady Danika said. "If we're to stop Serina, we must breach the Godswall. We've trusted Fioni this far. We must have faith in her seamanship skills."

#

Several hours later, Owen remained leaning over the gunwale, watching the Mouth and listening to the constant crashing of the waves. Far to the east, a red glow penetrated the mist that surrounded the Godswall. *It will be sunrise soon*, he knew, *an hour, maybe less.* At the peak of high tide, when the sun was directly overhead and the waters much more calm, they'd row past the teeth and into the Mouth of the Gods—*and then on to Torin Island.*

Most of the others remained awake, sitting in the dark, chatting softly or, like Owen, staring breathlessly at the dark Mouth. He would have thought sleep impossible, but Fioni lay nearby, curled up in a blanket, snoring softly. Ekkie lay beside her, guardedly watching Owen. "You don't like me, either, is that right, girl?" he softly asked the wolfhound.

She huffed in response and then lowered her head onto her massive paws.

He watched Fioni sleep. She was a skilled skipper, he knew. If anyone could slip through the Mouth and reach Torin Island, it would be her. It all seemed so impossible. He didn't know if Father Craftsman was watching over them, this far from home, in such a strange, otherworldly place, but he whispered a quick prayer just the same. *And if we do destroy Serina,* he mused, *what then? What will become of Dilan? Can we—*

He felt a chill rush over him, and he gasped for breath. Pushing himself away from the gunwale, he felt a rush of dizziness threaten to send him reeling to the deck. He saw the same fear mirrored in the eyes of the others. Even Ekkie whimpered, visibly trembling in terror.

It was the Dread.

"Fioni!" He shoved her. "Wake up! Hurry!"

She jerked awake with a start, sweat beading on her forehead, her eyes wild. "No!" she yelled, trying to shove him away from her, still half-asleep. "I'm not going down those stairs."

He caught her wrists and held her hands as she tried to strike out at him. "Fioni, it's me, Owen. Wake up, before it's too late."

She peered at him in confusion for a moment, and then understanding filled her eyes. "Awake," she mumbled.

Letting go of her wrists, he bolted up the wooden steps to the raised stern platform. The crew member on duty stood frozen, drool running down his beard, his hand on the tiller shaking visibly. Owen dodged past him and climbed up on the sternpost, searching the dark sea behind them. Just as he had feared, two shapes materialized out of the mist: *Thunder Killer* and *Iron Beard.* "To arms!" Owen yelled. "The enemy is on us."

Time seemed to freeze, as if a spell trapped the crew. They stood in place, staring about one another, incomprehension on their frightened faces. Then Fioni was among them, screaming orders, galvanizing them to action, and the spell broke. The crew jumped to obey, throwing themselves onto the rowing benches while others prepared for battle.

"Move, move, you sons and daughters of Fenya!" Kora screamed. "If you'd live to see the sunrise yet again, move!"

Fioni joined Owen, shoving the crew member on duty away and taking over at the tiller herself. She stared wide eyed at the two ships closing on their stern and shook her head. "Gods help us, how does this keep happening?"

"Can we get away?"

"And go where, Owen?" Her gaze darted from the two longships to the thunderous noise of the Mouth. Just for a moment, indecision flitted across her eyes, before cold resolve flashed in them. "Go get your lady," she said through gritted teeth, pulling on the tiller. "Time to find out if her sword is aptly named."

Fen Wolf's prow ponderously swung toward the Mouth as Owen dashed away.

"Row!" screamed Kora. "Faster."

A shower of arrows fell among them, hitting several of the rowers in the back. The ship faltered but only for a moment as others took the place of those hit. *Fen Wolf* sped closer to the screaming Mouth. Owen found Lady Danika. "My lady, we need to borrow the sword. Fioni's going to try the Mouth right now. She needs it to see the way."

The noblewoman bobbed her head quickly, and with Owen shielding her from the arrows with his body, they ran back to join Fioni at the stern. A handful of warriors armed with shields opened for them, letting them in among them and then facing outwards again as the arrows thudded into their shields. The roaring of the waves grew in volume, making speech difficult. Cold spray soaked them all. Bright-orange light blazed from the ship's prow where Kora and another held brightly burning lanterns over the gunwale, exposing the churning maelstrom of sea and rock into which they sailed. "Here!" screamed Lady Danika, seawater running off her chin as she thrust Sight-Bringer's hilt at Fioni.

Without taking her eyes off the prow, Fioni grasped at the white stone handle of the Illthori sword and held it tight against the tiller. She inhaled deeply, her eyes widening. "Wodor's balls," she swore and then immediately pulled back on the tiller, groaning through clenched teeth. The ship's prow drifted to port—away from the colossal fang of rock hundreds of feet high that they had been heading toward a moment ago.

The Mouth of the Gods loomed before them.

Chapter 29

Serina

"Hurry," Serina urged Galas.

Their prey pulled away, heading for the Mouth of the Gods, a turbulent storm of waves and freestanding spires of jagged rock haphazardly blocking the opening between the cliffs of the Godswall. Excitement coursed through her, making her feel alive once more. *The legendary Torin Island.* It seemed like a dream. *This is Ator's will,* she realized. *He wishes me to find this sacred place. It's fitting that here, where his hated brother and sisters once lived among men, I will end the Dain bloodline.*

On the decks below, warriors crowded near the prow, intent on finally capturing and killing their prey. Those with bows loosed arrows on the smaller longship, causing havoc among its rowers. The last of her ghouls, less than fifty of them, stood in silent, massed ranks near *Iron Beard's* towering mast. *Thunder Killer*, with Dilan aboard, raced ahead of them. If Dilan could board the other ship, his presence would slow them down long enough for *Iron Beard* to ram them, letting her ghouls clamber onto its decks. Then this damnable chase would finally be over. *And I can drink that Dain bitch's hot blood. Feel it splash onto my breasts.* Serina ran the tip of her tongue over her fangs. "I told you, Stron," she whispered to herself, "fifty years ago, when I pinned that damned sword of yours through your foul heart, that I would end your foul bloodline. I will keep that promise today. And when I'm done with your stupid niece, I'll go after your king."

"Fioni's heading for the gap in the cliffs!" yelled Galas from where he stood nearby. "Is she insane?"

"No, she's brave. I think I like your cousin, this *Fioni Ice-Bound.* Are you sure you wish to waste such a warrior as a broodmare?"

Galas's mouth fell open, his disappointment written across his rugged features. *Such a handsome man,* she thought, *but so inept at keeping his thoughts hidden. His lust controls him. Have I misjudged him?*

"My queen, I *must* have her."

Must?

Before he could blink, she washed up against him, gripping him by the sword belt, and crushed him against her breasts. His blood pulsed in his neck, reminding her of how long it had been since she had last fed. She wrapped a single leg around the back of both of his and pulled his groin in tightly against hers, grinding their sexes together. He moaned in terror as she buried her face in his neck and slowly ran her tongue over his hot skin, savoring the salty taste of his fear. "Then stop her, Yarl Galas Gilt-Mane," she whispered, "*before* she reaches the Mouth of the Gods. If she drowns, you'll never bed her. Worse, I'll lose my chance to drink Dain blood one last time. And if that happens…"

"Please… please, my queen," he practically squeaked.

She released him, and he fell away from her. She considered him then, admiring his long blond hair, his ruggedly handsome features. She glanced disdainfully at her new blood thrall, Dey, who knelt nearby, staring at his hands. *This one won't last,* she thought. *But then the pretty ones rarely do.* She pulled her gown open, exposing a single white breast and pink nipple, already hard. "Should I give you the gift of my milk, Yarl Galas? Could you please me? Would you like to bury your sword between *my* legs?"

"Please no, my queen," Galas whispered, his eyes round with horror.

"Then catch your cousin," she hissed, pulling her gown closed once more. "Thus far, she's out-sailed you every chance you've had, and I tire of your constant failure. Maybe *she* should be yarl of the Waveborn."

Galas ran to the railing and began to scream at the rowers, spit flying from his mouth. "Faster! Row faster, you get of diseased whores!" He then jumped down the wooden steps and ran among them, waving his sword. "I swear by Wodor, I'll kill any man I think is slacking."

Iron Beard surged forward.

Chapter 30

Owen

The narrow Mouth of the Gods seemed to rush upon them as *Fen Wolf* sped toward the gap between the Godswall and the numerous rocky, fanglike spires thrusting out of the water. The thunderous crashing of the waves became impossibly loud, drowning out all but screams. Owen, standing behind Fioni, held on tightly to Lady Danika, who gripped him around the waist. Fioni, still holding Sight-Bringer against the handle of the tiller, stood tall, staring at the hazard before them, her mouth open in incredulity. *Fen Wolf*'s prow rose and then crashed down again, jarring their bones. Water sprayed in their faces, the mist ever-present in the cataclysm they sailed into. Lady Danika's grip around his waist tightened, and Owen watched in horror, his mouth dry, as *Fen Wolf* thrust forward—heading straight for the closest rock fangs—a rocky pinnacle easily twice the width of the ship. Time seemed to slow.

Fen Wolf's stern rose as a wave pushed them up, sending the longship sliding straight down at the fang. Seawater crashed over the prow. Teeth clenched, Fioni screamed as she pulled back on the tiller, "Hard to steering board!"

"Hard to steering board!" Kora repeated, her voice barely audible over the din.

The crew on the port side lifted their oars completely out of the water, holding them straight up. Those on the steering board side thrust their oars deep, hauling back on them. And, impossibly, *Fen Wolf* skewed to the right, at the last moment slipping past the rocky fang, so close that had the oars still been in the water, the fang would have snapped them into kindling.

A moment later, they sailed into the Mouth.

The steeply sided cliffs of the Godswall rose up around them, now towering over them. The frenzied waters gripped the ship, tossing it about and sending crew members falling atop one another. Owen, holding onto a guide rope with all his strength, only just managed to stay upright. Waves cascaded over the hull, filling the ship ankle-deep in sloshing water.

"Hazard, ho!" Kora screamed.

Fioni pushed forward on the tiller, steering *Fen Wolf*'s prow away from another of the rocky fangs. More spires sped past on either side, blurring by in a moment. Ahead, two particularly large spires, each hundreds of feet high, created a gateway of sorts, but the waves crashed between them, impossibly powerful. Fioni adjusted course, aiming straight between them.

"*What are you doing?*" Owen screamed, half-choking on seawater.

Fioni howled in laughter, her eyes wild.

"The other ship!" Lady Danika yelled in Owen's ear, grabbing his head and turning it to face behind them.

While *Iron Beard* had pulled to before the Mouth, *Thunder Killer* was still coming. In a moment, it would be at the gap in the Godswall. A single dark figure stood at its prow. *Dilan, it has to be!*

Then *Fen Wolf* hit the raging maelstrom between the fangs. The longship, literally lifted out of the water by the force of the waves, flew past the two massive rocky fangs before hammering down again on the other side, shooting out impossibly fast. The cliff faces that had towered over them only moments ago sped past, revealing a sky already turning crimson with the rising sun of early morning, leaving only dark shadows around them. Like magic, the violent waters just… calmed as *Fen Wolf* skipped over the waves, like a stone thrown by a child. The sail, deprived of all wind, went slack. Before them, rising out of the calm water, was a vast dark shape: a mountain surrounded by water and the sheltering ring of the Godswall around it.

Torin Island—the Gateway to the Gods.

They had made it.

The island was like nothing Owen had ever seen before: its sides steep and covered in thick forest, but its summit was gone, as if a giant's blade had cut it away, leaving only a flat rim. In the glowing dawn, he could just make out long, deep crevices—ravines—cut into its steeply sided slopes. Lightning flared behind them, now clearly showing the metal towers set at regular intervals along the rim of the Godswall. The air thrummed with occult energy, causing his skin to pebble and leaving an acrid stench in the air.

Behind them, he heard a sudden horrific splintering sound, followed immediately by weak screams. Climbing up on the sternpost, he saw *Thunder Killer*'s prow disappear beneath the turbulent waters of the Mouth. The ship must have struck one of the rocky pillars and just… disintegrated. A moment later, the screams had ceased as well.

He stared in horror.

Dilan.

Stunned silence gripped the crew for a moment, but then *Fen Wolf* came to an abrupt halt, sending the entire crew flying, with some going over the side of the ship and into the water. The sounds of wooden beams splintering and breaking crashed over them as the hull fell apart, ripped away in a single heart-wrenching moment by something beneath the water. The impact ripped Owen free of the sternpost and sent him flying forward into the stairs leading up to the steering platform. Men and women screamed in terror and pain as cold water rushed over the hull and sprayed up from beneath them as the sea rushed in. The ship spun sideways, shuddered, and began to tilt. Owen staggered to his feet, looking wildly about for Lady Danika and Fioni. He saw neither, but he did see Gali huddling against the gunwale, terror on her face. He splashed toward her, the water already up to his knees. Beneath him, the hull continued to crack and break apart, causing him to reel. Fen Wolf *is dying,* he realized. *We hit something and ripped out the hull.* As the ship began to tilt, the mast began to crack and splinter just above the heavy mast fish attached to the deck. As it broke free, ropes whipped about like angry snakes, with one tearing a woman's head from her shoulders. A thunderous crack reverberated throughout the hull as the mast began to fall—directly toward Gali.

He hesitated. His duty was to Lady Danika, not this foreign girl. When he heard her scream in terror and raise her hands over her face, his indecision vanished. Charging forward, he collided with her, carrying both of them over the side of the ship and into the cold, dark waters.

Gripping her around the waist, he kicked wildly with his legs, trying to dive deeper to escape the mast. The falling mast hit the water above him, knifing through it as it came at them. At the last moment, it swept past them. His relief was short lived, though, as in the rush of its passage, the sinking mast grabbed them both in its wake, dragging them along with it into the depths.

Chapter 31

Galas

Galas, his hand upon the tiller, watched Serina, who stood motionless, staring over the gunwale at the churning waters in the gap in the Godswall and the bobbing flotsam that was all that remained of *Thunder Killer*. Knowing there was no way the much less maneuverable *Iron Beard* could possibly follow where *Thunder Killer* had failed, Galas had given up the chase, heaving to instead. Serina might kill him, but the Mouth of the Gods certainly would.

When she spoke, her voice trembled with effort, and perhaps a hint of disbelief. "Yarl Galas, your failure to catch our foe requires an... *amendment* to our pact. Your continued failure is deeply disturbing— and while I should pull your spine from your body—instead, I will offer you one final opportunity to serve me. Succeed, and I will still make you first among the other clans. Fail me again, and..."

"I... yes, thank you, my queen." Relief flushed through him. He wasn't going to die this day after all.

"But your remarkable cousin, this Red Wolf, she is now mine. Such bravery, such skill. She shall replace my own dear Auslaug, murdered so many years ago and taken from me."

"I… yes, my queen. Yes, of course." *Damn Fioni, and damn Serina. The bitch has to pay for what she's done to me! This isn't fair.*

"Lower your anchor here."

Galas, no fool, rushed to obey. In moments, *Iron Beard*'s heavy anchor, attached to an equally strong chain, was slipping into the waters. At first, he wasn't sure the chain would be long enough, but just before it ran out, the anchor struck the seabed. This close to the Godswall, the seabed was higher than he would have thought. The anchor held the massive drake-ship in place before the thrashing waters. With the dawn's promise lightening the sky, Galas could now see the shape of the island protected by the Godswall. *Torin Island, the Gateway to the Gods. Who'd ever believe such a thing?*

His destiny was singing in his ears, promising him great things.

Serina glanced toward the east, where the sun's rise now made the mist glow golden. Bolts of lightning continued to strike the peaks of the Godswall every handful of minutes. "How long until high tide?"

Galas hesitated while he made a mental assessment. Already, the water was rising in the Mouth—and as it did, the gap widened and the waters were becoming less turbulent. Soon, he'd be able to safely row past the fanglike spires blocking the gap. "An hour, maybe two—just to be safe."

"One hour, no more. The niece of Stron already has a considerable head start."

"But they don't know where to go, my queen. Without your map, they'll have to search the entire island."

She shook her head, watching the eastern sky. "The map beneath Serl's shield was almost a half century old. Besides, it doesn't show where my heart was hidden, merely this island and what looks like… ruins. In truth, my heart could be anywhere. Worse, whatever magic keeps the Feral Sea shrouded in fog also keeps the sky over Torin Island clear and cloudless. When the sun rises…" She sighed. "No,

Dilan and I will have to remain in the hold until nightfall. You must run down our foe. Besides, Dilan and I have already been awake since early yesterday. Such efforts are… draining."

Galas stared at her, his lip quivering. "My queen… your servant was aboard *Thunder Killer*. He must have—"

At that moment, *Iron Beard's* anchor chain rattled and began to swing wildly. The crew muttered nervously, and Galas, his heart leaping into his throat, moved to stare over the hull at the length of chain. At first, he saw only dark waters, but then, a shape materialized, hanging from the chain and slowly making its way up it. Galas stumbled back, recognizing what it had to be. *Gods, help me.*

The blood fiend called Dilan pulled himself hand over hand up the length of the chain, climbing up *Iron Beard's* hull. The crew fell away in horror as he—*it*—climbed over the side, still wearing a heavy ring-mail coat. Serina drifted over, and the monster buried his curly head in her bosom. "It's all right, Dilan," she softly said, brushing his wet hair. "It's an island. They're not going anywhere."

She met Galas's eye, and a shudder coursed through him. "The very moment the tide is high enough, go after them. Send *all* your warriors this time. Leave no one behind. Whatever you do, you must stop them from reaching my heart and using Sight-Bringer on it."

"My ship…"

"Leave behind only the last of the Windhelm prisoners. When Dilan and I awake, we shall be… *ill tempered* to demonstrate restraint."

Dey stumbled forward, his gaze locked on her feet. "What… what would you have of me, my queen?"

"You must go with Yarl Galas, my pet. As fond as I am of your ministrations, it will not be safe for you either when I wake. Help catch those who would do evil to your queen."

"And once I catch them, my queen?" Yarl Galas asked. "What then?"

"Do as you will, although I would recommend keeping at least some prisoners for the long voyage home. But bring me the niece of Stron and your cousin. The Dain woman I shall consume, ending her foul line. Your cousin will be turned and become my new commander."

Galas bowed his head. "As you command, my queen."

Without another word, Serina and her blood fiend childe entered *Iron Beard*'s hold, the hatch doors slamming shut behind them.

Chapter 32

Owen

Owen's boots slammed down into something hard on the bottom of the seabed. Rocks or a reef, the water was too dark and dirty to ascertain what exactly, but he suspected whatever it was had also ripped out *Fen Wolf*'s hull. Mad with panic, Gali thrashed against him, flailing at him with her fists. Tightening his grip around her waist, he shoved off the rocks, following the air bubbles up, dragging the struggling young woman with him. Just when he thought his lungs would burst, their heads broke free of the water. He inhaled deeply, holding Gali against his chest as she coughed and moaned. If she was coughing, it meant she'd live.

Nearby, the ship continued to sink. It was mostly underwater now, but those on the deck were still standing above water, helping others. He caught a quick glimpse of Fioni, heard her screaming orders to the crew to swim for the beach. Still holding Gali against his chest, he rolled onto his back and kicked for the shoreline, maybe a hundred paces away. The beach was grey with the sunrise and ringed by thick dark woods.

"Don't fight me, Gali. Be calm. I'll get you to land."

In response, she only moaned.

The waters were surprisingly calm, with little to no surf, a result of the protective Godswall, but swimming with Gali was still exhausting work. Then his boots touched bottom, and he could stand with his head above water. "Be calm," he told Gali. "We're almost there."

She answered in Hishtari, but soon she could stand as well. Then they were struggling out of the water and onto the shoreline, safe for the moment. She collapsed onto the sand, but he stared back at the sinking longboat. Only *Fen Wolf*'s curved prow and stern now remained above the water. He still heard Fioni's voice giving commands, saw a flash of her red hair near the stern. Others were in the water now, each man and woman pushing... something through the water as they swam for the shore. He squinted and then recognized the objects: shields, loaded with weapons and other supplies. Fioni was trying to save what she could.

He ripped his boots free and then tore his shirt over his head. He laid both beside Gali and then undid his sword belt, putting the weapon in her hands. He leaned over, placing his hand on her shoulder. "Stay here, keep this safe, but help the others reach the beach if you can. Do you understand?"

Her eyes were large with fear, but she bobbed her head in understanding. He turned away, making his way back into the water, and swam for the sinking ship. After only a handful of strokes, he passed a clearly miserable Ekkie. The dog whined once as she paddled past him. He rolled over again and began to pull himself through the water with long, steady overhead strokes.

Where is Lady Danika?

Then he saw a woman's face framed by long dark hair plastered to its sides. She was swimming toward him, pushing a wooden shield on which balanced several fighting axes. Relief washed over him, and

193

in two quick strokes, he reached her. "Are you all right?" he asked.

"Fine. I'm fine," Lady Danika said breathlessly. "Help Fioni."

"Sight-Bringer?"

"I have it. Go!"

She kicked away from him, headed for the beach. He watched the back of her head for a few moments and then swam for the ship. Most of the ship was beneath the waves, but Fioni and several others still moved about. Fioni hung to the sternpost, giving orders to Kora and a handful of the crew who were trying to save what they could. The crew was still able to stand on the submerged deck and keep their heads above water, but for how much longer, Owen didn't know.

Kora pushed a wooden plank, part of a rowing bench, over the submerged hull. A lofty pile of weapons and armor sat atop the bench, held in place by a length of rope. "What do you need?" he called out to her.

"Save whatever you can," she said breathlessly, "but focus on weapons." Her gaze darted to the Mouth of the Gods in the distance behind them. "The tide is rising. When it's high enough, *Iron Beard* will come."

As she kicked away, he climbed onto the submerged deck, the water up to his neck. He thrashed about, heading toward the spot next to the fish mast where he had tossed Vory's ring coat, praying it was still there. He ducked under the water, searching for the coat unsuccessfully. He surfaced, took several deep breaths, and moved a few feet farther away before diving under again. This time, his fingers brushed the sleeve of the coat where it was stuck beneath a bench. A feeling of giddiness coursed through him, and he surfaced once more, grasped at a broken length of wood several feet long floating nearby, and dragged it to him. Once more, he dove beneath the water, pulling the coat free of the bench and piling it atop the wooden board.

Looking about him, he saw Fioni was no longer atop the sternpost. A quick flash of red hair in the waves was likely her. Beneath him, the ship shuddered, and a loud crack resonated through the deck boards beneath the water. Water and air bubbles cascaded near him. A moment later, the ship sank, leaving him grasping at the wooden board upon which lay his coat. *That's it then,* he thought. Fen Wolf *is gone.*

And with it, any chance we had of getting off this island.

Pushing the board ahead of him, he swam for the shore.

#

Owen joined Fioni, Kora, Lady Danika, and Erik on the beach. He had donned his ring-mail coat and retrieved his sword from Gali. Fioni was the only other person wearing ring mail, having recovered her own coat before swimming from *Fen Wolf.* The crew—a quick count showed him sixty-one of them—sat about on the sand, recovering their strength or tending to wounds, while others laid out the weapons and supplies they had managed to salvage. The water where *Fen Wolf* had sunk wasn't that deep, and the best swimmers had already made several more trips out to dive for supplies. The problem was that they were running out of time.

"How many did we lose?" he asked Kora.

"Two of the wounded and three others. Everyone else made the swim to shore easily enough. As far as shipwrecks go, we were lucky."

The look Fioni gave her could have melted steel.

"Sorry," Kora mumbled, looking away.

"What of weapons?" Fioni demanded.

"Not so lucky," admitted Erik. "A couple dozen shields and axes, ten of the Wolfrey swords, a handful of long-knives, maybe a dozen spears, and… not much armor, unfortunately."

"What of the crossbows?" Fioni asked.

"Five of them," said Erik.

"That could be worse," Fioni said hopefully.

Erik looked crestfallen and shook his head sadly. "We found only two bundles of bolts, less than thirty missiles."

"Wodor's balls," swore Fioni. "That'll barely slow them."

"It gets worse," said Kora. "We have only a day's worth of fresh water and less food. We'll need to hunt to stay alive if—"

"No, we'll need to *fight* to stay alive," said Fioni, looking past Kora to the Mouth. As the tide rose, the gap between the Godswall widened. "Galas will be coming soon."

"The sun is up," said Lady Danika. "There's no fog over the island, so Serina can't come after us until nightfall. There's that at least."

Fioni snorted. Owen glanced from the Mouth to the dark interior of the island, to the steeply sloped flat mountain rising before them. "We can't stay here," he said to Fioni.

Her eyes narrowed. "Why not? We hit Galas as he tries to come ashore, when he's vulnerable. As long as he can't get his men onto the beach, he can't overwhelm us."

Owen shook his head. "That won't happen. Galas will move farther down the shoreline—where we can't stop him. He'll bring all his men ashore, form ranks, and then march on us. We'll be overwhelmed."

Fioni's face darkened in anger. "He's already lost an entire ship. How many more men can he have?"

"I think Owen's right," said Kora in a neutral tone. "Just to sail *Iron Beard*, he must have a hundred or more men. And all of them will have shields and armor, not to mention bows. If we had more to fight with…"

"He also has Serina's ghouls," Lady Danika said. "You said yourself they didn't stop with the dawn when they hunted you at the Fist of Wodor."

Fioni glared at them, looking from one face to another.

Owen looked past her into the forested interior of the island, thickly overgrown with brush and pine trees. Marching through the island's interior would be arduous work, but they had no real choice; to stay and fight here was certain death. *Fioni must see that.* A far too warm breeze caressed his face as he watched her struggle with the inevitable. *How is such weather possible this far north—and at this time of the year? We should be seeing snow, but it's like an autumn day.*

Fioni ran her hands back through her wet hair. "You're the idea man, Owen. What do you suggest?"

"What about a shield wall?" offered Erik. "If we put the crossbows on the flanks, we can—"

"No, we can't," Owen insisted. "We don't have enough shields for everyone. Even if we did, Galas would come against us with a longer wall and envelop us. Once his men are behind us, your crew will break and run."

"We Fenyir are no cowards!" Erik insisted.

"It's got nothing to do with bravery," Owen said. "It's about tactics and human nature. No one will stand and fight against a foe to their front while another enemy savages their rear. If we fight here, we die." He met Fioni's gaze. "We need to head inland and find a more defensible location, one where they can't use their numbers on us. Here, the terrain favors him, not us. Half of winning a battle is choosing where to fight it. This is *not* the right place!"

"He's right, Fioni," said Kora. "We can't defend here."

"I'm tired of running from my cousin," said Fioni. "I've been running from him since he betrayed his own clan and murdered my father."

"This is crazy," said Lady Danika, pushing her way between them, forcing them to look at her. "Listen to yourselves. This isn't about Galas Gilt-Mane. The real foe is Serina Greywynne, *the Blood Queen.* We cannot win against her through any battle—no matter where we fight. We need to find your uncle and use Sight-Bringer on her heart. Everything else is pointless."

"Aye, listen to her," said Owen.

Kora leaned in and gripped Fioni's wrist, meeting her eye and shaking her head. "Don't let your pride choose the rapids over the calm deep water. We can't kill Galas on the beach. You know this to be true."

"Nightfall," said Lady Danika softly. "That's as long as we have, and we're wasting time arguing about it."

Fioni closed her eyes, her chest rising and falling. When she opened them again, she stared at Owen. "All right, Northman. Where?"

Owen's gaze drifted to the steeply sloped mountain. "If nothing else, we climb for high ground."

Fioni locked her gaze on Owen. "If you're wrong again, we're all dead."

"The fact that you're still alive to hate me proves I wasn't wrong the last time," he said, his own anger flaring in challenge.

Just for a moment, he feared she'd strike him. Instead, she turned to Kora, her voice tight. "Get the others ready. We move before the sun hits the high hand."

"*Iron Beard!*" someone yelled from the beach.

The prow of the drake-ship appeared through the gap in the Godswall. Long rows of oars pulled it into the calm waters, where it slowly began to turn toward them.

"Maybe he'll hit the reef as well," Erik said.

"No," said Fioni, shaking her head. "The Mouth broke us, smashed us against the reef, but it's as Serl wrote in his journal—at high tide, the Mouth calms. It would seem the gods wanted *us* to sink, not my cousin, damn his eyes." Fioni pulled her sword several inches from its sheath and then slammed it back in, her face dark with anger. "We move now."

Chapter 33

Galas

Iron Beard's hull was too deep to bring the drake ship up onto the beach, so Galas ordered his men to drop anchor about twenty feet away, where the water rose only to a man's chest. He stood on the shore, watching as his crew, over a hundred warriors, made a human chain in the surf, offloading weapons and supplies. Nearby, standing about and doing nothing while his men worked, were the remainder of Kory'ander Dey's Hishtari soldiers, now less than two dozen men. He glared at them, snorting contemptuously. The Hishtari were guppies, of no real consequence in the coming battle.

He stared into the woods in the direction Fioni and her crew had disappeared. His men had found their trail within moments of hitting the beach. It would be child's play to follow them through the thick bush. Fioni and her warriors were shipwrecked and without supplies. Galas had almost twice as many fighters—*all strong men.* Half of Fioni's crew were only split-asses, good for only one thing. Serina had told him to take prisoners, and he would, but first they'd suffer. And—despite the queen's wishes—Fioni was going to die this day as well. While he'd prefer to keep Fioni alive long enough to suffer and give him sons, there was no gods-damned way he was going to let Serina reward her with eternal life. He'd have to make up a story about how his cousin had *unfortunately* died in the fighting and there was nothing Galas could do about it… *blah, blah, blah.* His blood began to throb, his erection grow, when he considered what he'd do to Fioni, but then his eyes fell on that weasel, Dey, standing apart from his men, and his mood darkened once again. *He'll be a problem.* Galas sucked his teeth. *He'll tell on me—and then Serina will kill me.* Galas considered Dey. He could have his men attack, kill all the Hishtari at once, but then he thought about Serina's last blood thrall, Modwyn Du'Aig. Modwyn had possessed inhuman speed and strength. He had killed two guards with his bare hands, ripping their heads and spines from their bodies like pulling a weed from a garden. *No, if Dey is the same as Modwyn, he'll kill me in a moment. Unless…*

He turned away, strolling along the beach as he considered his options. The early-morning sun beat down on him already, heating his ring-mail coat, soaking his thick wool gambeson with sweat. The weather was unseasonably warm. *This is unnatural, as is that constant fucking lightning along the Godswall, the bright-blue sky overhead but fog everywhere else. We need to leave this place—soon!*

He heard heavy steps behind him, turned, and saw Aegrism approaching, his bald octopus-tattooed head gleaming in the sun.

"Well?" Galas asked.

"We're ready," Aegrism said.

"The ship?"

"Just the last of the Windhelm prisoners, six girls."

Galas sighed. "What a waste." He turned and stared into the woods. "We're sure we can track 'em?"

Aegrism nodded, his pleated black beard swaying. "Grotlin grew up hunting deer with his cousins on Macklin Island. He reckons he can follow almost a hundred clansmen through woods well enough."

"If he can't, I'll gut him myself." Galas ran his fingers over the hilt of his sword. Under his arm, he held his speckled iron helm. He donned it now, tying the leather straps beneath his chin. "Let's go say hello to my cousin, then."

He approached his men, all grouped together on the beach and waiting for him. Standing separate were Dey and his Hishtari soldiers. Dey had donned one of their ridiculous brightly colored gambesons and had strapped a long curved sword to his waist.

As Galas was about to address his men, Dey stepped forward, a sneer on his blue lips. "You took too long preparing, you Fenyir dog. Those we hunt have now gotten too far ahead."

An angry murmur swept through his men, and their eyes hardened as they glared at the Hishtari soldiers, now glancing at one another in fear and backing away from Dey.

Galas, once again remembering the sight of Modwyn holding two severed heads, considered his words carefully. "No one cares what the queen's fuck-boy thinks. Be glad I'm letting you tag along at all."

Dey's smile was a hollow thing as he slipped closer, coming within inches of Galas's face. His heart leaping into his throat, a cold sweat coating his skin, Galas forced himself to remain where he stood. To flinch would not be manly, nor would his men understand why; they hadn't seen what Modwyn could do.

"The plan has changed, Yarl Galas Gilt-Mane," Dey said, an insane glint in his dark eyes. "*I* will lead the hunt now."

His men swore angrily, but Galas held his hand, knowing that, despite appearances, his life hung by a thread. "That's... that's not what the queen wants," Galas said, hearing the tremor of fear in his voice and hating himself for it. His men stared at him in disbelief. "She ordered you to help me."

Dey leaned in closer, and it took every ounce of self-control Galas possessed to not fall back. Dey whispered into his ear, "I *am* helping you, dog, by not killing you in front of your men."

"Don't be stupid," Galas said softly. "I only have to give the word, and—"

His words died in his throat as Dey reached out impossibly fast and gripped Galas's cock, squeezing it and the thick fabric of his wool breeches with his fist. Before Galas could do or say anything, Dey grinned and squeezed. Pain flashed through Galas, but he kept his arms by his side and remained still. His men surged forward, anger on their faces. "Wait!" Galas practically shrieked. "Do nothing."

Dey, a wry grin on his delicate features, leaned in and placed his blue lips against Galas's neck. "Listen to me very carefully, you fucking Fenyir animal. With no more effort than it would take to wipe my ass, I'll rip your flaccid little excuse for manhood right from you."

Galas trembled. "The… the queen—"

"Sleeps. And when she wakes, I will give her the Dain woman. With her enemies dead, do you really think she'll be angry because I embarrassed you? No, she won't punish me. She'll reward me. But you'll be a eunuch."

"You're making a mistake."

"No, I'm changing my fate. *I am the Moon Lord of Daenipor.* I will no longer be her... her… No, *I* will lead the hunt, not you. Do you understand?"

Galas bit his lip and inclined his head. "Go on then, *Moon Lord.* Lead. We all want the same thing, after all."

"Tell *them.*"

When Galas hesitated, Dey squeezed his cock once more, causing him to gasp in pain, his vision blurring. He raised his voice, practically panting. "Listen… listen to me. Kory'ander Dey, the Moon Lord of Daenipor, is now in charge. Obey him as you would me."

His men stared at him in disbelief and then contempt. But Dey released him, sending relief flooding through Galas as he rubbed himself, falling back from Dey, spots of light in his vision.

"Just so," said Dey magnanimously, turning about and addressing all the men. "The queen wishes I lead the hunt. Your yarl understands I am—by far—best suited to do so." He paused, raising a thin eyebrow at Galas.

Galas, feeling overwhelming shame, looked away.

"Now," said Dey. "We hunt."

The Hishtari soldiers stared at Dey with a mixture of awe and fear, as if Dey were one of their honored ancestors brought back to life. The hunter, Grotlin, led the way into the woods, with Dey and his men following. Galas's crew stood in place, staring at Galas with something decidedly less than admiration. Aegrism stepped forward, his mouth still open in disbelief. "What—"

"Just go, gods damn it!" snapped Galas, spittle flying from his lips. "Follow them. And if anyone ever speaks of this to me again, I'll kill him."

Aegrism grimaced but turned away, leading the men into the woods. With no other choice, Galas followed.

Chapter 34

Owen

Fioni led her crew through the thick woods, following one of the many ravines cut into the mountain's slope. As Owen had expected, the bush was thick and difficult to break through, so when he pointed out a deer trail that meandered its way along the ravine, Fioni gladly accepted his suggestion to follow it. Knowing she was still in a dark mood over her ship and having to run from Galas, Owen kept to the rear of the party, watching for the inevitable pursuit.

The Fenyir, terrible woodsmen, made too much noise, so he remained back, watching their trail from cover, listening intently to the forest around them. He heard birds, squirrels chattering, and the soft creak of branches, but no sign yet of Galas and his men. Satisfied for now, he slipped away, easily catching up to the others not that far ahead. He heard the stream before he smelled the fresh water, feeling relief his guess about the deer trail crossing water at some point had been correct. Fioni had taken advantage of the water and had called a quick break. Men and women clustered on hands and knees before the stream, drinking, their faces flushed from the exertion. He heard Kora call out to Fioni in an excited voice, motioning her over to where she stood in the thick grass behind a bank of the stream. Ekkie was beside Kora, barking furiously. Fioni and Erik pushed through the grass to join Kora. Owen joined them.

When he was within a dozen paces, the stench of rotting flesh wafted over him, followed immediately by the angry buzzing of hundreds of flies.

The three Fenyir warriors stared down at the corpse of a large wolf, but the carcass seemed… odd somehow, as if it had shrunk in on itself. The wolf's dark-brown fur was almost black with rot. Its brown eyes bulged in death, its once-pink tongue now swollen and sticking out from the muzzle.

"Just a wolf," Erik said, glancing at Owen.

A heavy sense of unease settled in Owen's gut. "What kills wolves?"

Kora shook her head. "I was just thinking the same thing. Bear?"

"Could be, but I've seen no bear spoor." Owen dropped down on one knee, gripped the animal's maggoty hide, and flipped it over, surprised at how light the carcass was.

"Gods' balls," said Erik, holding his mouth and staggering back.

Owen forced himself to breathe through his mouth as he examined the carcass. The wolf's wide chest was… gone, replaced by a tunnel-like wound larger than his arm penetrating the chest cavity. Ekkie lowered her head and whimpered. Maggots wriggled and fed in the exposed flesh. He drew a dagger and used its edge to examine the wound.

"A spear-thrust?" suggested Erik. He glanced at Fioni. "Your uncle?"

"This is no spear wound," mused Owen. "The opening is far too large. I could stick my entire arm in there and still have room."

"No bear, then. What could do such a thing?" asked Fioni.

Owen suddenly understood why the carcass appeared shrunken. "The blood is gone."

"Gone?" asked Fioni. "What do you mean *gone*?"

He prodded the edges of the wound, exposing raw pink flesh but no blood.

Kora walked about around the wolf, examining the ground, pushing aside the stalks of grass. "There's no blood on the ground, either."

"Blood fiend?" asked Erik.

"Blood fiends bite the neck," said Owen. "Don't they?" He saw the indecision on their faces. Turning back to the carcass, he pushed the fur aside, examining it. "I see no other wounds."

"You're the woodsman, Owen," said Fioni. "What do you think?"

He wiped the tip of his dagger against the dirt before returning it to his sheath. "The maggots aren't yet cocooned, and the carcass is mostly stiff. Normally, I'd guess less than a week. But…"

"But what?" asked Erik.

Owen sat back, rubbing his beard. "By now, other scavengers should have picked it apart, but they haven't touched it. Why just bugs? Where are the birds, the rodents, the foxes? Why have they left the carcass be?"

"Maybe there are no bears or foxes on this island," said Kora.

"An island without scavengers?" Owen shook his head. "Something is very wrong here."

Fioni looked past him to her crew and then to the mountainside they still had to climb this day. "Leave it alone," she said curtly. "This island can keep its secrets. We need to find my uncle before nightfall, or we're all dead."

As she led her people farther up the side of the ravine, Owen stared at the dead wolf. When the last of the crew had disappeared from sight, he remained in place for several minutes, sweeping his gaze about the dark, silent forest.

Nothing, he thought. *Is it too quiet?*

#

As they pushed through the woods, steadily climbing the ravine up the mountain's steep slope, the sun beat down upon them. Morning passed into early afternoon, and still they were only partway up the mountainside. Now, the trees began to thin out, replaced by bushy cliffs, gullies, and ravines. They found a path—although it was so overgrown and wild, Owen couldn't tell if it was natural or manmade. Fioni led the others along it as it cut back and forth up the mountainside. The higher they climbed, the harder the march became, and soon everyone was drenched in sweat.

Owen shaded his eyes from the sun as he estimated the distance until they reached the rim of the mountain, still high above them. When he saw Lady Danika and Gali, both struggling along, helping the other, he wondered how much longer either of them could keep going.

He paused, remaining in place and listening to their rear once more. Just over an hour ago, he had heard the first sign of their pursuers—a man's shout carried unnaturally far by a sudden wind. His gaze went from the woods behind them, to the two women, to a natural switchback and thickly wooded gully to their front.

They're going to catch us, he realized.

The terrain sloped steeply on the mountainside of the gully. *I'd wager there's another deep ravine just on the other side of that slope.* Just before the switchback, the ground funneled in and became much more restricting. Thick bushes and boulders lined the slopes of the gully, providing cover from casual observation—especially if someone was following a trail. He thought back to the tactics discussions he had held with Keep-Captain Awde, using their impromptu sessions to work through this particular problem.

"All right, Owen," he said softly to himself. "If Keep-Captain Awde was here right now, how would the conversation go? Start with the problem," Owen answered himself. "Lay it all out."

Okay, we're not only outnumbered, we're blind and handicapped by our wounded. But Galas only needs to catch up to us.

"Okay, what happens when he does?"

He felt the crushing certainty of the answer.

They take us in the rear while we're strung out. It's inevitable now. As people start screaming and dying, panic spreads up the line. Some, like Kora and Fioni, will turn and try to fight, but it'll be too late. They'll be overwhelmed. Then the others will break, bolting ahead or trying to slip away down the side of the mountain.

"And?"

And Galas's men hunt down the stragglers one by one.

"It'll be a slaughter."

Yes.

"So what can be done?"

We can ambush Galas here. This is as perfect a killing ground as any I've ever seen.

"How?"

The slope—a small party remains behind, hiding in the bush at the top of the slope. They can push boulders down the slope, use the crossbows. At this range, shooting from elevation at a massed foe below… they can't miss.

"But the missiles."

Doesn't matter. There's more than enough to bloody them, force them to slow down.

He saw the ambush unfold in his imagination, heard the screaming of the wounded, and pictured the confusion and anger among the enemy as the missiles savaged them.

"Okay, how long do we have?"

Not long. He estimated their slow rate of march then guessed at how long it would take a hundred healthy men, rested and well fed, to catch up to them. *At best, we have an hour or two.*

"All right, so the ambush goes as you plan—not that that *ever* happens—but what then? To what end?"

Buy time for the others to find better ground.

"Is that it? Is that all we can accomplish?"

Yes.

"Okay, Owen," he said, nodding to himself. "Does Fioni understand this?"

Resignation and hopelessness swept through him as he shook his head. *No. She's a raider, a pirate, not a soldier. She'll never understand, not until it's too late.*

"So convince her."

I can't. She doesn't trust me anymore, not after Rolf and the others.

"And what happens if you don't convince her?"

He ran his hands over his face, wiping the sweat away, knowing with absolute certainty that his assessment was correct. *Everybody dies.*

"Everybody dies," he repeated.

He took off running along the trail.

He *had* to convince Fioni.

#

He caught up to Fioni just before the switchback cutting along the mountain's slope. Fioni had called another halt, waiting while the stragglers caught up. She, Kora, and Erik knelt in conversation, their heads closely together under the shade of a small copse of trees. Several dozen paces behind them was a large wagon-sized deadfall, a collection of fallen trees, broken branches, and pieces of bushes caught up against the rocks of the switchback behind it. At his approach, they all looked up at him. Ekkie, who had been lying nearby, lifted her large head and growled at him, still no doubt sensing Fioni's mood. Fioni reached out and scratched behind Ekkie's ears. "Something's wrong. What is it?"

He took a deep breath and then set about explaining why and how they needed to set up an ambush here. When he was done, he simply stressed one point. "They're going to catch us, Fioni. I'm certain of that."

"That's what I've been saying," said Kora, raising an eyebrow at Fioni.

"What do you know of such things, Northman?" asked Erik. "I thought you were a knight, not a scout."

"I've followed your plans too many times now," snapped Fioni coldly. "People die following your plans."

Kora advanced on her. "*Fenya's tits, Fioni!* You're being a walrus's ass. People die no matter what. *No one's* plans can change that—not yours and not his!"

"I'm not wrong about this, Fioni," he insisted. "They're coming. If we don't slow them down with the crossbows…"

She cupped her hands over her face, groaning softly and shaking her head. "Owen… even if you're right, I can't risk the crossbows. They're the only real advantage I'll have when we finally fight back."

He dropped down in front of her, took her hands, and held them while he stared into her face. "Fioni," he said softly. "If we don't use the crossbows now, there won't be another fight."

She ripped her hands free from him, stood up abruptly, and spun away, her shoulders trembling. "Here we go again, *Sir Owen Toscovar*, the mighty kingdom knight who knows everything."

He climbed his feet and reached a hand out toward her shoulder but let it hover over her instead. "Fioni…"

She spun on him, her voice angry. "Whoever stays behind to carry out this ambush will almost certainly die."

"They may be able to… slip away down the other side of the cliff—while Galas's men are climbing the slope. Maybe meet back up again with the others later on."

She snorted in derision, her eyes flashing. "Do you really believe that?"

"We have no choice," he said weakly. "It needs be done."

"And who am I going to ask to do such a thing?" she demanded. "You? You're the soldier. It's your plan—again! Will you do this thing that *needs be done*?"

His cheeks burned, his arms hung at his side, and his throat felt thick as he spoke. "I... I can't. You know that. I can't."

"Can't what? Leave your precious noblewoman?"

"I'm bound to protect her," Owen said weakly.

"Fioni!" snapped Kora, stepping between them and jabbing Fioni in the chest with her finger. "Owen can no more abandon his oath than Rolf or the others could throw away theirs. I know what's really happening here, and you're drifting before the storm."

"Don't you tell me what—"

Kora shook her head. "Stop acting like a girl with her first blood."

Ekkie began to snarl, the fur rising on her hackles. Owen watched the animal with trepidation. The wolfhound weighed more than a hundred pounds and could easily kill a man. Yet the dog was facing *away* from him, toward the deadfall, her haunches trembling. The sun, overhead now, cast shadows across the two arguing women. A sudden coldness hit his core as his gaze swept down Fioni's body, to the longsword sheathed to her waist and the blood gem embedded in its hilt that seemed to be softly glowing in the shade.

"You don't lecture me," Fioni snapped at Kora. "I'm *Fen Wolf*'s master, not you. If Vory was alive—"

Kora barked in laughter. "He'd put you over his knee and heat your butt with his palm. Besides, *Fen Wolf*'s gone. You can't even master your emotions."

Owen stepped forward, between the two women, who glared at *him* now. "Something's wrong—"

Ekkie lunged forward, jarring all three of them aside as a nightmarishly large spider—its bloated orange-and-purple body as big as Ekkie—exploded from the tall grass behind them. Ekkie and the spider collided in a frenzy of fang and gnashing mandibles. Owen recovered first, whipping his sword free and rushing forward, but in the mad, chaotic battle between spider and dog, he was unable to strike without hitting Ekkie. The spider chattered in fury, an inhuman screech that sent a chill down his spine. As he moved around them, one of the spider's three-foot-long legs whipped out, almost striking him. He swept to the side, pivoted on his hips, and cut down hard, severing the spider's shiny black leg at the joint. Pale-blue blood sprayed through the air. Erik joined him, his fighting axe held at the ready as the other man looked for his own opportunity to strike. But then the spider managed to pin Ekkie with two long legs. Before Owen and Erik could take a step to help, the spider buried its fangs in the wolfhound's chest. Ekkie's yelp was heart wrenching.

"No!" Fioni screamed, throwing herself atop the spider, thrusting her sword into one of its huge eyes.

The spider shrieked and bucked, releasing Ekkie and ripping the sword from Fioni's hands. It spun about in circles, screeching and pounding the ground with its remaining legs. Erik stomped on one of the legs, immobilizing the spider as he buried his axe in its bloated body. Several crew members armed with spears began stabbing it repeatedly, and soon it ceased all movement. Blue spider blood coated their spearheads, dripping in gooey drabs like thick gravy.

"Is everyone all right?" Erik asked breathlessly.

Lady Danika hurried over, her face ashen. "Father Craftsman, help us. That's a nell spider."

Fioni knelt next to Ekkie. Kora took one of the spears, hooked it around the crossguard of Wave's Kiss, and pulled Fioni's sword free. The gem embedded in the hilt continued to glow softly.

"Be careful," Owen said, staring at the gem. "There may be more."

Using his sword point, he brushed aside the tall grass where the spider had been hiding, revealing the opening in the deadfall wedged against the rocks. *No, not a deadfall,* he realized as he came closer and saw the web silk interwoven among the branches and tree trunks of the opening—*a nest. We were talking right in front of its nest.* Sweat ran down his spine as he bent over, peering into the opening. *There's something there,* he realized.

"Gods, Northman," said Erik in disgust behind him. "I'm sorry I ever doubted the size of your balls, but don't get any closer."

Owen waited while Erik, holding one of the bloody spears, used its point to push aside the webs around the opening, exposing the interior of the nest and revealing the pillow-shaped milky-white egg sac the size of a man's head that sat cocooned by webs within it. Owen's revulsion grew when he saw the movement within the sac: dozens of baby spiders. And, from deep within the sac, came a soft, pulsing red glow. He stared in confusion at it.

"It's another blood gem," Lady Danika said from just behind him. He hadn't realized she was there.

"My lady, please. Go back. What if there's more?"

"There won't be. Nell spiders kill anything that comes near their nests—including other nell spiders. That's why the blood gems are so hard to harvest."

He didn't argue with her but stared in revulsion at the egg sac. "How do you know?"

"Kalishni'coor. He liked to brag. The gems glow when near one another, but what they really do is store occult power, allowing sorcerers to cast powerful spells. This is how Serina removed her heart. But according to Kalishni'coor, the gems are only harvested in the Fallow Desert."

Erik spun his spear upside down and drove it into the dirt. "And here as well, it would seem."

"Indeed," said Lady Danika softly.

"Well… now we know the mystery of the wolf," said Erik.

Owen shook his head, still staring at the egg sac in revulsion. The spiders within it were clearly only partially formed, no larger than his fist. "No. The wound was far too large for a spider bite. There's something else on this island, something we haven't seen yet."

"I'm beginning to hate this place," said Erik.

"What I don't understand," said Owen softly, trying to peer past the moving spiders within the sac, "is how the nell spiders get the gems within their eggs."

"I don't think that's it," said Lady Danika.

Owen inhaled deeply, suddenly understanding. "*They're not gems at all!* They're like pearls in an oyster. The spiders lay them as part of their egg sac."

Kora joined them, her face white. "Gods, that's revolting."

"How is Ekkie?" Lady Danika asked.

Kora shook her head. "Dying."

#

Fioni knelt with the wolfhound, holding her head in her lap. The wolfhound whined, clearly in agony. Kora knelt beside Fioni, wrapped an arm around her shoulder, and placed her cheek next to hers. "Let her go, sister."

"I understand," said Fioni softly, her voice breaking as she stroked the dog's head. She held her hand out, and Kora handed her a long knife. Placing the point over the dog's heart, Fioni softly spoke into her large ear. "Know that you were loved." Her hand tensed.

"Wait!" said Owen, reaching out and catching her wrist.

Emotion surged in Fioni's face. "She doesn't need to suffer."

He shook his head, his eyes locked on hers. "I think... maybe she's *not* dying."

"How can you be so certain?"

He leaned in closer, placing his nose over the bloody puncture wounds in the dog's chest, and inhaled deeply. Instantly, a wave of nausea swept over him, and he swayed dizzily. Kora caught his arm, holding him upright. When the nausea passed, they were all staring at him in confusion. "There's poison in the wound," he mumbled. "But it might be like the Marsh Tick Queen's poison that Modwyn used."

Confusion flitted over Fioni's face. "I don't—"

"Modwyn soaked face masks with poison from the Marsh Tick Queen we killed, told us it would protect us from 'foul vapors,' but it only made us sick and helpless while he woke Serina. It paralyzed Keep-Captain Awde and Lord Palin, put them into a sleep-like state, but I never trusted Modwyn, so I pulled my mask free. It still made me sick, though. Maybe... the spider's poison works the same way. If we can drain the wound, Ekkie might live."

Fioni's gaze darted about and met the gaze of Kora, who said, "It's worth a try."

Together with Kora and Gali helping, they pressed pieces of cloth against the bite marks while Owen gently kneaded the fur around the wounds, trying to coax the poison out. But after only a few minutes, Ekkie ceased moving, and her eyes closed.

"Gods, no," whispered Fioni.

He looked up at Lady Danika. "My lady, may I borrow Sight-Bringer?"

She handed him the sword. With its magic coursing through him, he placed his ear against Ekkie's chest. The dog's heart throbbed slowly but clearly, and he exhaled, handing the broken sword back to the noblewoman. "She's alive, but barely."

"Will… will she wake?" Fioni asked.

He bit his upper lip and shook his head. "I don't know."

"Thank you, Owen," Fioni said softly. "We'll build a stretcher."

Owen stood up and looked back down the ravine in the direction they had come. "We've been distracted too long already. We have to mount the ambush—right now!"

"Whoever stays behind will almost certainly die," Fioni said miserably.

"Everybody dies, Fioni," said Kora. "This is destiny. *I'll stay.* If I can find two or three volunteers, I'll ruin Galas's day."

Fioni reached out and cupped Kora's cheek with her palm and then shook her head. "Take Ekkie and the northerners. Find my uncle."

"Don't be a goose," said Kora. "You're *Fen Wolf*'s master and daughter of the yarl. You need to lead the crew."

Fioni shook her head. "You said it yourself. *Fen Wolf* is gone. My father is dead, and I suspect the gods always intended the line of Serl to end on this island. Save as many of the crew as you can."

"Fioni, this is—"

"Destiny—*my destiny*—yours is somewhere else, Kora Far-Sails. Go. Find four volunteers, but hurry. Owen's right. We're running out of time."

"I'll stay," said Erik. "And, as luck would have it, there are still three more Windhelm clansmen. She's right, Kora. If this isn't fate, I don't know what is."

"Are you sure, Erik?" Fioni asked.

"We owe you our lives, Fioni Ice-Bound. Because of you, we can die as free Fenyir warriors, not oar slaves. We're sure."

His men clustered behind him, their faces solemn as they nodded in agreement.

"Fioni," said Kora, anguish in her voice. "This isn't…"

"You're wasting time you don't have, Kora," said Fioni, embracing her friend hard. "If you love me, obey me. Go now!"

Owen stood silently watching them, unable to meet Fioni's eyes. He pointed to the rocks and bushes atop the slope, where Fioni and the others could easily hide while Galas's men became bunched up in the narrow, confining space before the switchback. "Wait until they actually cluster here. Then take your time with your shots and—"

Fioni gripped Owen by the collar of his ring mail, pulled him against her, and kissed him hard. He stood motionless, too stunned to move. Then she buried her face in his neck. "Go tell your grandmother how to suck fish bones, Owen Northman. I'm the daughter of Yarl Taios Oak-Heart, and I know how to die."

His throat constricted, he couldn't say anything as she spun away from him. In moments, Erik and his men had taken possession of the remaining crossbows and bolts. While the others made an impromptu stretcher for Ekkie with two spears and a blanket, Lady Danika stepped up next to Owen, held his hand, and peered sadly into his face.

Without another word, Kora led the crew past the switchback and on toward the mountain's summit. Lady Danika waited with him, watching him. Fioni led three of the Windhelm volunteers up the steep slope, pulling themselves up by grasping clumps of weeds and bushes. Erik tilted his head as he watched Owen. "It isn't too late to change your mind, you know. Stay with her."

"I... I can't," Owen answered, his voice thick. "Don't... don't let Galas..."

"Don't worry, Northman. If it comes to that, I'll do it myself. Besides, maybe we'll slip away after all before they reach us. I'm a fair woodsman myself, you know."

Owen smiled despite the loss shuddering through him. "I know you are. Erik... I was wrong about you."

Erik flashed his white teeth at him. "So many are. Don't fret. We'll get drunk together in Nifalgen. You'll see. You may only be a kingdom-man, but Orkinus is wise. He'll make an exception for you and let you into his watery realm." He turned away, his crossbow over his shoulder, and began to climb after the others.

Owen remained in place, feeling his world spinning away from him. *Duty is a double-edged sword blade.*

"We have to go," Lady Danika said sadly.

"Aye," he whispered, turning away and following her up the mountain.

Chapter 35

Kory'ander Dey

Kory'ander Dey paced ceaselessly as the Fenyir tracker examined the forest floor. *What foolishness!* Even he, a pureblood Hishtari prince, saw the clear boot prints of dozens of people, the broken trail that led through the steeply sloped ravine along the mountainside. "Well?" he snapped, his irritation mounting.

The tracker, an ugly, gaunt man with a thick, hairy mole on his cheek, glanced at Dey from beneath hooded eyes before turning his attention back to his task. Dey's body trembled in rage. With barely an effort, he could break that cretin's neck. *Ancestors, I could pull his ugly head from his body!* Instead, he turned away, fighting down his rage. This trail was obvious now, but it might not always be so. His men were soldiers, not woodsmen. Had he had a real tracker days ago, he'd not have fallen for the Red Wolf's firetrap. That failure had fueled Serina's anger toward him, clouding her judgment, turning her against him. *No, I need this dog… for now.*

"Answer him," Galas Gilt-Mane, standing nearby, ordered.

"The trail is clear," said the tracker, speaking to Galas. "They continue up the mountain."

"How far?" asked Galas.

"Not far." The tracker pinched some dirt between his fingers, leaving a dirty residue. He smelled his fingertips. "Blood."

Galas smirked. "She keeps her wounded with her, slowing down everyone. Fioni is as weak as I always suspected. This is why women shouldn't command ships."

Dey stamped a boot in the ground, immediately regretting having done so and now appearing like a spoiled child. "*When?* When will we catch them?"

The tracker peered up at the sun through the branches overhead. "Before nightfall, maybe sooner."

"We'll do better than that," said Dey, motioning toward his new captain, a tall, broad-shouldered, and thick-nosed man who, while he didn't come from a noble family, understood his place better than the last captain. Dey laid out his plan. "The trail is clear, so my men and I will move forward on our own. My men are soldiers, not sailors. We're much faster than you are. We'll run them into the ground."

Galas stared at his hands, his expression properly subservient. "If you think that would be best."

Dey beamed, now knowing his lesson to Galas had worked. *The trick in handling any dog,* he knew*, is teaching it to fear its master.* He turned to his men, two dozen brave Hishtari soldiers. They'd be outnumbered, but the enemy was already on the run. With his gifts, they'd be more than enough to strike the Red Wolf's unguarded rear. If his ancestors were watching, as he was sure they must be, he might even capture the Dain woman amidst all the confusion. Once he had her, he could pull back and let the Fenyir slaughter each other, as befitted such base people. Dey turned to his new captain. "We'll move forward on the run. If we're fast, we can come up on them before they can raise the alarm. Take only the Dain woman or the Red Wolf prisoner."

The man's thick peasant face took on a pale cast, but he bobbed his head in understanding. "Yes, Moon Lord."

Dey drew his scimitar and began an easy lope along the trail. Behind him scurried his men, their weapons and armor jingling. Soon, he heard their ragged breathing and smiled. Days ago, that red-haired Fenyir bitch Fioni Ice-Bound had thrown a spear through his leg, but now, he was faster and more agile than soldiers were. Angry with him, the queen had humiliated him. But if he pleased her, gave her the Dain woman *and* the sword, she'd be certain to reward him.

Will she make me like her, he wondered, *immortal?*

He increased his pace.

Chapter 36

Danika

Danika struggled near the rear of the column that slowly crawled up the twisting mountain pass. Owen remained behind with her, stopping every few minutes to watch and listen to the trail behind them. Gasping, she paused to lean over her knees and catch her breath, watching him out of the corner of her eye, recognizing the guilt that washed over her. *Why* does *he serve me? Is it his oath or duty, or am I using him? It isn't affection—not for me. That much I do see. Nor does he do it just for personal gain. Maybe at first, but not now. I'm certain of that.* Her father had been wrong to sentence him to service as a guardsman. It had been one more example of the kingdom's at times unjust laws. *Owen defends his sister from his bully of an older brother—and for this—he's guilty of a crime?*

And we call the Fenyir barbarians.

Watching Owen pace, his hands clenching into fists, listening for the sounds of battle that would herald the death of Fioni, she suddenly understood what she had to do, what she should have done weeks ago.

"Owen," she said softly.

Turning, he glanced at her and then at the others already far ahead. "My lady, we should catch up before—"

"I'm sorry, Owen. I'm so sorry. I didn't think I had any other choice, but the truth is... I was afraid, too frightened to do this alone. It was wrong of me. Thank you for my life. Thank you for everything."

Owen's face was crestfallen, and he placed his hands on her shoulders, staring down at her with tired eyes. "My lady, we can't stay here. At best, Fioni and Erik can only delay Galas."

She pulled one of his hands from her shoulder and gripped it between hers, marveling at the roughness of his skin. *A warrior's hands... just like Brice's.* "Listen to me carefully, Owen. Brice was right when he compared duty to a double-edged sword. Duty stopped me from running away with my lover when I had a chance. I did my duty, but my brother still died, as did Brice. I had no choice... but you do."

He shook his head. "Duty binds us all. I promise you, I will see you safely home."

Reaching up with one hand, she cupped his bearded chin. "You're a good man, Owen Toscovar."

"My lady..."

"I, Danika Dain, last surviving member of House Dain, Guardians of Wolfrey, Lions of the North, release you from your oath of service."

His eyes narrowed. "My lady, I don't—"

"I'm not *your lady* anymore, Owen."

"This is madness."

"Brice was right about the cost of duty, but he missed an important part of it: duty must also be about *choice*. Fioni, Erik, Rolf... all the others chose their own path, but I took that choice from you."

"No," he whispered. "I chose to fight Orin. I didn't need to break his leg. I was angry, and I went too far. I see that now."

She kissed his knuckles. "You are free, Owen Toscovar. Free to set your own course in this world."

"My place is with you, my lady."

Chapter 37

Fioni

Fioni and the others had been in place, hiding behind rocks along the slope's summit, when they heard the sounds of snapping tree branches in the woods below. Owen's tactical sense had been sound, and from here, they had an unobstructed view of the narrow gap, the deadfall containing the nell spider nest wedged against the rocks on the opposite side of the ravine, and the switchback just past the rocks leading farther up the mountain. The slope had been difficult enough just to get up here. It would be murder when she and the others were shooting crossbow bolts and heaving stones down upon those trying to scale it.

The one thing Owen had been dead wrong about, however, was his suggestion that they could retreat down the other side of the slope. There was no other side, just a dead drop of at least a hundred feet overlooking a pine-tree-filled ravine cut into the mountain's roots. While Owen might have been able to scale it, there was no way they could. When they had first looked down upon it, Fioni had joked about having "run enough from Galas for one lifetime," and they had all shared a laugh, but in truth, it was no joke: the time for running was over.

The sounds of breaking branches grew in volume, and she pushed the stock of her crossbow tighter into her shoulder. *Galas and his men aren't even trying to be stealthy. Good. Keep coming, you kin-murdering bastard.* She thought of her father then and smiled in memory of him. They had fought far too much after her mother and brother had died at sea, but she was certain he'd forgive her. *We can get drunk together in Nifalgen, you old walrus. I'll tell you then how sorry I am, how much I loved you.*

Maybe Vory will be there too.

That thought filled her with warmth.

"Be ready," Erik said softly. "Make every bolt count."

Her six bolts lay wedged against her knee. She'd take her time. There'd be little reason to hurry. After the bolts were gone… well, they'd run out of rocks long before they ran out of enemies. She regretted arguing with Kora—especially over a man. Kora had been right; she had been behaving like a lovestruck girl, jealous of the noblewoman and Owen's loyalty to her. *Of course* Owen had chosen duty over her. *And why not?* she mused. *It wasn't as if we were long-time lovers. In truth, you barely know the man, Fioni. You lay together only one night.* She wiped the sweat from her eyes, smiling at the memory of a naked Owen. *It was a good night, though.*

"Here they come," said Erik, snapping her attention back.

Time's up, she realized. Her heartbeat hammered beneath her ring-mail coat, and she took long, deep breaths. She met Erik's eyes. "Your father, Yarl Vengir, would be proud of you, Erik Gull-Song."

"And yours as well, Fioni Ice-Bound."

Then they saw the first of their pursuers break from the woods: Hishtari soldiers in brightly colored gambesons, their animal masks hanging around their necks. Her eyes narrowed in confusion. *Where are Galas's men?* Then, in disbelief, she saw Kory'ander Dey running along with them, more than twenty Hishtari soldiers moving in a disorganized clump, with stragglers in the rear struggling to keep up. Dey ran with a scimitar in hand, its naked blade flashing in the sun. *Not Galas, but he'll do.* She took aim upon his chest. "Wait until I shoot."

"What a yarl you'd have made, Fioni," Erik softly said. "Die well."

Her throat tightened, and she swallowed, focusing on Dey.

Faster than the others, Dey reached the switchback before the deadfall first. He stopped there, staring up the trail the others had taken, waiting for his men to catch up. She aimed at his back, right between the shoulder blades. The distance was far but not too far, perhaps a hundred paces. She squeezed the trigger lever, and the weapon jumped in her grip as the limbs snapped forward. The shot was good, but at the last moment, a Hishtari soldier stepped in front of Dey, spinning about like a child's toy before crashing into Dey and knocking him down.

Damn it!

Erik and the others released their own missiles, sending more Hishtari soldiers reeling. Screams of pain drifted up to them, and the Hishtari soldiers looked about wildly in all directions, panic on their faces. Fioni reloaded and tried to find Dey again, but in the press of bodies, she couldn't discern him, so she shot at the confused mass, feeling immense satisfaction at the sight of a head turning into a bright-red spray of blood and gristle. She reloaded. The survivors ran for cover, understanding they were under attack. They still didn't know where the missiles were coming from, and some hid on the wrong side of trees. Fioni pinned one such soldier to a trunk, his legs dangling beneath him. She reloaded. This time, one of the Hishtari soldiers must have seen her, because he began screaming and pointing at her. "Tattletale," she said as she put a bolt into his gut, sending him flying backward as though kicked by a horse. She reloaded, feeling *very* satisfied. "That's for my ship."

A handful of the soldiers dashed out from behind cover and ran screaming at the slope, led by Dey himself. Fioni loosed a bolt at him, but he somehow slipped out of the way. She reloaded as Dey hit the slope and, impossibly, seemed to scurry up it like a barracuda going for something shiny. She shot at him again, and again he dodged out of the way. She gaped in disbelief. Erik loosed a bolt at the Hishtari Moon Lord, now only paces away, but Dey's scimitar flashed, cutting the bolt apart in a shower of wooden chips. *No one is that fast.* Dey's face was a mask of rage as he fell upon Erik. She grasped for another bolt, only to find they were all gone. Dropping her crossbow, she drew Wave's Kiss, but she was far too late. Dey's scimitar swept up and down, cutting Erik in half from skull to groin.

She screamed in rage as she attacked, but he was already turning, catching her blade on his and pushing it to the side. Before she could react, he elbowed her in the jaw, sending her reeling to the ground. She tried to rise and fell, and then managed to reach her knees as the last three Windhelm warriors converged on Dey all at once with their Wolfrey swords. Dey skewered the closest through the throat—a perfect thrust! Then he pivoted away while taking another man's arm off at the elbow. His reverse cut opened the wounded warrior's throat. Blood sprayed Dey, covering his upper body. The remaining Hishtari warriors were fleeing back the way they had come, perhaps not realizing their master was winning. Dey's scimitar flashed down on his last opponent, shattering both his scimitar and the Wolfrey sword the man had been using to block, before its jagged remains ripped the man's chest and stomach open, spilling his intestines.

She stared openmouthed at the Hishtari prince, who had just slaughtered four warriors in moments. She staggered upright, intent on dying on her feet, her sword held before her with both hands. Dey raised a single mocking eyebrow and then swept in, ripping the sword from her hands and once again slamming her to her back. He stood over her now, her own sword at her throat, blood dripping off his chin. "She has plans for you, you stupid bitch."

"What… how?" she mumbled.

"But I only need to leave you alive, not all in one piece." His face twisted into a mask of rage as he dropped down, ramming his knee into her solar plexus, knocking the air from her lungs. She gasped in agony, unable to do more than make mewling noises as he stepped on her ankle, holding her leg in place, and readied her own sword to cut down at her. "You stabbed me in the leg. *Me, the Moon Lord of Daenipor!* I'll give you to the queen, but you don't need your feet."

He cackled like a madman—and she realized he probably was. "You… weren't… Moon Lord," she gasped. "Just… puppet."

He cocked his head, leering at her. "I like your sword." He held the hilt up to his eye. "Why is the gem glowing?"

"It's a pearl, actually," said Owen from behind him.

Dey turned just as Owen threw the glowing nell spider egg he had carried up the slope. It shattered against Dey's chest, covering him with shards of white crystalline and slimy ichor. Dey staggered back, releasing Fioni. He stood shaking with rage before Owen, yellow goo dripping off his chin. "How dare—"

He froze, his mouth hanging open, as dozens of baby nell spiders scurried over him. Dey screamed as they began to bite him. He dropped Fioni's sword and began slapping wildly at the spiders. Some he crushed against his skin, leaving a gory smear, but others darted under the collar of his gambeson and ran down his back. Frantic, Dey tried to pull his gambeson over his head, but as he did, Owen surged forward and kicked him in the small of his back, sending him flying down the incline. As he tumbled head over feet, his screams grew dimmer.

Then Owen was pulling her to her feet. She grasped at his arm as he bent down and picked up her sword. "Why?" she whispered. "Why did you come back?"

Shaking his head, Owen slid her sword into her scabbard before pulling her against him. "Why do you think I came back, you damned frustrating woman?"

"But… your oath?" she whispered, staring wide eyed at him.

He kissed her, crushing her lips against his.

She pulled away just as Galas and a small army of warriors emerged from the trees below. They began to climb the slope, murder in their eyes. Owen gripped her hand, pulled her along with him as he ran to the cliff behind them. "Do you remember the Rose Palace, when I asked you to trust me? I need you to trust me again."

"I remember I fell."

His eyes shone with amusement, and he cocked his head, raising a single blond eyebrow.

He thinks this is funny—and he calls me *frustrating.*

"Fioni, do you trust me?"

Breathless, still in a state of disbelief, she squeezed his hand. "With my life."

He ran for the cliff. Without hesitation, she jumped with him, and they both flew out into empty air. She felt a momentary wave of weightlessness as the treetops rushed toward her.

Chapter 38

Galas

Galas peered over the cliff, staring down upon the pine trees below. Fioni had chosen death over capture. In truth, he really didn't blame her. "Farewell, cousin," he said softly, turning away.

Aegrism searched the corpses nearby, one of the intact crossbows over his shoulder, several of the iron-tipped wooden bolts clutched in his large hand. Along the trail at the base of the slope, his men continued their search for survivors of the ambush. Fioni's attack had been surprisingly effective, and corpses of Hishtari soldiers littered the ground before the switchback. Miraculously, a handful of the guppies had escaped injury and sat grouped together on the trail below with their wounded. Others probably still fled through the woods, wild eyed, with shit running down their legs. When Serina had first brought Dey and his men aboard *Iron Beard*, Galas had thought it a mistake, assuming the inept empire soldiers would only get in his way, but he had to admit now that he had been wrong: if nothing else, Dey's headlong charge had sprung Fioni's trap, sparing his own men.

Near the bottom of the slope, a half dozen of his men formed a circle around Kory'ander Dey. Galas whistled a Fenyir shanty as he made his way back down the steep slope, Aegrism trailing along behind him. As he came nearer, he saw some of his men stamp the ground near the still-thrashing Dey. Galas shuddered. *What a way to go.* The once-handsome nobleman's face was now swollen and red, oozing pus from numerous small punctures. His eyes were unfocused. "Help...help me," Dey whispered through blue lips now swollen to twice their size.

One of the spiders scuttled closer to Galas's boot, and he stomped it repeatedly in disgust, leaving a wet smear on the bottom of his boot that he wiped against the grass before squinting up at the sun. "How many hours, do you reckon, until sunset?"

Aegrism sniffed, wiped the back of his hand against his nose. "This far north... four, five hours."

"It was a good ambush site," Galas admitted, glancing toward the trail cutting around the rocks and up the mountain. "It'll be several hours at least before we catch up to the Dain woman."

Dey lifted a hand out to Galas, his fingers trembling. "Yarl... Yarl Galas," he mumbled. "She'll...reward you... help."

Galas held his hand out to one of his men standing nearby, leaning on a spear. The warrior upended the weapon and handed it to Galas, who then cautiously moved closer to Dey.

Dey's eyes widened in understanding, and he shook his head. "She'll... be... angry."

Galas sighed happily, feeling immense satisfaction warm his nuts. "I doubt it. You're seeing things all skewed, *Moon Lord of Daenipor.* You see, despite my advice—and Serina's instructions—you took charge, unfortunately leading your men into a trap, which *is* true enough. By the time my men and I could come to your rescue, it was far too late, which *isn't* quite as true but does make for a far more satisfying story, don't you think?"

Dey shook his head.

Without taking his eyes from Dey, Galas said, "Kill the others."

Aegrism turned away to carry out Galas's orders. Moments later, the Hishtari soldiers began to scream. Galas grinned as he thrust the spear into Dey's groin, skewering his genitals. Dey, still paralyzed, could only howl like a tortured dog. Galas saw the nervous glances his men exchanged; several unconsciously stroked their manhood in sympathy. He smirked. Lessons were important. Galas thrust the spearhead repeatedly into Dey's genitals, shredding his tiny eel. Eventually, Galas grew bored with the mewling noises Dey was making and stabbed him in the throat, finishing him. He'd have preferred to leave him to suffer, but he couldn't take the chance that he might somehow live long enough to tell on him to Serina.

He was about to turn away when he saw something flash in the sun on Dey's corpse. Plastered against his side by goo and webs was a small red gem about the size of his thumb. Using the spear's tip, he pried the object free, dragging it toward him. He wiped it clean, revealing what had to be a blood gem like the one on Taios's sword. He had always admired that sword and, just for a moment, considered sending men to search the base of the cliff to recover it from Fioni's corpse, but then discarded the idea. There was no time for such things.

He still had to kill the others and capture the Dain woman.

Chapter 39

Owen

Owen lay next to Fioni amid a massive pile of pine needles and broken branches. He felt as though a wild stallion had just run him down, but when he flexed his fingers and toes, he found everything still moved. He pushed himself up into a seated position and waited until his vision stopped spinning. Lying atop his legs, Fioni groaned in pain. Blood ran freely down her scalp, soaking her neck. "Can you move?" he asked, holding her against him, running his hands over her body, looking for broken limbs.

"I can move," she mumbled. "I just don't want to."

He helped her into a seated position. When she tentatively brought her fingertips to her scalp, she winced in pain. He gently pried back her hair, softly probing her scalp. "It's not that bad," he said. "Head wounds always bleed a lot at first."

"Hurts," she said.

He used his dagger to cut away a portion of his padded gambeson beneath Vory's ring-mail coat and then pressed it against the cut on her scalp. "Don't be such a guppy," he said.

She snorted, frowning at him. Then she bent back, staring up into the thick pine branches above them that obscured the cliff they had just jumped from. "How did you know?"

He helped her to her feet, holding onto her as she stumbled against him. He watched her face with concern, but after a few moments, she was capable of standing on her own. "Know what?"

"That the pine tree branches would break our fall, slow us down."

"I didn't," he admitted, staring in wonder at the pile of needles and tree limbs lying about. They had hit the branches within the first few seconds, snapping through them, each one slowing their fall. "But we'd have died for sure if we didn't try. I think our armor helped protect us, as well."

She groaned, rubbing one of her buttocks. "I'm so tired of falling from heights with you, Owen."

"No more. I promise."

Then she wrapped her arms around his neck and kissed him long and hard, his body stiffening in surprise, before she just as abruptly pulled away again, leaving him standing there in confusion. "I can't believe you actually touched that foul thing. How did you know the spiders would hurt him?"

"I didn't," he admitted. "But I know Serina... changes her servants, somehow. When I saw Dey dodge the crossbow bolts, I knew I couldn't fight him any more than I could Modwyn."

She pulled the wad of cloth away from her forehead. "The bleeding is slowing already."

They took stock of their belongings. Both were armed with sword and dagger. She had flint and stone. He carried a small skin of water and some dried fish, but she had only her flask of flame-rot, and that was half-empty. They finished the water and fish, wolfing both down. He scanned the terrain around them as they ate. The forested ravine they had fallen into cut into the roots of the mountain. "You're the woodsman. What do you think?"

He considered the mountain. "If we're lucky, maybe we'll find a path back up to the trail, or even another way up the mountain."

He felt her eyes on his back. "What is she to you really?" she asked softly. "I need the truth."

Turning, he met her gaze, and then struggled to explain how he felt, not truly understanding it himself. "I don't know. She's all I have left of Wolfrey and home. I'd be lying if I told you I had no feelings for her, but it's not like with you. She needs me, but so did you—and I couldn't let you die."

Her face softened, and she rushed forward, embracing him. "Let's go find my uncle and the others. Everything else we can work out later."

They slipped through the forested roots of the mountain.

Chapter 40

Danika

Danika followed the others up the path cut along the side of the mountain. At regular intervals, they came across the remains of smooth stone platforms where the trail cut back, zigzagging along the mountainside. In addition, the path they trudged along was now lined with cut stones and irregular but clearly built steps, removing any doubt that this path was unnatural. Someone had built it, albeit hundreds of years ago. With each step now, Danika's leg muscles burned. She paused, her chest heaving with exertion as she took in the view of the magnificent primal forests far beneath her, and the shadow cast by the mountain as the sun moved west. *It has to be late afternoon already,* she agonized, *but we still haven't reached the summit.*

When she heard the tinkling of running water cascading over stones, her thirst peaked, and she pushed herself on, catching up to the others taking a rest break alongside a stream that had cut through the path, leaving a gap several feet wide. The others made way for her, and she fell to her knees before the stream, cupped her hands in the cold water, and drank greedily.

A hand fell upon her shoulder. "Go slow," Kora said. "You'll cramp."

With considerable effort, she pushed herself away from the water, wiped her mouth with the back of a filthy arm. "We should keep going."

"We've time for a break. I sent back two of our fastest runners to watch for sign of Galas. They've yet to report back."

Danika remembered passing them now, a young man and woman, both unarmed. She had thought that odd at first, but now she understood why: so they could run faster. "Do you think... Can Owen, Fioni, and the others..."

Kora's frown deepened as she sat back against the rocks. "I think... maybe, we need to focus on ourselves, on finding Fioni's uncle. Otherwise—"

"Otherwise, their sacrifice will have been wasted."

They sat in silence for a few minutes. At this height, the wind blew over the Godswall, caressing her sweaty face and sending her long hair flapping. "How do we know Denyr even made it this far?"

"We don't, but what choice do we have?"

The wind gusted, whistling softly, the only response.

#

Not long after that, they came upon the black stone pyramid and the white statue built atop it. The pyramid, identical to the one they had found in the ruins of the Illthori fort beneath the atoll, was four sided, with a narrow, flat top. Built entirely from an unrecognizable seamless black stone, it sat atop one of the switchback platforms built along the mountainside, giving it a commanding view of the path and the surrounding terrain. Danika stood next to Kora, staring in mounting unease at the statue, placed upon the pyramid like a pedestal. A woman, but not human, with the same catlike features and bizarre beastlike legs as the Illthori corpses they had found underground. She faced the forest below, her arms outstretched, as if to say, "All of this is my domain."

"Well," said Kora softly. "Now we know Serl and Denyr came this far at least."

Danika bit her lip and nodded in agreement. *Iron Beard*'s strange figurehead was clearly modeled on this statue, as was the white stone woman on Sight-Bringer's hilt. Was she an Illthori, or one of their gods? The answer, Danika suspected, would remain a mystery. What was clear, though, was that Serl had been here, and had been so inspired by this strange statue that he had it replicated in wood on the prow of his prized vessel.

The rest of the crew edged farther away, keeping their distance, whispering prayers or gripping the Wodor hammers that hung from their necks. It was the pyramid, Danika knew, not the statue, that they found so disquieting. The structure was identical to the one they had found beneath the ruins, but infinitely more... disturbing. Despite the unseasonable warmth, frost coated its dark stone sides. She could feel the chill from where she stood. More than ten feet tall, and half as wide at its base, its sides sloped upward to the narrow flat summit upon which stood the statue. Large double doors, made of the same black stone but bound with rust-free steel and equally coated in frost, faced the trail, with the strange Illthori glyphs running around the outer seam of the doors.

"What is it, and why here?" Danika wondered.

Kora shook her head.

"First we find an Illthori fort, now this... I understand none of this."

"This island was once home to our gods," said Kora. "Our myths said nothing of the Illthori. Could they have been servants?"

"Those markings are like the ones on the portal I activated with Sight-Bringer."

Kora turned to face her with wide eyes. "*Activated?* What do you mean?"

"When I touched Sight-Bringer to them, they began to glow. That's when the portal opened. Do you think…"

Kora glared at her in disbelief. "No. *No, I do not think*," she said quickly but firmly. "Whatever its purpose once was, it has sat here for hundreds of years. Leave the damned thing be. It gives me shivers just looking at it."

"There are mysteries here," Danika said, staring up at the statue. "The small folk say that Sight-Bringer—as well as the rod and the crown—were gifts from our creator, Father Craftsman, but this isn't true, at least not in the sense that they literally came from the hand of our deity. All three were found almost a century ago by children playing in a half-submerged cave along the coast—a coast that sits perhaps two weeks' sail to the west."

"They all possess magical powers, don't they?"

"Scholars claim that everything the Illthori created was magical, but I've always thought they were only guessing. I really don't know, either. While the sword has power over the undead and enhances the wielder's senses, the other two are equally wondrous, if not more so. The rod can control the weather. This is why the harvests are so bountiful in King's Hold, why the king is so wealthy. The crown is said to bring insight to those who wear it, which certainly hasn't hurt his long rule."

"Is that true?"

Danika shrugged. "The seasons *are* beautiful in King's Hold."

"And the Raven's-Eye lets one find the sun."

"Indeed," said Lady Danika softly. "Do you think Serl found it here?"

"I don't think so. I think he had it long before he sailed here."

Danika snorted. "Perhaps he found it in a cave as well. We should keep moving," she said, glancing up at the sky, which was now much lower on the western horizon.

240

"Do you know what I don't understand?" Kora asked, peering at the black pyramid. "You said the rod controls the weather and the crown gives wisdom, but why create a sword with power over the undead?"

"What do you mean?"

"Serina became a blood fiend through ritual sacrifice to the Dark Shark, one of *our gods*, not your Father Craftsman, not some long-forgotten Illthori deity. What possible reason could they have had for such a weapon?"

Before Danika could answer, they heard one of the crew cry out in excitement and point back down the path where a young man ran toward them—one of the two scouts Kora had left to watch Galas. The young man was lean and fit, with unusually dark hair for a Fenyir. Kora moved to meet him, and Danika followed closely behind. Sweat drenched the young man, plastering his long dark hair to his face. Kora handed him a waterskin, from which he drank. When he was done, she conversed briefly with him. Her face tight, she turned and addressed the crew. "Galas and his men are coming."

#

Now, the pace Kora set was almost more than Danika could bear. Fortunately, they had been closer to the summit than she had realized. Kora led them over the rim, coming out on a path that led between two sheer rock faces, carved out of the mountain, wide enough for two wagons. *A gateway,* Danika realized, *but to where?* As the others passed through the opening, they began to point and cry out excitedly. When she too crossed under the shadow of the gateway, she immediately understood why: The mountain, shaped like a bowl, was hollow in its interior. Its rim, much like the Godswall, sheltered the remains of an ancient stone city. In the center of the city, rising above all the other ruins, casting a long shadow in the setting sun, was an impossibly large green pyramid. Steps built into one side led up to a flat summit crowned by still-standing stone pillars. Despite the Fenyir legends about Torin Island being the "Gateway to the Gods," she knew in a moment that those myths were false. This island had never been home to the Fenyir gods.

It was an Illthori city.

The first anyone had ever seen.

Chapter 41

Owen

The forested ravine cut into the side of the mountain like a wedge, leading Owen and Fioni deeper into its shadow. Just ahead, partially obscured by trees, Owen saw a dark form, a structure of some kind. Although dusk was falling, the structure seemed unnaturally wreathed in shadows, as if it leached the surrounding light. Owen glanced at Fioni and saw the same apprehension on her face that he felt. She drew her sword, and he did the same. Together, they stalked closer, moving around the trees for a better view: it was another of the black pyramids, identical to the broken one they had found beneath the ruins, but this one was intact still, with steel-bound double doors covered in a layer of frost.

"I don't like this," whispered Fioni. When she spoke, he could see her breath before her face.

More of the bizarre Illthori runes had been etched into the frame of the stone running around the doors. The ground before the doors had been trampled smooth; someone had been here recently. Edging closer, he trailed his fingers over the barely discernible seam between the two doors, snatching his fingers back immediately. It was like touching ice.

"Owen!" she whispered sharply.

She held her sword upside down, its hilt before her eyes. Once again, a soft red glow emanated from the blood gem. His fear spiked, and he spun about, looking in all directions for a threat, expecting another giant spider to launch itself at them.

The forest was silent and dark with the growing shadows.

"I don't understand," she said. She moved away from him and the pyramid, and as she did, the glow in the gem faded. White-faced, she looked from him to the pyramid. When she stepped closer again, the glow returned.

He shook his head in confusion and then slowly circled the pyramid. There was nothing around the back of the pyramid, but perhaps two hundred paces away, he noted a second, identical structure, also obscured by bushes. Even farther away, he recognized a third. All three were in line, like a soldier's defensive post. "How many are there?" he wondered out loud.

"I don't know," she said, "but I don't like them. We should go."

With every step they took away from the pyramid, they felt more relief.

#

The ravine led deeper within the mountain, leaving all the trees behind and becoming stonier, with tall, cliff-like walls on either side. Owen found a small cold stream, and they drank their fill. He said nothing to Fioni, but he hadn't seen any animal sign near the water, nor had he seen any since passing the line of black pyramids. It was as if the animals avoided coming near the mountain.

Just ahead, a narrow crevice cut right into the mountain, with towering walls on either side. The sky was red, the shadows lengthening. *When will Serina awake? Soon*, he imagined. *An hour, maybe two.* He stood before the crevice. The opening was wide enough for a wagon, but it narrowed the farther in one went, disappearing into darkness. The stench of rotten eggs drifted from the crevice. "Gods' balls, what is that?" Fioni asked.

"Smells like yellow-stone."

"What?"

"Yellow-stone, also called Drake's-Blood."

She shook her head, her face wrinkled in distaste.

"Well, you find it in caves up north, sometimes. Looks like yellow crystals or cake. Mix it up with dung, and it makes decent fertilizer. Old wives say if you burn it in a home, it'll drive away evil spirits and pests."

She snorted. "It'd drive *me* away."

"We'll need a torch," he said, staring into the dark crevice.

He pulled handfuls of moss from nearby stones while she looked about for a suitable tree branch. By the time she returned with a thick branch, he had a large pile of moss strips ready. Taking the stick from her, he wrapped the moss shreds about it, until the head of the branch was thick with tightly bound moss. "I'm going to need your booze."

She made a face but handed the small flask over. He poured its contents over the moss, soaking it thoroughly. The moss caught fire with a single spark from her flint, casting a bright-orange light on the stony walls of the crevice. Holding the fluttering torch out, he led her into the crack in the mountain. The stony ground was worn smooth, as if it had once been a passage. At several points, the passage twisted, changing direction, with overhanging rock completely obscuring the sky above them the farther in they went, before becoming a true tunnel, seemingly carved out of the side of the mountain. The air became moist, with droplets of water running down the stones. The passage narrowed, requiring them to turn sideways to keep going. Fioni brushed up tightly against him, clearly uncomfortable with the tight space. The stench of yellow-stone grew stronger, the air thick with warm moisture, creating a glowing halo around their torch. There were cave systems like this in the north, with secret grottos, long-valued by northerners.

"Owen," said Fioni, a trace of surprise in her voice. "Look at the walls."

He had already noted the clearly worked walls ahead of them. Someone had used tools to chip away the stone, widening the passage. "I had suspected as much," he admitted. "I think this is another passage into the mountain."

"Why is the air so wet?"

For the first time in days, he felt a surge of happy expectation. "If this is what I think it is, I think you're about to find out."

A series of oddly paced steps led down into a vast natural chamber filled with steam and hot, moist air. He led her down the steps, taking her hand and pulling her along with him across the vapor-filled air. Hundreds of paces wide, the chamber had been expanded, its walls and floor worked smooth with tools. And, just as he had suspected, sitting in the center of the chamber, lined by regular white stone blocks, was a massive steaming pool of water sunken into the stone floor. Heat trails drifted from the water.

She inhaled in sudden surprise. "Gods, what is that?"

He led her closer. "A hot spring. I suspected as much but didn't want to get your hopes up."

She made a face of distaste. "For what?"

"You don't have hot springs in the islands, I assume?"

"I've never even heard of such a thing," she said with wonder.

A crust of white minerals had formed around the waterline of the pool. Water dripped and burbled. And while the stench of sulfur was strong, so was the damp smell of wet rocks and rich mud. Fioni moved past him and knelt beside the stone-lined pool and then dipped a finger into the water, quickly yanking it back again. "It's hot," she said as though she didn't believe it.

He smirked, shaking his head. "That's the point."

He left her there while he crossed the cavern to its far side, where another tunnel led farther on. At the opposite end of the tunnel, steps led back up, twisting and climbing. He moved back to join Fioni, thrusting the lit torch between two stones to hold it upright. "I think the passage has cut right through the side of the mountain. It must be a shortcut, much faster than climbing the pass the others took. I think we're ahead of them now."

"What now?"

He stripped off his sword belt, sat down on the lip of one of the carved stones lining the pool, and began to pull off his boots.

Her eyes tightened as he pulled his ring-mail coat over his shoulders, piling it atop his boots before undoing the string on his breeches. "What are you doing?"

"Taking a bath."

"In that?" She stared in disbelief at the steaming pool.

"Trust me."

Completely naked now, he dipped his foot in the water, sighing in glorious satisfaction. Then, without pause, he climbed all the way in, feeling hot gravel lining the base of the pool beneath his toes. The silky hot water baked his skin as he lowered himself into a seated position, resting his back against the hot stones lining the pool. Fioni continued to stare at him in disbelief, and he winked at her before dunking his head beneath the waters. Rising again, he watched her, tasting the bitter tang of minerals on his lips. He leaned back, extending his arms out to either side to rest against the mineral-coated stones, feeling the release of tension in his aching muscles.

She stood at the edge of the pool, arms crossed before her as she stamped her boot. "There's no time for this."

"If we're ahead of the others, as I suspect, we have time."

"This seems frivolous."

"I thought you said you'd sleep with a bear for a hot bath?"

She frowned at him, cocking her head. "Just like a man to hear what he wants to hear."

He watched her, water dripping off his chin, his once-short hair now dripping down his neck. "Fioni, the last few weeks have been… horrific. I've been poisoned by a traitor, hunted by islanders, and almost molested by a degenerate thief, not to mention shipwrecked. It seems everyone I meet wants to kill me—except you, who only wants to kill me sometimes."

"Owen…"

"In an hour, maybe less than that, Serina will awaken and come after us. There's an excellent chance neither you nor I will ever see another dawn. Do yourself a favor and experience this bliss at least once in your life."

She looked away at the fluttering torch then, shaking her head, sat down on a rock and began to pull off her boots, followed by her sword and armor. Owen watched her undress, enjoying the sight, feeling his breathing increase. He shifted in place as his erection sprang up on its own. She gingerly placed one foot into the water and then frowned at him. "What are you staring at?"

"Your legs," he answered. "You have nice legs for a pirate."

She glared at him, her face red. "Look away."

Now she's shy? He shrugged and glanced away, but he still watched her out of the corner of his eye as she climbed into the pool. Immediately, she groaned in pleasure, a beatific smile on her face. "Oh gods," she sighed, sinking all the way to her neck. "That may be the most wonderful thing I've felt in weeks."

"Told you," he said.

She closed her eyes and dipped her head underwater. When she surfaced, he was standing only inches before her. She stared at him, suddenly trembling. *So strange,* he thought, *for such a bold woman to be so coltish.* He took her in his arms, pulling her tightly against him. She moaned, thrusting herself against his erection and burying her face in his neck. He cupped her face with his palms and stared into her green eyes. "I came back because I'm in love with you, you damned insufferable woman."

"Well, of course you are," she said as she pulled his head toward hers, crushing their lips together.

Breathless, he ran his hands down her body, desperate to touch her. Her tongue was in his mouth, sharing the tang of minerals. She shoved him back against the stone bench, and the two of them were so clumsily desperate for one another they almost fell. She straddled him, and he gasped, his nerves on fire. He ran his palms over her nipples, squeezing her firm breasts before pulling her thighs wide. She reached down, grasping him and guiding his erection toward her. With a single thrust, he entered her, and she threw her head back, moaning in pleasure, scoring the skin of his arms with her fingernails. Breathing heavily, they kissed, mashing their teeth together, breathing into one another's mouths. Then they began to rock together, like long-time lovers moving in perfect symmetry. He grasped at her buttocks, pulling her in tighter against him, thrusting harder and faster as they moved toward their inevitable mounting orgasm. When it came, all too soon, it shuddered through them, their cries echoing off the cavern walls.

They could have been the only two people in the world.

Chapter 42

Danika

Irregular stone steps led down from the rim of the mountain, cutting back and forth to the stone ruins of the city below. At each landing, they passed stone markers carved with the elaborate Illthori markings Danika recognized from Sight-Bringer's blade. With an entire city filled with relics of the dead, scholars might now be able to learn to read those markings, translate the sword's meaning. What other arcane secrets did these ruins hold?

Although the spacing of the steps was jarring, they allowed the party to make good time on their descent down the interior rim of the mountain. As night fell, Kora led them down the last of the steps and into the ruins, long since reclaimed by the wilderness.

The crumbling stones filled the interior of the mountain. Tall, still grass and thick clumps of weeds shot through the broken stones. Long snakelike vines strangled fallen columns. Even trees had somehow burst through the stones. As with the fort on the atoll, only the shells of buildings remained, crumbling walls long devoid of ceilings. A clear, bright moon and stars bathed the ruins in a silvery glow, highlighting the remains of beautiful marble sculptures.

Danika recognized the remains of what must have once been courtyards, many retaining shards of once carefully set multicolored tiles, etched in stunning geometric patterns. *Even now,* she marveled as the others slowly filed past—*after centuries*—*it's still breath taking.* An eerie silence filled the city, broken only by the clap of their hobnailed boots on the crumbling stones. To Danika, standing here among the ruins felt like a dream, one lost in time.

They could see the top of the vast pyramid in the center of the dead city. After a brief discussion with Danika and the others, Kora led them toward it. They had no idea if Fioni's uncle Denyr was there, but it was the most prominent feature in the city, and one of the few structures still standing.

As they slowly made their way past the shattered stones, cold sweat glistened over Danika's skin, and she found herself stopping to stare behind them. Galas and his men weren't that far behind them, she knew, but he was the least of her fears. With the sun now fully down, Serina must be awake. Blood fiends possessed superhuman speed and strength. How fast could she cross the island? While it had taken *Fen Wolf's* exhausted crew an entire day to make the trek, she doubted Serina and Dilan would take even a fraction of that time. If they didn't find Denyr and use Sight-Bringer on Serina's heart soon, she'd catch them and slaughter all of them. Then thousands more would die when Serina once again invaded the kingdom.

"My lady," said Gali, interrupting her thoughts. "Please. The others go ahead."

Now realizing the others were far ahead, Danika increased her pace. "I'm coming."

They caught up to the others as Kora led the crew onto the shattered remains of what had once been an impossibly wide stone avenue that must have cut across the city, heading directly toward its heart—the green stone pyramid. Kora wiped her mouth with the back of her hand before handing a waterskin to Danika. As Danika drank, Kora stared at the pyramid rising in the distance, so large it blocked out the stars in the clear night sky. "You're a noblewoman. What do your kingdom scholars have to say about the Illthori? A temple, do you think?" Kora asked her.

"I don't know. No one does. All we know of the Illthori is conjecture, master magic-users and artisans, but we know nothing of their gods—if they even had gods."

"Could they have been servants to... *others?*"

Danika's lips pressed together as she watched Kora's face, recognizing what Kora was truly asking. The Fenyir clans believed Torin Island to have been the abandoned home of their gods, not a long-dead Illthori city. *Kora and the others have bound this island in religious knots, tying into it all their beliefs—and those knots are now unraveling before them. The dissonance must be soul wrenching.* "Kora, this place... the Illthori... you must see that I can't—"

"Don't. It's not a question for you to answer. It's for our holy men." Turning away, she stared at the pyramid. "Whatever its purpose was, it remains high ground. We'll make our stand there."

#

A scar shattered the broad avenue where the ground had seemingly been wrenched apart, leaving a deep tear in the stone. Had they rope, they could have tried climbing down and then back up again, but the rope had sunk with *Fen Wolf.* With no other choice, Kora led them east, back into the ruins, in an attempt to circle around the shattered land. Kora called a short halt in the remains of what had once been a walled courtyard with a broken fountain, now covered by weeds and vines. Danika glanced uneasily at the night sky. Although she was just as tired, desperation and fear gave her strength. They needed to keep moving. Serina was coming.

Kora stood atop a broken wall across the courtyard, staring out at the pyramid, now looming before them, just on the other side of another broken compound. Danika joined her, easily pulling herself up beside the other woman with just her arms—a once-impossible feat. This voyage had changed who she was, she knew, both good and ill. Now, she was not only far stronger than she had ever been, but also much lighter. She had lost at least ten pounds, and maybe more. Each day, the ends of the strings that held her breeches up seemed to grow longer as she tightened them in the morning. In truth, she was barely recognizable as the pampered noblewoman who had set out with her brother months ago on an expedition to Greywynne Island.

"We should press on," Danika said.

Kora bit her lip, her eyes hard. "How fast can blood fiends—"

"I don't know, but fast—very fast."

"I heard they can… fly."

Danika shook her head empathically no. "My uncle Stron kept a war journal. If such a thing were true, he would have mentioned it. There were—are—many tales about blood fiends. It's often hard to sift through what is true and what is legend. And even then, much of what we once thought was true wasn't. When Stron and his battle-mage, Belion, confronted Serina in the Great Crypt, they did so during the day, assuming she'd be asleep and vulnerable. She was waiting for them, still awake."

"Aye," said Kora softly. "It was daytime still when *Thunder Killer* caught up to us, bringing the other blood fiend, this… *Dilan*, did you name him?"

Danika closed her eyes, feeling a rush of sadness. "Dilan Reese."

"Bringing this Dilan Reese against us."

"I've wondered at that myself. It was daytime, but there was no sun, not with the fog overhead. I think, maybe, it's the sun that hurts them, not the time of day." She glanced up at the clear night sky. Far away, lightning struck the Godswall again, arcing up into the dark, roiling clouds that surrounded the island.

"You think that's why Serina and Dilan didn't—"

She dropped down suddenly, pulling Danika with her to lie atop the wall. Danika's fear spiked wildly, sending her heart thudding into her throat. Had Galas somehow gotten around them, or—worse— Serina? But in the ruined compound ahead of them, she saw nothing but dark shadows. She listened intently, hearing nothing but her heartbeat. She stared at Kora's face inquisitively. Kora slowly placed her lips near Danika's ear. "I saw something moving behind the stones of that compound. I'm sure of it."

"Galas?" Danika whispered.

"Kersta and Vadik would have gotten word to us."

Perhaps, Danika thought with growing concern, neither of the two scouts was able to bring warning. Remaining behind to spy on Galas and his men was dangerous, even from a distance. The athletic young man and woman could easily be dead by now. She watched the anguish on Kora's face as she likely considered that possibility as well.

"*I* find out who it is," whispered Gali from just behind them, startling Danika, who hadn't heard her climb up onto the broken wall.

Kora watched Gali intently as she considered the young woman's offer. She bit her upper lip and shook her head. "I'll go."

Gali smirked, cocking her head. "I was best slip-thief in Bent Men. All know this as true."

"It's too dangerous," Danika whispered.

"She is part of the crew now," replied Kora softly, "with or without a ship." She reached over and gripped the back of Gali's head, bringing her closer. When she spoke, Kora's face was granite. "Listen carefully, my little Hishtari mouse. Go around to the left of that wall, just beyond the broken archway. Do you see it?"

Gali bobbed her head, her eyes shining in the moonlight.

"To the right of the archway is where I saw movement. It might be an animal, although I've seen none here. Look and then come back and report. Do nothing else. In a haunted place like this, a life can end in a moment."

"In *any* place, death hides," Gali whispered.

She tensed to move, but Kora gripped her wrist, stopping her. Then she slipped a long knife into the young Hishtari woman's hand. Gali stared at the weapon and then squeezed the haft. Without another word, she slipped over the wall, silently dropping down on the other side like a cat. In moments, she was just another shadow, darting from stone to stone. Danika quickly lost sight of her.

"Wodor's balls," whispered Kora. "She *is* a quiet little mouse. Maybe she could take *Iron Beard* back for us."

Then, remembering she still had Sight-Bringer's magic to help her, Danika drew the broken sword, bringing the ruined compound into stark relief against the star-filled sky. But, despite the sword's magic, she still saw no sign of the young woman. "Should we—"

Kora shook her head. "To lead is to trust. We wait."

The minutes stretched, becoming unbearable. Sweat ran down Danika's back as her anxiety mounted. *It's taking too long. Something must have—*

Then Gali appeared once again, stepping out from behind the archway, waving enthusiastically at them, motioning them to come forward. Kora and Danika stared at one another in confusion. "I don't see anything, anyone else," said Danika.

"The little mouse has found some cheese, I think," said Kora softly, rising and dropping down over the side of the wall. Danika dropped down beside her and then heard the noise of the rest of the crew following behind them. Kora was the first to reach Gali, whose teeth flashed in a grin. Danika stared in confusion at the young woman, and then sudden fear as two shapes stepped out of the shadows behind her.

Her fear transformed into breathless joy when she recognized Owen and Fioni.

"You're alive!" she cried as she threw herself into Owen, almost knocking him down. Tears welled in her eyes as she squeezed him through his ring-mail coat. Owen stiffened in surprise but then wrapped his arms around her, hugging her back. "I told you I'd see you home yet," he said softly, his voice breaking with emotion.

Fioni stood nearby, her hip cocked jauntily to the side, a wry smile on her face. "*I'm* alive, too, my lady of Wolfrey."

Chapter 43

Dilan

Dilan bolted upright, a pain-filled emptiness burning within him. He was always thirsty upon awakening, but this was far worse. Now, his bloodlust made his head spin. His vision flared in bright hues of red and gray. Serina had warned him it would be so. *We can stay awake during the day,* she had told him, *but it is draining. The fog will protect us from the sun, but the lack of sleep comes at a cost.* He felt that cost now, his hunger a sharp spike that threatened to cut him in half. Then he saw Serina, and his heart surged with love, despite the pain. She stood before him, naked, as he was, and covered in filth and congealing blood. He reached for her but fell. "Mother…"

She caught him, held him in her arms, and whispered into the top of his head. "I know, my childe. I know. I feel it, too. You must drink—as much as you can hold. The pain will pass."

She lifted him, held him in her arms like a babe, and carried him up the steps of the hold to the moonlit deck above. As the cool night air swept over his naked form, he stared in confusion at the angry open gash in his right palm. The skin around the cut was black and flaking, like charred wood. He made a fist, and his entire hand

257

throbbed with pain. The other wounds, the two crossbow bolts that had impaled him, had healed completely. The other day, he had even regrown missing fingers, but this small cut remained. "Mother," he whispered, staring at his palm.

She carried him to the last of the bound prisoners. "Sight-Bringer," she said. "During the war, the small folk named it *Blood Fiends' Bane*, because it was so lethal to our kind. The wound will heal… after you have gorged yourself. And after tonight, it will never threaten us again."

"It… I…"

She carefully set him down before the prisoners, a handful of young women. Normally catatonic, the women tried to draw away now, perhaps sensing their doom. They trembled and wailed, eyes wild, fouling themselves in their terror. "Drink, my brave hero. Be strong again."

Dilan, his thirst a red fire, crawled atop the closest prisoner, slamming her onto her back. With her arms bound behind her, she was helpless as he drove his fangs into her soft neck. She screamed, arching her spine beneath his weight. Dilan drank, immediately feeling joy spread through him, abating his pain. When the first rush of hot blood began to slow, he gripped her chest and began squeezing her heart through her rib cage, forcing the blood to keep flowing. Her screams ceased, became soft moans of pleasure. And then she was dead.

Dilan rose on trembling legs, feeling so much better already.

Nearby, Serina had buried her face between one of the prisoners' thighs, drinking from her femoral artery. The woman's mouth opened and closed in ecstasy.

Dilan, still hungry, advanced on another prisoner.

Chapter 44

Owen

"I feared you dead for certain," Lady Danika said, finally releasing Owen and stepping back to regard him.

"I'm fine, my lady," he said, surprised at the emotions running through him. Before departing Castle Dain, he had never said more than two words to her, nor her to him; now he felt a powerful need to protect her.

Fioni frowned at Kora and the rest of the crew, standing around them in a circle. "What? No hug for me?"

Kora gripped Fioni's arms and placed her forehead against Fioni's. "How did you get away—"

Fioni snorted and glanced at Owen. "I learned how to fly." She drew away from Kora, her eyes falling on the still-comatose Ekkie on her makeshift stretcher. "Is she any better?"

"The same," said Kora sadly.

"Galas?"

"Still on our trail. I have Vadik and Kersta watching his men. Every two hours or so, one of the two will run forward and report."

"The last report?"

Kora bit her lip. "A few hours ago."

Fioni's smile disappeared. "Do we have torches?"

"A few. I didn't want to risk the light."

"Risk it," Owen said, stepping forward. "We need to move faster now. We're running out of time."

With the light of burning torches, they sped through the ruins, with Fioni explaining how she and Owen had cut through the crevice and the hot springs, entering the city before Kora and the others. Since then, he and Fioni had been moving toward the largest still-standing structure, the pyramid. They had had no idea Kora and the others were anywhere nearby until Gali had suddenly sprung up behind them, surprising them.

The pyramid rose before them, much closer now, surrounded by a half dozen smaller pyramids, all with flat tops. "What did your great-grandfather say in his journal about these ruins?" Lady Danika asked Fioni.

"He didn't. His last entry of this island noted a mountain pass and a statue of a strange woman. He didn't say this in his journal, but I suspect he thought it a likeness of Fenya, one of our gods."

"He didn't go any farther?"

Fioni shook her head. "His crew refused. Some… *thing* unnerved them. Denyr, a holy man, went on alone."

"We found the statue," said Lady Danika, "and another of those black tomb-like vaults. *It* unnerved me."

"Really?" asked Fioni, surprise in her eyes. She glanced at Owen. "We found several as well."

"I think," said Owen, speaking for the first time, "they ring the mountain."

"Why?" asked Lady Danika.

He shook his head.

They carried on in silence, soon arriving at the base of the pyramid. Stone carvings of snarling animal heads had been affixed along its base: snakes, wolves, bats, and—most prominently—birds.

Lady Danika approached a large snake's head, taller than she was, and ran her fingers over it. She turned to one of the crew standing nearby with a torch and asked him to let her have it. She held the flaming brand closer to the snake's jaws and then turned to Owen. "The stone around the animals' mouths looks discolored."

"Discolored how?" he asked.

"I think that when it rains, the water must run down these funnels cut into the side of the pyramid and behind the heads." She swept the torch along the ground where a dark, equally discolored stone trough ran to a ruined fountain.

Owen rubbed his fingers over the discoloration and then stared at the oily blackness on his fingertips. "Why's it so filthy then?"

"It's been centuries, Owen," she answered.

"I guess," he said as he peered intently at one of the heads, a fierce bird of some type with a massive pointed beak. "But I don't know how much rain this island really gets."

"What do you mean?"

At just that moment, another of the lightning bolts struck the cliffs of the Godswall far in the distance, highlighting the dark clouds that seemed to flow around the island. He considered his words, searching to explain his guess. "I think…" he began, "that whatever magic is at work with the Godswall, the lightning, and the fog, somehow also keeps the weather so mild, so unseasonably warm, and the sky overhead clear of clouds. I don't think this island sees much rainfall."

"That's just not possible," she said.

He shrugged. "Some rainfall must blow in over the Godswall, or else there'd be no trees or vegetation at all."

"That makes no sense," said Fioni, joining them.

"Nothing on this island makes sense," he answered. "But we can't stand around anymore, and it is high ground, the most defensible terrain I've seen all day."

"Agreed," said Fioni, staring up the steps to the top of the pyramid. "And it's as good a place as any to search for my uncle." She took the torch from Lady Danika and began to climb the stone steps. Owen waited for Lady Danika and then followed her. The others came behind, a long line of exhausted crew members trudging up the scores of steps. By the time they neared the top, Owen was breathing heavily, his heart pounding beneath his armor. It would be worse, he knew, for an attacker to climb all those stairs while defenders threw stones and hindered their way. About twenty steps below the summit, a long, wide stone landing, like a massive balcony, circled the top. *Here,* he told himself, *is where they'll pause, re-form their lines, and ready themselves for the final push up to the top. We'll hold the high ground... but for how long?*

He climbed the last of the steps, coming out with the others upon the pyramid's flat summit, at least a hundred paces wide and lined with stone columns that had once held a stone walkway, and was now only rubble.

Well... at least we won't run out of stones to throw.

The pyramid must have been a temple after all, because a large black stone altar sat in the center of the smooth tiled surface, surrounded by more rubble. The surface of the pyramid was easily large enough to hold hundreds of spectators around the altar.

He paced along the top of the stairs, mentally measuring the length of a shield wall they could place here. Unfortunately, there was far more open ground than there were crew members—especially crew members with shields. *They'll move quickly up the stairs, and by the time they reach the landing below, they'll be tired, and we'll be throwing stones the entire way, but they'll pause and re-form their lines before coming against us.* In his mind, he once again relived the many tactical discussions he had held with Keep-Captain Brice Awde, examining the battle from all angles. "*Fight the battle first in your mind, Owen,*" he remembered Keep-Captain Awde telling him repeatedly. "*How does it end?*"

It ends, he knew, *with Galas's men swarming around our flanks to strike our rear and shatter us. Tired or not, there's just too many of them.*

"We can't defend here," he whispered, recognizing the truth of it the moment the words slipped past his lips.

"Owen!" Gali yelled from behind, excitement in her voice.

The young woman rushed over, grabbed his wrist, and pulled him along with her toward the dark stone altar. "Come quickly. Fioni found something."

Broken stones lay near the altar, where Lady Danika, Fioni, and Kora stood, examining something alongside the altar before them. Fioni held a fluttering torch, her face grim; as Gali drew him closer, he saw why: sitting back against the stone altar, almost in repose, were the skeletal remains of what had once clearly been a man. An age-browned skull rested atop the rusting remains of a ring-mail coat and rotten shreds of dark clothing and boots. A hole the size of his hand had been punched right through the rusted ring-mail links, directly over the skeleton's ribcage, leaving the shattered bones visible. Several feet away from the corpse, an elaborately carved wooden staff had been thrust between stones so that it still stood upright all these years later. The top foot or so of the staff had been broken. It was still attached but leaned away from the rest of the staff at an angle. Even from here, he could see that the runes carved into the length of the staff were Fenyir. He turned to Fioni, cold understanding rippling through him. "This is *him*, isn't it, your uncle?"

She nodded, her lips mashed together. "It's Denyr."

"But…" said Lady Danika, her voice faltering, "if someone killed him, why break his staff and leave it standing like that all these years?"

Owen stared at the corpse, his anguish mounting. "The jewel case—"

"Isn't here," she finished for him. "Serina's heart is not here."

"Then," said Kora sadly, "that means…"

"That we can't stop Serina," said Lady Danika. "We've failed."

Lightning crackled across the sky.

Chapter 45

Galas

"You said we'd catch up to them before nightfall," Galas admonished his tracker, Grotlin. Night had fallen, and many of his men now carried lit torches. Another of his men held a torch for Grotlin while the tracker knelt on all fours on the broken stone avenue that ran through the ruined city.

"Was *before* they jumped up the Hishtari guppies," the tracker answered as he peered intently at one of the rare boot tracks left among all the stones. He snorted in amusement. "Was a nice piece of work, though."

"Not so nice that Fioni ain't dead for it." Galas tamped down his mounting agitation, grinding his teeth. This was all taking too long. The queen would be on her way by now. If she had to finish his work, she'd be displeased. She might even start asking questions about how Dey and all his men had died. He needed to give her the Dain woman to play with. "How much longer?"

Grotlin stood, noisily hawked a mouthful of snot, and then swallowed it instead of spitting. Galas watched in disgust as Grotlin pursed his thin lips. "Each time we make up ground, they go faster. Someone's tellin' tales on us, I figure."

"You're sure?" Galas asked, now feeling unseen eyes on him. He spun about, looking in all directions, feeling suddenly vulnerable, as if one of the powerful Kur'teshi crossbows were aimed at his back right now. *No,* he realized. *They barely had enough bolts for the ambush; I doubt they held any back.* Still, just the same, he slipped between Grotlin and his first mate, Aegrism. Aegrism, no fool, shifted uncomfortably, his captured crossbow resting across his thick shoulder as his gaze darted about.

"I think I sees 'em a while back," Grotlin said, scratching at the thick mole on his cheek. "If I was a gamblin' man, which I is, I'd say they hidin' over there." Without pointing, he looked toward a cluster of fallen stones ahead and to their right, with a commanding view of the broken avenue.

"Is that a fact?" Galas thrummed his fingers on his sword hilt.

"Ayup," Grotlin grunted.

"That new toy of yours..." He turned to Aegrism. "How many bolts you find?"

"A few," Aegrism answered with a sly grin.

"All right. We're going to set a large fire right here, act like we're setting up for the night. You, me, and Grotlin. None other."

"We want prisoners?" Aegrism asked.

Galas sucked on his front teeth as he thought about it, and then shook his head. "Later, after we got the kingdom bitch and the sword."

#

As ordered, his men built a large fire, set to cooking stores for dinner, while Galas, Grotlin, and Aegrism slipped away into the dark ruins, slowly circling around the collapsed building Grotlin thought the most likely place for scouts to be hiding. Galas was no woodsman, but when necessary, he could be stealthy enough. He had learned long ago that the unseen knife striking from behind was often much more effective—and less dangerous—than direct confrontation, although there was a time for both. Aegrism, by comparison, was surprisingly quiet, nearly more so than Grotlin. Galas made a mental note of this little fact; knowing who could and couldn't quietly slide a blade between your ribs was potentially crucial knowledge.

They circled around the rubble, a collapsed tower of some kind, coming in on it from behind. With luck, the scouts would be watching the campfires—if Grotlin had been correct. If he was full of shit, Galas might be looking for a new tracker this night.

Grotlin paused often, remaining motionless, listening to the silent city around them. The only noise Galas heard came from his own men, laughing and talking around their fires. At the edge of the ruins, Grotlin dropped down on his belly, and Galas and Aegrism did the same. They slowly crawled forward, keeping behind cover whenever possible. Finally, Grotlin stopped entirely, turned, and slowly motioned to a gap between two large stone blocks sitting near the top of the fallen tower. Galas stared, not seeing anything. But then, he caught a quick flicker of movement. One of the shadows between the blocks had shifted. Grotlin held up his thumb and forefinger, silently mouthing the number two. Now, Galas was able to see two distinct forms kneeling amidst the rubble, watching his men around their fires. He turned to Aegrism, who was slowly fitting a bolt to his already cocked weapon, and nodded.

Aegrism rose into a kneeling position and pulled the stock of the weapon in tightly against his shoulder, aiming down its bolt. Soon, Galas knew, they'd take up the hunt again, and this time there'd be no one to warn Fioni's crew. By the time Serina arrived, they'd have the Dain woman, the sword, and all the prisoners they'd need for the voyage home.

The arms of Aegrism's crossbow snapped forward, sending the deadly bolt cracking off into the night.

Chapter 46

Owen

With Denyr long dead and no idea what had befallen the jewel case containing Serina's heart, all outcomes seemed dark. While Fioni, Kora, and Lady Danika debated the next course of action, Owen moved away to consider how best to fight Galas. Even if they had found the jewel case containing Serina's heart, just sitting there waiting for them, they would still have had to deal with the warriors coming to kill them. He took a torch from one of the crew and stalked back and forth along the top of the wide stairs that covered the entire side of the pyramid. The problem he needed to work out was how to stop Galas and his men from spilling around the side of their shield wall and enveloping them. The obvious answer was to construct obstacles and funnel the attackers in where they could hold them. Much of the rubble lying about the outer rim of the summit was small enough to move by hand. In time, they could easily move enough of the rubble to create barriers on their flanks, but they didn't have that much time. It would take at least a day of hard labor. At best, they had hours—and maybe not even that long.

He moved down the stairs to the wide landing before the summit.

His intuition told him this landing, perhaps a dozen feet wide, would be key to the battle, not the summit itself. *But why? What am I missing?*

Once again, he pictured Galas's men storming up the steps: tired, angry, entirely focused on Fioni's crew, who would be raining stones down upon them. He imagined them hitting the landing, re-forming ranks for the final push. And then… Sudden understanding swept over him. *I'm coming at this wrong,* he realized. Now, he remembered another impromptu lesson with the Keep-Captain. "*The best obstacles,*" Awde had said, "*are the ones the enemy sees but disregards as insignificant until it's too late. If you can break up an attacker's momentum at a critical moment in the battle, you can seize the initiative from him.*"

His gaze went from the rubble lying about on the summit to the vital ground before him as he assessed how long it would take to do what he wanted. "There's time," he said to himself, "if we get started right now."

And *if* he could convince Fioni.

Lightning flared, illuminating a solitary figure struggling up the steps. He realized in a moment it had to be one of the two scouts, come to report on Galas's men. "Someone's coming!" he yelled to the others.

Still holding the torch, he moved down to meet the scout, recognizing Kersta, one of the two crew members Kora had said she had left behind to spy on Galas's men. She stumbled and fell forward, blood on her face, and he rushed to help her, hearing the footsteps of others coming behind him. He wrapped an arm around her shoulder, lifting her up again. "You're bleeding."

She wheezed for air, clearly physically spent. "Vadik's… dead… Ambushed us. They're… coming."

"Wodor's balls!" swore Fioni, taking Kersta's other arm and helping Owen bring her to the summit. "How long?"

Kersta shook her head. "Don't... know... I ran... all way."

"I see torches," said Owen, staring down into the ruins below. "They'll be at the steps in a handful of minutes, I'd guess."

"How many?" Fioni asked Kersta.

"At least a hundred, Waveborn... but scum of... clan."

"That seems about right," Fioni said. "How about the Hishtari?"

Kora had handed Kersta a waterskin, and she drank greedily and then wiped her mouth with the back of her hand before shaking her head. "Only Galas's men."

"How do you want to do this, Fioni?" Kora asked her. "We can meet them with sword and axe as they reach the summit. If we move farther back until they're almost on us, they won't be able to use bows."

Fioni's face registered her uncertainty. "If Galas brought all of his men, maybe we could slip away, try and get around him and take back *Iron Beard.*"

"We can't leave!" insisted Lady Danika. "Not until we've destroyed Serina's heart."

"There is no heart!" snapped Fioni. "Besides, we're outnumbered almost two to one—and each of Galas's men will have both shield and armor. Even with the high ground, I don't think we can win here."

Owen stepped between them, placing his hand on Fioni's forearm. "You can. I know how."

Fioni watched him, uncertainty flitting across her features. "Owen..."

"I have a plan. I think it might work."

"Another plan, Owen," she said sadly. "And who will carry it out this time?"

"*I* will—with your permission."

All discussion ceased as the crew silently stared at Owen and

Fioni. *She still doesn't trust me,* he realized, feeling a sinking sensation in his gut. There was nothing more he could do, though. It was her crew; the decision was hers. Her eyes softened, and she smiled. "All right, Owen. I trust you."

He'd have kissed her right there if the others weren't all standing about, watching.

"They'll be expecting a shield wall to meet them at the top of the stairs," Kora said.

He considered Kora. "Do your people know a swine wedge?"

Confusion crossed Kora's face. "A what?"

"It doesn't matter," he said. "We're only going to get one chance to get it right, anyway. For now, I need everyone to pick up stones and help me."

"There's no time for that now," insisted Fioni.

He lifted a chunk of broken rubble the size of his head. "Hurry, all of you!"

Chapter 47

Dilan

Dilan stood behind Serina, considering the black pyramid with the statue of a strange beast-like woman atop it. The pyramid's ironbound doors stood open, its empty interior wafting with the unmistakable aroma of dried blood. They had crossed the island as fast as the ghouls could move—which was snaillike in comparison to how fast the two blood fiends could have moved without them, but Serina had insisted they might yet need soldiers this night. Now, several dozen ghouls remained, a silent, unmoving mass of walking corpses, among whose ranks were the women whose blood Dilan and Serina had just consumed. While he watched, Serina softly swayed before the pyramid, her eyes closed in concentration, her arms held out to the side.

Something felt… *wrong* here. "Mother, what…"

"It's magic, Dilan, the residue of eldritch power—a magic so powerful it has stained the ground." She inhaled deeply, her red eyes flashing open. "This is *a tomb*, my childe!"

He stared in confusion at the empty vault. "Why here, overseeing a mountain pass?"

She entered the vault, turning about and inhaling deeply. "I don't know, but the connection to the dead is clear. Such magic, though. I've never experienced its like before." She inhaled deeply, exposing her fangs, her red eyes shining with awe. "This island hides wondrous mysteries. Once we deal with our enemies, we must unravel them." Without another word, she stormed off, gliding up the mountain like a beautiful, terrifying dream. She paused again when they came out from beneath a massive arch, the silver-bathed city ruins lying below them.

"She's down there," she said softly. "Your bloodline ends this night, Stron."

Chapter 48

Owen

All too soon, Galas's men were halfway up the steps, glaring in hatred.

Owen stood with Fioni's crew in a two-rank shield wall twenty men and women strong along the top of the stairs, waiting for their foe. There were only enough shields for the first rank, armed with long-hafted fighting axes and the remaining Wolfrey longswords, so those in the second rank carried the eight-foot-long ash-wood spears with leaf-shaped iron blades. In the press of battle when the two forces met, the spears would be long enough to thrust over the heads of those in the front. Owen stood now in the center of the first rank, where most could see and hear him. Whether his plan worked or not depended entirely on how fast the others backed him up. If they hesitated—or failed to see him move—he'd die in moments, followed shortly after by everyone else.

Fioni stood on his left, Kora on his right—the iron core for the shield wall. All down the line, each warrior overlapped his or her stout limewood shield with that of the warrior just to the left, creating a single armored mass. Fewer than ten men and women were left to act as reinforcements when warriors fell, or to harass Galas's force with stones. *There's not enough of us,* Owen knew, *not when the screaming and the dying start.* He ground his teeth together as he watched Galas's force steadily climbing toward them, completely filling the stairs with their numbers. If he had even twenty more men, enough to form a third rank or extend his wall, he'd have been content to fight a defensive battle. But with the odds stacked against them, he knew how this fight would unfold. Without a third rank to shore up the first two ranks, to push upon the backs of those in the front, they'd slowly give way to the enemy. Battle between opposing shield walls was, in truth, a shoving match, with each side straining to push back and break apart the other side.

If our wall breaks first...

Those too injured to fight, as well as Lady Danika and Gali, hurled stones down the steps. Most missed, but a few crashed into the enemy, crushing bones and sending men tumbling into one another. The enemy came forward, their front ranks almost at the landing where Owen knew they'd pause and form their own shield wall. He had made his preparations as well as he could in the time he had; now it was up to fate. "*No plan of battle survives the first clash of sword,*" Keep-Captain Awde had always said.

As expected, each of Galas's men carried a shield, with many in leather or hide-armor as well. Their ranks bristled with spears and axes. Although Owen could hear Galas's voice behind his men, egging them on, he couldn't see him.

"Be ready!" Owen screamed above the insults and taunts of Galas's men. "They'll throw spears just before they come on."

The front rank of Fioni's crew began to bunch together as each warrior unconsciously pressed his or her unprotected side closer behind the shield of the warrior on their right. "Keep your pacing!" Kora admonished them. "There is no safe place this night. If you die, know that the crones spun your destiny the day you came into this world, screaming for your mother's tit. Wodor, Fenya, and Orkinus are watching. Give the kin-killing traitors the sword's sleep they've earned!"

The crew cheered.

"Stand fast, true Waveborn!" Fioni's voice rose above the din. "Avenge your yarl and make corpse beer of your foes!"

Again, the crew cheered, a hysterical tint to some of their voices. *Good,* mused Owen. *Anger is better than fear. Fear kills more men than spear or sword.*

The first of Galas's men reached the landing, huddling behind their shields as they waited for the others to catch up, all the time screaming obscenities, telling the women what they'd do to them after the battle. They threw their lit torches forward to land among the steps, casting a bright-orange glow upon the steps. In moments, the enemy's own shield wall took form. Four ranks deep, and wider than their own, the enemy's shield wall pushed the front rank closer to the low pile of broken stones and rubble near the end of the landing—just before the lip of the steps leading up to the summit. The obstacle, if you could even call it that, was barely the height of a man's ankle. Anyone that saw it would easily step over it—but only *if* he saw it in time. Hopefully, the enemy's attention was entirely upon the shield wall awaiting them. Those in the enemy's second or rear rank would be entirely blind to the hazard.

Or so Owen prayed.

Now he saw Galas behind the first two ranks. He wore a speckled helm and stood next to a bald brute of a man bearing one of the Kur'teshi crossbows. Upon seeing Fioni, shock filled Galas's eyes, replaced almost immediately with a leer of satisfaction. "Still alive, cousin? You'll soon wish you weren't."

"Come, craven!" Fioni yelled back. "No one else needs die this night. Let's you and I dance the blanket together."

Galas barked in laughter. "That's not what we'll do beneath the blanket, cousin."

She leaned forward, straining against Owen's shield. "Be calm," Owen admonished. "He's trying to draw you out."

"Tell me," yelled Galas, looking about his men. "Where's that fat whale who taught you how to fight, Vory Eel-Gifted? *He'd* be worthy of dueling, not some fatherless split-ass."

His men cheered, smashing their weapons against their shields.

"Ignore the pile of whale-shit," Kora yelled over the clamor. "He already knows Vory's dead, else he wouldn't dare make the challenge."

Owen saw the signs of the enemy's rage building as they prepared themselves for the violence to come. The front rank began stomping their left boots on the landing and beating their shields in a steady cadence that promised blood.

"Be ready," Owen warned the others, unsure if they could even hear him.

A single warrior broke out from the front rank, darting forward to launch a spear through the air. As the shaft seemed to hang in the air for a moment, the moonlight glinting off its leaf-shaped blade, Owen recognized it was coming for him. He braced himself, waiting until the very last moment. Then he leaped up into the air, letting the spear hit the stones where he had been standing, clattering away harmlessly. A cheer erupted from Fioni's crew, and they began hammering their own weapons against their shields.

"Kill them!" Galas screamed, his face red with rage. "Break them!"

An entire volley of spears flashed through the air just before the enemy surged forward. A spear struck his shield, burying its metal head into the limewood, but Owen cut it loose with his sword. The front rank of the enemy hit the low obstacle, stumbling into it, with several men falling forward unexpectedly. Some had seen it and stepped over it, but in doing so, they slowed down the others, who pushed upon them, stumbling into one another. The enemy faltered, but it would be a fleeting thing, lasting only moments.

"Now!" roared Owen, charging forward down the steps.

He didn't hesitate to see if the others followed him in the Swine Wedge formation that he had drawn out for them with pebbles, showing how it was supposed to work. The Swine Wedge formation was like a spear thrust into the enemy's ranks intended to break shield walls. But if the others weren't with him, he was going to die. He had gambled their lives, trading the high ground for a desperate attack against a superior force, something only a fool would attempt, but something Galas would never suspect. "*And one should never do what the enemy thinks you'll do,*" he heard Keep-Captain Awde's voice in his memory.

His heart surged with pride when he heard the war cries of the others right behind him, and he leaped through the air over the last few steps, a Wolfrey battle cry on his lips. The two forces collided in a bone-shattering crush of shield, steel, and muscle. When Owen smashed into the enemy's ranks, he knocked several men back. A tall man with tattoos covering his forehead and cheeks stared wide eyed at him, but Owen rammed his sword point into the man's mouth. Then he was among the enemy. With his shield before him, he cut over its rim at another man, who also seemed to melt away, without Owen being sure if he had struck him or not. Another man replaced that one, and Owen hammered his shield into his face, knocking him down and stamping over him to get at yet another man. Owen pushed on, shoving and hammering at those before him, using speed and violence to carry him on, trusting Fioni and Kora to safeguard him from the sides. If he didn't cut through Galas's force, they'd be surrounded, and the attack would fail. He was vaguely aware of Fioni and Kora just behind him, the tip of the spear, fighting on either side as he stabbed forward. Men screamed in pain and rage. Spears, swords, and axes flashed in the torchlight. Several times, he felt pressure and blows against his ring mail, but he ignored everything, always pushing forward, always cutting and hacking and stabbing and shoving. It felt as though he were being buried in bodies, the screams and pandemonium deafening. Then he split the skull of a man before him and stepped out past the press of bodies.

Free! I'm through.

Without pausing to appreciate what he had just accomplished, he spun and lashed out at the enemy's rear, striking men down from behind. A moment later, Fioni and Kora were with him, also attacking the enemy in the rear, followed shortly after by even more of the crew. *We've split his shield wall!* When the awful realization of what was occurring spread through the enemy's ranks, many of whom couldn't even defend themselves in the press of bodies, panic began to take hold. *Men don't fight when surrounded,* he knew—*not if they can run.*

The landing, slick now with blood and guts, sent men slipping and falling. Disemboweled men screamed in agony, thrashing about among the severed arms, legs, and heads, further discombobulating Galas's ranks. The fear began to build, spreading now like the fire they had set days earlier. Galas's men began to bunch together for protection, but under assault from front and back, they were so densely packed together even the dead had no room to fall.

They broke.

Those on the periphery fled back down the steps, practically falling over themselves to get away. Others tried to climb over their mates, all pretense at reason gone. A handful tried to put up a defense, locking their shields together. Owen hooked the bottom rim of his shield over theirs to pry open a gap and then cleaved through a man wearing baleen and leather from clavicle to belly button. As his body fell apart, the man's guts poured out like oats from a split sack.

A moment later, their courage shattered, they fled as well.

It was a complete rout.

Owen, his heart pounding painfully in his chest, let his shield slip from its straps to clatter on the steps, and then held his sword between his knees while he quickly patted down his limbs, looking for wounds. Miraculously, he was unharmed.

Fioni collided into him, almost knocking him down in her enthusiastic embrace. "We did it!" she cried, turning and waving her bloody sword at the fleeing enemy. "Run, you craven bastards! Run!" She gripped his chin and kissed him, her lips tasting of blood.

"Are you hurt?" he asked.

"I'm fine," she answered. "I was wrong about you, Owen. I'm sorry. You *are* a battle wizard."

Kora was there a moment later, blood dripping down her forehead. "What now?" she asked Owen.

"Now we go after them," he said. "Organize the crew into groups of at least five. Hurry. The next few minutes are crucial. We can't rest. There're still more than enough of them to reorganize and come back again—and we can't do this twice."

Fioni bit her lip. "I understand, but those men are still Waveborn. If they surrender, we take them alive. Galas, on the other hand..." She scanned the dead and wounded.

Owen saw no sign of Galas, but he did see both Lady Danika and Gali moving among the wounded, helping them. *Thank Father Craftsman for that.* They retrieved the fallen torches and, minutes later, in small handfuls of warriors, began to move down the steps. Near the bottom, they found the first enemy, a man speared through the leg. Fioni spared him, having the others only seize his weapons and bind his wrists. They began to fan out, searching for others.

They froze when they heard a scream of horror in the darkness, followed by an inhuman staccato cry, like nothing Owen had ever heard before. He turned and stared wide eyed at Fioni. Then they heard other men screaming, their cries all too quickly cut off. Something was killing Galas's men. The crew began to edge together, once again becoming a single mass.

"Is it the Blood Queen?" someone asked in a trembling voice.

"Owen," said Fioni. "My sword."

The blood gem in the hilt glowed.

A moment later, a dark shape the size of a bear detached itself from the night, moving forward into the torchlight. Hunched over, with two massively long arms ending in knifelike talons that trailed along the ground, it shambled forward on thin stork-like legs that should not have been capable of bearing its weight. Shiny black feathers at least a foot long covered its torso, leaving only a bare red patch over its wide chest. In the center of that chest sat a glowing red eye. *Another blood gem,* Owen realized in confusion. The creature's large raven-like head swiveled back and forth over the men and women, its small black eyes shining in the torchlight. Its pointed beak—at least two feet long—glistened with dripping blood. Once again, he saw the massive gaping hole in the wolf's torso, the ancient mummified corpse of the Illthori, and the skeletal remains of Denyr, and he knew in a flash of insight how they had all died.

The monster paused, raised its bird head high, and once again emitted that hideous staccato warbling. Dozens of other beasts instantly answered its call, their angry cries echoing around them.

Chapter 49

Danika

While Owen and Fioni had led the others down the steps of the pyramid, Danika and Gali remained behind, helping tend to the wounded. Five of the crew had died during the fighting, with eight more wounded, several so badly they'd die before the sun rose. Galas's force had lost easily three times that. Owen's plan had worked perfectly, achieving a stunning victory that would have made Brice proud.

Danika held the hand of a young man as he bled out, his left leg gone below the knee. Neither she nor Gali was a physician, and applying a tourniquet above the wound had barely even slowed the gush of blood. He cried out a woman's name repeatedly, trying to rise, but she pushed him back down and whispered soft words into his ear as she caressed his forehead. Moments later, he lay still, his eyes open. Melancholy and relief struggled within her as she leaned over and kissed his forehead. *At least his pain is over. How old had he been? Eighteen, younger? Far too—*

A scream of pure, tortured agony shattered the night, followed moments later by more howls of pain rising from the base of the pyramid where the others had gone to hunt down Galas's survivors.

Gali's head snapped up, her eyes wide. "That… what…"

"That's not battle," said Danika, jumping to her feet and dashing to the edge of the pyramid's summit, looking down the steps. From this high up, all she could make out below were the torches and shadows of the crew clumping together in one large mass near the base of the steps. With trembling fingers, she drew Sight-Bringer. She gasped, her skin suddenly clammy, when she saw the dark, menacing shapes converging on the others. "Father Craftsman, help us!"

"What is it? What's wrong?" Gali demanded.

"Run!" Danika screamed. "They're coming!"

Too late, the closest of the… monstrous creatures shot forward, launching themselves on the crew members, tackling them and pinning them to their backs. Now, their own comrades screamed in agony. Danika staggered away from the steps and faced Gali in bewilderment.

"What is happening?" Gali whined, her voice breaking in terror.

And then Sight-Bringer throbbed with occult power, sending a vibration coursing up her arm, washing away her terror. Twice before, the Illthori weapon had saved her life: The first time had been when Modwyn had tried to trick her into opening the gates of Stron's Watch. That time, the sword had revealed Modwyn's hidden force of rebels waiting to storm the fort. The second time had been in Kalishni'coor's occult chambers in the Rose Palace, when he had cast a spell immobilizing the others. That time, the sword had not only freed her from his magic, but had also given her the strength to drive its jagged blade through his black heart, ending his foul life.

Now, it once again warned her. But to what end?

Once, when she had been maybe six or seven, her father had taken her to see a water diviner find a new well in one of the local villages near Castle Dain. He had held a double-forked hickory branch before him as he slowly turned about, all the time chanting a spell. When the forks began to tremble, the mystic smiled broadly, declaring the men needed to dig there. Sure enough, they found water. All her life, she had secretly suspected the mystic had already known where the groundwater lay, and that it had all been a charade, a show for the small folk and children like her, but she mimicked him now, gripping the sword with trembling hands and holding its broken point out before her. While the others screamed and died below, she turned in place. Another jolt of energy shot up her arms when the blade swept past the dark altar atop the summit. *There. There's something there.*

She ran for the altar.

Chapter 50

Owen

Without warning, the monster shot forward, moving far faster than Owen would have thought possible for such a large creature. It slammed into one of the crew, a stout young woman named Helgin who could burp names, knocking her onto her back and pinning her to the ground with its oversized arms. Before Owen could take three steps to help, the monster raised its bird head and rammed its beak through her chest, just above the heart. She screamed in agony, her arms and legs flopping helplessly as the creature began to slurp noisily through its beak.

Owen charged, screaming in fury as he brought Brice Awde's lion-marked longsword down upon the monster's feather-clad back with both hands, aiming for its spine. His sword rocked back, as if he had just struck stone, sending spasms coursing through his forearms as he staggered back in disbelief.

The monster continued to drink, unconcerned.

Now, others charged forward, dozens. Each monster bowled over a crew member, pinning him or her down before ramming its foul beak through their chests. A cacophony of pain-filled shrieks filled the air.

We're being slaughtered!

Nearby, Fioni repeatedly slammed her sword against the back of another monster, to no discernible effect. She staggered back, terror in her eyes as she took in the scene of horror. "Get away!" she shrieked. "Back up the stairs!"

As Owen and the others ran for the stairs, none of the monsters attempted to stop them. Each was too concerned with draining the blood of his friends. *That can't last,* he knew. *They butchered Galas's crew in seconds.*

The survivors flew up the steps, almost climbing over one another. They had lost half the crew in moments, and now, overcome by panic, they practically clawed at one another to get up the stairs first. Fioni came last, with Owen. He turned and saw one of the monsters, its beak still dripping blood, charge up the stairs straight at Fioni.

"Look out!" he cried, knowing it was already too late.

She spun about just as the monster slammed into her, pinning her to the steps. Time seemed to slow: the monster lifted its beak, Fioni roared in defiance, and Owen charged, his sword drawn back. As the monster reared back, it exposed its chest and the glowing blood gem embedded in its center. Owen thrust his sword forward, driving the blade's point into the gem. The impact shuddered up his arms and down his back, and the tip of Brice Awde's sword snapped, but the gem shot free in a shower of sparks. The monster froze, its beak pointed toward the moon. Then, without a sound, it fell off Fioni, tumbling down the stairs and shattering into ashes and black feathers. Owen looked at the broken sword in his hand, the feathers drifting through the air, and then at Fioni. He gripped her hand and pulled her to her feet. "Can you move?"

She stared at him, her eyes wide.

Is she in shock? "Fioni!" he said, shaking her.

She jerked upright, as if suddenly waking. "Go," she said as she picked up her sword with its glowing blood gem. "I'm right behind you."

The dozens of other monsters, already finished with their victims, had paused at the base of the stairs, their heads pivoted toward him, their black eyes shining in the moonlight. Owen flew up the stairs, no longer tired.

Gali met him at the top, her face white. "Hurry! Come with." She grabbed his wrist and dragged him with her.

Owen took one final look over his shoulder to see the monsters climbing the stairs, clearly in no particular hurry. *And why should they hurry? Where are we going to go?*

Gali dragged him to the altar in the center of the summit, where Fioni, Kora, and the others clustered together, now less than half of those who had gone into battle only minutes ago. As he came around the rear of the altar, where shattered stones covered much of the summit, he saw Lady Danika on her knees, an expanse of stones perhaps four feet by four feet cleared around her.

In the light of the torches, he saw that she knelt before a white stone triangle set into the base of the pyramid's summit, ringed by Illthori runes. It was another portal, he realized, like the one they had found on the atoll. They had missed it earlier because of the rubble covering it and because they had been so focused on looking for Serina's jewel case with her heart. Lady Danika held Sight-Bringer's tip near the runes, activating them, causing them to glow with eldritch radiance.

Fioni grabbed his shoulder. "Owen, they're coming!"

The first of the monsters shambled over the lip of the stairs, pausing for a moment as it swung its birdlike head about, its beady black eyes seeking them. A shudder ran through Owen as its gaze fixated on them. It warbled its staccato cry before shuffling forward on its arms and legs. Others answered the cry, appearing behind it. Owen braced himself, gripping his broken sword in both hands, knowing they were all about to die. A grinding noise filled the air behind him, and a quick glance over his shoulder showed the portal sinking. Now, the closest of the monsters was only twenty paces away, shuffling forward. "Is there a way out?" he yelled.

"The portal opens onto a slide of some kind!" Danika yelled. "But it's too dark to see where it goes."

Fioni moved up beside Owen. "It doesn't matter. Take it."

Owen braced himself as the monster shuffled closer.

Then, with Fenyir war cries on their lips, a handful of warriors ran past him, attacking the monster. The creature tackled one of them, pinning the young man to his back before driving its beak through his chest and ignoring the others as they pounded helplessly with axes and spears upon it. Moments later, more of the monsters rushed forward and tackled them as well, killing all of them in moments. He had *never* seen such bravery. His heart was in his throat with helpless frustration as Fioni pulled him away from the carnage. "We have to go."

The others, led by Kora, were already gone, leaving only Lady Danika, Gali, Fioni, and a handful of others awaiting their turn to go down the slide. Owen stared at the triangular opening, more than wide enough for a man like him but too small for those monsters. Just as Kora had said, a stained-black metal slide disappeared into the darkness beneath the opening.

"I can't see where it goes," Gali said to Fioni in panic.

"Away from here," she answered as she picked the young woman up and unceremoniously dropped her onto the slide, where she immediately slipped away, a cry on her lips. Moments later, the last of the crew jumped through the opening, leaving only Owen, Lady Danika, and Fioni.

"Go, my lady," he urged. "I'll be right behind you."

He spun as one of the monsters, finished with its meal, advanced on them. He threw his broken sword at it, but the steel merely rebounded, clattering against the stones.

"Here." Lady Danika tossed Sight-Bringer to him.

He caught the broken sword by the white stone hilt, felt its magic course through him. A moment later, the noblewoman jumped into the portal, leaving only Fioni. She stared at the pile of their dead lying beyond the steps, and the litter that still held the comatose wolfhound. Fioni's anguished eyes met his. "Ekkie…"

"Go!"

"I can't leave her."

Owen slammed into Fioni, knocking her onto the slide, where she disappeared with a whoosh. The monster darted forward, once again moving faster than such a large, ungainly creature should have been able to, but he dodged beneath its outstretched talons, coming up behind it and lashing out at it with the broken tip of the Illthori sword. This time, the blade cut through the rocklike body. The creature lifted its head and screeched in agony as smoke rose from the wound, before falling away and crumbling into ash and black feathers. But dozens of others had circled Owen, and they rushed forward. Owen leaped for the opening, slamming belly first onto the metal slide. In a moment, he was gone, surrounded by darkness and whipping air. It wasn't a slide, he realized, but a metal tube, twisting and turning, tossing him helplessly about as he hurtled down it, faster and faster, desperately holding Sight-Bringer away from him so he didn't impale himself.

Ahead of him, he heard a loud grinding noise, like stone being crushed in a mill. Then he heard the screams rising out of the darkness.

Chapter 51

Dilan

Dilan felt Serina's unease, waiting silently as she looked out over the dead city. The ruins, shining silver under the moon's radiance, extended before them, completely filling the rim of the mountain. Dilan, seeing with the perfect clarity of a night owl, saw every rock, every shattered stone and fallen tower. He inhaled deeply, immediately catching the scent of blood wafting through the still night, as well as... *something else*. Perhaps sensing his concern, she shook her head. "There's a power here I don't yet understand—and *that lack of knowledge* could prove fatal, even to you and me, my childe. We must move with caution. Death walks this island."

He stared at her in confusion. "But we are immortal."

The smile on her lips might have been the saddest thing he had ever seen. "If only." She returned her gaze to the dead city. "These ruins are Illthori. What a discovery. Now that Kalishni'coor is dead, I probably know more about that long-dead race than any scholar does, but even I know very little that I can point to and say is truth. In the centuries since they vanished, they've only left behind relics and myths. Kalishni'coor was fascinated with them, insisting they were the source of magic on this world. He wasted much silver buying every trinket said to be Illthori, but I think they were mostly fake." She was silent for a few moments. When she spoke again, it was only a whisper. "Perhaps I was the fool."

"No," said Dilan quickly, "you are perfect."

She slipped away, ghosting across the ruins toward the vast pyramid in the city's center.

#

Not long after, in the ruins of a courtyard near the base of the pyramid, they found the first corpse, the body of a Fenyir warrior completely drained of blood, a massive hole punched through his chest. Dilan knelt next to the still-warm corpse and pried open the wound with his fingers. "The heart is… gone, Mother. What could have done this?"

"Kalishni'coor mentioned servants the Illthori used. Sentinels called…" She paused, lost in thought for long moments. "Shrikes. He called them shrikes."

"Like the birds of prey that—"

"Impale their victims on thorns," she answered.

Just then, a man stumbled out of the shadows near the entrance to the courtyard, staggering off a broken archway and falling to his knees. Dilan leaped to his feet, but she stopped him, placing a hand on his shoulder. The smell of blood in the air was intoxicating. The man, one of Galas's crew, crawled forward, clutching at a wound in his side. The man, overcome by the terror of whatever chased him, still didn't realize that only a dozen paces away stood two blood fiends and more than thirty ghouls. When a monstrosity lurched out of the shadows behind him, Dilan understood why the man was so terrified. A creature of nightmares pursued him: more than two or three times the size of a man, with long arms ending in talons, stork-like clawed legs, and the head of a bird—including a foot-long pointed beak. The man screamed as the monster surged forward, knocking him down, and then impaling him with a single thrust of its beak. He continued to scream as the monster began to feed.

"Shrike," Serina whispered in awe. When Dilan began to edge forward, she held him back. "Wait." She turned to her ghouls, and without a word of command from her, they stumbled forward.

The shrike, intent on its meal, completely ignored the ghouls until they attacked, throwing themselves upon it and bearing it to the ground with overwhelming numbers. The shrike reared up, tossing ghouls away, ripping at them with its talons and tearing flesh from bone. But the ghouls, already dead, ignored the horrific wounds and rushed back in, seizing its limbs and holding it in place.

Serina slid forward, and Dilan rushed to her side, terrified it might break free of the ghouls. His fear was well founded, as the shrike abruptly ripped an arm free, sending two of the ghouls flying to smash against a nearby wall with a sickening crunch. Before Dilan could move, it lashed out at Serina—but with no more effort than it would take to overpower a toddler, she caught the arm and held it still over her head. Dilan took hold of the shrike's arm, freeing her to examine the beast. Her fingers trailed over its feathered chest, resting atop the glowing blood gem embedded there. "What *are* you?" she asked it, staring into its glassy black eyes.

Dilan grunted, straining to hold the beast's arm in place. "It's strong, Mother."

"*Death magic.*" She reached up and ran her fingers over the shrike's glistening beak before placing her bloody fingertips in her mouth. She gasped in sudden understanding. "*It's a flesh simulacrum, Dilan*, a necromantic construct like my ghouls. But it's so much more than that. It's also like *us*, Dilan, kept alive through blood consumption." She laughed, clapping her hands in delight. "Imagine,

Dilan, centuries after its creators have become dust, this wondrous sentinel continues to guard the city!"

Other shrikes were approaching now, at least a dozen of them. "Mother," he said, a note of caution in his voice.

She ignored him, instead gripping the blood gem embedded in the shrike's chest. Up close, Dilan now saw it was attached to a metal frame of some kind, a golden triangle hammered into the shrike's dead flesh. With a single soft grunt, Serina tore the gem free from the shrike's chest, the gem trailing small hairlike threads. The shrike stiffened and dissolved into ash and black feathers.

The other shrikes surged closer, fanning out within the compound. Dilan hissed at them, baring his fangs. The ghouls spread out to stop them as Serina stared at the blood gem in her fingers, seemingly oblivious to the danger. "Mother," he repeated, more urgently this time.

She glanced at him. "Be careful, my brave childe. They were designed to go for the heart first, and if they impale yours..."

The ghouls rushed forward to grasp at the shrikes, which, in turn, knocked down the closest ghouls and used their beaks to impale them. But the ghouls' hearts no longer pumped blood, nor served any other purpose, and the impaled ghouls kept fighting, reaching up to grasp at the shrikes. The other ghouls rushed in. In moments, each shrike battled several ghouls in a silent but no less violent battle.

Dilan attacked, hissing as he leaped among them.

Chapter 52

Owen

Hot, dry air blasted Owen's face as he hurtled down the tube, surrounded by darkness and the growing intensity of the grinding noise and the screams. Then the screams stopped, and just as abruptly, he burst out of the darkness and into a vast chamber lit by torches, revealing a monstrous machine of giant rotating stone cogs directly in his path. The tube led to a ramp that, in turn, sat upon a metal frame, a ramp placed at the edge of the machine so that it fed into the rumbling stone cogs. The cloud of dust hovering over the machine did nothing to obscure the grinding stone cylinders that now glistened wetly, and he knew in a single heart-wrenching moment why the screams had stopped. Helpless, he watched Fioni ahead of him as she slid toward the ramp and the cogs.

It's going to crush her!

Kora, standing at the side of the ramp, swung a long-hafted axe at one of the metal struts holding it in place, sending it tilting lopsided with a crash.

Fioni smashed into the stone side of the machine instead of the cogs.

A moment later, Owen slammed into Fioni. Pain lanced through him as he flew up over her, knocking the breath from his lungs as he struck the edge of the machine and began to slide face first into the cogs. Hands grasped his breeches, half-yanking them around his buttocks as someone hauled him back. He fell once more atop Fioni. "Gods, get off me, you musclebound whale!" she groaned, shoving him away.

Lady Danika was before him, helping him sit up, her brown eyes filled with concern. He didn't resist as she pried Sight-Bringer from his grip and slid it into the sheath on her back. He shook his head as the chamber continued to spin about him. "Fine. I'm fine," he mumbled as the dizziness ebbed.

Fioni was sitting up as well now, running her hands over her body. "What is this?" she asked, looking about her. Including Kora and Lady Danika, Gali and fifteen crew members stood about in dazed shock, several still somehow holding the torches they had slid down the tube with.

"The city's underground, I think," said Lady Danika.

"Gods," said Fioni in anguish as she took in the survivors. "The others…"

Kora, her eyes filled with sorrow, softly shook her head.

Fioni's shoulders trembled. "So few?"

"We were lucky," said Kora. "The machine didn't start at first, not until most of us were already down and moving about. Gali, Vadik, Hain, and Dagmar, though…" She looked away, her face pale. "They were standing atop the cogs when the machine came to life. Gali jumped away, but the others… *didn't.*"

"What is this horror?" Fioni demanded, rising to unsteady feet and moving about the chamber, slowly circling the machine, its stone sides as high as her waist, its giant cogs still grinding away. He noticed, with some relief, that the gem on the hilt of her sword was dark once more, which hopefully meant none of those monsters was nearby.

Owen followed her, his mind reeling. The rounded stone ceiling above them was at least twenty feet high, the chamber itself over a hundred feet wide. The walls, built from thick stone blocks, curved inward at the top. The metal tube they had slid down hung from an opening in the ceiling and fed into the ramp and the cogs. The machine took up most of the chamber, but around its edges sat ancient, dusty worktables holding tools, rusted chains, and other detritus. Along the curved ceiling and down the walls ran corroded metal pipes, which still dripped fluid. At opposite ends of the chamber stood two six-sided tunnels leading on into darkness. As he followed Fioni around the edge of the machinery, he trailed his fingers along its humming exterior, mystified at its role here beneath the temple's summit.

"Fenya's love," whispered Fioni just ahead of him, her voice filled with horror as she stared at something on the far end of the machine.

He hurried forward, recoiling in disgust when he saw the obscene mound of what looked like black gravel piled up before them— covered by a glistening new layer of wet blood and shards of gleaming white bone. "Father Craftsman, save us," he whispered. *It's crushed bone.*

His gaze snapped from the obscene mound, to the machine, to the tube from the temple's summit. The machine began to slow and then ground to a halt, dust still in the air. "They… *sacrificed* victims up there," he said in disbelief.

"What kind of a civilization murders so many people it needs a machine to dispose of the remains?" Fioni asked bitterly, making fists of her hands.

"We should go," Owen said. "Those monsters may have another way down here."

"Which way?" asked Fioni, glancing at the two tunnels.

"It doesn't matter," said Owen, staring at the bone pile, "as long as it's away from here."

#

Fioni chose a tunnel and led the survivors away. Unlike the tunnel beneath the atoll, these passages held no glowing runes along their walls to provide light. Whatever magic had still been somehow working then, now their only light source was the few remaining torches, which were already beginning to sputter; they needed to find their way out of the underground before the torches died.

Ankle-deep pools of foul-smelling black water filled entire sections of the passageway, soaking their boots. At regular intervals, small chambers holding ancient cabinets and rusted tools sat silent and dark, blanketed in a glistening coat of dust an inch thick. At other times, they slipped past vast chambers filled with long-dormant machines. Along the sides of the passageway ran corroded metal pipes. Once, Owen paused, placing his ear against the pipe. At first, he heard nothing, but then, almost imperceptible, a soft musical trilling echoed in his ear; a moment later, the pipe was silent once again. *Shades of a long-dead race?*

He shuddered, hurrying after the others.

Glistening spiderwebs, some ten feet in circumference, blanketed the passageway, and Fioni used her sword to pull them away, but within a handful of minutes, they were all trailing webs anyway, brushing furiously at their heads and necks. Owen, remembering the nell spider, tried to look in all directions at once, especially the tunnel's ceiling.

They passed rusted handcarts and barriers so old the wood had petrified, becoming stonelike. Fioni paused before an intersection of identical tunnels, and Owen slid up next to her. He noted the flickering flames on her torch. "That way," he said, following the bend in the flames.

"Are you sure?"

"Not even a bit."

Her lips tight, she moved down the passageway.

Minutes later, they entered another large, open chamber filled with silent, rusting machinery, all covered by a blanket of sparkling dust and cobwebs. Across the chamber, they saw a flight of stairs leading up into the darkness. Fioni took the stairs, which led to another passageway. Here, the air—although stinking of rusted metal, damp earth, and rot—also carried the promise of fresh air. Fioni moved quickly down the passageway, her torch flickering. She began to trot, no longer concerned with the spiderwebs. The only sound was the steady pounding of their boots, their strained breaths, and the constant drip of water from the pipes overhead.

Thick tree limbs, some several feet wide, had grown through the walls here, crushing the stone apart and growing across the passageway, slowing them down while they climbed over them. Giant luminous mushrooms sprouted atop the roots.

"Does this mean we are close to top?" Gali asked hopefully as Owen hoisted her over one of the larger roots.

"It must," he said while suspecting the roots grew much deeper than he'd like to admit.

Then he noticed for the first time that the air had grown moister, warmer. Another chamber lay ahead of them, the largest they had seen yet and filled with ancient machinery, long rows of rusted metal containers, each adorned with glass faces covering dials and knobs. Copper tubing and metal wires—even thinner somehow than the finest ring-mail coats—ran between the machines, stringing them together. He touched one of the machines, instantly yanking his hand back when power flowed through his fingers and up his arm, so similar to the energy that flowed from Sight-Bringer's hilt. *It's the same magic—still there, but… sleeping perhaps, despite the centuries.* Lady Danika joined him. The noblewoman reached out her hand. "My lady," he cautioned.

She touched the machine and, just as quickly, yanked her fingers back. She turned in place, her gaze drifting over the seemingly endless banks of machines. "What is all this?"

"I don't know," he said helplessly, feeling insignificant, "but I think maybe these machines are connected somehow to the weather, the lightning?"

Gali's face paled, and she trembled like a leaf. "Ancestors, help us."

"The others are getting ahead," he said, motioning for the women to hurry along.

At the far end of the chamber, Fioni and the others clustered in heated conversation before an ancient metal scaffolding, now almost completely rusted through, that led up to another passageway with stairs.

Hope gave him energy. *Up means out.*

Owen and the two women joined the others, examining the scaffolding, a series of rusted struts and supports. It could fall apart under their weight in a moment, he knew. "What do you think?" he asked Fioni.

Fioni snorted. "I think you go *last*, Northman."

She locked her fingers together, made a cup. "You first, little mouse," she said to Gali.

Without hesitation, Gali stepped onto her cupped hands, and Fioni hoisted her up onto the scaffolding. It creaked and groaned as she began pulling herself up it, climbing like a lizard. A metal strut popped beneath her weight, but she was already pulling herself up onto the stairs. He watched the still-shaking scaffolding with concern.

"Don't go far!" Fioni yelled to Gali.

"Just a peek," Gali answered, her voice trailing off as she disappeared from sight.

In silence, they all watched and waited, the remaining torches little more than sputtering flames, casting only a dim light. Owen fidgeted, softly grinding his teeth. "I'm light," said Kora. "Hoist me up."

Fioni raised her palm to silence her. A moment later, Gali's beaming face was back. "It's the surface, thank the ancestors."

Fioni motioned to Kora. "You next."

Kora dropped her fighting axe on the stone floor, stepped into Fioni's cupped hands, and sprang up the scaffolding, once again sending it rocking. As with Gali, it held, and moments later, Kora was on the stairs.

Fioni cupped her hands for Lady Danika. "My lady of Wolfrey."

The noblewoman scrambled up the scaffolding. Kora reached down, grabbed her hands, and pulled her the rest of the way up. The rest of the women went next, followed by the smaller men. Each time, the scaffolding creaked and strained, vibrating under the weight, but it held. Soon, only Fioni, Owen, and a handful of the larger men remained. Owen eyed the rickety scaffolding. "Maybe you should go next," he said to Fioni.

"Maybe you should remember who's in charge around here," she shot back, gesturing to one of the men to go next.

As the larger man climbed the scaffolding, it swayed and creaked, almost screaming in protest. Another strut broke free, but the man was soon at the stairs. Only one torch remained now, flickering softly. The other men climbed up, but each time, Owen was certain the entire structure was going to fall apart. Then it was just him and Fioni. He leaned in closer to her, lowering his voice so that only she could hear. "What do you want to do when we get to the surface?"

Her eyes were filled with regret. "I know your lady wants to keep looking for the heart, but..."

"I know. We can't search an entire city."

"Not with those *things* out there, not with Serina also looking for us. I made my father a promise, but... I just don't see how I can keep it now. I have a responsibility to save as many of my people as I can." Her voice trailed off.

His despair was crushing, but he was all out of clever plans. "I understand, but you didn't answer my question."

"Are you coming?" Kora called down.

"We find our way back to the beach. We might be able to take *Iron Beard* and sail from here. Maybe we can even trap—" Her eyes widened as she stared at the glow coming from the gem on her sword hilt.

"Damn it," he said, spinning about.

Red lights glowed from the far end of the chamber. A moment later, at least a dozen of the monstrous bird-bear creatures shambled forward out of the darkness. Owen picked up the axe Kora had dropped. "Climb now!"

"What is it?" Kora demanded.

Fioni's gaze snapped from the approaching beasts to Owen, to the scaffolding, and then to another passageway, nearby. He understood her consternation: there was only time for one of them to make the ascent before the monsters caught the other. "Fioni, go!" he urged.

Shaking her head, she looked up at Kora. "Take the crew and head for *Iron Beard!*"

"What? No!" Kora shook her head in disbelief. "Wait! I'm coming back down."

"Sail from this place and never return," Fioni said as she kicked at the scaffolding, sending it shuddering. Flakes of rust and broken struts fell. Owen slammed his axe into the struts and then yanked

Fioni back as the entire thing came down with a screech of twisting metal. Then, coughing and choking, he saw the flicker of the torch on the stone floor. Still holding Fioni's arm, he picked up the dying torch, and they staggered away down the other passageway. A dozen red eyes pursued them.

Chapter 53

Serina

Serina stood back, watching the battle. The ghouls, possessing supernatural strength and savagery, threw themselves relentlessly upon the shrikes, trying to overwhelm them with numbers. The shrikes, however, shrugged off the ghouls' attacks, methodically pulling the undead men and women apart. It was like watching a full-grown warrior battle toddlers. In frank fascination, Serina slowly circled the fighting, watching these amazing creations: bear, bird, and gods only knew what else. While one of the shrikes struggled with several ghouls, Dilan, taking advantage of the distraction, swept in and ripped free the blood gem embedded in its chest. In a moment, the shrike disintegrated in a cloud of dust and feathers.

Nearby, another ghoul, one of the young women they had drained earlier, tried to leap atop one of the shrikes, but the shrike caught her and ripped her in half. Her bloodless organs spilled out in a rush. Another shrike, this one with three ghouls hanging from its back, spun about, sending the ghouls flying. One of them, a rotting Kur'teshi mercenary, smashed into Dilan from behind, knocking him down. Before Dilan could recover, the shrike shot forward, pinning him and drawing back its beak to strike.

No!

Serina swept forward and caught the shrike's beak, holding it in place above Dilan's chest. Then she ripped it free with a single wrench before using it to club away the disfigured shrike, sending it smashing into an ancient fountain. She dropped the beak and pulled Dilan to his feet. "Mother, we must run," he said.

"I do not run from battles."

Even now, the shrikes were finishing with the last of her ghouls, tearing them apart as if they were only paper. *Now we know why the Illthori needed weapons like Sight-Bringer,* she realized, *in case they lost control of their sentinels.* Great sorcerers the Illthori may have been, but they had also been necromancers—like her. Despite surviving all these centuries on the blood of animals, the shrikes were still just necromantic creations—not true blood fiends.

And if necromancy had created them, necromancy could destroy them.

She began to cast a spell, a variation on one used to sever souls from the realms of the dead. Occult energy flowed into her, like a river into the sea. Shivers of ecstasy coursed through her, far more satisfying than coitus could ever be. Long before Ator had rewarded her with the blood-fiend kiss for the souls she had sacrificed to him, Serina had been a master witch, far more powerful than any mage she had known—including her one-time ally, Kalishni'coor, despite what that fool may have believed. Now, as the shrikes advanced on her and Dilan, she reached the pinnacle of her spell, sending invisible tendrils of dark magic spiraling out from her fingertips in a web that swept over the glowing red blood gems embedded in the chests of the shrikes.

Standing protectively before her, Dilan hissed in challenge.

Serina, her head tilted back, shrieked as the spell rippled outwards, expanding in a concentric eldritch wave that washed over the nearby ruins and on into the city. The force of the spell cracked each gem into shards and shattered the closest ruins. Serina fell to her knees as the shrikes turned to ash and feathers, the broken blood gems tinkling onto the stones of the courtyard. Dilan knelt and wrapped his arms around her, his concern strong through the bond they shared. "Mother..."

"It's all right, my childe," she whispered. Holding onto his arm, she staggered to her feet and buried her face in his neck. "We must keep going. My heart is near. I can feel it now, calling to me."

"What about those things?"

"Gone... but I must learn this island's secrets. Such wonders."

Chapter 54

Danika

Danika stumbled up the stairs, torn by the need to go back and save Owen and Fioni and her duty to find Serina's heart. When she heard the metallic clamor of what could only have been the scaffolding collapsing, she knew there was no longer anything she could do for Owen and Fioni. They were on their own once more. Kora swept by, grabbing her arm and pulling her along. "Hurry! Move!"

"But where?"

"Away from this cursed place."

They came out through a wide, broken opening into the cool night air and a star-filled sky. The stairwell had come out in the midst of a shattered shell of a ruin, now overgrown by weeds and choked by snakelike vines. The rusted remains of Illthori machines surrounded them. Danika, loss wrenching her heart, spun in place, trying to find her bearings. There, rising nearby and blocking the stars, was the giant temple pyramid.

"I think we're north of where we entered the city," she overheard Kora saying to the others.

"What are we going to do?" one of the others asked, a plaintive whine in his voice.

What indeed?

"What about Fioni?" another asked.

"Fioni will catch up to us if she… if she can. For now, her orders were clear. We're to head back to the beach and take *Iron Beard*."

"That's suicide," another woman said. "There's less than twenty of us. We can't take that ship."

"We take that ship, or we die!" Kora's voice became heated.

Danika stepped in front of her, forcing her to face her. "And what if you do take the ship, what then?"

"Then we sail from here and never come back."

"You can't do that! We have to find the heart."

"No, we don't. I'm sorry, but this time, I'm going to obey Fioni. I'm going to save as many of the crew as I can. We're done here. This quest is over." Kora spun away.

Suddenly overwhelmed, Danika was barely aware as Gali took her arm and led her away to sit and recover as Kora and the others made their plans. *We're leaving. We've failed.* She sat there, hugging herself, feeling feverish with manic energy. *Serina will kill thousands.* She drew Sight-Bringer and held the jagged blade up before her eyes, staring morosely at the moonlight glinting from it. "Why did you come to me?" she whispered. "I don't understand how we can come this far…" The constant lightning over the Godswall flared once more, clearly showing the tower in the distance with its top broken and hanging at an angle. Danika inhaled in sudden realization as Sight-Bringer throbbed with occult power, sending a vibration up her arm. Once again, she saw the skeletal remains of Denyr and his broken staff thrust upright into the stones—its tip broken so that it hung at exactly the same angle as the tower. *He must have known those things were coming for him. He was trying to leave a message.*

"Are you okay?" Gali stared at her in concern.

"I'm fine," she lied. "But thirsty."

"I go find water," the young woman said before darting off.

While Kora and the others conversed about the best path back to the beach, Danika rose and slipped away into the ruins, heading for the tower.

Part 4:
Promises

Chapter 55

Owen

Owen and Fioni had been running down the passageway when the entire underground rocked violently, sending them reeling. Dust and stones cascaded down onto them, coating them. The glow from the gem in Fioni's sword abruptly disappeared, leaving only the guttering remains of the torch Owen held, which would die out in minutes at best. "What was that?" Fioni asked, coughing and hacking. "It was like the entire city just ran aground."

Owen pulled her to her feet and dragged her along with him, dust and gravel continuing to sift down upon them. "Once, in Wolfredsuntown, when I was little, the ground shook like that. Homes fell apart. Men said that a part of the mountain had collapsed."

"You think a mountain fell? This island *is* a mountain."

"I don't know what happened, but we need to find a way out of this underground now."

They came to another intersection. Fioni stared at Owen and then the flickering tongue of flame on the torch. "If we choose the wrong way, there may not be enough—"

The torch went out, plunging them into complete darkness.

Fioni exhaled. "Fenya's tits!"

"This way," said Owen, still holding her wrist and pulling her to the left. "I think the flame was blown out, which means fresh air… *maybe.*"

They shuffled along the left-hand tunnel in darkness. He kept his grip on her wrist and trailed his axe head along the wall, expecting to see the glow of red eyes behind them at any moment. He stopped abruptly, smelling fresher air. "Do you—"

"I do. Just ahead."

When his foot struck something, he fell forward, slamming into what felt like steps, smashing his elbow and knee. His axe clattered against the stones, and it took some grasping about blindly before his fingers touched the wooden haft once more.

"Are you all right?" she asked in amusement.

He was probably lucky she couldn't see his face in the dark. "I'll live," he said as she helped him back up. "Stairs."

"Then let's go up."

As they mounted the steps in the dark, he found himself imagining broken sections of stairs where he'd fall, but then the stairs came out on a landing, twisted about, and carried on, exposing the opening and the stars above. Clean, fresh air caressed his skin—they had somehow found another exit. "Thank you, Father Craftsman," Owen whispered.

Fioni snorted as she pulled herself free of his grip and began to climb the steps. "Your god has no eye on this land, Owen. You'd be better off thanking mine—Wodor, Freya, and Orkinus… although truth be heard above the wind, I don't think they'd give a whale's wet turd what some kingdom knight had to say."

"I'll thank whoever gets me back outside."

He followed her out into the open, to the rubble of another fallen Illthori structure, barely the shell of what had once been a large stone building. "What now?" he asked, looking about him.

"I don't know," she answered with resignation. "Nor do I know why those monsters just stopped pursuing us."

#

Owen and Fioni moved slowly through the ruins, searching for Kora and the others, who must have come out of the underground nearby. After the complete darkness of the underground, the starlight and moon provided more than enough light to make their way. They neither saw nor heard any sign of the monsters, but just the same, they both kept a watchful eye on the gem in Fioni's sword, which, thankfully, remained dark.

When he saw movement in the shadows nearby, he grabbed Fioni's arm and pulled her down beside him, hiding behind a shattered stone column. He put his lips near her ear. "There's someone there, but I think they dropped out of sight at the same time I saw them."

She put two fingers into her mouth and whistled into the darkness, a short trill that he had heard many times before aboard *Fen Wolf*, usually when someone wanted to get the attention of someone farther forward, or up on the mast. A moment later, they heard an answering whistle from the shadows. Owen's pulse raced. "Does Galas—"

"Maybe. If I take a crossbow bolt through the mouth, you'll know to run." Before he could stop her, Fioni climbed to her feet, sword in hand, and advanced forward.

Owen, grinding his teeth in exasperation, gripped his axe and hurried after her. Then a shadow detached itself from the darkness ahead of them, materializing into a person. Moments later, more shadows appeared. "Fioni?" Kora's voice called out hopefully.

Relief coursed through Owen, and Fioni rushed forward, embracing her friend. More of the crew appeared now, slapping him on the back and welcoming them.

"What about those monsters?" Kora asked.

Fioni shook her head. "Don't know. They stopped after the ground shook."

"We felt it, too."

Gali appeared, tugging frantically on his arm. "Do you see lady?"

"What do you mean?" Now, for the first time, he noted the absence of Lady Danika among the crew. He stared at Gali's worried face. "Where is she?"

"We don't know," answered Kora. "It took us a few minutes before we even realized she was gone. We've been looking for her, but..."

"Damn it," said Fioni softly.

"I'm sorry," said Kora. "She was unhappy when I told her we were going back to the beach."

Owen stared about the ruins, his thoughts racing. *Why would she just run off?* Fioni was staring at him, her eyes shining in the starlight. He watched her, feeling his helplessness welling within him. "Fioni, I —"

She sighed, smiling at him. "We'll find her together."

"Please," interrupted Gali. "I see lady's face when sky light up. There was a tower, that way," said the young woman, pointing into the distance.

Owen stared, seeing nothing now but darkness. Just the same, he felt certain Gali was right.

"Well," said Kora, "let's go find her."

"No," said Fioni with finality. "You're taking what's left of the crew and heading back to the beach."

"Fioni," said Kora, heat in her voice. "You can't—"

"I can. I've lost too many people already."

"Damned stubborn goose, this is crazy!"

"Am I still *Fen Wolf*'s master?" Fioni demanded. "Do I still have your loyalty?"

Kora inhaled deeply and then looked down, practically grinding her teeth. "You are. You do."

"Then you will take what's left of the crew and take back *Iron Beard*, before Galas and his men—if any still live—make it back to the beach as well."

"This is a bad idea."

Fioni's white teeth flashed. "I'm the queen of bad ideas, Kora Far-Sails. Give us until high tide tomorrow. If we're not back by then, sail from here."

"I can't do that," Kora said in anguish.

"You *can*. Do it for me."

A long, heavy moment passed in silence, and then Kora's shoulders slumped. "Aye, I'll do it," she whispered.

"We need to go now," said Owen.

Fioni turned to follow him, but Kora shot forward, embracing Fioni and burying her face in Fioni's neck. "Someday you and I will swim together as black fish," she said, her voice breaking.

"If the gods are kind," Fioni whispered, kissing Kora's cheek before turning away to follow Owen.

Chapter 56

Danika

Danika stood beneath a broken archway, gazing upon the dark tower. It stood at the far end of a shattered courtyard filled with statues of the strange beastlike Illthori women. A ten-foot-tall vine-covered wall surrounded what must have once been a special place to the Illthori centuries ago. At the far end of the courtyard, a large stone bridge spanned the remains of a deep moat that, in turn, circled a small hill upon which sat the solitary tower. Six-sided, like the strange passageways the Illthori built, the tower was seven stories tall, with narrow, triangular-shaped windows running diagonally up its side. Vines grew in and out of the windows and the wide cracks in the tower's walls, giving it the appearance of being woven from vines. The uppermost level of the tower leaned at an angle, as if ready to fall off at any moment.

"You left a clue after all, Denyr," she whispered. "You did your duty."

How long, she wondered, *did you survive here on your own, hunted at night by those monsters—a day, two… longer?* A shudder coursed through her.

Lightning flared, once again turning night to day, revealing the courtyard, its statues and broken fountains, and what must have once been a beautiful mosaic set into its surface, thousands of meticulously placed colored tiles forming a winding pattern, like the eye of a storm. Sight-Bringer's magic flowed through her, bringing the shadows and tiles into sharp relief. She smelled the intermingled scents of mildew, stone, dirt, and rotting vegetation of dead leaves captured in the depths of the moat.

It's in there, she knew, her vision tunneling in on the tower. *Serina's heart—the end of this quest, revenge for my brother, my father...* Brice. All she need do was step forward. Yet she remained in place, frozen in fear, rivulets of sweat running down her spine, her lips trembling. Her hand clutching Sight-Bringer shook so forcefully, she had to grip it with her other hand to hold it steady. "Duty is a double-edged sword," she whispered breathlessly before stepping into the courtyard. Only the stone faces of the Illthori statues saw her, mute witnesses to her courage.

#

On the far side of the stone bridge, a terraced stone path led up to the tower on the hill. Danika climbed the path, her thoughts a storm of emotions. The entrance to the tower had collapsed long ago, leaving a ten-foot mound of ruins: loose stones, weeds, and broken pieces of wall. Winding completely through the mound, like a spider's web, were the same thick vines that choked the tower. Atop the mound, a wide fallen gap in the wall led into the tower's dark interior.

Facing the mound, she considered how best to climb it. She'd need both hands, so she slid Sight-Bringer once again into its sheath, immediately regretting the loss of its magic. She inhaled deeply before grasping one of the thick vines with both hands, intending to use it to pull herself up the steep bank. A moment later, fire burned through her palms. She cried out in agony, dropping the vine and staggering back. At first, she thought something had bit her, but then she realized it had been the vine. It had burned her palms somehow. Waves of pain coursed up her arms, filling her eyes with tears. *The vines are poisonous.*

"No," she said through gritted teeth.

Her fingers trembling, she drew Sight-Bringer and used its razor-sharp edge to cut away strips of cloth from her shirt before wrapping them tightly around her hands. Once again, slipping the broken sword into its sheath, she glared at the vines. "You're not stopping me."

She gripped the vine and began pulling herself up the steep bank hand over hand, climbing as quickly as she could. Her skin, through gaps in the strips, burned with the vine's poison, but she forced herself to keep going, to keep pulling herself up, knowing she'd never be able to do this again if she quit now. She cried out in agony, pulling herself up atop the mound. Drenched in sweat, she threw the vine away and fell to her knees, moaning, squeezing her fingers, and sobbing. Had Kalishni'coor's torturers possessed these vines, she'd have broken the first time they used them. The pain was indescribable. "It's too hard, Brice," she moaned, eyes closed. "Please help me. I can't do this by myself."

There was no answer.

When she finally felt capable of moving again, she slowly drew Sight-Bringer, but numb with pain, her fingers could no longer grasp it, and it fell between her knees. Moaning in frustration, she forced herself to pick it up again. Balancing it atop her palm, she somehow managed to wrap one of the cloth strips around it, securing it to her hand. Then she glared at the opening in the tower, breathing deeply as she struggled for the strength to carry on. "Duty," she whispered as she staggered through the tower's fallen wall.

Chapter 57

Owen

Owen and Fioni stepped onto the tower's courtyard as lightning flared once again over the Godswall, highlighting the broken tower. "Does that tower—"

"Denyr's staff," Fioni said softly. "Danika was right, and I was wrong. Denyr must have hidden the jewel case with Serina's heart in the tower and left his staff upright as a clue. I'm sorry, Father. I was going to betray my promise."

"Let's find Danika—and Serina's heart. We can still finish this."

He led her onto the courtyard, past the broken fountains and among the statues of a long-dead race, whose oversized feline eyes even now seemed to follow their path. Fioni stood before one of the statues, staring up at it. Behind them, near the entrance to the courtyard, Owen thought he heard something. He spun about, staring into the darkness but seeing nothing.

"What?" she whispered.

"I thought I heard something, a creaking noise."

He listened for several moments, but the night was eerily silent.

"A tree branch in the wind," she finally offered.

There was no wind, nor had there been since they had passed through the Mouth of the Gods. A nagging familiarity tugged at him. He knew that sound, but he was so tired, he wasn't thinking clearly. Then his eyes widened in surprise when he saw a soft glow coming from the gem in Fioni's sword. *There's another blood gem nearby!* At that exact moment, his thinking clarified, and he realized what he had heard—the sound of someone spanning a crossbow's arms.

He threw himself atop Fioni, bringing her crashing down as a wooden bolt exploded into shards against the marble statue where she had been standing a moment before. They scurried behind the ruins of a waist-high stone fountain as another bolt cracked over their heads, winging off into the night. They huddled together behind the fountain when a mocking voice called out from the other side of the broken archway, "Are you still alive, cousin?" Galas asked.

"Come find out!" she yelled back.

Galas laughed in response. "I'm glad," he called out, his voice echoing across the courtyard. "This is the way it should end, don't you think, just you and I?"

Owen peered around the stone, searching for Galas. There, near some rubble just beyond the archway, a soft red glow shone. "He must have a blood gem," he whispered, "although I can't imagine where he found one."

"How many?" she asked, peering around his shoulder.

"I don't know. But if we can see him, he can see us—get back!"

Another bolt smashed into shards against the stones behind which they hid.

"Well," he said. "There's at least one other with the crossbow."

"Come, Fioni!" Galas called out. "This has gone on entirely too long. Let's you and I settle this, man against… well, woman. Have the same courage your lover Talin had—before he cried for his life. What say you?"

"He's trying to draw you out," Owen warned. "The moment you step out, the one with the crossbow will shoot you."

"*I know,*" she answered in anger.

Owen turned around, scanning the courtyard and its high walls. *There,* he noted with excitement, *a portion of the wall has collapsed, enough to slip through.* "Keep their attention," he whispered. "I'll slip around behind them, try and get the one with the crossbow."

"Be careful."

"I'm always careful," he said, lowering himself to his belly and sliding forward.

Fioni, keeping below the rim of the fountain, yelled out to Galas. "Okay, I agree! Let's you and I settle this between us."

"Good. Come out, and let's get this over with!" he yelled back.

She laughed harshly. "You think me an idiot? The moment I stand, your man will put a bolt through my face."

Owen slid closer to the wall, expecting a bolt through his spine at any moment.

"Not true!" Galas yelled. "You have my word."

This time, Fioni's laugh was genuine, and when Galas spoke again, fury laced his voice. "Come out, cousin. The queen's coming, you know—and she wants *you.* For the blood we share, I'll give you a quick death. Tell her you gave me no choice."

Fioni snorted. "I thought you wanted to marry me and give me babies. You shouldn't play with a woman's affections, cousin. It hurts my feelings—you kin-killing sea-snake!"

Owen slipped sideways through the crack, holding his axe one-handed. Just for a moment, he became stuck, but he wrenched himself through, slipping onto the weed-covered cobblestones on the other side. He crouched, his eyes searching the dark rubble and listening for any sign they had seen or heard him.

"I like that," yelled Galas, his voice distorted over the wall. "*Sea-*

Snake, a much better name-gift than *Gilt-Mane*, don't you think? I've never liked my name-gift; it has no style, no originality."

"I think, cousin, that after tonight, you'll no longer need a name."

Keeping low, he began to slide along the wall, making his way along it to the entrance where Galas and his archer hid. He walked on the outer edge of his boot, slowly rolling his foot forward so it made no noise. When the lightning flared once more, it exposed the tall bald man with the crossbow standing only paces away, also sneaking along the wall, coming toward him.

Both men stared at one another in shock.

Chapter 58

Danika

A set of broken stone steps wound its way up the six-sided tower, with a tangle of thick vines snaking their way over the steps, up the walls, and out the wide cracks filled with starlight. Had it not been for the cracks in the walls and Sight-Bringer's magic, Danika would have been blind, tripping over the poisonous vines. She saw just enough to make her way up the steps, avoiding the vines. Thick spiderwebs stretched from wall to wall, glistening in the moonlight. High above, she could see a large gap in the tower's walls where the top had broken away, leaning precariously at an angle.

When she reached a landing partially blocked by fallen stone, she sat and rested, dizzy with exhaustion and pain. Then she heard angry voices from the courtyard below, including a woman's. *Fioni!* she realized. *It's Fioni. Is Owen with her?*

Hope surged through her. She didn't have to do this all by herself after all. A moment later, she recognized the other voice, *Galas Gilt-Mane*, and her hope vanished, replaced by terror. If Galas was here, so was Serina. She jumped upright, rushing on to the tower's summit, pushing through the spiderwebs, letting them trail behind her.

She reached the summit, where the final section of tower hung at an angle. Staring about her in mounting fear, she saw the landing was empty. Only broken stones lay about. The jewel case wasn't here after all. Her despair drove her to her knees. *No. How is this happening? It has to be here. Why else would Denyr have left his staff like that?*

The obvious, chilling answer was that he hadn't, that someone or something had played a cruel joke on her. Tears ran down her cheeks in her frustration, and she buried her face in her hands, sobbing with the unfairness of it all.

When she opened her eyes again, she noticed the soft red glow coming from a pouch attached to her belt. She stared at it in confusion for a moment, before realizing what it was—the blood gem they had found beneath the Illthori fort on the atoll. With her hands burned, all she could manage was to pull the pouch away and upend it, spilling the glowing blood gem onto the stones.

She stared about her in confusion, before seeing a slim crack of red light slipping through an opening at the very end of the tower, where the top portion hung at an angle.

Leaving the blood gem, she staggered upright again and cautiously pulled herself over the rubble, climbing up the broken section of the tower on hands and knees, Sight-Bringer still tied to her palm. At any moment, she expected the tower to fall away under her weight, but the vines that snaked around it must have been holding it in place. The higher she scampered up its length, the more clearly she saw the red glow coming from an opening at the very top. Once, stairs must have reached all the way here. She pulled herself up through the opening, groaning with the effort, and found herself within a final enclosed chamber of the tower, mostly in ruins now, with thick spiderwebs stretching across its length, looking like crimson curtains in the glow.

And there, only feet away from her, sitting atop a mound of

broken stone, was a golden jewel case a foot wide and half again as tall. Although it was covered in dust, she saw it was stunningly beautiful, etched with a woman's naked form across its front.

She stared at it in wide-eyed disbelief.

Denyr *had* been here. *Thank the Craftsman!*

But the case was closed, its latch secured. The glow she had seen wasn't coming from the jewel case and its treasure of blood gems, she realized in sudden confusion, but from the round shape covered in spiderwebs that sat just behind the case. Peering at it in the darkness, she felt her skin crawl with sudden revulsion, recognizing it as another nell spider egg a moment before she heard the scrambling of arachnid legs and the angry hissing above her.

Chapter 59

Owen

The man Owen faced was as tall as he was, with a thick plaited beard and bald tattooed head. As he raised his crossbow into his shoulder, Owen did the only thing he could: he threw his axe and charged. The weapon, a long-hafted fighting axe, was meant to be used with two hands, not as a missile—but Fioni's gods must have been watching, because the handle of the axe cracked into the crossbow. The bolt flashed past Owen's ear as he collided into the man, bearing them both to the stones. Owen tried to knee him in the groin, but the other man turned his hip, so Owen struck only muscle. The man hammered a powerful blow at Owen's ribs, and Owen felt something give, followed immediately by a lance of agony burning through his side. The man followed up by grasping at Owen's neck, trying to drive his thumbs into his windpipe. Rather than trying to pull away, Owen drove forward, ramming his forehead into the man's nose, feeling a satisfying crunch. The man howled in pain, releasing his grip, and Owen chopped down with the edge of both hands at the nerves on either side of the man's thick neck, abruptly cutting off his scream. The man's mouth and eyes opened wide in shock, and Owen braced his forearm under the man's chin while grasping the back of his head with his other hand. Owen grunted as he threw all his weight back, dragging the man's head forward against his forearm, hyperextending his neck, and crushing his windpipe. A surprised, pain-filled grunt slipped past the man's lips. Breathless, Owen staggered to his feet, retrieved his fighting axe, and finished the man with a single blow to his forehead. As he wrenched his axe free, he heard the scrambling boot-steps of others, and a moment later, two more warriors ran at him, moonlight glinting off their weapons.

Chapter 60

Galas

After his last two warriors had sped off to help Aegrism, Galas glared in the direction of the red glow emanating from behind the ruins where Fioni had taken cover in the courtyard. *Bitch must have sent her knight around to do the same thing Aegrism was trying,* he realized. Gripping his sword hilt so tightly his knuckles cracked, he ground his teeth. *This voyage was nothing but whale-shit.* He had lost three ships now: his lovely *Blood Raven*, *Thunder Killer*, and *Hard Stone*. But, as galling as that was, after this disaster of a night, he no longer even had enough men to sail *Iron Beard*. He was going to die here, marooned. *It's all Fioni's fault. Everything is that cunt's fault. The queen's orders be damned. I'm going to kill her.*

That was when he saw the red glow coming from the leather pouch on his belt. He had been so occupied earlier with the sudden glow coming from the gem on the hilt of Fioni's sword as he and his men had crept closer that he hadn't even seen his pouch glowing. He stared at it in confusion now and then slowly drew it open, revealing the bright blood gem he had taken from Dey's corpse. His gaze darted back to the glow behind the rubble where Fioni hid. It appeared as though the two blood gems… glowed when in proximity. He gazed in wonder at the gem. "Fioni!" he called out. "Did you know the stones did… this?"

Then he heard the clash of steel upon steel coming from where he had sent Aegrism earlier. He stroked the black fish carving around his neck and considered his options. *Fioni is still hiding behind the rubble—unless she's clever enough to have left her sword behind—but she'd never do that, not Wave's Kiss. No, it's just that damned fool knight.* He turned and stared off into the darkness, where a man's sudden shriek of agony cut through the night. He inhaled deeply, his thoughts racing. *That bastard knight is a good fighter. I doubt he's good enough to best Aegrism and two others, but… if he does, then I'll be outnumbered.* He was the finest swordsman he knew, and although he was certain he could beat Fioni, he was less certain he could fight her *and* that knight. *I should go help them, and then we can come back and deal with Fioni.* His mind made up, Galas rose—

And saw Fioni standing before him, not five paces away. *How—*

She pulled her hand away from where she had cupped it around the red gem on the hilt of her sword, letting its radiance shine, turning her hard eyes red, reminding him of Serina. "Come, cousin," she said coldly. "Let us finally embrace."

Galas scrambled back as Fioni attacked.

Chapter 61

Danika

Danika fell back, thrusting Sight-Bringer before her, as the nell spider, the size of a dog, smashed into her, driving the sword's broken blade deep into its tooth-filled maw, swallowing both blade and hilt, clamping shut over Danika's hand, and driving its fangs deep into her forearm. The spider shrieked in agony, the broken tip of Sight-Bringer having burst out the back of its bristly-haired head, and violently threw itself away from her, tearing the sword from her grip despite the cloth she had wrapped around it. Still shrieking, the spider spun about, drumming its legs against the stone floor in a pain-filled cadence, cocooning itself in spiderwebs it tore free of the walls.

Danika scrambled back, grasping at her hand as the spider thrashed and convulsed. Then the spider drew back into a corner, beneath some rubble, and curled its legs beneath it. Moments later, it ceased moving entirely, blood pooling around its web-wrapped form.

Danika squeezed her forearm, breathing deeply as waves of pain coursed through her. Without Sight-Bringer's magic, the chamber was now much darker, the chest barely discernible in the red glow.

Terrified that the egg might hatch more of the spiders, she scrambled past the jewel case and kicked it, sending it sliding across the floor and through a wide crack to plummet through the air and crash against the stones at the base of the tower. The tower was plunged once again into darkness. Her fear spiked when the fingertips of her right hand became numb. She stared in shock at her hand, feeling blood dripping down her arm. Vertigo swept over her when she tried to rise, sending her crashing back down again to her knees. She shook her head, overcome by dizziness as the numbness spread up her arm. *Father Craftsman, no, I've been poisoned—just like Ekkie!*

"Move. Finish this," she mumbled.

Gritting her teeth, she crawled toward the chest, barely visible now in the starlight slipping through the cracks. Each inch she moved seemed so hard, nearly impossible. She should lie down and rest, she knew, just for a moment or two… until the dizziness passed.

She closed her eyes.

Chapter 62

Owen

The two warriors came at Owen, timing their attacks so that the closest thrust a long leaf-bladed spear at him while the other followed up with shield and axe. Instead of meeting their attacks, Owen dropped down on one knee, the spear's head scoring off the armor of his shoulder as he swung the fighting axe one-handed in a low vertical arc that cut the spearman's leading leg away at the knee, sending him tumbling. The axe-man cut down at Owen's overextended axe, hitting it on the shaft and ripping it from his fingers. Rolling away, his ribs on fire, Owen heard the man's axe whistle through the air and slam into the stones, sending sparks arcing into the night. Owen scrambled to his feet. The axe-man, taking his time now against an unarmed opponent, paused, readying himself behind his shield for what Owen knew would be the killing blow. Time slowed as both men stared at one another, taking their measure. Then the man whose leg Owen had just cut away began to howl in agony, and the axe-man's eyes darted from Owen to his comrade.

Owen charged, kicking the bottom of the man's shield so that its iron-rimmed edge flew up, smashing into his jaw and sending him staggering back. Owen followed up with a palm strike into the man's now-unprotected nose, knocking him onto his back. Owen ripped his shield free, breaking the straps and lifting it above his head with both hands. The man's eyes widened in alarm just before Owen rammed the shield edge into his face, caving it in. He brought it down repeatedly, shattering his entire head like a melon.

Dropping the gore-covered shield, he picked up the fallen spear and, with a single thrust, killed the other man, silencing his screams. The discarded Kur'teshi crossbow lay nearby, beside a single remaining iron-tipped wooden bolt. Owen let the spear fall as he reached for the crossbow instead. Now, he heard the ringing clash of sword upon sword.

Fioni!

Chapter 63

Fioni

Galas moved from the rear guard to sweep his sword up and at Fioni's head. She caught his attack with a hanging guard, her blade dangling over her face, before smoothly transitioning into a lunge, sliding forward and shoving her sword point into his face, aiming for the openings in his speckled helm, hoping that even if she missed, her blade's tip might slide along the metal grooves and dig into his eye. But Galas was already disengaging, skipping back out of the way.

Instead of pressing the attack, she slid into a middle-guard position, holding her sword hilt with both hands near her stomach as they circled one another, their breathing wild, their faces drenched in sweat. In the space of less than a minute, they had already come at one another with half a dozen quick exchanges. So far, neither had been able to slip past the other's sword. For all his many faults, Galas was a superb swordsman, and he flashed his teeth at her now, but she saw the trace of spittle that ran from the corner of his mouth into his flawlessly maintained beard. "Getting tired, cousin?" he asked.

"Not even a bit," she lied.

Fighting was always exhausting, but never more so than when the battle was between two skilled fighters. He launched himself at her again, and their blades clashed in a flurry of feints, attacks, and ripostes before locking in a bind, each blade holding the other while they strained at one another. He tried to overpower her with his greater size and strength, but she danced back, disengaging and switching to the rear guard, forcing him to change his stance as well to counter it. *He's faster than I would have thought,* she grudgingly admitted. Her muscles were already tiring, and she was beginning to slow down. *If I don't at least cut him on the next exchange, I think I'm going to lose this fight.*

"Your lover Talin didn't do nearly as well as you, cousin," Galas sneered with just a trace of breathlessness, "especially after I cut several fingers from his sword hand. After that, he just begged." He snorted, shaking his helmeted head. "It was pathetic. Such a worm was beneath you, Fioni, the great-granddaughter of Serl Raven-Eye. You should have thanked me."

She knew he was trying to goad her into a mistake, but her temper flared regardless. "Talin was a better man than you," she snarled as she launched another attack, swinging her blade up and aiming for his outstretched sword-hand, where even a small cut would be his end. But he had already slipped back, while cutting low against her now-exposed front leg. She was already drawing her leg back, but tired now, she moved too slowly, and the tip of his blade cut into her thigh. *Stupid, Fioni, stupid,* she admonished herself as she hobbled back. She already felt the blood trickle down her knee and calf.

He could have finished her while she was off balance, but instead he taunted her again. "I don't hear any more fighting, cousin. Does that mean your knight is dead?"

Tentatively, she placed some weight on her injured leg. There was a sharp spike of pain, but the leg held, which meant the cut couldn't have been that serious. But, serious or not, it would slow her down, and against a swordsman of Galas's skill, that meant the fight was a foregone conclusion now. She forced bravado she didn't feel into her voice. "Maybe it's your men who are dead. Maybe you should run away—*again*."

He shook his head, his eyes shining happily. "It's over, Fioni. Drop your sword, and I'll make your death fast. Keep fighting, and I'll give you to the queen, although I'm not sure she'll want you after I'm done. I'll start with giving you what you've always needed and split you in two."

Despite the dire situation, she sighed, shaking her head in exasperation. "Oh, Galas, please, stop it with the ridiculous bragging. Women talk, even ones that would lie with you. I know all about you. You couldn't split an orange with that little thing between your legs. *Galas Snail-Dick* should have been your name-gift."

His eyes filled with rage. "She-wolf bitch!" he snarled as he rushed in, just as she had hoped he would. She easily caught his thrust and pushed it away before bringing her sword up and around in a desperate reverse cut that, while it probably wouldn't work, was her last chance. But then he did something she hadn't expected—he dropped his sword and gripped her wrist, immobilizing her sword as he stepped to the side and smashed his other palm into the back of her hand, sending Wave's Kiss flying away from her to clatter amongst the stones. Sweeping back in, his arms snaked around her in a wrestler's stance where he could flip her over his hip and drive her into the ground. "Here's your embrace, cousin!" he snarled.

"And here's yours," she answered as she stepped into him, slipping her leg behind his and kicking it up as she twisted her hips, throwing him into the air.

His back slammed into the rocks, smashing the air from his lungs. His speckled helm flew off, the chinstrap broken. Without pause, she slipped forward and caught one of his ankles, immobilizing him while spreading his legs. She stepped between them, still holding his ankle, controlling him. His eyes widened with terror. "No—"

She stomped down three times on his testicles, hopefully crushing them.

His screams turned into a tortured mewling as she let go of his ankle and he rolled over onto his side, curling into a ball. She retrieved Wave's Kiss and stood over him, shaking her head. "When I was eight, Vory Eel-Gifted—a far better fighter than you—taught me to wrestle. Mostly, he taught me how to outmaneuver larger men."

"Wa...wa...wait!" he managed to sputter, holding one hand out.

She drew her sword up over her head with both hands. "You should have kept the sword." The pattern-welded blade swept down, cleaving through Galas Gilt-Mane's perfect blond hair and into his skull.

#

Fioni stared at the dead man for long moments before she noticed the black fish sigil around his bloody neck. She bent over and yanked the cord free and then held it, spinning, before her eyes. *Father, wait for me in Nifalgen. Someday, we'll swim the oceans together.* When she heard running boot steps behind her, she spun about, her bloody sword held ready before her. Owen dashed out of the night, concern on his features, a loaded crossbow held across his chest. When he saw her, a smile lit up his face. She flew into him, staggering him. "You're hurt," he said, his voice thick with relief.

"I'll live," she whispered into his neck. "And you?"

"I'll live."

She drew back, held him at arm's length. "Galas's men?"

He shook his head. "They were kind enough to return one of our crossbows, though, but I could only find a single bolt. We're going to have to ask the Kur'teshi for more."

She laughed as she wrapped his arm around her, using him to help support her. "You'll find we Fenyir have the best woodworkers. I may even know a man who can duplicate the weapons themselves."

They hobbled across the courtyard and approached the bridge. On the other side was the broken tower, silent and dark. "We'll find her," she said, seeing the worried cast to his eyes.

As they stepped onto the ancient stone bridge, she glanced nervously over its crumbling side, seeing the empty moat was much deeper than she had at first realized—certain death if they fell. She had never been particularly frightened of heights, but a debilitating fear swept over her now. Her skin turned clammy with cold sweat, and her pulse began to race like a gull sweeping over the waves. Her heartbeat pounded in her ears, and she froze, staring at Owen, seeing the same fear in his eyes. "Owen, what…"

"The Dread," he whispered through trembling lips.

They turned. Serina and Dilan stood at the end of the bridge, silently watching them. Dilan, in his torn ring-mail coat and hate-filled red eyes, was terrifying, but it was Serina, the Blood Queen, who commanded her attention. She was beautiful and terrible, like a perfect steel blade poised to strike, and her pale skin seemed silver in the moonlight. She wore a dark fur-trimmed cloak over a beautiful blue gown and high otter-skin boots. Her blond hair, interwoven with gems and chains of silver and gold, was tightly braided. Intricate tattoos covered the upper half of her face, resembling a beautiful death mask. When she spoke, Fioni felt as though ice-cold hail lashed her skin. "Where is the niece of Stron?"

Fioni pulled away from Owen and drew her sword, but her fingers couldn't hold the weapon, and it slipped from her grip, clattering onto the stones of the bridge.

Serina raised an eyebrow. "You threaten your own queen?" She raised a single hand at them, and the Dread suddenly increased, like the weight of a mountain, crushing down upon her, driving her and Owen to their knees. Helpless, her heart hammering in her chest, Fioni watched Serina slide across the stones of the bridge, with Dilan following.

Serina looked down her long, narrow nose at Fioni. "So you're the one who's given me so much trouble."

Fioni's teeth clattered together, resonating in her ears.

"I met your father, you know—a traitor to his people, as was your foul great-grandfather Serl. Before I make you love me, you should know your father's soul suffers. For plotting against his queen, I have damned him. Taios Oak-Heart will never see Nifalgen, never be reborn as a black fish. You, however, shall not suffer his fate. I have special plans for you, *Red Wolf*. You shall serve me as my new general. As my beloved Auslaug was, so shall you be."

"Bu… burn, witch."

Serina snorted in amusement. "No, not I, but my enemies will burn—and *you* shall light the fire, Fioni." Turning away, she stood before Owen now. "Who is this handsome one, Dilan? He has the look of an islander but not the smell."

"Owen Toscovar, Mother," Dilan answered coldly. "He was the one who took the sword from the Great Crypt."

"Ah," Serina softly exclaimed, trailing her fingers through Owen's hair as if he were a pet. "Such a powerful destiny the crones have woven about you, Owen, to bring you all this way. Tell me, kingdom man, where is your Dain noblewoman? Where is Sight-Bringer?"

Owen shook his head. "Dilan, help…"

Serina turned her red eyes upon the tower. "No matter. I feel my heart calling out to me. Do you know how *hollow* I've felt all these decades? It felt like a part of me was missing—and it was. Of course, I had to do it to protect myself, had to remove my heart and sacrifice all my childes to power the spell, all for this, to finally be free of any threat."

"Dilan," pleaded Owen.

"It's time," Serina said softly, almost to herself. "The end of the Dain line is personal, Dilan. Stay here while I deal with Stron's kin."

She slipped past them, ghosting toward the tower, and as she moved away, Fioni felt the debilitating fear begin to recede. She flexed her fingers and then made fists. Wave's Kiss glittered in the moonlight, only inches away. Dilan, however, remained standing before her, watching her and Owen. "Mother?" he called out.

Serina's voice drifted across the night. "Go ahead and drain the man, Dilan, but leave the woman. I'll turn her later."

Dilan bared his fangs hungrily.

Chapter 64

Danika

Danika lay on her side next to the jewel case, her numb fingers brushing against its closed hasp. She had drifted off, she was certain of it, but then, abruptly, her eyes had just snapped open again. Vaguely, she remembered a voice... calling her, drawing her from her dream. Realizing where she was in a heartbeat, and galvanized by sudden fear, she had dragged herself across the sloping tower wall to the chest. But now, her numb fingers wouldn't work the clasp, couldn't even flip it up. When her hand fell away for what felt like the tenth time, she moaned in frustration, tears running down her cheeks. *Try again, Danika,* she admonished herself. *You can do this. You* have *to!*

The sword!

If she could retrieve Sight-Bringer from the nell spider's corpse, the magic might counteract the poison, even if only a tiny bit, and let her get the hasp open. The nell spider's cocooned carcass lay wedged behind some fallen rubble. With what little strength remained in her legs, she pushed herself along the floor, scrabbling forward by inches. In moments, she was drenched in cold sweat once again. She could see the carcass more clearly now, and the white stone of Sight-Bringer's hilt jutting out past the still-dripping fangs. *Move, Danika! Move!* She reached out, moaning as her fingers brushed against one of the bristly legs—and then a soul-crushing despair came over her, as if the gates of the underworld had just opened before her.

"Niece of Stron, your quest is over," a woman's soft voice said.

Serina.

"No," she moaned.

"Oh, but yes," the woman mocked in the darkness. "Are you hurt? Are you dying? Shall I end your pain for you?" Ice-cold fingers brushed Danika's cheek. "I almost feel sorry for you, to come so far, so close. Your Father Craftsman can be as cruel as my master, Ator."

Serina approached the jewel case, unlatched the hasp, and flipped the lid up, bathing the chamber in the bright-red glow of hundreds of blood gems. Atop the gems, still glistening wetly, was a severed human heart, covered in fresh blood. Serina trailed her fingers over the heart, smiling before turning her attention back to Danika. The tattoos on her forehead seemed to flow and alter on their own, but that could simply have been a trick of Danika's poison-addled mind.

Danika fought to speak, her lips trembling. "No... No."

"It probably would have been better for you had you died," Serina said simply. "Tell me, where is the sword? What did you do with Sight-Bringer?"

Danika closed her eyes. *Brice, help me, please. Give me strength.* "Gone," she finally managed to squeak. "In… shipwreck."

Serina sighed, as if at a willful child. "I very much doubt that. No matter. I'll find it. After sleeping next to it for half a century, I've become… *attuned* to it. Even now, I can feel it nearby. But I must thank you, niece of Stron. Once I've consumed your blood and recovered my strength, I'll prepare the counter-spell and return my heart to my body. Then, once I am complete again, I shall turn over every stone on this island and discover *all* the Illthori's occult secrets. With such power, I can conquer *all* of the kingdoms: Hishtar, Lyr, and even Xi'ur—all shall fall before me. And you, descendant of the coward Stron, *you* led me here."

Danika moaned. "Please... no."

"Now that I have everything I've ever wanted, you'd think I'd enjoy this moment more. But no, looking down upon you, I feel... nothing."

"Brice..."

"Brice? *Brice Awde?* Was he something to you? Were you the reason he betrayed me, throwing away the gift I gave him? I should have known as much. Always, your foul family has stood in my way—no more."

Danika's terror spiked as Serina swept forward, her fangs now bared. With no more effort than lifting a babe, she wrenched Danika up, holding her against her. Serina gripped the front of her tunic and tore it from her, as if it were nothing more than paper. Holding her in place, one hand gripping her breast, she began to suck and lick at her neck, flicking her tongue over the throbbing vein in her throat.

"Please, no," Danika whimpered.

"When Stron and his foul battle mage, Belion, came against me in my fortress fifty years ago—before I rammed Sight-Bringer through his own cowardly heart—I promised I'd end his line. This night, I keep that promise."

"No..." Danika begged.

"Yes, niece of Stron."

She opened her mouth wide, her fangs glistening. In one pain-filled moment, her head darted in, and she drove her fangs deep into Danika's throat, ripping through the vein. Danika cried out in agony, feeling her hot blood splashing down her neck as Serina began to drink, sucking at her. With the hand grasping her breast, Serina began to squeeze, pumping more blood through Danika's heart, forcing it to flow faster. And then, far more horrific than any pain, Danika began to feel the first stirrings of lust, sensations she had only ever felt before with Brice, and unable to help herself, she moaned. Serina, her eyes shining, pulled her blood-soaked mouth and chin from Danika's neck and then kissed her greedily, like a lover, slipping her tongue into her mouth, filling it with the sour taste of her blood. As Danika's vision began to grow dim, Serina began to drink again, once more painfully compressing Danika's heart. Danika, feeling her body begin to shut down, closed her eyes and felt her heartbeat slow.

I'll find you in the afterlife, Brice, my love.

Chapter 65

Dilan

Dilan's thirst for blood was like a living thing, an insatiable monster. He advanced on his one-time friend.

"Dilan, wait!" Owen pleaded.

The red-haired Fenyir woman grasped for the crossbow lying nearby, but to Dilan, she moved as if underwater, far too slowly. Disdainfully, he kneed her in the face, sending her falling over the crumbling lip of the bridge. She grasped at its edge, just catching herself as she hung swaying from the fingertips of one hand. Owen threw himself at her, skidding forward and catching her wrist just as she let go.

Dilan glared hungrily at Owen, bared his fangs, and prepared to throw himself atop the helpless man.

"Owen, let go!" she yelled. "Save yourself!"

"No!" Owen groaned, trying to wrench her back up.

Dilan froze. Shocked by the sudden memory of his dream and… *Artur*. Dilan had been hanging from the bridge, Prophet's Bridge. Once again, he heard the roaring river, saw his brother, Artur, in Owen's place, holding onto Dilan's wrist as he swayed from the bridge. He saw the rebels rushing forward.

345

"*Let me go,*" he had begged Artur.

"*Never,*" answered his brother—just before the spear thrust that had killed him, sending Dilan falling.

Dilan stared at his clawlike hands, now forever stained with the blood of the innocent. "Artur," he whispered in revulsion. "What have I become?"

Owen's grip failed, and the red-haired woman fell—but only for a moment before Dilan caught her in a viselike grip. He pulled her up easily, holding her at arm's length before him, her feet dangling above the bridge. Why had he done that? Owen scrambled to his knees while Dilan stared at the throbbing pulse in the woman's neck. His hunger spiked once again, driving away all thoughts of a bridge and a brother. He opened his mouth wide, staring hungrily at her throat.

Something hammered into his chest, knocking him back and sending the woman flying away from him to roll along the bridge. He stared in confusion at the feathers of a wooden crossbow bolt jutting from his chest where it had punched through the steel rings of his armor.

Right through his heart.

Owen lowered a now-empty crossbow as Dilan's vision began to grow dim. "I'm sorry. I'm so sorry," Owen said, his voice echoing as if in a tunnel.

His last thought before his world went black was to wonder why Owen looked so sad. Then he was falling, spinning and twisting in the darkness. Once again, he remembered falling from Prophet's Bridge, and he knew he should have died that day, with Artur. Then a familiar voice called his name, and he was no longer falling but standing on a hill, an autumn breeze blowing the tall stalks of grass around him. He didn't question how he had come to be here or why he was suddenly a young boy again. It just felt… *right.*

"Come on, Dilan!" Artur yelled at him again from the field below, where he played kickball with a group of other boys. "Hurry, or we'll lose!"

"Coming!" Dilan yelled, his heart filled with joy as he raced down the hill.

Chapter 66

Serina

The Dain woman's blood was wonderfully filling, particularly after Serina had drained herself casting the spell that had dispelled the shrikes. She paused now, drawing back and savoring the moment, knowing that the last of Stron's line was ending. Although her victory was complete, Serina still felt as if she had missed... *something*, some nagging detail. The Dain woman had been weak, barely able to move when she had caught her, but the only injuries Serina could see were oozing punctures on her—

Vertigo swept through Serina, causing the chamber to tilt and spin. Her fingers suddenly clumsy, she dropped the Dain woman and staggered back, feeling as if she were drunk. "What... what's happening to me?"

She looked about in astonishment, now paying attention to the spiderwebs for the first time. Her gaze snapped to the Dain woman, still somehow alive and fumbling before a... *a nell spider carcass*! Wedged behind rubble and wrapped in webs, it had escaped her notice before. *But...* She inhaled in ice-cold realization. "You were poisoned."

Now I'm *poisoned!*

She heard a sucking noise as the Dain woman suddenly pulled something free of the carcass, then she lifted Sight-Bringer into the air, its broken blade dripping with blue spider blood. Attuned to the occult, Serina felt the sword's magic flow through the woman, giving her strength. Her rage flared, and she darted at the woman, but instead she fell to her knees. "Kill you... thousand times, Dain bitch," she snarled as she pulled herself along the stone floor. "I'll—"

The final death of Dilan Reese ripped through her, tearing apart their psychic connection, as if someone had just ripped an unborn babe from her womb. She screamed in pain and loss, her anguished howl reverberating within the enclosed space. When she could finally speak again, her lips were numb and thick from the poison. "Strip... skin from... bones, niece of Stron."

But the other woman now knelt before the jewel case, holding Sight-Bringer with two hands, its jagged knifelike point over her still-beating heart. Terror swept through Serina for the first time since she had become a blood fiend in the monastery on Echo Island when she had sealed her bargain with Ator, the Dark Shark, ritually slaughtering not only the kingdom's foul, bleating monks, but also the sons of the Fenyir chieftains sent to learn the monks' ways. She held out a trembling hand in a desperate attempt to forestall the woman. "Wait, niece of Stron."

The woman glared over her shoulder at her with hard brown eyes. "My name is Danika Dain, and your family's line will end before mine." She plunged the broken sword into Serina's heart.

"No!" Serina screamed in agony, her chest a burning brand of fire where her heart should have been. Her outstretched arm turned to dust and fell apart. Her last sight was of bright-green flames shooting up around her heart and Sight-Bringer, as a triumphant Danika Dain fell away. Then blackness consumed her, and in a single horrific epiphany, she understood the full price of the bargain she had made so long ago. Her soul—stained with Ator's dark kiss as the first blood fiend—was banned from Nifalgen and the afterlife. Because she had given herself willingly to her dark master, she'd never be reborn as a black fish, never find peace. Then, whipping past her, she felt the euphoric release of hundreds of souls, all those damned by her magic. Their cries of joy flayed her as they escaped. Chief among them were the yarls Taios Oak-Heart and Vengir Flat-Nose, laughing as they swam to Nifalgen to embrace their eternity.

Chapter 67

Danika

Danika fell to her side as green fire consumed Serina's heart. Sight-Bringer remained upright in the case, the occult flames blackening its white handle. Without the sword's magic, her fatigue rushed back on her, forcing her eyes to close. She lay there in darkness now, barely breathing, so... cold. She had done it: Serina Greywynne, the Blood Queen, was dead. Then strong fingers gently took her hand, held it in the darkness. She shuddered in joy at the touch of that calloused hand she knew so intimately. "Said... you were... leaving."

Brice Awde pulled her into his lap, wrapping his arms around her and holding her as he had so many times before. His lips pressed against hers in a perfect kiss. "I couldn't cross the Golden Veil," he breathed into her mouth, "not without you."

She snorted softly, smiling despite the cold. "Knew... it."

He held her in silence for a time, her heartbeat slowing. "I did it, Brice," she whispered, no longer certain if she had actually spoken aloud. "Me."

"I'm so proud of you. You did your duty."

"Yes... What... now?"

351

"Now you keep your promise and come with me."

"Yes."

His love was a bonfire, banishing the chill of death as they slipped away together.

Epilogue

Owen

Owen stood atop *Iron Beard*'s towering steering platform, leaning over the gunwale, staring morosely at the island. Emptiness consumed him, an aching hole gouged out of his soul. The Dains were gone, their line ended. Danika's safety had been his responsibility, even if she had released him from his oath.

And he had failed her.

Once again, his gaze fell upon the grassy bluff overlooking the beach. They had buried Danika there next to a single pine tree, Sight-Bringer's blackened hilt atop her chest as befitted a dead knight. After all, if the sword belonged to anyone, it belonged with her—the true hero of the Dain family. The jewel case and blood gems remained in the tower, untouched, forever tainted by Serina's evil. They could remain there until the world moved on and Torin Island sank beneath the waters.

He felt Fioni watching him from behind, her hand resting upon the steering tiller as what was left of *Fen Wolf*'s crew, helped by a dozen of Galas's men, rowed the drake-ship toward the Mouth of the Gods and the Feral Sea.

Kora and the others had found *Iron Beard* abandoned. Later, when Galas's men straggled out of the forest, they easily took them prisoner. When Owen and Fioni had finally made their way back to the beach as well, Fioni had accepted their surrender and ordered them freed, insisting they were still Waveborn, and with Galas dead, it was time to forgive. Owen didn't particularly trust them, but they had no real choice. Even with their help, sailing *Iron Beard* with so few hands would be a challenge.

Fioni, however, had insisted she'd get them all home.

Home.

Ekkie's happy grunt dispelled some of his melancholy. She lay near Fioni's feet, and Owen found himself smiling despite his heartache. After Fioni and he had made it back to the ship, they had returned to the city, searching the temple and the ruins for more survivors, but the only one they had found was Ekkie, whining beneath a pile of corpses. Perhaps the poison had saved her life, fooling the monsters into thinking she was already dead. Owen didn't know, but it was a blessing just the same—something he desperately needed at this moment. The corpses of all the others, both Fioni and Galas's crew, they burned. No doubt, the souls of their friends were already swimming to Nifalgen.

"Owen," said Fioni hesitatingly, her voice filled with sorrow. "There was nothing you could do. You do know this, no?"

"I promised I'd bring her home," he said, pain shuddering through him.

"Oh, Owen," she said, leaving the tiller to hold him from behind, her arms around his waist, her face buried in his neck. "Some promises can't be kept."

His shoulders trembled, but he nodded. "She did it, destroyed the greatest evil the kingdom has ever faced—and no one will ever know."

"*We* know," she whispered into the back of his neck. "And we will *never* forget." She kissed his cheek.

He stared once more at the bluff, with its single lonely tree.

"What now, Owen?" she asked, a slight tremor in her voice. "I promised I'd bring you to King's Hold, bring you home."

Turning toward her, he cupped her chin and turned her face toward his, staring into her beautiful green eyes. "I *am* home, Fioni Ice-Bound," he said, knowing it for truth the moment he gave voice to it.

Fioni kissed him hard, crushing him in her happiness. Ekkie jumped to her feet and barked happily, jumping up against them. Owen winced. "My ribs, woman. Be careful!"

"Don't be such a guppy," she said happily.

He smiled, holding her as they approached the Mouth of the Gods.

THE END

<<<>>>

About the Author

William Stacey is a former Canadian army intelligence officer who served his country for more than thirty years with operational tours in Bosnia and Afghanistan. He is a husband, father, and avid reader, with a love for the macabre. Black Monastery, an Amazon 2014 Breakthrough Novel Award Quarter-Finalist, was his first novel.

Worlds of Dark Adventure

Visit him at http://williamstaceyauthor.com

ALSO BY WILLIAM STACEY

BLACK MONASTERY

An outlaw Viking clashes with a demon that flays and wears the skins of its victims...

Viking warband leader Asgrim has been banned from his homeland. His only hope of redemption is to raise a princely blood debt. When he learns of a great treasure hidden away on a Frankish Island, he thinks fate has given him one more chance. But Asgrim has been tricked. Deep beneath the stones of the mysterious Black Monastery, an unearthly evil has been set free. Asgrim must team with a suspected Frankish witch to stop a demonic force before it's unleashed upon the world.

STARLIGHT
(BOOK 1 OF THE DARK ELF WAR)

**A secret power. The revival of magic.
An ancient evil stirs.**

Twenty-year-old university dropout Cassie Rogan has returned to her small British Columbia home. Tortured by an accident that killed her parents, she drifts, failing life at every turn. When an impossibly localized lightning storm hits the surrounding forest, Cassie discovers her supernatural side. After centuries of atrophy, the forces of magic are flowing back into our world, and Cassie can wield arcane powers. Her life seems destined to turn around, until the downside of magic brings everything to a screeching halt. Horrifying mythical beasts now prowl the northern wilderness—including the Basilisk—an enormous eight-legged lizard that can turn its prey to stone. Recruited by a secretive agency, Cassie must quickly master her powers to protect mankind. As she develops her skills, a dark power secretly watches from the shadows. The Fae Seelie (a.k.a. the Dark Elves)—humanity's ancient enemy—have returned to settle the score.

CPSIA information can be obtained
at www.ICGtesting.com
Printed in the USA
FFHW010714120319
51040561-56445FF

9 781547 021277